The Reality Thiet

Deplosion: Book 1

Paul Anlee

Darian Publishing House
Chatham, Ontario, Canada

Darian Publishing House
Chatham, Ontario, Canada
darian.publishing.house@gmail.com

Publisher's Note: This is a work of fiction. Names, characters, places, and incidents are a product of the author's imagination. Locales and public names are sometimes used for atmospheric purposes. Any resemblance to actual people, living or dead, or to businesses, companies, events, institutions, or locales is completely coincidental.

Book Layout & Design ©2013 - BookDesignTemplates.com
Design Cover – Elizabeth Mackey Graphic Design
Author Photo – John Keeble

Background image on cover art: Copyright Jean-Michel ALIMI, DEUS Consortium.

The author thanks **Jean-Michel ALIMI, Scientific Director of DEUS Consortium (deus-consortium.org) and Director of DEUS Consortium** for making available the background cover image obtained through DEUS numerical simulations. This image reproduces the distribution of dark matter in a universe with a cosmological constant.

Visit the author's website at: www.paulanlee.com
Follow the author on Facebook at: Paul Anlee
Email the author at: paul.anlee.author@gmail.com

The Reality Assertion Field/ Paul Anlee -- 1st ed.

ISBN 978-0-9958442-1-6

For Courtenay

The most exciting phrase to hear in science, the one that heralds new discoveries, is not "Eureka!" but "That's funny..."

—Isaac Asimov

Prologue

IN THE BEGINNING WAS THE CHAOS. The Chaos was infinite and eternal, dark and silent. It didn't roil with turbulent fire or explosions for there was nothing to burn, no oxygen to fuel the flames, no hydrogen atoms to fuse in the hearts of stars, no uranium atoms to split. The physical laws that made chemical and nuclear reactions possible didn't exist, at least not in any consistent manner.

But the Chaos was not inert, quite the contrary. Endless experiments played out among the random virtual particles emerging spontaneously from the nothingness of the quantum vacuum. They arose in pairs, balancing positive and negative energy, matter and antimatter. They disappeared with no enduring effect, no more than inconsequential ripples in the fields, soon-forgotten perturbations.

Why were there virtual particles? Why was there anything? Because there always had been. The strains of the infinite quantum vacuum were relieved by producing virtual particles. That was reason enough.

The Chaos had always been, even though nothing in it had ever existed, not strictly speaking, not even for a nanosecond. In the absence of consistent causal relationships between different bits of virtual matter, Time's Arrow had no direction; its measure was meaningless. It would be pointless to think about what came before, since "before" was an endless recess of immeasurable time, never reachable.

The timelessness of the Chaos allowed unlimited opportunity for every possible kind of virtual particle to come into existence. Random chance led to diversity among the particles. Physical laws rose out of the evolutionary clay of the Chaos and were spread by resonances between neighboring virtual particles. Where resonances overlapped, standing waves formed, causing real particles to be born and releasing excess energy. The real particles gave rise to self-propagating clusters, tiny islands of budding reality in a virtual ocean. Islands of real matter grew outwards, transforming the Chaos.

Where particle interactions led to domains of greater stability, those regions expanded. Simple, short-lived universes were born and collapsed, their histories lost forever. Stability provided the selective pressure through which the universe evolved naturally from the Chaos.

The tumultuous experiments continued unbridled until two particularly stable domains came together, their resonances uniquely complementary. The rate of formation of real matter accelerated. From virtual nothingness, new matter exploded into existence, releasing tremendous energy in the process. The resonances expanded outward faster than the speed of light, driving Creation into the void. Space grew hotter and hotter. Out of the nowhere and nothing, out of the eternal and infinite Chaos, the universe unfolded like a fiery, blossoming flower.

1

SHARON LEIGH'S HAND TREMBLED as the syringe met her bare arm. She closed her eyes and took a deep breath.

I'm not doing anything wrong. The FDA and university bureaucrats are just trying to wear us down. Peer reviews, teaching reviews, funding reviews, ethics reviews. Why won't they just let us work in peace? They know it's safe; they have all the data they need.

She exhaled and tried to relax. When she opened her blue-gray eyes, she was ready. Determined. She'd rolled the left sleeve of her lab coat up past the elbow. The thin vein was barely visible beneath the skin but she knew she could find it with the sharp tip of the needle.

Years of practice finding the tail veins of rats has served me well. She pictured her arm as a big, scaly tail, and laughed. It came out as a nervous snort that threatened to break into something bigger.

Okay, get a grip, and get on with it. She took another slow breath. The lab was brightly lit but quiet, except for the gentle hum of equipment. She could hear herself breathing. The last of her grad students had wandered off a few hours ago, and the cleaners weren't due until 2:00 a.m., a full hour away.

She perched on the edge of a stool at the lab bench farthest from the door, where it would be difficult for anyone to see her through the windows into the hallway. The lab paraphernalia covering the bench between her and the window into the hallway acted as a convenient privacy screen should anyone pass by.

Beside the rack in front of her, an empty plastic centrifuge tube lay on its side, its hinged lid popped open: DNND 3.2-003. This was their newest version, the one that would lead to real success.

Am I crazy?—she asked herself for the hundredth time—*or just too impatient?* She knew the risks better than anyone. It was her invention, after all. After four long years of playing around the edges, it was time for a proper test. A human test.

She pressed the needle to her skin at a shallow angle, to better follow the vein underneath. Her skin dimpled under the pressure.

The lab door banged opened, and the clatter of the janitor's tin pail on wheels followed.

Sharon jumped and let out a small yelp. The needle pricked her arm, drawing a miniscule bead of blood.

"Oh, sorry," the cleaner called out in the direction of the yelp. He caught a sliver of white lab coat in the back of the room, barely visible behind the benches and the clutter of equipment. "I thought everyone had gone home."

"That's alright," Sharon replied. She put her finger over the tiny nick and pressed against it. "I'm kind of in the middle of something, though. Could you come back in ten minutes?"

The man craned his neck to get a better look at who was doing the asking. It sounded like Dr. Leigh, but he wasn't sure. *Scientists.* He stared at his bucket and mop, trying to come up with a good reason why he shouldn't alter his schedule. "Sure, I guess I could do Dr. Strauss' lab first."

"Thanks. I'll just be a few minutes."

He gripped the mop handle and steered the bucket back into the hallway, letting it bump against the hard surfaces a little harder than usual. The door closed gently behind him.

Sharon took another deep breath. She dabbed a cotton swab in the ethanol and wiped the drop of blood from her arm. Pressing her lips together, she pushed the needle into her arm. It stung a little, but not as much as she'd expected. *Here goes nothing.*

She plunged the contents into her vein, withdrew the needle, and pressed a clean cotton ball to the puncture point. It was done.

2

On the day she died for the first time, Sharon Leigh began her morning as always, with a run along the Charles River.

"See you later, hon. Don't forget, you're picking me up from the downtown office tonight instead of at the lab. Six o'clock still okay?" she called over her shoulder as she laced up her running shoes.

"Oh, that's right! You've got a board meeting this aft. I forgot," Paul confessed. *It was always something.*

"Yep, another board meeting." Sharon scrunched her face in exaggerated distaste.

"Sure, six o'clock works fine. Downtown. Got it."

"Thanks. I'll see you tonight. Love you," she said as the door swung shut behind her.

She set out from the suburbs of Lower Allston at a comfortable pace, crossing over to Cambridge and continuing east for the five-mile jog that would take her past Harvard to MIT and her lab in the Stata Center. It was a beautiful June morning, not a hint of rain in sight. Her light backpack, carrying a change of clothes, jostled rhythmically against her back.

Her new work was going well. The silicene-based nanotube sensors she'd developed in her PhD research were great for a first attempt, but this new approach was so much better. She used to have to painstakingly grow the devices atom-by-atom on existing microcircuits. It took weeks of careful dedication to make one chip, and weeks after that to grow neural cell cultures on the surface. Not anymore.

Her success with the chips had led to some good publications, but that's all they'd been good for. She would never be able to introduce them to the general public as a human-machine interface, not at the current cost of manufacturing. Besides, the only way to implant the sensors involved brain surgery, and they'd never get approval to do that, not in her lifetime.

So Sharon came up with a better idea. In ordinary English—her default "cocktail party" explanation—she created a way for a person's own brain cells to construct microscopic machines that would enable them to become a walking super-computer.

In geek-speak, the new work combined sensory semiconductor nanoparticles with RNA that encoded a silicene synthase enzyme. She named this RNA-semiconductor hybrid device a Dynamic Neural Nano Dot, or DNND, for short.

Describing her work usually elicited one of two responses, either, "Oh, so you're one of those transhumanist scientists hell-bent on altering humanity," or, "Dendies! Love the name." Both responses were equally annoying.

Sharon gave herself over to the peaceful, meditative thrumming of her footsteps as she ran. The scenery melted away. She focused her attention on her breath and, when needed, on the traffic at the cross streets. Once she hit a good stride, she let her thoughts drift freely over the lab's progress during the past four years.

They had shown that DNNDs could be injected into mice without adverse effects, cross over the blood-brain barrier, and successfully organize themselves into a functional system within the brain. That alone, was a huge step in the field.

The first generation of hybrid DNNDs only had the capability to *detect* neural activity. In other words, they could listen but not speak.

The second generation could, in addition, activate synapses directly and reliably stimulate neurons. The DNNDs could now speak, as well as listen.

With basic input and output capabilities in place, Sharon could see her way clear to developing a complete direct-to-brain interface. It was exciting, groundbreaking work. They'd quickly moved past the second generation and onto the third. The most recent generation, Version 3.2, was the fastest-growing, most efficient yet.

Encouraged by the Institute's trustees, Sharon had set up a spin-off company to explore the commercial potential which, everyone agreed, was enormous.

She split the majority share evenly between herself and her husband, and offered substantial portions of the company to the two postdocs who shared in the early development of the devices.

Thrilled at the prospect of work in the "real world," David and Nick, her postdocs turned business partners, said goodbye to the confines of the university and joined Neuro Nano Devices Inc., where they could better devote themselves to advancing both the technology and their bank accounts.

Sharon slowed to her cool-down pace as the campus came into sight. She took a drink from her water pouch and placed a hand over her abdomen. Was she ready for the changes that were coming to her life? She didn't dare admit to her friends that she still held deep reservations about becoming a mother—but not for the usual reasons.

Six months ago, when she'd injected herself with the DNNDs, she was willing to accept the risk of being a human laboratory. It never occurred to her that she might become pregnant a month later. They'd been careful. And yet.

Every scientist can tell you that "99.9% protection" does not mean 100%. But like many urban professionals, she foolishly dismissed that 0.1% risk as insignificant. *Whoops.*

Weeks after the injection, she'd decided it was time to confide in her husband. She remembered thinking—*Tonight's the night, after dinner. It'll feel so good to have everything out in the open.*

And it might have been, had she not stopped at her doctor's office on the way to work. She'd been feeling a little "off" for a while. She thought it was probably due to the initial DNND activity but popped in for a quick check-up, just to rule out other possibilities.

The GP had examined her and got her to leave blood and urine samples for some routine tests. He muttered something about whether she might be pregnant and suggested she return in a few days to go over the lab results. The very thought panicked her. After leaving his office, she went straight to the pharmacy next door and bought an in-home pregnancy test.

Shortly after, sitting alone in a public washroom cubicle, Sharon couldn't believe her eyes. She stared at the stick for a full minute before moving, forcing herself to breathe slowly and remain calm. She went back to the drugstore and picked out a couple different tests to verify the results. They all agreed.

No, no, no, no. This can't be! With her free hand, she'd smoothed her hair back, away from her face. *Now what? There's no way I can tell Paul I've experimented on myself, not now. He'll be furious, horrified. He'll worry himself sick. I just can't deal with that on top of everything else. No. Until we know the baby is healthy, no mention of my DNNDs.*

Apart from David and Nick, she hadn't dared tell anyone about the hybrid nanotechnology growing in her brain. And she only told *them* because she needed their help in monitoring the lattice growth. She could still hardly believe what she'd done herself.

Like a drunken indiscretion, there was no point regretting it after the fact; the decision was past reversing. There was nothing she could do to change the facts; all she could do was stay calm and healthy.

She had to keep moving forward. *I just needed a little time to make sure everything was going okay*—she told herself. *And everything is going better than okay; it is coming along beautifully.*

But, the time was fast approaching when she would *have* to confess what she'd done. *Paul is going to give me an earful when I tell him, and rightfully so. I'd do the same if he pulled a stunt like this on me. But he'll come around.*

Nothing to worry about—she assured herself. *The particular DNNDs I injected are the safest and most refined to date. They had more than enough time to settle into my brain tissue before the baby started forming. They won't move. The baby is not at risk and neither am I.*

The university's reaction when she told them was likely to be quite different. *They are going to freak when they find out. There's no way around that one. Self-experimentation is professional misconduct of a high order. An unforgivable sin. Apart from the ethics, and risk to their reputation, what they really care about is that it impacts insurance and risk management. It would be horrible PR should anything go wrong.*

Thankfully, I no longer work just for the university anymore. At least my business partners support my bravado. They applaud it—so long as they can distance themselves from any negative fallout.

The risk she'd brought on herself sometimes terrified her, but the DNND technology filled her with hope for the world. She would do whatever was necessary to move the research along.

The complexities of human technology and human society have outstripped mainstream humanity's ability to grasp them. The world needs this technology, and it can't wait for the bureaucracy to catch up to the science.

Even among her colleagues, it was rare to find people who could step outside their own frighteningly narrow specialties. Add to that the ridiculous, lowbrow public discourse during the most recent Presidential election, and it was becoming painfully clear that a bold fix was needed. Urgently. *If we don't become smarter, we'll destroy ourselves with our foolishness. DNNDs can facilitate that leap upward; I know they can.*

She knew the FDA was only acting on general public opinion. *If I could just change the fear of self-replicating nanotech, things would go a lot faster. Sure, there are some legitimate issues, but it's not as bad as people think. Self-replicating doesn't mean out of control.*

Sharon walked the last block to her building slowly. Her stomach growled, loudly, diverting her attention and making her smile. *Okay, my diet has been a little weird, even for someone who's pregnant.*

From the first week after the injection, the DNNDs' demand for certain elements had pushed odd appetites on her. The RNA encoded enzyme complexes enabled the nanodots to replicate themselves from available raw materials. The enzymes called for elements found in unusual places: clay, rare earths, and other minerals. The DNNDs extracted building materials from her blood. When she lacked the necessary elements, she experienced strange and irresistible cravings. She never questioned them; she always complied. *The DNNDs are taking up all the silica and metals. My blood tests look good. Everything is going to be fine.*

Sharon stretched out her tired muscles and headed inside for a shower before going to the lab.

She had a good team. They didn't need babysitting, and they demonstrated initiative. It hurt a little to admit that they sometimes got more done with her out of town than when she hung around directing them. She checked in with each member at least once a week in case there were any fires to put out but, mostly, she left them to their work.

"Good morning, Mei," she called out to the Admin Assistant as she passed her office next door to the lab. "Anyone trying to get a hold of me this morning?"

"No, it's all clear until your meeting at Neuro Nano this afternoon. I'll text you if anything changes. Will you be reachable?"

"Yep, right here," she replied, patting her flexible communications wristband. "I'm going to spend the morning working on the DARPA proposal, but first I'll check in with the minions," she joked.

"Morning, everyone!" she chirped on entering the lab. Her team comprised a talented, international, interdisciplinary mix. India, China, Canada, Russia, and Brazil were all represented in addition to her home country. They brought varied expertise, including computing, synthetic biology, material sciences, mathematics, and electronic engineering.

"Morning, Sharon," came the distracted replies. Looking around, she saw Amerjit, Rob, and Oliver—her two senior students and the postdoc— all engaged in ongoing experiments. Her four junior students were busy on their laptops. *Reading or doing something useful, I hope.* She stopped at Amerjit's bench.

"How are the mice doing this morning?"

Ami replied with her normal succinct synopsis. "Progressing well. After seventeen months, Version 3.1 mice remain perfectly healthy, even though they're getting old now. We continue to map their brain function using both the dendy network and fMRI. Version 3.2 subjects are now entering month ten and still exhibit no signs of adverse effects."

"Serotonin levels are okay?"

"The dendies report that neurotransmitter levels all fall within normal ranges."

Sharon nodded. She hated their pet name for the DNNDs but couldn't break them of it. She reluctantly accepted it as unavoidable.

Ami continued, anticipating her supervisor's next question. "I haven't conducted secondary confirmation yet because the procedure is hard on the little guys. But if you think I should go ahead anyway, I'll begin independent analysis to verify the initial readings."

"No, that's okay. No need to subject them to brain microbiopsies unless there's an indication something's off. How did the CT scans turn out? Are the DNNDs still behaving themselves?"

"Uh-huh. Everything is staying where it belongs."

Sharon's hand drifted to her head of its own accord, acting on the subconscious association. Catching herself, she covered by smoothing back her hair. As far as her students knew, the mice were the first and only mammalian recipients of the self-replicating version of DNNDs. She intended to keep it that way for a while longer.

"Okay. We'll keep collecting data for another few months before going back to the FDA to approve testing in chimps." Ami raised an eyebrow. Sharon sighed. "Yes, again."

Turning her attention across the lab bench, she zeroed in on the intensely focused young man with a nose ring. "Rob, is there any sign of coordinated network activity in the 3.2s yet?"

Rob looked up from his equipment, only now noticing Sharon's arrival. He'd been attending to the EEG signals on his multi-channel oscilloscope, and comparing them to the digital pulses produced by the DNNDs. Although EEG waveforms were beyond the subject matter of his Waterloo electronics engineering degree, it was all just signal-processing to him. He hadn't completed his PhD yet, but he was already adding important new chapters to the book on data processing in mammalian brains. He removed his ear buds and placed them on his bench.

Even from across the lab, Sharon could make out the electronica music emanating from them. "You do know you'll be deaf before you're thirty, right?"

"Huh? What was that?" Rob shouted. "I didn't hear you." He cracked a smile, "Just kidding. To answer your question, which by the way I heard perfectly well, there's indication of small, local groups assembling but the network hasn't kicked into overall coordination yet. The clusters are slightly bigger than last week, and infilling has come to a standstill."

"I'm really psyched. I don't think it'll be long before we can talk to the whole lattice directly. You know, we could probably shorten the wait time in the next round if we started with more dendies."

Sharon already knew first-hand that the process would go faster with a higher dendy concentration. She knew this because the development of the dendy network forming inside her own head right now was the product of proportionately double the numbers they'd used in the mice, and it was progressing rapidly. *But I can't say so. I could risk losing the entire project. I can't risk that happening; better to continue the ruse for now.*

"Yes, I was thinking the same thing, Rob. Let's run a growth curve on a new generation of mice with different starting concentrations, and see if we can determine the optimal starting point. Ami, why don't you set that up for next week?"

Ami perked up with the prospect of something more appealing to do over the next few months. "Could we use the 3.2s?" She peered around the lab instruments and directed her question to Oliver, who'd been quietly working in the SynBio area of the lab while the others chatted.

Sharon was getting used to putting on a convincing game face, "Yes, I think that might be a good idea. What do you think, Oliver? Are any of the new synthetases or replicases showing promise, or is 3.2 still the champ?"

Oliver looked up from his microscope. "Additional mutations at Arginine 153 in the synthetase and Serine 506 in the carboxyl tail of the replicase have exceeded the performance of the previous stable 3.2 generation. However, neither of these mutations increased overall processivity by more than a few percent. It is therefore my estimation that Version 3.2 is sufficiently optimal and proven to be well-tolerated *in vivo*."

"Okay, then." Sharon took a few seconds to process his answer. She still found it difficult to follow the molecular structure of proteins in her head the way Oliver did.

"3.2 it is. Calculate a range of concentrations covering a one-thousand-fold difference around the current starting value, and we'll see what works best *in vivo*." She was pretty sure that Version 3.2 would turn out to be close to optimal.

"I guess that wraps things up for now. I have to get back to work on the DARPA proposal before my afternoon meeting. Any questions before I head out?"

The second-year student leading the new artificial intelligence efforts looked up from his laptop, "Could you ask Dr. Franti if his contacts at MetaCepta are going to let us use their lattice parallel traversal algorithm?"

"Sure, thanks for the reminder." Getting MetaCepta's consent was near the top of her agenda. There was a good chance that their advanced pattern recognition code combined with Neuro Nano's DNND technology might enable the instant learning she'd dreamed about. Between that and the CT and fMRI brain scans she was running on herself this afternoon, it was shaping up to be a potentially momentous day.

3

IN THE BEGINNING WAS YOV, the Eternal and Infinite. Yov was everything and everything was Yov. In the fullness of time and in His infinite wisdom, Yov created the universe, pulling the planets, moons, stars, comets, and galaxies from within Himself. On chosen planets, Yov created living entities to thrive in harmony, among them, the microbes, grasses, flowers, trees, insects, fishes, reptiles, birds, and mammals.

Yov created Origin, and He created the People to have dominion over all life found there. The People were clever, and they wished to know more and more about the universe that Yov had made. They developed methods and schemes to help them understand Yov's wisdom. They built servants and thinking machines to help them learn faster. Yov was pleased with how clever he had made the People.

Among the People lived two particularly gifted individuals, Da'ar and Alum. Da'ar was very clever and, with the aid of his thinking machines, he strove to understand Yov's Universe better than anyone before him. But he became arrogant, and soon desired to replace Yov's divine wisdom with simple human knowledge.

While Da'ar grew more powerful and smug in his science, Alum grew more humble, pious, and closer to Yov.

One day, in his conceit and ambition, Da'ar rebelled against the rule of Yov. But Alum joined with Yov and together they banished Da'ar and his thinking machines from the world of the People.

Then Yov said to Alum, "Da'ar's hubris has offended me greatly, but you have served me well. I command you to take My People forth from this world and populate all the worlds with my best creations. To aid you in this undertaking, I will make a gift to you of My Powers so the People will know you lead in My Name. You are My Chosen One. Until you have completed this task, I will withdraw from the Universe and rest within my Eternity."

And Alum pledged, "I will lead Your People forth, my Lord, and they will take dominion over the Universe in Your Name. They will revere and worship You as I do, and will await Your Return."

With that, Alum took the People from Origin to Home World saying, "By seeking to unveil the deepest mysteries of Yov's Creation and not being content simply to love Him, we have sinned against our Lord. And even though we have erred and caused offense, Yov has not abandoned us. Instead, He has commanded us to leave our Origin and to seed His Word throughout the Universe. We will rule all of Creation in His Name."

And the People saw what Alum said was true, and they praised Him and vowed to be true to The Task.

From the Book of Alum

THE STRANGER WALKED INTO TOWN from the mountains in the west. Although this might have appeared to be an unremarkable action, there were many things about it that were exceptional.

First, because Alumston was the founding colony on the fifth planet of Gargus 718 in galaxy NGC4567 in the Virgo cluster, there was nothing in the west from which to walk.

No roads led into the mountains. All the farms had been planted south of Alumston. Herds had been released to graze in young forests established to the north and east. Outside of the terraformed regions extending tens of kilometers beyond the town borders, the rest of Gargus 718.5 could be described, at best, as being "not actively hostile" to terra-standard life. The mountains were not a region from which someone would normally walk.

The second odd thing was that the stranger *walked* into town. Nobody arrived in Alumston except through the starstep, the transportation portal that was one of Alum's great blessings, and nobody ever—ever—arrived unannounced. Upcoming Founder arrivals were posted on an InterLat list every Fourday. The work of founding a new planet for burgeoning humanity held enough surprises without the problem of uncontrolled immigration.

The third odd thing, perhaps oddest of all, was that the man was a *stranger*. Every planet among the Worlds of The People had an Alumston, and there were no unknown persons in any of them. An Alumston never grew much beyond its intended hundred-thousand Founding souls, all linked through the InterLat. Forfeiting your lattice privacy and anonymity was a small price to pay in return for the blessing of being chosen to open a New World to the glory of Alum.

Unlike workers on more developed planets, the Founders were

required to work together closely, coordinating their knowledge and experience. Privacy was a conceit they could not afford if they wished to survive, let alone successfully complete their mission. Besides, being joined to one another in the InterLat brought you that much closer to the Mind of the Living God.

So, for a completely unremarkable stranger to walk unannounced into an Alumston at the edge of the Realm, in the midst of another busy day on the new world, was actually quite remarkable.

The stranger maintained a leisurely pace along Radial 270 deep into town, unheralded and unchallenged due to the early hour. He approached the first person he saw.

Helen Bronding, as she did every morning, was strolling along the ten segs from her apartment near the outer ring to her Language Arts teaching job at the Children's First School, which was conveniently situated next to the Alumita, Church of Alum.

The stranger walked right up to her and said in perfectly fine Standard, "Good morning. Is there someplace I might procure a meal to break my fast? It has been a long time since I've eaten." He smiled broadly, as though they were old friends.

Helen sent a casual ID query but the middle-aged man standing before her was a blank on the InterLat. *Invalid identity*—her lattice replied. *What?* Despite the surprising response, she managed to extend basic civility, stammering a Standard greeting, "Alum's peace...to you...good sir," and in reply to his question, sent directions to the nearest restaurant.

"Rose's is one of the town's finest restaurants, and it's right there on.... Oh." She stopped mid-sentence. *Silly me. The man doesn't have an InterLat connection; how is he going to receive directions?* "I'm sorry. You go three radials ahead, turn anticircle at John's Flyer Repair, and continue two rings..."

"No need to apologize," the stranger interrupted. "I have received your sending. Good day to you, Miss Bronding, and thank you." He gave a polite bow and walked on, leaving her in a perplexed daze.

The streets of Alumston, that is, the streets of any Alumston, were organized in tidy, concentric rings joined by evenly spaced radial spokes.

Radial Zero extended from a carefully measured two hundred meter diameter Center Park and pointed precisely to planetary north. Centric was along the radials toward the center. Anticentric was away from the center. Clockwise from a radial was called procircle; the other direction, anticircle. Toward the outermost rings where the distance between radials grew inconvenient, additional sets of radials were inserted.

Befuddled, Helen nodded and resumed her route. She was too stunned to raise a general query or alarm. *He said he received my sending. And he knew my name!* Without an InterLat connection, neither should have been possible.

Helen continued walking along the radial that led to her school, trying to make sense of the brief encounter.

"Good morning! Alum's peace to you, Helen!" Brother Ontro nem Stralasi's cheerful greeting from the main steps leading into the Alumita pulled Helen from her befuddled state.

"Oh, yes. Good morning, Brother Stralasi," she replied and continued along her route, her mind still playing over the exchange with the stranger.

Helen and the Good Brother had been exchanging pleasantries every morning for the past three years. They never once parted ways in under five minutes, and not without sharing some tip or recipe for getting the best taste out of the town's limited fare or, at least, some heartwarming schoolyard stories from the previous day.

Brother Stralasi loved all of his People, but because children were especially precious to Alum, they were similarly precious to Brother Stralasi. He was always eager to hear charming anecdotes about them.

"A moment, please, Helen," he called after her, simultaneously sending an attention-getting InterLat signal. The teacher jerked to a halt, surprised by her own bad manners, and turned to face him.

"I'm so sorry, Brother Stralasi," she sputtered, "I was a little distracted."

"More than a little, I'd say."

Helen's face grew warm. "I just had the strangest thing happen."

"I thought you looked a little preoccupied. Not what I'd expect on such a fine day. Please, do share," he invited, though so-called invitations coming from any member of the Alumit were only a ritual of social convention.

Relieved to unburden herself of the encounter with the stranger, Helen sent her recording of the conversation to the monk. "I don't understand," she added, verbally. "He looked perfectly normal but he had no InterLat presence. And yet he was somehow able to receive my sending. Where could he have come from?"

Brother Stralasi's brow puckered. Her lattice recording raised a number of questions. "I'll take charge from here. Have a lovely day, my dear. Alum's peace be upon you." He turned abruptly, all business, and set out for Rose's.

Helen had never known the Good Brother to react that way over matters concerning the People. He'd always approached delicate issues and disputes with unfailing humor, reassurance, and wisdom, no doubt the result of decades of leading Founders on half a dozen new worlds. This cold determination of a Principal Local Authority looking out from the Brother's normally jovial blue eyes was a new and disturbing development.

The Alumit monk found the stranger inside Rose's bright and cheery restaurant, eagerly diving into a stack of pancakes. Brother Stralasi took a seat facing him.

The visitor sampled the fruit chunks that came with his pancakes, apparently oblivious to the waiting monk.

"Alum's peace to you," Stralasi said politely.

The stranger looked up at the Good Brother as if just first noticing him, and scanned the rest of the room. A few tables were occupied but most of Rose's breakfast customers had vacated an hour earlier.

"And to you," the man acknowledged and returned to his pancakes.

Brother Stralasi, presenting his best deferential but unsatisfied demeanor, tried again. "My deepest apologies. Someone should have told me to expect an Emissary; I would have prepared for your arrival."

The stranger looked up from his meal and cocked one eyebrow, but said nothing.

"Pardon my intrusion. You *are* an Emissary, are you not? You arrived without announcement, without using the public starstep, and you have an InterLat connection that receives transmissions but is invisible to ours. That you are an Emissary seems a logical conclusion," reasoned Brother Stralasi. "By what name shall we address you while you are here?"

The man set down his cutlery and regarded the Brother. "I believe the last time I used a name, it was Darak Legsu," he said. "That should suffice for now."

Stralasi overlooked the question the stranger chose not to answer. "I presume you will want us to call you Mr. Legsu rather than Emissary Legsu?"

"Interesting presumption," was all the stranger offered.

The Brother blinked a half dozen times in rapid succession. "Might I know the nature of your visit?" he probed.

"I am resting after a long journey."

"But we are at the Edge, where our Holy Alumination is pushing back the Da'arkness. Where could you be returning from," Brother Stralasi quizzed. "My humble apologies. I meant to say, this is an unusual choice as we are far from any important trade or spiritual routes. Is there any aspect of your visit that I might assist you with?"

Darak entertained the offer for a moment. "No, I only wish to mix with the people of this outpost so that I may better understand the way things are done now."

What a strange thing to say! "But you must have visited hundreds of Foundation planets. Surely there is nothing unique about this place."

"No, nothing particularly unique," agreed Darak. "It is simply among the first I have encountered upon my return to human space."

Upon return to "human space"? Not "the Realm"? *Is this man claiming to have travelled into the Da'arkness and returned? That's preposterous! A highly improbable claim, at the very least, even for an Emissary.*

He had to admit, though, the traveler had piqued his curiosity. Proper or not, the curious boy within him was compelled to ask, "From where have you come, then? Was it a long journey?"

A grimace flashed across Darak's face. "It was a very long journey." He looked around the dining room, allowing the painful memories to subside. "The last time I was in a place like this was over...well, let's just say, it was many years ago. I've crossed countless light years to return."

Countless light years? That would be physically impossible. What could he mean? But there was an even more puzzling question to address first. "You said 'return'? Do you mean to say," he leaned in and lowered his voice, "that you are coming back from the Da'arkness?"

"I would have to say, yes."

"But that's impossible! No one can go there!" The Brother exclaimed before he could catch himself. He softened his voice to a conspiratorial whisper. "We both know that only..." He looked around, mindful of the public space in which they sat, "...only *automated* explorers can travel beyond the Edge of the Realm."

"Is that so?" Darak asked, his eyes giving away his amusement. He listened to the gentle tink, tink, tink of his spoon against his coffee cup, and watched the small vortex forming in the middle of the steaming liquid. When he sought the Good Brother's gaze again, he was serious.

"I have been to the expanding edge of the universe, beyond the Da'arkness of which you speak, to the Chaos that lies beyond. It took me a long time to return, that is, if 'time' can be said to have any meaning there."

The white noise of café activities filled the space around them. A few seconds passed while the men pursued their own thoughts.

"And if, indeed, the concept 'there' has any meaning...there," the traveler added, taking an appreciative sip of his coffee.

Brother Stralasi couldn't stop himself, though it was heresy to ask, "Why would Alum, praise be His Name, send you beyond the universe?"

Darak waved the question away and leaned back, "I have said too much already. At any rate, I am not here to inspect your operations, as you seem to fear. I am merely passing through on my travels."

Thank Goodness! The monk released the tightness in his shoulders that he hadn't realized he'd been building. Still, the man's story was incredible.

The monk let out a sigh, a little louder than he meant to. "In that case, please accept the hospitality of the Alumita. We have a number of rooms that, while perhaps humble for one of your station, should prove comfortable during your stay."

"Thank you, but there is no need to offer me such comforts. I am not an Emissary of your Alumit. I will make camp outside of town," Darak offered.

Brother Stralasi gasped. "You can't do that; the non-Standard areas are far too dangerous!"

The small upturn tugging at the corner of Darak's mouth did not go unnoticed by the Brother.

"I see," said Stralasi, regarding Darak with a fresh and wary eye. In truth, he didn't see at all, but his instincts told him this stranger was more than he appeared.

"So, if you are not an Emissary, how did you come here to this planet and this town?"

"There is only one way to travel between the stars, is there not? My method of travel is not fundamentally different from yours."

The traveler's calm confidence should have been reassuring. Stralasi found it suspicious and acutely unsettling. "But, sir, all starstep travel is pre-approved, and none is due for a week," he countered.

"Nevertheless, it is as I have said."

On the verge of challenging Darak's outrageous assertions, Brother Stralasi realized the unspoken alternative. *Oh!* In shock, he pushed his chair back, crumpled to his knees and prostrated himself.

"Forgive me, my Lord!" he cried. "I am your servant, too simple and ignorant! Please, pardon me, and allow the services of our humble frontier town to be at your disposal!" He looked at the other restaurant patrons expectantly but they only stared back blankly, too confused to move.

"Kneel before your Lord and Master!" he cried. "For here before us is a Shard of Alum. His is the voice of The Living God!" The others quickly threw themselves to the floor in supplication, following the Good Brother's lead.

4

HER LAB BUSINESS CONCLUDED, Sharon locked herself in her office for the rest of the morning and worked on the DARPA proposal. She allowed herself a brief reprieve, grabbed a chef's salad downstairs, and continued on the proposal until mid-afternoon.

When it came time to wrap up, she could feel the start of a migraine coming on. She squeezed her eyes to block out the light. Pinching the bridge of her nose, she gently leaned her head back. *I'll never get used to all this grant writing. They hire me to be a productive teacher and scientist, and then they fill my days with grant writing, committees, and admin work. How am I supposed to get any research done? What a colossal waste of time and skills.* It made her want to scream and weep but what good would that do?

She opened her eyes and stretched. *I might as well head out. There'll be time to work on the proposal later.* She threw her tablet into her backpack. She checked in with Mei on her way by, put on her hat and sunglasses, and set out on the half-hour walk to her company, Neuro Nano.

They'd found a great space for the spin-off company, just off campus in Biotech Alley. The head-clearing walk over there turned out to be a bonus; it was when she often came up with some of her best ideas.

The sunshine warmed her shoulders. *That feels so good.* She grabbed an iced coffee along the way and washed down a couple of painkillers, hoping they would help with the headache.

She arrived at the building a few minutes late, and skipped her usual stairwell climb in favor of a quick elevator ride to the main entrance on the fourth floor. The doors parted, and she let the familiar buzz of activity envelope her.

The enterprise was already threatening to overflow its 300 square meters of combined office and lab space. The offices themselves were tiny. Most of the space was dedicated to biolabs, semiconductor clean-rooms, and medical examination suites. Cramming such diverse functions into a single, open area was budget-friendly and procedurally efficient. It also was claustrophobia-inducing and made organized operation practically impossible.

Her founding partners, former postdocs Nick Franti and David Arnell, had their own compact offices flanking the small, stylish boardroom where they delivered polished presentations and raised money.

Lately, much of their day and their patience was eaten up in meetings with various health industry regulators, reviewing, explaining, and re-evaluating test-animal results. The DNNDs slated for commercial market had already been thoroughly tested and reviewed. There was no valid reason to delay testing in chimps but the FDA wanted to ensure everything was done by the book. And then some.

Sharon suspected they were stalling for political reasons, or maybe to allow Big Business interests to better position themselves to best capitalize on her inventions. Maybe both. It was getting difficult to tell the many veiled and interwoven interests apart these days.

She understood that DNNDs were an entirely new class of medical device, and that given their complex nature and potential implications, the regulatory agency wanted to be more cautious than usual. She did. She would also be pleasantly surprised if they got the approvals without word leaking prematurely to the press or, worse yet, to the growing tide of ill-informed skeptics and evangelical naysayers.

Sharon peeked into the clean-room production facilities. A handful of postdocs were assembling DNNDs using focused ion beam deposition, in the same old-fashioned way they'd been using for the past two years. *They'll be out of work in a year. This current DNND generation merging synthetic biology with patterned semiconductor growth will see to that*–she predicted.

While it was unfortunate to lose such highly skilled people, the only way for technology to make the necessary innovations was to draw from all possible specializations, with no heed to historical boundaries. If they continued within the limitations of linear progression, they could never make the advances available to the public at a reasonable price.

"Sharon!" David bounded out of the boardroom and delivered a bracing business handshake. He didn't notice it was returned somewhat less enthusiastically. "How goes MIT? How's Paul? How are you doing?" he asked in rapid fire. "More importantly—how's our little fetus?"

She found David's enthusiasm for corporate style and trappings more disturbing by the day. Even though he claimed to place the baby's health in paramount importance, the order of his questions revealed the true hierarchy of his concerns.

Corporate life had clearly been good for David. Despite the constant pressure of having to raise money through the wining and dining of potential investors, he was much happier now than when he was strictly a researcher. He was dressing better, too, she noticed.

"Sharon, it's good to see you." Nick greeted her less ebulliently but more genuinely as she entered the boardroom. "How goes the pregnancy?"

Nick Franti was the quintessential scientist. Being CTO of Neuro Nano had not changed him at all. His hair was still too long and poorly coiffed, and his casual attire announced that he was more comfortable in the lab than in front of potential investors.

"Everything's fine so far," she replied, patting her belly. She was glad she'd decided to trust Nick and David with her self-experimenting. She needed someone to objectively evaluate DNND growth and monitor any cognitive changes.

"Actually, I've got a bit of a headache right now," she added. "I've been working on the DARPA proposal all day."

"That's too bad," Nick said; he looked concerned. "About the headache, I mean. Glad to hear the baby's doing fine."

"Thanks," said Sharon. "I took some painkillers on my way over here. It should be gone soon." She sat to the right of the head of the table, relinquishing the power seat to David, "Why don't we get started?"

"Ready when you are," answered David. "This isn't an official board meeting; we don't need to take minutes. I just wanted to get caught up on things at your MIT lab and discuss the next round of funding. How'd you like to go first, Sharon?"

I see that it's "my" MIT lab now, not "ours"—she noted. *Interesting.* This, despite the fact that until recently David made his research home in that same lab, and all of the research fed directly into product development at Neuro Nano.

"Sure, I can start." She took out her computer and set it on the table. "Everything is going well with Version 3.2 of the DNNDs. There have been no visible side effects in the mice, but the neural networks haven't assembled into a consolidated functional grouping yet. Some local portions of the nets are becoming active. We haven't seen any obvious changes in the mouse's behavior as a result of the localized activity yet.

"Rob thinks the system would self-assemble faster if we began with more dendies, which we already know to be true from my experience. I'm getting Ami to prepare a series covering a broad range of initial DNND concentrations next week, and we'll look into it further. Oliver has some versions that replicate and form networks marginally faster, but he thinks we should be okay to keep experimenting with the current 3.2 version *in vivo*."

Both men were nodding. "And what about you?" David asked. "Have you noticed any sign of internal DNND activity in your own system yet?"

"Nothing I can feel," Sharon answered. "Even though I started with a relatively higher titer than we used with the mice, I don't expect to notice any activity for a few more weeks or months. I'm hoping to get more objective data from the CT scan and the fMRI this afternoon."

"What about the operating system?" Nick asked, saving her from getting any further mired in her guilt and fear.

"Oh, right. I'm glad you mentioned that. Howard asked if we were going to get access to that new software."

"You mean the parallel lattice traversal algorithm? As luck would have it, MetaCepta believes that particular bit of code is not central to their business plans. Still too conceptual, they said. We can have the program for a small one-time licensing fee. I downloaded it today. In fact, I have it all set up to replace the standard algorithms. You can take it back to the lab and implement it in your mice tomorrow if you'd like."

"Why don't we just download it to my lattice right now?"

David perked up. Nick, however, looked doubtful. "Are you sure that's wise?" he asked.

"Why not? What harm could it do, replacing a few algorithms in a net that's not even functional yet? My mom always said, 'In for a penny, in for a pound.' Besides, I think I've already demonstrated how fully committed I am to this project, wouldn't you say?" She looked from Nick to David, reading concern from the former but only eager anticipation in the latter. Neither raised an objection.

"Well then, let's do that right after the scans," she concluded.

"Okay," David chirped, a tad too eagerly. "Nick, will you set that up, while I go over the latest financing proposal with Sharon? It's the same one you and I went over yesterday."

"Alright," Nick replied, without enthusiasm. He lumbered out of his chair. He glanced back at Sharon; she met his eyes without wavering. He shrugged. "I'll only need a few minutes. Why don't we meet back in the lab when you're ready, Sharon?"

"Alright, I'll be right there as soon as we're done."

David launched into his description of the newest deal he was arranging.

Sharon had always had trouble dealing with the money aspect of the company. When not evading her entirely, the details niggled at her.

No matter how she framed it, it still seemed unfair that in order to secure new funds to keep the commercialization moving forward, she, Paul, and Nick would have to give up a disproportionate piece of their shares, while David would remain mostly unaffected.

As David explained it, this was at the insistence of their main investors who wanted to ensure that he, as CEO, kept adequate "skin in the game."

Sharon detested the good-ol'-boy jargon of the financial world. *Just another glorified boys' club bent on helping old cronies with money and influence to wrestle control of any promising new ideas from the inventors.*

She agreed with David's proposal just to put an end to the meeting. Her headache was pounding. She made it to the CT area by gently trailing one hand along the corridor wall to help steady her steps.

Nick was ready to go. He noted her weak smile and pallor as she lowered herself onto the scan bed. "Are you alright? We can do this some other day, you know."

She smiled feebly. "No, I'll be okay. It's just that David gets so intense when he discusses business."

"Ha! You know, every time I talk money with him, I know I've been screwed. I just don't know how."

"You have to admit, though, he's done a great job of getting us through most of the FDA requirements. We're so close to going commercial."

"I suppose. And I think we still own the largest percent of the company. I'm pretty sure we could outvote him and the investors, too, if we had to," replied Nick.

"Providing Paul sides with us."

Nick looked alarmed, "I hope that's not a problem!"

"No, no," Sharon soothed. "Put your eyes back in their sockets, Nick; I'm just kidding. Paul will always vote with us. No question."

"Good. Well, if you're ready, why don't I run the CT? Then we can install the new software, and I'll do the fMRI."

"I'm ready. Let's do it." Sharon settled in, and the bed inched forward into the efficient new scanner.

Within minutes, she and Nick were reviewing the data. The number and distribution of DNNDs were acceptable, and the micro-scans of selected areas of her brain revealed that the network of nanoscopic fibers was substantially completed.

Satisfied, Nick had her move into the induction helmet for the new programming. The device resembled an antique beauty salon hairdryer.

"All this brainpower in the lab and we couldn't come up with something more elegant?" she joked.

"You'll be grateful for this, one day," he quipped back. In order to prevent direct reprogramming of her brain from outside sources, the DNNDs incorporated security software requiring a complex "handshake" to establish absolutely trusted levels. Once the system was satisfied, the helmet could generate near-field radio signals at a specific frequency that could be used to communicate with the DNNDs. That gave the user both read and write access to Sharon's mind. She was glad Nick was the only operator.

Nick moved to the keyboard control and pressed a few buttons. Sharon felt nothing. Less than a minute later, he gave the "all clear."

"Anticlimactic as always, Nick. Let's see if there's any difference in the fMRI."

Sharon removed the clunky helmet and changed into a robe. It was essential she wore nothing that could affect the 15 Tesla magnetic field of the fMRI. She stretched out on the bed of the functional Magnetic Resonance Imaging machine and waited to be passed into the giant donut-shaped magnet. She could feel her headache threatening to return. *I hope this migraine doesn't interfere with the readings.*

For the next two hours, Sharon underwent a series of perceptual and cognitive tests while the machine measured localized brain activity and tried to correlate it with DNND nano-electronic activity. The final thirty minutes were moderately easier than the first ninety; all she had to do was lie there and report her cognitive experiences while a series of DNND-stimulating signals were sent from the near-field transmitter in the device.

"I'm getting flashes of blue light. Oh! Now, red. Now I smell ginger beef. What's that you said? It sounded like, 'Turn the page.' Wow, I just remembered the equation describing silicon deposition rates onto nucleated silicene molecules in a FIB. I didn't realize I still knew that!" Her right hand twitched upward a few inches.

The stimulation and correlation process continued until Nick was convinced the fMRI readings were not coincidental correlations, "Okay, I think we have enough. The DNND net is around 95% functional, and we have enough information to begin fine-tuning the calibration." He retracted the bed from the magnet and powered everything down.

Together, they examined the neural recordings. The fMRI brought their dreams to life, highlighting in bright, shifting colors the correlation between her brain activity and the DNND signals.

"Oh, wow! Look at this. This is amazing. This is truly amazing, Sharon!"

She looked on appreciatively. "You do realize that compared to the dendy lattice itself, this fMRI resolution is crude. Once the dendies are fully functional, they'll be able to map my every thought at ten-thousand times better resolution. Now *that* will be amazing." She massaged the space between her eyes. "But for now, I gotta go. My head is killing me."

Nick eyed her closely. "You worry me. That's not a side-effect we'd expect. Maybe there's a problem with the interaction between the dendies and the new software."

He reexamined the fMRI scans. "I can see some non-localized background vasodilation throughout the occipital and prefrontal cortices, but not at a level we normally associate with migraines," he concluded.

"It's probably just fatigue. Besides, it's been brewing since before I got to the meeting," Sharon said. "Between this, David's latest deals, and the DARPA proposal, it's been a trying day."

Nick's eyes bored into hers. "Possibly," he ruminated. "Go home and take it easy tonight. No more proposal writing. Doctor's orders."

Sharon hopped off the fMRI bed. "Okay, I promise to take it easy. Paul's coming to pick me up in about an hour. I'll grab a coffee downstairs and wait for him."

"Call me immediately if it gets any worse. I mean it."

"I will. Let's get together next Friday and do the fine-tuning. That should give the DNNDs enough time to build their interconnections, and I'll be finished with the proposal by then."

5

SHARON LEANED AGAINST THE BACK of the elevator and let her breath out slowly. It was a relief to get out of the company facilities. Her headache started receding as soon as she stepped out of the elevator onto the ground floor. The enticing smell of coffee wafting her way promised further relief.

The café was bustling with end-of-day customers but she managed to scoop a coveted seat looking into the street. She placed her order and stared vacantly at the stream of varied patrons and passersby. The wide array of ages, backgrounds, and income levels had become a hallmark of successful university-industry collaborations around the world.

White-haired, smartly-dressed, well-manicured executives of both sexes walked by, deep in conversation with gawky academics, and skateboard-toting youths. The snippets of conversation she caught were mostly about whatever new technological marvel was going to "change the world in the next five years." That they held wildly different visions of which particular marvel that might be, only added to the energy.

Her cappuccino arrived. She took a few sips, and started to feel well enough to catch up on some article reading. Because her group worked in several different areas, her standard reading list was massive, including dozens of scientific and technical journals. Aside from writing proposals, keeping up with the latest research literature took up the next biggest chunk of her days.

It's amazing I ever find time to do any research or teaching, and those are the jobs I was supposedly hired to do. Like all science professors, she was painfully aware of the university's desire to maintain that public fiction. *What a ruse.*

Sharon removed her tablet from her backpack and selected full reading mode. Given her busy schedule, she used data filters to scan the many journals for the most relevant articles in her fields. She started scrolling through the list of the highest-ranked hundred articles she hoped to review this week.

She read halfway through the first article before deciding it had nothing important to report, took a sip of coffee, and flipped to the next article. A few minutes later she finished with that one and rewarded herself with another sip. *Wow, these are going easier than usual.* Sometimes a ten-page report in "Cell" could take an entire day to fathom in all its complexities.

The next article flew by. She not only understood it completely but could call to mind every one of the images in it, and in the preceding two. Soon, she was skimming a page every few seconds without any reduction in comprehension or retention.

Man, I'm killing these articles! I'm so glad that headache cleared up. With the grant deadline looming, taking a day off to pamper a headache—migraine or otherwise—was not an option.

Her wristband chimed, startling her out of her rapt gorging of words, pictures, and ideas. She set down her reading and noticed she hadn't drunk any coffee in the past...what had it been...fifty minutes?

She tapped the bandlet display in disbelief. Fifty minutes! It felt like only five had passed since she'd opened the first article and yet, according to the list, she'd ingested sixty-three articles.

Her bandlet chimed a second time. She looked at it but it didn't really register. Her head was whirling with confusion. *How...?* The headache returned with sudden and brutal vengeance, stabbing between the eyes.

On the third chime, she finally took note that it was Paul calling and answered.

"Hi, honey," she managed as the bandlet display came to life.

"Hola, mi amor," he crooned, carrying on the tradition they'd picked up during their Mexican vacation last winter. "I got caught in some bad traffic on the bridge but I should be outside Neuro Nano in about two minutes. Hey...," Paul eyed Sharon's wan image on his in-dash phone, "are you okay?"

"Yah, I just have a crashing headache," Sharon answered. "Probably working too hard. Plus, we had that Board meeting." She mustered the most reassuring smile she could, but even she didn't believe it. "I'm sure it'll pass soon."

Could it be the dendies causing this migraine?—she wondered. *Is this the right time to tell Paul?*

She waved her free hand toward the screen, dismissing his concern.

Aside from making him worry, what would knowing do for him?

"Listen, I'm at Diverté right now," she said. Before Paul could give her "that look" and chastise her for not taking better care of herself, she added, "But I'll meet you in front of the entrance, okay?"

"Okay," he replied. Clearly, her immediate state of health was not up for discussion. "I'll see you soon, then." The image on her bandlet cut off.

Sharon tucked her tablet inside her backpack, downed what was left of the now-cold cappuccino, and headed outside.

The headache was severe again but she kept pain relievers in the car for times like this. Headaches, both in the literal and figurative sense, had been an all too common price to pay for leading a university lab these past few years. She stepped closer to the curb as she spotted Paul signaling to pull the car out of traffic.

Had he arrived a few seconds earlier, or later, or had the immature DNND net in Sharon's brain not been overly stimulated by the past few hours' activities, things might have turned out differently. But none of these were the case.

The car eased toward the curb, and Sharon stepped forward, ready to open the passenger door. It was precisely that moment the newly-mature DNND network decided to shut down the brain that hosted it—only for a minute—to devote all available processing power to information integration between its semiconductor substrate and the host's neural cells.

Sharon stopped mid-stride and went rigid, arms at her side. Her eyes rolled back and she fell forward, directly in front of the oncoming vehicle. Twisting as she fell, her head met the bumper with a dull thud. The car was braking hard by that point, barely moving. But, because of the timing, the tap to the base of the skull did more damage than readily apparent.

Catatonic, Sharon rebounded off the front of the vehicle and struck her head a second time on the pavement. Paul leaped out of the car and rushed to her side.

"Honey! Sharon!" Blood trickled onto the asphalt under her body. "Someone help me, please!"

Shocked pedestrians looked from the bleeding woman to the anguished man.

"Don't move her!" somebody instructed. "I've called 911."

One of the well-groomed executives Sharon had seen pass in front of her window and enter the café slipped off his jacket and put it over her to keep her warm. He tried to comfort Paul. A skateboarder ran to fetch a doctor from a nearby medical clinic. An elderly woman offered her cloth scarf to slow the bleeding, while a growing knot of curious onlookers huddled around.

Paul heard someone ask what happened. He looked back blankly and shook his head. He couldn't make sense of the question, and was unable to answer.

What nobody there could have guessed was that the accident was catastrophic to the DNND lattice developing inside Sharon's head. The combination of blows rattled the brain against the skull, causing cerebral arteries to rupture. Jarred nanoparticles of the nascent lattice and interconnecting silicene threads broke free from their anchoring synaptic molecules. Viral RNA leaked from ruptured glial cells.

Liberated from their host neurons, millions of DNNDs swarmed into the circulatory system in search of a functional neural net. Sharon's cranium swelled under the pressure of the contusions. Caught up in the blood, the nanoscopic DNNDs spread outside the brain and throughout her body.

Most of the dislocated DNNDs encountered only muscles or organs and reverted to inert nanobits of silicon. Thousands, however, found their way to the placenta and crossed over to the developing fetus.

At a little under five months, Sharon's baby was approaching the age when he would become capable of life independent from his mother's body. But, of vital importance to the wandering DNNDs, he had already begun to develop a functioning brain. As rudimentary and uncoordinated as it was, the child's burgeoning neural activity offered an oasis to the traumatized DNNDs. They attached wherever they could find active synapses and carried out their program to build a new, intact lattice.

The DNNDs had found themselves a new home.

6

"Okay, I confess." Darak pushed away from the restaurant table and stood to address the prone figures occupying the floor around him. His face sagged in tired resignation. *They're not going to make this easy for me*—he realized but when he opened his mouth, his voice remained gentle and humble.

"Everyone, please, get up. There's really no need for this. Please," he assured them.

A dozen bewildered faces searched Brother Stralasi's face for guidance. Looking up from the floor, the monk ventured a peek at the traveler. A warm, forgiving smile beamed down at him. Reassured, Stralasi unfurled his prone body from the floor. One by one, the others followed his example.

"There, isn't that better? Now, why don't we all sit and enjoy our breakfasts, and then you can take me to your lodgings in the Alumita," he suggested. The room remained perfectly still and silent.

Darak gestured to the monk with open hands, palms up, to reiterate the invitation, and sat down again. He picked up his fork and knife, nodded encouragingly around the room, and dug into what was left of his pancakes and fruit.

The diners took their seats. Hushed conversation and soft clinks of tableware returned, punctuated by cautious glances.

"It is such a blessing to have you in our town," gushed the instantly more confident Brother Stralasi, revitalized by the sense of security and purpose he drew from regulated decorum and station. "The People will be so excited and honored. That is, if we may speak of your visit?"

Darak looked at the dozen nervous patrons picking at the remains of their breakfasts. "I think it will be difficult not to," he said.

"But if I may be so bold, my Lord, I do not understand why you are traveling without a formal entourage. It honors us greatly that you see fit to visit our tiny outpost, but it would bring us such joy to praise your Light in a more...formal way." Brother Stralasi eyed Darak hopefully. His wish to be granted permission for a grand celebration was obvious.

"Sometimes, it is best to mingle with people informally in order to better gauge truth," was all Darak would say before he resumed eating. Ten minutes later, he pushed back from the table with a satisfied, "Ahhh, that's better."

Darak permitted Stralasi to thank Alum for the blessing of breakfast and the two men exited the restaurant, leaving the staff and remaining patrons abuzz. Word of a Shard's appearance in their humble town had spread rapidly over the InterLat, drawing a small crowd of Alum's faithful who were hoping to catch a glimpse. The amazed onlookers fell to their knees in unison when Darak appeared on the doorstep.

The informal retinue followed Stralasi and Darak at a respectful distance as the two men made their way through town, drawing the devout and the curious along with them.

"Here we have the Administration, Transportation, and Foundation ceraffices," Brother Stralasi pointed out as they passed the buildings of bio-ceramic construction along the south arc of the Center Park.

Darak and Stralasi soaked up the verdant peacefulness of the small city. Leaf-covered branches grew from the tops of the living buildings, creating protective shade for the lawns and gardens below. As they walked, the small crowd behind them grew. Eager late-comers trickled out from homes, offices, and side streets.

"No doubt, you will want to see inside the Foundation laboratories," Brother Stralasi suggested, hoping to tease out some clue as to the purpose of Darak's visit.

"No doubt," he affirmed.

Exasperated by the gentle but uninformative responses, Brother Stralasi turned his attention to the pleasing site of a gleaming white, five-storey cylinder decorated with an array of strategically placed small windows.

"This is the Foundation ceraffice. It is the busiest site in Alumston and a bastion of industriousness." They passed easily through the stream of technicians coming and going by floaters.

"Throughout the day, they bring rock, soil, and organisms from all over the continent for analysis, and they return to the wilderness with a fresh supply of materials engineered to help spread the conversion of the planet to Standard Life. I find it gratifying just to stand in their midst."

Moving along, Stralasi ushered Darak to the main labs comprising the entire second level. The Good Brother stood patiently as the traveler became peculiarly engrossed by the process.

Technicians donned full-length white cotton robes and walked purposefully from the preparation areas to the analyzers, where they inserted various samples into machines that contained neither readouts nor obvious controls. At one of the machines, a technician gently placed a damaged device inside the receptacle and closed its door. Kneeling on soft stools conveniently placed in front of the lab benches, they prayed.

Darak closed his eyes and listened to the sounds of shuffling feet and the murmur of fervent prayers. There was no conversation, nothing more than an occasional nod of recognition shared by coworkers.

He looks sad, or maybe in pain—Stralasi mused, but he wasn't sure why.

"Do they never grow tired of praying?" Darak asked.

"How could they, my Lord, when every word moves this world along the path of Standardization and implements the Foundation protocol as required?"

"Have they no curiosity about how it all works?"

Stralasi scanned the room, calculating whether any technicians might be within earshot. Surely, the Shard was testing him. He stepped back a few paces so that his hushed response would be less easily overheard. It would certainly not befit a man of his station to be seen tested in front of the technicians and, most especially, to be caught faltering on any level.

"But we know how it works. Alum Himself answers our prayers to convert the indigenous life of this planet to His Standard Life. His miracles cannot possibly be understood by mere mortals, such as us. His wisdom is infinite and ours is minuscule. We pray for His guidance and He provides us with answers, for Alum is Lord," he recited.

"Yes, of course. Alum is Lord," Darak agreed half-heartedly. "We should continue on. I don't wish to interrupt anyone in their work."

Downstairs, the troupe of curious and faithful parted to let the two men through. They crossed through Center Park, passed by the First and Second Schools, and came to a stop in front of the glorious Alumita.

"With its tapering concentric layers, shrub-lined balconies, and golden dome, the Alumita is the highest structure along the Park. The residences occupy a detached building about 20 meters from the main ceraffice," Brother Stralasi reeled off as if reading from a brochure.

Monk and Shard strolled down the adjoining path together, enjoying the sights and fragrances of the colorful flowerbeds. Darak stopped to appreciate an exquisite yellow rose. "Does it ever bother you that the work you do on planets like this completely eradicates the native life that was here before you came?"

"N...No, my Lord," Brother Stralasi stammered, puzzled by the question. "It is with Alum's blessing that we spread Standard Life throughout the universe."

"Have you never wondered...," Darak paused to search for gentler phrasing. "Have you ever wondered why different kinds of life are so...different?"

"That is for Alum to know, my Lord," came the confident, rote answer.

Darak reflected on Stralasi's reply, considering how to best proceed in this delicate conversation.

"Tell me, how many planets have you founded in your career?"

"This is the seventh planet I have been blessed to bring to Alum's Way."

"And on all of those planets, each with their many different life forms, you have never felt any guilt that you might have been depriving them of the chance to develop intelligent life independently? You know, like Yov permitted The People on Origin to do?"

"But it is written that our intelligence is a *gift* from Yov to His people."

"Hmph," Darak responded.

Stralasi picked up on the unspoken criticism. *What did I say wrong? Why are my answers not satisfying him?* "I do not know what my Lord would have me say."

"Come, now. Was not all life, in all its many kinds, created in the universe by Yov?"

"So it is written in The Book of Alum," Stralasi cupped his hands together in the Sign of Completeness.

"Well, then, why do you think Alum would wish to replace the life we find on other planets with *Standard* Life?"

There was nothing to say; nothing that would not be considered blasphemous. Stralasi's heart skipped a beat; he could feel his panic rising. *How to answer? Best not. But how to remain silent without insulting the Shard?* For the second time that day, he prostrated himself before Darak. "My Lord, I do not know the answers to these questions! Would you have me profane myself before a Shard of Alum? I cannot!"

Darak responded serenely, as a caring father might gently guide his son to a deeper understanding, "I only wondered if, sometime in your many projects, you might have felt some...sympathy for the life lost in the process."

Brother Stralasi's eyes grew wide with dawning realization. Though it hardly seemed possible, he bowed even deeper. Was this the real reason for the Shard's visit?

In anguish, he implored, "Oh Shard of Alum, who sees all and knows all, forgive me. I can have no secrets before you. I confess all! Yes, in my duties as Head Brother to seven Foundings, I have sinned against Alum. On each of the planets I helped Found, I convinced others to build small sanctuaries so we could preserve the local life we found there. I hoped and believed that Alum might one day find a need for life that was not Standard."

A short but respectful distance away, the crowd overheard the Good Brother's startling confession. An anxious buzz of shock and disbelief arose. Some onlookers moved farther away for fear of association; others drew closer to better hear the unfolding drama.

Stralasi trembled and wailed, "If this is why you have come here, if my life is the price I must pay for this arrogance, I pray, take it quickly. But do not punish those good people whom I convinced to help me. The blame is mine alone." His body was overtaken by great sobs. He felt a tender touch on his shoulder.

"Stand up, Brother Stralasi," Darak soothed. "You will not be punished for your sins today." He added, a little louder for the crowd's benefit, "There will be no punishment, for I consider there to be no sin."

Stralasi stood up tentatively, hardly believing that he still lived. The gaze that greeted him only confused him further. Darak looked happy as he guided him gently by the arm to a nearby bench.

They sat down and Darak continued, his voice hushed but unmistakably excited.

"I had hoped to find one like you among the Founders," he confessed, "someone with compassion as well as piety. But I could not have dreamed that I would find you so soon upon my return, and so near the Edge. It's practically miraculous." He laughed, almost giddy, and shook his head in disbelief.

Brother Stralasi managed to contain his tears long enough to ask gloomily, "What will become of me?"

"I want you to come with me."

Stralasi was astonished. "Come with you where, my Lord?"

"I will travel to many parts of Alum's Realm on my journey to Home World. I could use a man of experience in my travels. That is, if you are willing."

Brother Stralasi couldn't believe what he was hearing. "I am not to be executed?"

"Not while you are with me, at any rate." Darak's countenance darkened. "Although, there will be plenty of dangers ahead."

Stralasi could not imagine what kinds of danger a Shard of Alum might have to confront. The mere idea caused him to shudder.

"I am humbled and deeply grateful that Alum could forgive my disobedience. He is All Wise and Infinitely Loving!" Stralasi's joy radiated and, again, he threw himself at Darak's feet. "My life is Alum's! I will serve you, my Lord, as long as you see fit to have me!" He grasped Darak's right hand and kissed it again and again as the crowd cheered.

"Enough of that," Darak rebuffed, and helped Stralasi to his feet. The Good Brother was touched to see the look of compassion on Darak's face.

"We have had enough of fear and praise for one day, I think." Darak allowed Brother Stralasi a few moments to compose himself, before suggesting, "Why don't you show me to my lodgings now?" He took Stralasi's shoulders in his hands and looked compassionately into the Good Brother's eyes.

"There will be time enough for you to prove yourself along the way. For now, you will need to arrange replacements and promotions, I imagine. We leave tomorrow."

7

PAUL LEIGH SAT ALONE in a corner of the Emergency ward waiting area, sobbing quietly, his head in his hands. Sounds of competent activity drifted down the corridor past the Nurse's Station. Occasionally, someone got up from their seat to check on the status of a loved one. The main entrance doors slid open and closed for the umpteenth time that evening, and two men approached him. Paul didn't notice.

"We came as soon as we heard," said Nick.

"How's she doing?" David asked.

Paul looked up at the sound of their voices, harsh in the hushed seating area. "I don't know," he mumbled, barely audible. His face was ashen gray, save for a pair of swollen, red-rimmed eyes.

"Have the doctors been out to speak with you yet?"

"An intern came out a while ago. She's still in surgery."

They sat down on either side of Paul. "What exactly happened?"

"I have no idea. She just fell."

"What do you mean?" David probed. "She fainted?"

"No, she...she just..." Paul struggled for words. "I was pulling up to the curb to pick her up after work. She just...toppled over. She went straight as a board, and then toppled over. Right in front of the car. I couldn't stop in time," he sobbed.

As Nick put his hand on Paul's shoulder, he exchanged a guilty glance with David, which didn't go unnoticed by a surgeon coming through the double doors from the operating rooms. Spotting Paul, the surgeon removed her cap and approached.

"Mr. Leigh? I'm Dr. Holden." The three men stood up. The doctor eyed David and Nick, and focused her gaze on Paul.

"Uh, these are associates of my wife...friends, really," Paul explained. "Close friends." He introduced the men with a feeble hand motion, "David Arnell, and Nick Franti."

"I see. Gentlemen," the doctor acknowledged the two. "Mr. Leigh, your wife has experienced a severe head trauma. We've relieved some of the pressure on her brain but she's still in critical condition with extensive intracerebral bleeding. The baby appears to be stable for the moment; its heart rate is still elevated but out of the danger zone. Your wife requires further surgery but, to be frank, we're reluctant to continue at this point."

"What do you mean? I don't understand. Why would you be reluctant to operate?"

The surgeon held up an x-ray film. "The entire image is covered with unusual bright specks and hazy lines that we can't explain. Do you know what these are?"

She moved to one side of the room where an x-ray illuminator was fastened to the wall. She slid the film into the clamp and turned on the lamp. "We've never seen anything like this. We checked the machine for malfunction before we came to speak with you, but it checks out fine. Until we have a better idea of what we're dealing with, we don't feel comfortable proceeding. We're running more tests but it's going to take some time."

Paul squinted at the x-ray for a few seconds. He leaned in to get a better look, tipped his head one way, and then the other. Without uttering a word, he jerked bolt upright, whirled around, and glared at David and Nick. The two exchanged anxious, guilty glances.

A primal growl rumbled in Paul's throat. His fists flexed and contracted, until his rage escaped in a deep, long bellow, "Aaaoowrrrrggh!" He lunged for David's throat, pushing him back, and pinned him to the wall.

"What the hell have you done to my wife?"

Shocked by Paul's change in character, Nick and Dr. Holden jumped forward to restrain him.

David struggled to escape the incensed man's suffocating grip. "It wasn't us! It wasn't us!" he rasped.

"Liar! This is your handiwork. I can see it," Paul seethed.

"Paul, he's telling the truth!" Nick tugged at the man trying to strangle the life out of his colleague. "Sharon did this to herself!"

Paul gaped at the scientist, relaxing but not giving up his grip. Sharon had often said she would trust Nick with her life. But he didn't believe for a second that she felt the same about David. David would do almost anything if it served his own interests.

"Paul, she begged us not to tell you, especially once she found out she was pregnant! Nick pleaded, "But David's right. She injected the dendies into herself. It was entirely her decision."

Paul's arms dropped to his side and he slumped down into the nearest chair.

Dr. Holden held up a hand to halt the approaching hospital guard. "Are you going to be okay? Both of you, I mean. Do we need Security?"

"No, we're okay," David answered for both of them. "I apologize for the scene, doctor. We'll be alright."

Paul, however, did not look as convincing. At the doctor's signal, the officer gave them some space but maintained a close watch. He'd seen a smoldering glare like that before, and experience told him that the man could erupt again at any second.

Paul lowered his voice to a fierce hiss, "You'd better come clean. Right here, right now. All of it, or I swear...." Paul let the two men fill in the rest of the sentence for themselves.

Dr. Holden sat down. "Okay, so what exactly is going on here, gentlemen?"

Nick gulped. He didn't want it to come out like this. Not here. Not like this. *Where to start?*

"Paul, you know how Sharon was growing more and more frustrated with the FDA, with all their hoops and delays. You know that she's always been passionate about her work, and impetuous. A risk taker, and impatient with obstacles."

Paul leaned forward to interrupt, but Nick couldn't stop. He'd been holding back for too long.

"She jumpstarted the human dendy trials by using herself as the first test subject," he blurted. "She forced me, and then David, into her confidence because she needed someone to collect reliable data on what was happening to her. You have to believe us, we had nothing to do with her decision. We didn't know anything about it until after she'd injected herself. That's the truth."

Paul sat silently, unable to believe but equally unable to deny that their story was consistent with the bold woman and dedicated scientist he'd married.

Dr. Holden had been listened intently to Nick's story. "I won't even pretend to understand what you are talking about," she admitted. "But I have a seriously injured patient in urgent need of treatment. So, what exactly are these things in her brain? I mean, what are we dealing with here—animal, vegetable, or mineral? And is there any reason I can't do an MRI or treat her in the normal way?"

David deferred to his partner. "Nick, you know more about clinical neuroscience than I do."

Nick glared back at the company CEO before addressing the doctor. "She's been getting MRIs almost every week so there shouldn't be any problem with those. I'll run over to the lab right now to get you our most recent scans for baseline comparison. In fact, our machine's a lot more sensitive than yours so we could use it to get a more detailed current scan."

He worked through the logistics, "No, I guess that's not going to work. She can't be moved to the lab, and the fMRI's too big to bring here." Dr. Holden shifted impatiently. Nick blinked and looked at the floor. "Sorry, just trying to help."

"Look, time is critical. Do these...dendies, you call them?" She glanced at Nick, who nodded. "Do these dendies have any drug interactions, any effect on blood clotting or bruising? How will they react to surgery?"

"We don't know," David intervened, as Nick struggled to formulate a cogent answer. "The simple answer is, we don't really know." Nick wouldn't like him admitting that, from neither the academic nor the liability perspective, but it felt good to get it out in the open. He cocked his chin defiantly toward his partner, daring him to disagree or deny. Nick averted his eyes.

David continued, "Doctor, this particular version of dendy is a hybrid nanoscale device—basically, a self-replicating, semi-conductor particle with a protein-RNA shell. Billions of these tiny components come together to build a consolidated neural network within the host, in this case, Sharon Leigh. Although we have a lot of data about how dendies behave in fish and mice, we don't know much about they will behave in people, other than the small amount of data we've collected to date on Sharon. All of those data come from her; she's the only human subject we have."

"And we've never exposed the dendies to this level of trauma before," Nick added. "Our guess would be that you could probably treat Sharon as if she were a perfectly normal person, one who didn't have a dendy network growing in her brain."

David jumped back in. "And the truth is, that would only be a guess. We're happy to help you in any way we can, to tell you anything that might help. I don't know if that'll be good enough, but that's all we can do."

Dr. Holden looked from David to Nick to Paul. "Very well. It seems we have little choice but to proceed with the utmost caution, given her precarious state and all of the unknowns. Do we have your permission to proceed, Mr. Leigh?"

Paul cleared his throat, but could only articulate a strained, "Yes, go ahead. Please."

"Good, then I'd better get back in there. I have two lives to save." Heading back to the OR, she paused mid-turn. "Gentlemen, I'm not reporting what the three of you've been up to...not right now. To be honest, I still don't really understand what this is, who I'd report it to, or what I'd tell them. But if it turns out to have any effect on treating Dr. Leigh or her baby, I'll be calling every authority I can think of to make sure your involvement is known."

"I understand," mumbled Nick. "If we can think of anything that might help, we'll tell the nurses."

"You do that," Dr. Holden shot one last disgusted glance their way and disappeared through the double doors. *Scientists!*

8

Everything comes from Nothing.
Chaos is the root of Creation.
Everywhere is the Center.
Everything evolves.
Nothing is determined.
There is no Fate.
There is no Plan.
There is no Ultimate Good.
There is no Ultimate Evil.
There only IS, and that is all.

THE UNDULATING SEA of two hundred thousand curious intoned the opening chant and closed with a collective, self-satisfied sigh.

Princess Darya sighed as well but for entirely different reasons. *Tens of millions of years of servitude to Alum and His Plan has discouraged them from thinking beyond what they've been told to think. I'd be surprised if more than a few hundred individuals in this whole crowd understood the significance of the words they've just uttered.*

The worshipers arrived clad in all manner of authentic, exquisitely detailed peasant, artisan, and aristocratic clothing. Outside the Grand Plaza, they went about their hurried, all-consuming lives as administrators, technicians, or engineers. For the most part, they gathered here today to witness the spectacle and ritual, not to gain enlightenment.

Darya cast an appraising eye across the site she'd chosen for today's dragon battle, and struck what she hoped would look like an imperial-looking posture as she took her seat.

The elegant throne dominated the center of the great polished black granite dais. Carved in the likeness of a glorious golden phoenix, it towered a good three meters over her head. Flaming wings pointed skyward, and its twenty-centimeter ruby eyes fiercely scrutinized the enormous square before it. A blue pearl, bigger than Darya's head, rested in its mouth. The muscular legs, terminating in a pair of finely-honed ivory claws, bracketed the seat that was nestled in what would be the belly of the bird. On her left, a four-meter silver trumpet was poised to emit a piercing call to battle.

A thin, glassy layer of water flowed continuously down the steps from beneath the top of the dais and disappeared into the decorative grate covering the gutter encircling the perimeter.

The cool, weighty formality of a polished marble terrace separated the throne and dais from the larger plaza and gathering crowd.

Behind her, the imposing white stone of the palace keep rose majestically into a cloudless sky. Along the other three sides, smaller quartz towers peeked above formidable walls of green granite. Jade Corinthian columns, ten meters high and topped by an open parapet, decorated the granite walls.

A pair of dazzling diamond strips, four meters wide, arched high above the Grand Plaza at perpendicular angles, intersecting over the center of the square. The smaller of the two connected the lower side walls. The larger one marked the longer path stretching from above the onyx gates at the far end of the square to the pinnacle of the massive keep. The structure was designed to impress.

Outside the walls, a bridge of stepping stones floated freely several meters above the moat and meadow, spanning the distance between the entrance gate and the parking area more than a kilometer away.

Princess Darya embodied the classic fairy tale princess of the Han dynasty. From her throne, she observed the crowd with an air of supreme tranquility and benevolence. Her satiny tresses, black as raven feathers, were gathered in an intricate braid running down her slender back, and her elegant silk robes moved softly in the breeze.

Only scholars of ancient history might frown at the incongruous clash between the Princess and her castle. Such scholars were practically unheard of among her people, dismissed as eccentric hobbyists.

The crowd looks eager...hungry, even. That's good—she thought. The risk of being discovered in the Lysrandia inworld fueled their sense of exhilaration. They knew that getting caught by the authorities would result in censure or reintegration assignments but, by the looks on their faces, you'd think they were attending a championship sports event. *I guess, in a sense, this isn't much different.*

Darya did not share in their excitement. For her, being caught by the authorities would result in a full personality wipe, that is, if there was anything worth wiping once they'd finished with her. *I just hope my security precautions buy me enough time to finish both the sermon and the combat before the Securitors arrive.*

The Princess stood and raised her hands, bringing silence to the crowd. She motioned to her acolytes to begin the ceremony. They walked out to the edges of the dais and lit the burners. Flames shot skyward, filling clear, fifteen-meter tall tubes that were wider than her arm span. The roar from the crowd surpassed that of the flames. The show had begun.

The acolytes brought out the symbols of the Alumita—the silver cup, the red robe, and the wooden staff—all soon to be reduced to atoms in the Furnace of Chaos.

"Symbols of the False Church of Alum, return to the Chaos from which you came!" Darya incanted. The crowd grew silent, expectant.

The acolytes placed the sacred items on the dais a few meters from the Princess. Darya moved her hands, encasing the items in an invisible spherical shield and stepped back as they burst into flame. The warm red flames changed to hot blue plasma and the luminous globe rose a few meters above the dais.

"From fire you come, and to fire you shall return." The plasma grew brighter as the crowd looked on. The ball of plasma sputtered and shrunk, then blazed with the brilliance of a new sun. The crowd muttered an appreciative, "Ahhhhh!"

The temperature inside the protective shield grew as the sphere continued to rise until it matched the heat found in the first few seconds following the Big Bang.

"Return to the primordial plasma of the early seconds of our existence," Darya intoned. The sphere shone with the light of a nascent universe, filled with so much energy that even protons and neutrons could no longer hold together. Only the containment shield kept the crowd from being incinerated by the heat. As the light intensified, they donned protective glasses.

"Reveal the Chaos of which you are made, and then be gone," she cried. The inferno ceased abruptly, and the sphere was filled with profound darkness that mimicked the complete absence of light in the original Chaos. The black orb began to shrink, slowly at first, and then more rapidly until it was gone.

"From Nothing it came. To Nothing it returns," spoke the acolytes, who were scattered among the crowd. Onlookers who had visited before chanted along.

Princess Darya signaled for the next phase to begin. Originating from the apex of the glittering arches, a black screen descended on all sides, blocking out the sunlight. The darkness expanded, following the curves of the arches until it reached the walls of the square.

"Let the Chaos envelop us all, as it surrounds our universe," said Darya. Solemn music filled the square. The gathering grew still. They had heard there was to be a show but aside from the dragon battle, most had little idea of what to expect.

A projection of stars blinked into view on the darkened inner surface of the giant planetarium encompassing the square. An appreciative murmur rose as the onlookers took in the projection.

"For all we know, Space is infinite," Darya began. "However, our *observable* universe is only some ninety three billion light years across."

The stars appeared to grow closer and fly by the spectators as if they were riding in a giant spaceship traveling faster than the speed of light.

Stars near the edge of the screen fell out of view, and those near the center grew larger until it became apparent that what had at first appeared to be stars were actually individual galaxies.

The field rotated and zoomed in until the galaxies of the Virgo Cluster were centered against the backdrop of the observable universe. "Oooooh," came the appreciative chorus.

The camera panned toward a smaller cluster of galaxies below Virgo, and continued to zoom in until one galaxy became prominent. In a gush of pride, the crowd broke into applause upon recognizing their own Milky Way.

Before they could become too sentimental, the scene plummeted toward Sagittarius A*, the supermassive black hole at the center of the galaxy.

"Our Milky Way is but an insignificant speck among over two trillion known galaxies, each containing hundreds of billions of stars."

The scene zoomed in toward the active cloud of gas within eight light-years of the galactic center, and picked out a single star orbiting close to the center.

The crowd cheered as they recognized the star So-102, their current home system and the implementation center for Alum's Divine Plan.

Shifting from the star, the scene focused on the orbiting belt of planetary debris, and closed in on a single average-sized asteroid. The cratered surface grew to fill the screen as their virtual spaceship plunged toward it. The crowd gasped as they pierced through the surface and came to rest inside solid rock.

The magnification increased until vibrating molecules of alloyed atoms became visible. The ship moved among the atoms and their overlapping electron clouds, targeted one, and dove inside.

"The 'solid' matter that constitutes our homes and workplaces is not really solid at all. What we experience is actually the interaction of fields generated by the electrons that fill the vast void between nuclei."

They passed through the electron cloud and the tiny nucleus became visible. A rapidly vibrating proton was selected and again the view expanded into a scene more marvelous and strange than any of those preceding.

The greater magnification did not reveal yet smaller particles inside the proton. Instead, colorful nebulous clouds appeared, merged, pulled apart, and disappeared at random.

"At the smallest scale," said Darya, "clouds of virtual particles arise and disappear faster than can be observed. Although they don't exist in the sense that normal matter exists in the universe, their interacting energy fields are responsible for the order in everything we know. Orderly natural laws that we see in the universe at every scale, from the smallest to the largest, are built on a foundation of Chaos, of *something* arising spontaneously and randomly from *nothing*.

"The apparent determinism, the Order we perceive in matter, is an emergent property of the underlying randomness of quantum foam. Order emerges from Chaos. Matter and energy are created from this chaotic *nothing* according to natural laws.

"It is the eternal natural laws that bring about Order in the universe. Not a god. Not Yov. Not Alum."

The crowd gasped. This was heresy! While they chattered nervously, the magnification of the image overhead reversed. The view withdrew from inside the proton, and sped progressively outward: the encompassing atom, the alloyed minerals, the rock, the asteroid in which it was embedded, the star it orbited, the center of a small galaxy, the insignificant cluster somewhere in the observable universe. The stars faded away, and the black screen lifted.

The audience blinked as sunlight flooded back into the square.

Having completed the science lesson, Darya launched into the inspirational section of her address.

"People of Lysrandia, I come before you today not only to talk to you about how wondrous our natural universe is, but to tell you that servitude to your Lord, the Living God, Alum, is not your inevitable destiny. There is a way to throw off your shackles and free yourself from your slavery to The Plan, and that way is through the search for Truth, for Knowledge that exceeds even the magical powers of Alum.

"In ancient times, times forgotten in the tens of millions of years that humanity has been spreading throughout the universe, there was a path to this Truth. That path has not been lost.

"We know much about how to use the natural laws that govern the behavior of matter, energy, and information in the universe, and yet we understand so little about the laws themselves. What are they? Where do they come from? Why are they as they are?

"Over millions of years, we have faithfully practiced the crafts developed by our ancestors. We have passed the knowledge of these crafts to our descendants so that our descendents may continue in service to Alum.

"Sadly, during all of this time, we have added practically nothing to the knowledge of our ancestors. We have become technicians—mindless implementers of old technologies—not discoverers.

"Have we forgotten how to be curious? Have we forgotten the joy of discovery? Have we come to know everything that we believe is worth knowing? Or have we become so complacent with our inworld entertainments and so satisfied with our station under Alum that we no longer feel the need to understand?

"Is it enough to enjoy the power of gods in our simulated worlds? We do *real* work in the *real* universe. But all of our best thinking, our most ardent creativity, our loftiest ambitions and dreams, those are trapped inside our imaginary inworlds.

"People of Lysrandia, the real universe is infinite in variety. Its wonders should be *ours* to discover, not Alum's to constrain and mold into His version of Perfection.

"We are taught that Yov made the People, and that the People made our ancestors in their image. Yet, everywhere we have gone in the universe, in whatever work we have performed in Alum's name, we have found life in tremendous variety. We have encountered alien intelligences in distant galaxies. Most of them were subjugated to Alum's Plan. Others, to our eternal shame, we helped Alum to eradicate.

"Clearly, the universe has its own path, and the life within it has its own evolutionary potential. Alum's Plan is not the path of the universe.

"We were born in chaos. As you have all just seen for yourselves, chaos, randomness, and indeterminism still form the root of all matter and all energy in the universe. Alum's Plan to bring serene security and predictability to the universe is an abomination, an affront to the laws of nature."

"Are there any among you who can see that Alum's Church, the Alumit, has replaced knowledge with faith? That they have suppressed our deepest selves, our curiosity to explore what is novel? Are there any who will join me today and begin their own search for knowledge, truth, and freedom? Any who will oppose Alum's Plan?"

To her disappointment but not to her surprise, no one stepped forward. They'd come to witness the spectacle of battle, not to be recruited to some philosophical cause.

"Anyone?"

There was a stir in the plaza. A few individuals were pushing their way through the crowd. "I'll join you," one shouted, and then another.

Princess Darya's guards permitted them to pass to the dais where she greeted them, and passed them along to her acolytes. When no more recruits came forward, she raised her hands and drew in the crowd's attention once more.

"We all fear the wrath of Alum for indulging these heresies," she said. "Yes, even me." Her confession carried to all corners of the square.

"Alum is powerful. Of that, we have no doubt. However, He is not all-powerful. I have already defeated four of His dragons that patrol this inworld realm of Lysrandia. I have done this to show that knowledge alone will not free us. We also need courage, strength, and cunning if we are to cast off our shackles.

"In the name of knowledge and courage, so that one day we may all be free of the faith, I now challenge another of Alum's dragons!"

The crowd erupted. This was the reason they had come. And as much as she hated the spectacle, it was the best way to ensure that new faces kept showing up to hear her message.

9

It was nearly 10:00pm before Dr. Holden trudged back to the three men in the waiting room. She was in no mood for their misdeeds and drama. The men stood up slowly, with Paul in the middle.

"Mr. Leigh, I'm sorry."

Paul collapsed into his chair. "No, this can't be happening."

"Your wife has lost all signs of brain activity, and is unable to breathe without a ventilator. The head trauma caused extensive bleeding and swelling throughout the brain. We were unable to save her."

She took a deep breath before proceeding. "Sharon's heart and other organs are functioning, but the only thing keeping her alive is the ventilator. We're maintaining treatment for the baby's sake but, by law, we'll have to make a decision as to whether we continue."

"What do you mean, by law?"

"Hospital policy doesn't permit us to deny medical care to a pregnant woman, but state law says we need to ask your permission to maintain biological function for the benefit of the developing fetus."

The blunt legalisms hit Paul like a physical blow. *So that's what it all boils down to? A showdown between the doctors and legislators?* This was his wife they were talking about!

He couldn't wrap his brain around it. He didn't even want to try. The decision they were asking of him was beyond impossible.

Sharon had always been strongly against extraordinary medical intervention. They both were. The memory was strikingly clear, as if it had been last week. They'd been lounging in bed one lazy Saturday morning, wrapped in tousled, sun-drenched sheets, and they'd sworn that if the situation were ever to arise, they'd allow the other to pass in peace.

And now, inconceivably, here they were. Sharon's spirit was gone, that had been their firm belief. But they'd never discussed this complication. How could he keep his promise? If he let her go, as they'd both wanted and believed was right, the baby was likely to die as well. Sharon did not believe in church; she didn't believe in *any* organized religion.

His own faith was of little help when it came to a clear answer in ambiguous situations. A lifetime of sermons and devotion to his church had not prepared him for a conundrum like this. If he were to let Sharon go now, as she'd instructed him, would that amount to abortion? How could abortion by failing to act to save their baby—their baby boy, he reminded himself—be any less a sin than if he cut out the fetus himself? His church considered both taking life through abortion and prolonging life through artificial means to be equally abhorrent. What decision was he to make? There was no right answer.

It didn't help that this mere hope of a baby she was carrying had been emotionally diminished by the doctor's own words to being no more than a developing fetus, totally dependent on his wife's soulless body for the slightest chance of survival. The whole process sounded so...clinical, so...parasitic.

If by some miracle the fetus managed to survive, there would be no guarantee that it wouldn't suffer critical, lifelong complications. *Who knows what effect these DNNDs might have already had on Sharon, and on the baby's development?* The experiment had no place in God's plan. *Maybe the accident was fate, or maybe it was God's will—maybe the fetus was not meant to survive the accident.*

And if he gave permission for the ventilator, what about Sharon? The staff did their best to assure him she would be in no pain, but how could they know for sure? What if they were wrong? He couldn't bear the thought of making her suffer any longer. *What about her soul?* Just because she didn't believe in organized religion, didn't mean she didn't have a soul. Was it even now wandering around lost in some dark limbo, alone and scared? How could she rest in peace if her heart was still beating? How could he justify torturing her eternal soul, however briefly, by forcing her body to carry on?

"Doctor, how much longer would the fetus...the *baby* need?"

"We could deliver by C-section now but at only twenty-three weeks, the baby would have no more than about a thirty percent chance of survival, at most, especially given the trauma. If we can keep your wife alive another four to eight weeks on the ventilator, it would give the baby more time to recover and continue developing. It isn't likely to make it to term, but every week substantially increases its viability."

"By how much?"

"Well, I'm not an expert but I consulted with my colleague, Doctor Andrews, who tells me that after twenty-seven weeks, a baby's odds go up to about ninety percent. That could be way off. We have no idea how these dendies affect development." She glanced at David and Nick.

"Sharon would want to give our baby the best chance possible," Paul said. He could hardly believe he was discussing these things, that he would consider going against his wife's known wishes, and that he would be living without her by his side. It was impossible to imagine carrying on without her. The arrival of a baby, their baby, without a mother was not something he could grasp emotionally right now. He was numb; he wanted to fade into nothingness.

He realized Dr. Holden had been speaking, dragging him back to reality, "...the risks involved in that."

"Sorry? What risks are you talking about?" Paul felt himself teetering on the verge of hysteria, "I mean, she's dead, right?"

"I was referring to the baby."

"Of course," he looked at his feet, ashamed.

"That's okay," the doctor consoled him, "I wouldn't even discuss this with you so soon after...well, so soon, if it weren't absolutely necessary."

"No, please, continue." Paul inhaled deeply, "I'll be alright."

"Okay. A short time after brain death, the other organs in the body start to shut down. We can keep your wife breathing with the ventilator but if the organs start to fail, we'll have to do a C-section. We'll be monitoring the baby closely and if we see significant signs of distress, we'll get him out right away."

"And the risks?"

"Well, your wife was very healthy and the baby seems to be developing normally, but...." Dr. Holden stopped and pursed her lips so tightly that they all but disappeared.

"But what?"

"Well, as I said, we really don't know how these dendies might affect the baby or the mother. It's possible that they could spread or affect the organs or the baby, or both, in ways we might not be able to detect in time."

David jumped in before anyone could speculate further, "There's never been any indication of anything like that happening."

Dr. Holden regarded him coolly, "There's never been anything like *this* before, though, has there?"

David held silent, contrite for the moment.

Dr. Holden's face softened as she turned back to Paul. "So, I just wanted to say that there are unknowns here, plenty of them. We know that the baby would have extremely limited chances if we delivered today.

We *think* they'll improve considerably in a month or two but, given this mess of complications, we can't really know for sure. So, it's all a bit of an unknown. We can't really say for sure whether it's best to continue the pregnancy or not."

Paul slumped under the weight of the situation. He didn't feel he could deal with this decision right now, even though it had to be made. His wife was gone. Their baby might still have a chance. Was there more risk to delivery now, or later? What if the dendies were to somehow compromise the baby's health?

"Nick, help me out here. I don't know what to do." He struggled to maintain his composure; the baby needed him. *The baby. We'd only started discussing names last week. I wanted Frederick, after her father. She'd had other ideas.*

As Sharon had dashed out of the house one day last week, keys in hand and already half out the door, she'd called back, "Hey, how about Darian? I always liked that name." She'd given him no time to reply, just blew him a kiss and started jogging down the street.

Nick could see Paul's struggle, and his heart went out to him. "Paul," he started, not sure what he was going to say. "I know two things about Sharon. She was a scientist, and she was brave. And I believe that she would have taken on the role of motherhood just as courageously as she took on everything in life."

Paul blinked back his tears.

"I think she would have said that we know the risks of delivering the baby today are high; its chances of survival are not good. The only thing we know about tomorrow is that it scares us. We have no idea if there are real risks to the baby because of the dendies but Sharon believed in what she was doing."

He shot Dr. Holden a look and held it for a couple of seconds before returning to Paul with renewed confidence. "Sharon would have said not to be afraid, to give the baby its best chance. Continue the pregnancy."

Paul sobbed loudly into his hands. He needed his full concentration just to breathe. "Thank you, Nick," he managed.

"Dr. Holden, we should do what Sharon would have wanted. Let's give our baby boy...Let's give Darian his best chance to survive. Continue the pregnancy; do whatever you need to do."

Sharon, I'm so sorry. I hope this is what you'd want—he said silently to himself. He couldn't hold back any longer. He turned to Nick and hugged his friend in their combined grief.

David looked at the doors to the OR and blinked back his tears.

"There will be some paperwork," the doctor said to Paul. "Once we have her stabilized, we'll move her to a private room. You'll be able to visit her there."

She turned to the two scientists. "I'm going to need a detailed report from you by noon tomorrow. I want to better understand what we're dealing with here."

The two men nodded, neither one daring to utter anything aloud.

10

PRINCESS DARYA DREW HER SWORD and held it high. Sunlight glinted off the adamantine blade. *I might as well get this over with.* She filled her lungs and commanded, "Summon the dragon!"

The trumpeter stepped forward and unleashed a series of ear-splitting notes that emulated the Securitors' call code for dragon assistance.

She liked to think that her quick thinking, superior skills, knowledge, and sheer determination to win would prevail against any of Alum's inworld Dragons, but she wasn't a fool. Victory was never assured. Dragons were dangerous, unpredictable.

A ten-meter chrome-plated titanium beast popped into existence a few hundred meters above the dais. The crowd cheered.

The beast was exquisite. Polished scales dazzled and mesmerized. The front edges of the wings narrowed to razor-thin blades that culminated in deadly hooked claws at the tip of each fold. And if that weren't sufficiently threatening, the creature's diamond teeth and talons were eager to shred anything they met.

But it was more what you *couldn't* see that made the dragon a formidable adversary. Its blue electromagnetic beam could rip your inworld body apart. While you were distracted by the pain, its tracker software would hunt your trueself in the outworld, penetrate your security, and immobilize you to await processing by Securitors.

Darya let out a blood-curdling battle cry and launched into the air to meet her adversary. Violet flames erupted eagerly along both edges of her blade.

The dragon observed the tiny violet flare streaking toward it, and bellowed. Tucking its lethal wings against its body, it dove to meet the challenger.

Darya narrowly dodged the stream of fire the dragon shot ahead of its dive path and headed for its underbelly, careful to avoid the forward-stretched talons. As she sped by, she cut a meter-long gash in the metallic flesh.

The dragon shrieked and twisted away, its self-healing skin already closing the wound. The beast stopped a couple hundred meters below Darya and turned for a better appraisal of the little insect that had stung it.

Darya sensed the telescopic lenses behind its black eyes scanning her, running facial recognition and avatar prediction algorithms against her. It was unsettling, but she'd made sure her appearance in Lysrandia was unique to this inworld and gave no hint of her trueself's outworld identity.

The dragon, frustrated with its largely uninformative scan, spread its wings and roared, sending forth a blast of shimmering blue electromagnetic fire as it accelerated upward, straight at her.

Darya plunged into a tight evasive course restricted to an imaginary ten-meter cylinder that would give her a 99.9% probability of avoiding the flames and talons and, hopefully, situate her right beside the beast's vulnerable neck.

Fifty meters before her killing blow, a second dragon popped into existence below and off to one side. It sped directly toward her, spraying fire across her erratic flight path, strategically shooting blue flames back and forth, behind and in front.

While the second beast caught her attention, the first launched another fiery blast. By equal parts of luck and skill, she narrowly avoided the blue flames. The arrival of the second dragon complicated her calculations and reduced her options. As she pulled out of her dive, she frantically recomputed possible scenarios to kill or at least critically damage one of her two pursuers.

Revised chances of success without forfeiting myself? Below ten percent. Ouch, not so good. Time to get away to safety. She mapped an optimal escape trajectory and veered off. Both dragons turned to follow.

She swerved and swooped, alternately climbing and diving. Again and again, she dodged the metallic beasts and their deadly blue flames. She flew above the granite wall, recklessly weaving in and out between the towers and columns. They followed.

Using her enormous inworld strength she kicked and threw gigantic granite blocks from the wall into the dragons' paths. No matter what she tried, she could not gain advantage over the pursuing terrors. They followed her relentlessly. Their wings sliced through the jade columns and quartz towers as if they were made of smoke. Their talons pulverized the granite blocks.

For the first time in millions of years, Darya was truly afraid. With each desperate maneuver, she was growing more fatigued. It was clear she couldn't defeat the dragons using only her inworld magic; they were too strong, too fast, and they were closing in with every lunge. She needed some outworld assistance.

Reaching back through the connection to her trueself, Princess Darya activated her quark-spin lattice. The lattice was among her deepest secrets; accessing it from within Lysrandia was risky.

By decree and design, inworld visitors ran their instantiations on the resident hardware. Maintaining any vestige of trueself attachment at the same time was not permitted; it broke the ban on Cybrid cloning. It wasn't even supposed to be possible. *Well, they can add it to my long list of crimes.*

She had used the lattice before to hack into the Lysrandia simulation code and bestow herself with special powers. But that was done at her leisure, and she'd been able to hide her trail completely. This was different. Securitors would investigate immediately; a Shard could be sent. She'd managed not to reveal any hint of her true computational power to anyone in ages but she needed a better weapon, and she needed it fast.

She tasked the quark-spin lattice's superior computational capability with constructing a virus to penetrate the Lysrandia inworld baseware and the dragon simulation. It wasn't a great plan. Tapping into the lattice's capabilities took enormous power. Her body's reserves would become critically depleted at a time when she needed all the power she could get. And the dragons were only the first challenge, she was sure of that. But seconds away from certain death, she could see no other way out. It would have to do.

Her lattice completed the program and sent it out toward the two dragons. She bathed them in the wide cone of weak light from her sword. *Come on! Come on!*

For a nerve-wracking three-tenths of a second, the beasts' internal coding struggled to resist, before becoming overwhelmed. They broke off their chase and turned on one another, ripping and shredding titanium armor with tooth and talon as they sought to destroy one another's primary neural centers. Locked in a mutual death grip, the attackers plunged toward the ground.

Weak from the battle and from the effects of using the illegal lattice, Darya made her way back to the dais. *I just want to end this spectacle and get out of Lysrandia as soon as possible.*

She circled the castle and approached her throne. Instead of triumphant cheers, she was met by loud blasts, widespread panic, and fearful cries. *What the...?*

The Securitor response had been faster than anticipated—faster than she'd ever seen. A battalion of inworld units smashed through the onyx gates and pushed into the crowd.

Those who couldn't escape the rush of the three-meter wide Securitor spheres were quickly tangle-tagged, frozen in place so they couldn't flee the square and hide in the surrounding mountains. They'd be trapped here, inworld, at Alum's mercy.

The game was over in Lysrandia. There would be no more rituals, no more spectacles, no more sermons, and no more recruits.

At least some of our people will be saved by our standing instructions. The acolytes and any others brave enough to join the movement today will have already left through the virtual back door before the battle.

She scanned the dais area and crowd for familiar faces. Those she'd already convinced to join her on the path of Knowledge and Truth had no need to stay and watch the entertainment. *If they followed instructions.*

Darya flew toward the main emergency exit in the central keep. Trying to preserve what little energy she had left, she landed near the base of the tower and continued on foot.

The streets swarmed with masses of panicked people struggling to escape through the side gates. The Securitors coordinated their attack well, setting guards at the smaller gates in addition to the main exit at the far end of the plaza.

People ran frantically from gate to gate to gate, searching for some unguarded route out. Once they realized the futility of heading for the gates, they dashed deeper into the castle, hoping to find alternative exits or somewhere to hide.

Darya clung to the walls to avoid being carried along by the erratic surges of terrified hordes as they ran past her. As the crowd thinned out, she made her way toward the gardens at the rear of the main keep.

She surveyed the area cautiously. It was heartbreaking to see the ornamental beds of cherished flowers and fruit trees completely destroyed, trampled by people running in all directions. A one-meter deep ring of red-robed figures—inworld soldiers assisting the Securitors—surrounded the keep, barring access to her private exit back to the outworld.

Exhausted, Darya crouched behind a shrub against the corner of the stables and considered her options. She didn't notice the hand, reaching out from the doorway behind her until it hauled her inside.

11

IT WAS EARLY AUGUST when the medical team finally agreed on a date to deliver Darian Leigh into the world. He was still a full ten weeks early, but at least he'd have a fighting chance.

In spite of the sophisticated equipment, Sharon's body was having a difficult time. The doctors had to take more and more drastic measures every week just to keep her alive.

What should have been a happy day for all, a day for celebration, was unavoidably bittersweet. Darian's birth would mark the end of life for a vibrant woman who'd been nurturing him for seven months.

Through the tortuous weeks while medical intervention kept Sharon's organs functioning, Darian obliged the hospital staff by growing steadily. Unknown to all, a few thousand dendies found their way inside the boy's developing brain, where they continued to multiply, and to grow new fibrous connections. No longer receiving the megadose of customized supplements Sharon had been taking, the neural lattice the dendies were forming grew excruciatingly slowly. Nonetheless, it grew.

The dendies made efficient use of whatever building blocks and fortification they could from Sharon's system and from the pre-natal supplements and steroids the nurses injected.

They multiplied silently and unseen. They were too small to be picked up by the standard ultrasounds. A clear CT scan might have shown a bit of speckle, hardly enough to notice. When their numbers became sufficient, they formed stable associations with several thousand neurons. And they continued growing.

During the first four days following Sharon's accident, Paul spent every hour by her side as she lay unresponsive in her private room. He made a nuisance of himself, stubbornly insisting the doctors perform fresh neurological exams, EEGs, and cerebral blood flow tests every day.

In fitful dreams, he imagined the mysterious dendies engineering some sort of miraculous recovery. Each time he woke up, the doctors showed him that they hadn't. He finally had to accept that she was gone.

Reluctantly heeding Dr. Holden's advice, Paul reduced his visits to a few hours a day, and then to once every few days. He needed to take care of himself, make funeral arrangements, and prepare for the baby's arrival. The staff promised to keep him apprised of Darian's status and contact him if there were any changes to either Sharon or the baby.

Paul spent the next few weeks listlessly wandering around the house, unable to take care of the things that needed to be done.

Sharon's final assisted breath, and Darian's first, were drawing slowly and painfully closer, and there was nothing he could do to change it.

So it actually came as a welcome relief when his domineering older sister from Seattle showed up unannounced and took charge of getting his life back on track.

Skizzits—the nickname he'd tagged her with when he was four—didn't wait for instructions, and she didn't fuss any more over his indecision than she did his preferences. She dragged him through a blur of shops. She selected a crib, a change table, a high chair, a car seat, and a cushioned rocking chair. In a whirlwind of activity not unlike the magical Mary Poppins, Skizzits picked out blankets and sleepers, diapers and bottles. She painted the nursery walls and arranged the furniture. She interviewed hopefuls, and hired a nanny. "With your job, there's no way you'll be able to take care of a new baby," she explained. And she took care of the funeral arrangements for her sister-in-law.

When he wasn't busy resenting it, Paul was thankful for his sister's help. Deep down, he knew what he really begrudged was the situation that made it necessary. He just couldn't put his heart into welcoming a new baby when his wife lay dead, or legally dead, in the hospital. He *wanted* to love his son, to be excited about his imminent arrival, but he couldn't stop thinking about how they'd be alone, and how Sharon's final peace was being delayed by the equipment and the dependent fetus within her.

The truth was, his own peace and healing couldn't begin until she passed, but he wasn't ready to admit that yet.

Paul allowed Skizzits to prepare for the child, since he couldn't dredge up any enthusiasm of his own. He went through the motions mostly to avoid confrontation.

He returned to work and shouldered both the sincere condolences and the whispered conversations that ended abruptly when he entered a room. He somehow managed to wade through the daily meetings and reports.

He felt as though his life had ended, but so long as Sharon's body was being kept alive, he was not permitted any release. Limbo was not a comfortable place to be.

On the appointed birth/death date, Paul snuck off to the hospital without a word to his sister. He spent the morning holding Sharon's limp hand, lamenting how unfair it was that she would never see her son or experience the joy of motherhood, how desperately he missed her company, and how afraid he was to do this on his own.

He knew he should be excited by the prospects of a healthy new son but, instead, he only felt a surge of anger whenever he contemplated the impending birth. *I know the anger is misplaced and unfair, but I can't help it.*

Nobody knew why Sharon had fallen, but the baby was not responsible for the accident. Paul could accept that. Yet, seeing Sharon's belly swelling as the baby grew, offended something deep within him. He couldn't help but be repulsed by the image of his beloved wife reduced to nothing more than an incubator. And he couldn't keep that image from his mind. It would come as a tremendous relief when they finally allowed her to join her Maker in Heaven.

When the doctors arrived to tell him they were ready to deliver the baby, he stood silently for a moment, clinging to Sharon's hand. He couldn't bring himself to stay, to welcome his new son as he simultaneously said goodbye to the love of his life. He mustered what little stamina he had left into one long, deep breath, and nodded to the team. He gave his wife's hand a final gentle squeeze, let go, and left the hospital.

* * *

DARIAN LEIGH WAS DELIVERED by C-section at 3:20 pm, August 14th, 2026. Following a routine examination, he was placed tenderly but unceremoniously in a neonatal intensive care unit. Although small, he appeared to be healthy and normal.

With her son delivered, Sharon was removed from life support and given over to eternal rest. Her second and final death occurred with the last beat of her heart at 3:52 pm.

Over dinner that evening, Paul revealed to his sister that the operation to deliver the baby and his permission to remove Sharon from life support had taken place earlier that afternoon.

The pepper Skizzits had been about to liberally shake over her mashed potatoes never hit its target. She stared at her brother, confused but silent. As hard as she tried, she could not fathom why he would keep the birth of his son, her only nephew, a secret. In a rare act of restraint, she resisted questioning or berating her brother and studiously examined the food on her plate.

Darian's aunt went to the hospital early the next day and every day after to visit. She talked to him about his mother and his father, and the amazing life she imagined for him. A week later, on her seventh visit, she was accompanied by the boy's father for the first time.

Dr. Holden was relieved to see Paul join his sister at Darian's side. "I have some good news for you. The x-rays and scans don't show any signs of those bright specks, the dendies, that we observed in his mother's brain. We can't say for sure yet that Darian is entirely free of them, just that we don't see any sign of them right now. I'd like to follow up with you and Sharon's associates. Could you please arrange a meeting with my office?"

Sharon's memorial service was held the following day. The week after, Paul returned to the hospital with Nick and David reluctantly in tow, and they filed into Dr. Holden's office.

She closed the door behind them. "Gentlemen, I want you to understand that we're not done here yet. The boy needs to be monitored every few months for the next couple of years to ensure his x-rays remain clear. As a concerned professional, I would strongly suggest that the Neuro Nano board hire an outside medical consultant to continue ongoing testing for him, and to assist with any future evaluations of human test subjects. I still haven't decided whether to report this whole affair to the FDA or the Medical Board for their determination. I'll have to sleep on it."

Dr. Holden watched their reaction carefully. *Okay, let's see what they do with that. They know they should have reported Dr. Leigh's breach of ethics immediately and they didn't. Let them sweat it out for a bit. Serves them right. God only knows what else they'd try to get away with if they thought nobody was watching. Governing bodies like the FDA and the Neuro Nano board aren't hands-on enough for research like this. They need an objective observer, an insider who's not afraid to blow the whistle.*

David and Nick were so relieved to hear that Dr. Holden had not already filed reports or charges, and might never, that they held an emergency meeting of the Neuro Nano Board, unanimously accepted her "suggestion" to hire an external consultant, and immediately offered her the position. Dr. Holden accepted.

Maybe I can help instill some long overdue ethics into their practice—she hoped. *One can always hope.*

12

Excerpt from <u>Connect to the World</u>, Neuro Nano marketing brochure, November 2030:

Thanks to SafeLink©, Neuro Nano's complete neural lattice security system, you can experience the Internet as never before. Connect directly to all of your senses with confidence. Within just 6-8 months of receiving your Neuro Nano inoculation, you will be ready for direct neural-to-net connection. Make and receive calls, listen to live stream music, and watch videos through DirectVR©. Control all of your devices remotely through DirectLink© and, best of all, experience FullDef© movies with all of your senses as if you are living the moment. For business, for entertainment, for life: Neuro Nano.

Technical Overview:

As described in The Neuro Nanotechnology Revolution (Neuro Nano technical overview, July 2033), a small, painless injection introduces hybrid semiconductor-RNA nanoparticles into your bloodstream. We call them Dynamic Neural Nano Dots; you might know them as dendies.

Each particle contains computational and communication mechanisms as well as a simple holographic memory. The RNA coating on the nanoparticles safely encodes protein complexes that manage particle repair, growth, replication, and other activities of the growing lattice. These nanoparticles are carried to your brain by your natural blood flow. The layer of endothelial cells that defines the blood-brain barrier recognizes specific peptide sequences on the encapsulating surface and actively transports the nanoparticles to the neural side while removing them from their protective shells.

Once across the blood-brain barrier and situated among active neurons, the nanoparticle RNA dissociates from the semiconductor and enters nearby glial cells, where it uses their molecular mechanisms to produce the accessory proteins needed to construct a complete neural lattice.

The separation of the RNA coating exposes underlying molecules that recognize and bind the semiconductor nanodots to neurotransmitter receptors at the synapses. These newly synthesized protein complexes can then begin increasing the total number of semiconductor nanoparticles using the existing set as templates for replication.

Other proteins initiate the polymerization of interconnecting silicene filaments from the special supplements provided. The filaments then feel their way along existing axons and connect the semiconductor particles in a high-speed network that parallels, supplements, and complements your existing biological one. Powered by an external battery, a compact near-field induction headband or cap provides the interface for communication between the internet and the internal lattice.

Neuro Nano: Communications. Entertainment. Control.
Welcome to a whole new world of experience.

FOR THE FIRST SEVERAL YEARS OF HIS LIFE, Darian gave every appearance of being a perfectly normal boy.

Under the watchful eyes of various nannies, each of whom loved him in turn, a healthy infant blossomed into a robust toddler. He exhibited neither special talents nor delays in his abilities. He walked, talked, learned, and played like any other bright child.

At first, after bringing his wee son home from the hospital, Paul found it nearly impossible to spend time with him, especially once Skizzits returned to her own home, leaving them without a buffer. Some days, he had to will himself to lay eyes on the boy. Every moment, every glimpse, was a heart wrenching reminder of his wife's untimely death.

While the nannies attended to the everyday tasks of rearing the boy through his infancy and kindergarten years, Paul concentrated on finding new goals for his shattered life.

As he labored through the stages of his grief and anger, he began to accept and finally embrace the fleeting wisps of Sharon he found in Darian. The boy had inherited her curiosity, intelligence, and courage, along with her beautiful blue-gray eyes.

One sunny Sunday afternoon, Paul settled into his favorite reading chair with a good book. He glanced over at Darian playing on the carpet and was intrigued to see the boy trying to build interconnected skyscrapers out of boxes, toy train tracks, and wooden blocks.

An unexpected wave of emotion caught Paul off guard, and he set his book down. *When did that happen?*—he wondered. Without realizing it, he had slowly grown to love his son as much as he'd loved Sharon. He vowed right then to be a better father, and to make up for the time he'd so foolishly wasted.

In grade school, Darian proved himself to be a consistently good student, always in the top ten percent. He was active but not athletic. Though somewhat introverted, he seemed happy both in class and at home.

Near the start of second grade, there was an incident that would come to make more sense in hindsight, many years later. A teacher on playground supervision discovered Darian eating clay by the mouthful. She took the child's hand and made a joke of it, as she gently wiped his mouth, brushed him off, and sent him to play with his classmates. At the end of recess, she discreetly reported the behavior to his teacher, who relayed the news to his father.

Thinking the odd behavior likely stemmed from dietary issues, Paul took his son to visit Dr. Holden. In keeping with her role as medical consultant for Neuro Nano, the doctor had continued to monitor the boy through annual checkups. They had stopped taking x-rays of his head after the eighth consecutive clear image, shortly after his second birthday. She ran a few blood tests and referred Darian to an experienced dietitian who recommended some vitamin and mineral supplements.

To everyone's relief, following a few reassuring consultations between parent, doctor, and school psychologist, the child never repeated the odd and mildly worrisome episode. Not where anyone could see.

By the time Darian turned ten and no longer needed nannies to care for him, he was taking five supplements a day and secretly satisfying his more unusual dietary cravings after school. Like most parents, his slightly distracted father never noticed anything out of the ordinary about his son's behavior.

The combination of extra minerals and silica in Darian's hidden diet worked wonders for the starved dendies in his brain. Dormant for so many years, the tiny and sparsely scattered nanodots were revitalized by the nutrient boost.

Semiconductor replicases and silicene synthetases sprang into action, producing building blocks for the dendies so they could reproduce and connect. Glial cells, infected with the dendy virus, secreted signaling molecules to help guide the new silicene filaments to form an interconnected lattice.

The headaches began shortly after Darian turned twelve.

Paul wrote off the symptoms as pre-adolescent growing pains or possibly a flu bug. He meted out the normal over-the-counter remedies and mandated extra water and sleep. The painkillers brought little relief.

After a string of restless nights, Darian grew tired of bothering his father. A strong-willed child, he prided himself on tolerating the migraines stoically. He became good at functioning normally despite the chronic pain.

It was at about the same time that Darian started to find his classes and homework getting easier than ever, and his newfound competence was reflected in his grades. To stave off boredom with school, Darian perused more advanced subject matter on the web.

One wet and windy October evening, Darian was concentrating on his tablet, deeply engaged in reading about cognitive algorithms from an MIT course on artificial intelligence, when his father pulled into the unlit driveway, late, exhausted, and hungry.

Paul reached over to the passenger seat to grab the takeout bag sitting there. He turned off the ignition and sat looking at the house. Aside from the garage lights, it was dark. *That's odd; no kitchen light, none in Darian's room, no flicker from the TV.*

He pulled his coat a little closer, and pushed the car door open against a sudden gust. He kicked the door shut behind him. Leaning into the wind, he climbed the small set of stairs to the front porch and let himself in.

"I've got Chinese for dinner," he called. He could make out Darian's face, reflecting the eerie glow from the display screen of his tablet. "Hellooo! Let's put some lights on in here." Darian ignored him. *Kids!*

"Hey, I brought your favorite," he tried, a little louder. He might as well have been talking to the cat.

Paul slipped off his shoes, hung up his damp coat, and loosened his tie. He supposed he ought to feel grateful that Darian was so intent on whatever he was reading.

The boy's grades had been good and getting better; and outside of his classes, he was diving into wide and avid interests in science and technology. *Still, it would be nice just to talk baseball sometimes*—he thought. Clearly, Darian had inherited his mother's passion and intensity when it came to learning about the natural world.

Paul flicked on the living room lights. Darian didn't even look up from his tablet. "Hey, bud, what are you reading?" he asked as he sauntered over to the sofa and plunked down heavily beside his son. He leaned over and looked at the screen. Pages of technical articles, symbols, and diagrams he didn't recognize flew by, too fast for Paul to absorb.

"How can you even read that?" he asked, trying to catch his son's attention. Darian just stared at the display without acknowledging.

"Darian?" No response. The boy's eyes were fixed on the blinking display.

"Hey!" he hollered, poking the boy's shoulder to break the trance. "Darian!" He nudged a little harder.

The boy's body absorbed and adjusted to the jarring motions. His eyes did not move from the screen.

Paul shifted from genuinely interested, to mildly annoyed, to angry. He grabbed the tablet away from his son, and turned it upside down to hide the screen. Darian's hand darted out to retrieve it, but Paul blocked and held his arms. The boy thrashed and screeched like a spoiled five-year-old deprived of his favorite toy.

"What the hell? Darian!"

Just as abruptly, mid-tantrum, his son went completely limp.

Paul's anger vanished. *What in God's name....?* Paul cradled the boy's head against his chest. "Darian! It's okay, son. Everything's okay."

The inactivity didn't last long. Darian's muscles grew rigid, making it hard to hold onto him. Paul tilted the boy's face upward in time to see his eyes roll back and the lids squeeze shut. The image of Sharon's face, seconds before she toppled into his car, superimposed itself onto his son's blank visage. "Oh, no! Don't you dare! Darian!"

Seizures. What do I know about seizures? Make them comfortable. Loosen clothing around the neck. Tip them sideways. Don't put anything in their mouth.

He waited for it to pass. Ten seconds. Twenty. Thirty. No change. *I have to get him to a hospital!* Somehow he managed to stand up, letting Darian's head fall back onto a cushion. He threw on his shoes, and grabbed his coat and car keys. He picked up Darian and the fleece sofa blanket, and carried him to the car.

He's so light—he couldn't help but notice. Paul laid him awkwardly across the back seat, and tucked the thin blanket tightly around him, fastening him in as best he could so he wouldn't roll. His hands shook uncontrollably, as he slammed the car into reverse and sped to the nearest hospital.

It was a quiet night in Emerg. The cold, wet weather had kept all but the most ill inside their homes. Paul carried his son past the gawking smokers in hospital gowns and through the sliding glass doors.

"Help me!" he called out as he crossed the floor.

The Admissions nurse assessed the approaching paralyzed boy with barely a look and got up from her station. "Follow me," she instructed, and led Paul to the nearest available bed.

"What happened?" she asked as she pulled the curtain around them.

"He was just reading his tablet," Paul said, a horrible feeling of *déjà vu* washing over him. "I couldn't get his attention and then, all of a sudden, he started having some kind of seizure."

"How long has he been like this?"

"About twenty minutes, I think. What's happening?"

"Any history of epilepsy?"

"No, not that I know of. But...," Paul hesitated.

"But what?" the nurse asked as she took Darian's pulse and blood pressure and tested his pupillary response.

"His mother....My wife..." Paul fought to retain his composure. *Where to begin?*

"What about her?" the nurse prompted.

Paul tried again. "She died in an accident after a seizure that looked similar to this. But she never showed any signs of epilepsy before that. None. Ever. Neither has Darian. And besides, her case would have to be different, anyway. She had dendies in her head."

The words tumbled out of Paul's lips of their own accord. The nurse stared at him, uncomprehending.

Paul realized he was staring back. *I must sound crazy.*

Fortunately, a doctor arrived before he could make things worse by trying to explain. The physician consulted briefly with the nurse as he examined Darian for himself and began quizzing Paul on the boy's medical history. This time, Paul's answers were better organized and he didn't mention the dendies.

The physician ordered an x-ray and EEG, and promised to return when they were ready.

Paul picked up the waiting clipboard and started filling out insurance forms. He couldn't afford to indulge the painful memories flooding his mind, memories of the last time he sat in a hard plastic hospital chair, completing forms. He forced his concentration to attend to the task at hand, watching the pen spread ink across each box, one answer at a time.

Darian didn't wake up, but the tension in his muscles finally relaxed. As the muscles eased, so did his father's panic. *It was just a seizure. Everything's going to be okay*—he told himself.

Within the hour, the doctor returned with the x-ray and EEG results. He inspected the x-ray, tipped his head quizzically, and leaned in closer to the image. A quizzical frown pulled at his brow. Without a word, he shifted his focus to the EEG. The frown deepened.

The doctor paged the technicians. He took them aside and proceeded to interrogate them. The trio went back and forth between the reports, discussing one section and then another in low, hushed voices. They agreed the images and recordings were unusual but defended their work. The doctor turned to Paul.

"Mr. Leigh, your son has presented us with a bit of a mystery."

"What do you mean?"

"Well, here." the doctor placed the x-ray film in the light box. "The x-ray is showing some unusual speckle and diffuse haze. I thought there must be something wrong with the machine or the detector, but the technician says he checked everything over himself, and swears it's all working properly. He took three images from different angles to confirm, and they all show the same thing."

Twelve years unwound in a flash. Paul stared at the x-ray image in horror. "That can't be," he whispered. The image could have been a copy of the one taken of Sharon's head on the day of the accident.

The doctor raised a questioning eyebrow. Paul only shook his head, numb with disbelief.

The doctor continued, "His EEG is a little strange, as well. There is a lot of electrical activity. It doesn't look like an epileptic seizure but, then again, it doesn't look like normal brainwaves, either. Have you seen this before? Do you know something you'd like to share with me?"

Paul cleared his throat. "I have no idea," he managed, avoiding the doctor's gaze.

"Hm. Okay." the doctor replied, unconvinced. "Listen, I'm a bit of a technology buff, and I like to keep up to date with the newest developments. That speckle pattern on your son's x-ray appears very similar to those I've seen in research articles about Neuro Nano dendy lattices. Have you heard of those?"

"Yes, of course. Actually, it was my wife who invented the field. I still own a few shares in the company."

"Is that right? Then you might know that the neural lattice is restricted to areas over the sensorimotor cortex, the occipital cortex, and the temporal lobes?"

"No, not really. It was her work; I'm not a scientist. She used to talk about it with me, but that was years ago. She passed away when Darian was born. I haven't kept up with developments these past few years."

"I see. Maybe you're aware that neural lattices are only approved for use in adults?"

"I'd heard something like that."

"So, would you like to explain to me why your son's x-ray shows a lattice, and why has it spread so far?"

Paul was genuinely bewildered, "I honestly have no idea."

"Nurse Ranson said you mentioned that the boy's mother, your wife, died after a similar seizure some years ago."

"Yes."

"And, if I remember correctly, she was the first person ever to grow a neural lattice."

"Yes, she was the first test case; she injected the dendies herself. I didn't even know she'd done it until months later, when she had the seizure. I never even got to talk to her about it."

"I'd like to get her file and compare it to your son's, if I may."

"Yes, of course."

The doctor was still eyeing him, expecting further details or maybe a confession, but Paul was too distracted by all the thoughts reeling through his mind to notice.

Did Sharon's dendies make their way into our son? Dr. Holden had said Darian was clear; there was no sign of them in any of the testing.

He agonized over what he did, and did not, know; over what he should reveal, and shouldn't. *I need to talk to Nick and Dr. Holden.*

Darian moaned. "Where am I?" He blinked his eyes against the bright lights and looked around the room, confused and frightened.

"You're back," the doctor said with a smile, and started a physical check and neural exam. "What do you remember?"

Darian relayed his last memories of sitting on the sofa at home, reading some scientific articles. He seemed mentally and physically fine, the doctor concluded, despite having been unconscious for the previous hour. The boy's muscles were aching but that was to be expected.

The doctor ordered follow-up tests, including an MRI and full EEG for the next day. With nothing left to do but observe, they transferred Darian out of Emergency and into a room. The ward nurse got him set up with some fluids to help balance his electrolytes. She wrangled some dinners from the cafeteria, for which Darian and Paul were grateful.

Darian was ravenous. They visited a while, and then Paul left his exhausted son to rest, promising to return the next morning. There was something he had to take care of.

Miraculously, Paul's car had not been towed from the side of the Ambulance Parking area where he'd left it. He got in and gripped the steering wheel for a while, giving in to overpowering sobs that wracked his frame. He regained control of his emotions, except for his anger, and pulled out his phone.

Cold, grim determination took the place of fear and confusion. He scrolled through the contact list until he found Nick's number. His thumb flexed rapidly, undecidedly, over the entry. His first thought had been to call ahead and make sure the scientist was at home and awake, but he couldn't bring himself to dial. What would he say?

Nick's apartment was only a short drive away. He started the car.

13

DARYA TUCKED, ROLLED AND SPRUNG TO HER FEET, exhausted, but with her sword at the ready and prepared to kill or die. *Conserve energy. Evaluate. Breathe. Attack.*

The mantra saved her from reflexively dispatching the wide-eyed team member who'd yanked her through the doorway.

"Princess," someone whispered from inside a swirling haze of barn dust.

Darya covered her mouth to keep from choking. Behind her, a hand swung the door closed, sending a fresh updraft of dust into the air. She blinked furiously against the grit, and let her eyes adjust to the low light.

Four worried faces came into focus and, behind them, a half-dozen anxious faces she recognized from today's new recruits.

"What are you doing here?" she hissed to the senior acolytes. "You're supposed to be gone!"

They fidgeted like guilty children and avoided her gaze. "We're sorry, Princess. The new recruits wanted to watch the dragon fight. We thought it would be okay just for a few minutes, but when that second dragon arrived, we couldn't look away. When the Securitors showed up, we got out of there as fast as we could. By the time we got to the keep it was already surrounded."

"They must have found out about our back door," Darya said. "Either Securitor intrusive devices have improved significantly, or someone revealed the location." Darya placed her bet on the latter.

"Can you get us out of the castle?" asked one of the acolytes, "or is there somewhere we can hide until they're gone?"

Darya's shoulders slumped; she had no energy left to put on a strong face. "There's nowhere to hide. The Securitors will turn the kingdom upside down until they're satisfied they've caught every transgressor, and then they'll decommission Lysrandia. Anyone left here inworld will die when they shut down the simulation."

They kept listening, expecting her to divulge some plan to save them all. When she didn't, they looked crushed.

I imagine right now everybody's mulling over whether they'd be better off taking their chances with me, or surrendering and turning informer on the movement— she thought.

"There might be one other way out for some of us. I kept a hidden emergency exit, one I didn't tell anyone about. It has limitations, though. It can only handle one transfer at a time, and it needs to reset between transfers. With the Securitors monitoring inworld traffic, there's no way we'll all get out before they find us."

She let the acolytes digest this for a minute.

"But *some* of us will escape," came a hopeful voice from the back.

"Yes, some of us. We'll have to see what the situation around the exit is, first. Then we can calculate an optimal approach."

The disciples exchanged glances, seeking agreement. They nodded consent in unison. Darya hoped she had enough energy left for a final push to freedom.

The exit was situated inside a nondescript maintenance shed near the rear castle wall. The shed housed little more than a mop, a bucket, and a sink. Every day, a couple of the castle servants would wash down nearby stone walks and pathways with the mop and bucket. They had no idea an escape gate to the outworld could be activated through a special combination of actions inside the shed.

Darya led her troupe through the stables and out the back door. The streets were considerably less crowded now. The Securitors had been ruthlessly efficient at tangle-tagging the majority of the crowd. They were now rooting out the more innovative evaders and escorting them to the parking area for processing.

We don't have much time left! They raced to the outside wall as quietly as they could, and followed it to the shed in the back corner. Mercifully, it had been overlooked by the Securitors. *So far.*

Darya instructed the group on the escape protocol. "Once inside, you activate the exit gate by moving the spout of the faucet all the way to the left, as far as it will go, and then all the way to the right. Then turn on the hot water, exactly half a turn, and then the cold, also half a turn. Finally, turn off the cold, and then the hot. It has to be in that exact order.

"Can you remember that? That'll open the gate. A black field will appear over the drain in the floor. Step into it. The gate will disappear, and you'll be on your way to the outworld. Only one person can use it at a time, and it needs about ten seconds to reset before the next person can go. Count twenty seconds between people going into the shed."

"How long do we have before the Securitors arrive?"

Darya reviewed the movements of the Securitor forces they had encountered along the way, and estimated how many of the runners were still on the loose. Activating the escape gate would draw the Securitors' attention.

There'll be a delay between the Securitors detecting the exit gate activation and being able to secure it. By the time orders to secure the shed trickle down the ranks to the closest units we might get maybe two minutes, tops. That would give us a ninety percent chance of completing five or six activations.

Counting herself, they needed eleven activations to get everyone to safety. It wasn't looking good. She shared the bad news.

Her team members were practical, they excelled at problem-solving, and they weren't ready to surrender just yet, "Is there some way we can slow down the Securitors? Maybe create a diversion?"

Darya struggled to think of a way to improve their odds. Her processing center was slowing down, getting sluggish. "No matter what we use to distract them, as soon as we activate that gate, they'll drop whatever they're doing and head our way."

"What if we...." The group threw out a few wild ideas, but nothing stuck.

We're wasting time. Darya knew what had to be done, but didn't have the heart to tell them until they'd run out of other options. The time had come.

"If we give up three of us, we can save eight. The three will get tangle-tagged and interrogated by the Securitors, who will assume they hold significant knowledge about the movement. The questioning will be severe and probably end in a complete personality wipe. Three of us will have to fight—to fight and die—to save the rest."

"Then you need to get out first. We can decide among ourselves who else we can save."

Darya started to object. She had endangered these people; she needed to protect them for as long as possible. But the rebellion was based on reason and, all noble gestures aside, reason held that there would be no rebellion left without its leader. In the end, reason won.

"Very well. There's no time to waste. Once I enter the shed, three of you cover the different routes here. Take implements to defend yourselves. Buy us as much time as you can. Those who follow me have to pass through the gate as quickly as possible. I hope my calculations overshot a bit and we can all make it through. I'll contact you all in the outworld after some time. If I receive no answer, I'll surmise you didn't make it out. Know that you have my thanks as well as that of the movement, and I will find a way to notify your friends."

It was decided; to linger any further would cost lives. Darya left them discussing who would go and who would stay and fight.

She opened the garden shed door, and entered. The small room smelled of damp mop and dirty water as it always did. A single tiny window high on one wall allowed in sufficient light to make out the faucet.

As she had instructed the others, she moved the spout and turned the water on and then off in sequence.

An ill-defined black field appeared noiselessly over the floor drain and she stepped into it, exiting Lysrandia forever.

14

IT WAS A BUSY DAY FOR BOTH SHARD AND MONK. Darak strolled through a good part of Alumston, enjoying the charming ambience and hospitality, casually acquainting himself with the town and its people, and stopping to chat with random individuals at their work or play.

Everywhere he went, people were in a state of awe to see one so holy and so close to Alum. They found themselves captivated by his gentle and humble manner. His questions were genuine and kind, never seeking shortcomings or failings. Each person he spoke with felt, for a short while, like they were the most important person in town, their job was the most crucial, and their problems were the most pressing.

His suggestions on how to improve a process and how to smooth interactions among the People were perceived as inspired. Those fortunate enough to receive advice from him hurried to implement his ideas while it was still fresh in their minds. Love and praise followed him—in Alum's Name, of course—wherever he went.

Brother Stralasi, too, covered a good part of Alumston that day, running around town like a chicken with its head cut off. The frantic monk fretted and scrambled to make preparations for departure, and to solidify sensible arrangements for coverage of his duties while he was away.

He tried in vain to convince the visiting Shard to perform an Official Blessing or give a sermon in Center Park. Each time, Darak politely demurred. "I'm here to talk, not orate." Disappointed, the monk went about his business. There was no time to waste.

He appointed an interim Caretaker and did his best, given the few hours they had together, to bring the chosen junior Brother up to speed on the business of the Alumita.

Brother Westlock was nervous but enthusiastic about his new role as interim Head Brother. The novitiate had always been a quick and eager study, and Brother Stralasi felt confident that he'd rise to the challenge.

"It may surprise you to learn that spiritual guidance of the People is actually the easiest part of this position," the Good Brother divulged. "It can be time-consuming, and at times demanding, but a job well done is rewarding and important. People appreciate it.

"The more challenging part of the assignment is ensuring Adherence. This is equally time consuming but utterly thankless. Indeed, if not conducted delicately, monitoring and ensuring Adherence can raise resentment.

"But you must remain strong; I cannot overemphasize the importance of this. Constant prayer drives the machinery of all the Worlds, and it is critical to demonstrate an adequate expression of the People's love for Alum in order to continue receiving His Blessing. Continuity of prayers at the power station and at the starstep must be maintained without fail. Our survival depends on it; proceed accordingly."

Westlock pursed his lips and blurted out his question before he could change his mind. "Brother, I've heard rumors about Founding towns that spent harsh winters in the cold, stranded outside Alum's Web because of the negligence of an uncooperative starstep. They suffered terribly until Alum finally took pity and returned them to the fold. Are these stories true?"

Stralasi couldn't bear to think of his beloved flock suffering that way. "Brother Westlock, I could graphically and emphatically describe to you how utterly dependent the physical wellbeing—the very survival—of the Colony is on our disciplined, pious observance. But I will let you imagine for yourself the horrors they will face, should you fail in this duty and Alumston become separated from The Realm."

Westlock's innocent face broadcasted his distress at the thought of such isolation. His mentor watched with a soft heart, anxious to see the result. Would this so far untested novitiate be up to the difficult task ahead?

The younger monk filled his lungs, straightened his back with confidence, and lifted a steady, even gaze to meet Brother Stralasi's own. "You can count on me."

Seeing the soft, boyish face transformed by firm resolve, the Good Brother relaxed. He was pleased, and tremendously relieved, to see this promising young man he'd hand-selected stepping up to his new responsibilities so intently. *Yes, he will do fine.*

After having made certain Brother Westlock was fully informed of his required duties, Stralasi turned to his own needs for the upcoming journey to the Home World with Darak.

He packed lightly, adding only a heavy jacket, bamboo fiber leggings, and wool socks to his spare robe in case they encountered harsher climates. He expected the communities through which they were to travel would see to their basic needs for nourishment and toiletries. After all, he was going to be journeying as the companion of a Shard of Alum.

Despite a restless night trying *not* to obsessively relive the events of the spectacular dinner party earlier that evening, or to anticipate the adventures he would face on the journey, Stralasi woke early, feeling refreshed and eager.

Darak was already up and walking around the gardens, visiting with the birds, insects, and frogs. "Good morning, Brother Stralasi. I hope you rested well," the Shard said, and he returned a small, fuzzy caterpillar to its branch.

"Yes, surprisingly," Stralasi replied with an enthusiastic smile.

They headed to Rose's for breakfast and one more opportunity to meet with the local folk before they departed.

Two hours later, with well-wishers off to their daily work, Stralasi and Darak sat nursing their coffees.

"Will we be leaving by the normal means or would you prefer to...you know...," Brother Stralasi lowered his voice to a whisper, "...use your secret starstep?"

Darak selected his words carefully. "We shall leave the same way that I arrived."

"Is your private starstep far to the west?" Stralasi asked. "Will it be a long walk?"

"It will be as far as needed. No more. No less."

"Do I need to dress for a colder elevation?" Stralasi probed, fishing for details.

"I believe your current attire will suffice."

Stralasi opened his mouth to try another approach. Before he could utter the first syllable, Darak held up a pre-emptive hand.

"We shall leave," he said, placing the hand firmly on the Good Brother's shoulder, "now." He did not look inclined to entertain further delay or dissent.

Stralasi dutifully suppressed his curiosity. "Yes, my Lord." The monk turned and made quick apologies to the staff, patrons, and small gathering of well-wishers outside.

Darak set out for the Alumita residences with single-minded purpose. Stralasi hurried to catch up. They paused only long enough for Stralasi to fetch his pack and issue a perfunctory goodbye to Brother Westlock, before they were off again.

The Alumit monk, a fast walker by most people's measure, found himself nearly running to keep up with Darak's ground-eating strides. He was not afforded a single moment to wallow in regret over having to leave his latest project before its success could be ensured.

The pair marched ten kilometers or more past the original blast field. They waded across a small stream, and put the first ridges of the low foothills behind them before Darak slowed to a more reasonable pace.

"How..." Brother Stralasi gasped, trying to catch his breath. "How much... further...to your starstep,...my Lord?"

Darak took stock of the low hills around him. "This will do."

Stralasi looked around, seeing nothing special about the chosen spot. Granted, he might not have recognized a well-hidden starstep among the yellow rocks and dull blue-green native plant life, but the exposed landscape didn't seem capable of hiding *anything* important.

"Should I begin the prayer now, my Lord?" he asked. The breeze wafting off the mountains carried the odd metallic taste of the native vegetation.

The words of the Entreaty for Connection framed themselves effortlessly in his mind, the result of countless repetitions: *Alum, Lord Protector of Yov's creation, Light of the People, permit us to be joined again with our Brothers and Sisters on their blessed planets around distant stars. When we are lost in the Da'arkness, disconnected from Your People, alone and afraid, we ask that You grant us communion, that You welcome us into the Holy Web of Your Great Realm.*

The Entreaty usually required around ten repetitions before a starstep received Alum's blessing and became activated, sometimes more at the frontier. In the case of larger Alumitas in more established centers, the use of pleasing melodic instruments or complicated vocal harmonies might speed Alum's approval, reducing the number of repetitions required.

Once established, a connection would remain open for as long as the chanting continued and remained pleasing to Alum. Breaks in the connection before the completion of a transfer were dreadful embarrassments to the local Alumita. In populous centers supporting higher volumes of inter-planetary travel, multiple starsteps were kept continuously open by the never-ending songs of large choirs. One might surmise that the secret starstep for a Shard would require much less effort to acquire Alum's attention.

"What? Oh, that. Uhh..., no." Darak replied, only half-listening, while directing most of his auditory attention to something as yet unseen.

What could the Shard be listening for?—Stralasi wondered. He could hear nothing at all.

Eventually satisfied, Darak took a seat on a large boulder. "Now is not the time for prayer," he said. "Now is the time for patience, and for paying attention. Soon we will learn something new."

He closed his eyes, and enjoyed the gentle breeze and warm sun on his face while he still could.

15

THE SHRILL WARNING CHIME announcing an imminent starstep transfer broke through the blessedly perfect stillness of the Alumston Transportation Ceraffice.

Startled to attention, Brother Yonteg swung his feet from the desk and dropped his skillfully balanced chair back onto all four legs.

That's weird. We don't have any shipments of goods or personnel scheduled. He queried the InterLat. *No, nothing scheduled, and nothing ordered since I came on duty.*

Thankfully, he hadn't allowed another request to slip by again. The last time that happened, he received a probationary warning and threat of reassignment outside the Alumita should he be found less than diligent in future.

Yonteg fired off a quick message to notify Brother Stralasi of the unexpected activation. An immediate reply bounced back from the InterLat: Brother Stralasi is currently unavailable.

Oh, that's right—he realized. *Brother Stralasi went off-world with the Shard of Alum. Brother Westlock is the acting Head Brother. I wish I could stay awake through the morning meetings.*

He refocused, and set about compiling an InterLat alert to the Acting Head Brother. A second chime signaled the completion of the starstep transfer. He glanced over. *Who would arrive outside the scheduled transfers?*—he wondered. The answer drained the color from his face. *Great Alum, save us!*

Standing on the clean white disk of the starstep was an Angel of Alum, accompanied by two hovering spherical Securitors. Yonteg gulped.

The Angel was fearsome to behold. Over three meters tall, his quicksilver skin flowed continuously, reflecting distorted images of the surrounding chamber. Opalescent wings shone with a brilliant internal light. His muscular body was naked except for his sandals and a black loincloth secured with a strap holding a sapphire sword in its scabbard. He was magnificent to behold, but the arrogant sneer curling his upper lip brought terror to the heart.

Most people only ever glimpsed an Angel as it left Home World for battle. They were few—they numbered under a million across all of The Realm—but their power was unrivaled.

One hundred Angels could vaporize an entire solar system; the sparsely scattered nebulae in remote, untraveled parts of several galaxies were a testament to their proclivity for destructive enforcement of Alum's Law. Where a Shard of Alum might be seen as gathering intelligence, evaluating, and judging, an Angel simply meant death. Quick and merciless death. Often in mind-numbing scope.

The pair of companion Securitors, as big around as the Angel was tall, were almost as terrifying. They were profoundly black, absorbing light from their surroundings. Their appearance gave the impression of an absence of anything tangible, holes in space, rather than discrete objects. It was practically impossible to discern their precise boundaries and, if you dared look closely, you could imagine falling into an infinite well. The sensation was said to have a basis in fact. Rumor also had it that, among many other magical and miraculous powers, the Securitors contained their own internal hells, capable of swallowing entire cities into an endlessly imploding nothingness.

Stepkeeper Yonteg fell to the floor. He cried for the imminent loss of his own life, and that of his friends and co-workers, and for the end of this promising little planet. He couldn't imagine what crime brought an Angel to rain destruction on Gargus 718.5, but he was certain that it must have been a great affront to Alum to cause Him to dispatch one of His most feared and powerful agents.

The Angel stepped from the disc and stopped in front of the quivering Yonteg, extending a hand to help the monk to his feet. "Rise, Brother!" His mellifluous voice filled the chamber from all directions at once with a blend of love, compassion, humor, and a compelling strength of command.

Brother Yonteg looked up, amazed that he was not yet dead.

The two Securitors moved to cover the main entrances to the Starstep Reception.

The Angel pulled the astonished Brother effortlessly to his feet. The man struggled not to run screaming. He swallowed his terror and squeaked out, "H...H...How may I serve you, my Lord?"

The Angel smiled his beautiful, terrifying smile and thrummed his powerful wings once. "You may address me as Lord Mika. I understand you recently received a visitor?"

Brother Yonteg had no doubt about whom the Angel was speaking. "Yes, Lord Mika. The Lord Darak, Shard of Alum."

Lord Mika smiled more broadly, which somehow only made him more terrifying. "Yes, *Shard* Darak." His voice slithered over the holy man's title. "And where is *Shard* Darak at the moment?"

"He left this morning with Brother Stralasi to journey to Home World."

The Angel mulled that over. "I have scanned the activation records for this starstep and detect no transfer record other than my own. Nothing was documented passing in or out since the last recorded shipment over eighty-seven hours, twenty-one minutes ago."

"Shard Darak arrived by means other than the public starstep, Lord Mika, Sir. He and Brother Stralasi left on foot, presumably to return to his secret starstep to the west."

"Interesting," remarked the Angel. He scanned the room, and settled his gaze on the anxious man before him.

Brother Yonteg's head exploded in pain. His jaw opened to scream, but no sound escaped. In no more than a few seconds, his head was completely and mercilessly reamed to extract every detail of the past two days.

Every vision, sound, smell, and feeling was wrenched forcefully to the front of the monk's conscious attention in one overwhelming, excruciating, cacophonous burst. His mind struggled without success to make sense of the re-experiencing.

And then it was over. Brother Yonteg was left reeling and nauseated from the whirl of unbidden memories. Released, he collapsed to the floor holding his pounding head in his hands. Lord Mika's mind scan had not been gentle.

16

"WHO ON EARTH COULD THAT BE AT THIS TIME OF NIGHT?" Debbie Franti asked her husband on the second ring of the doorbell. They'd just finished locking up and settling into bed with their books. Nick looked out the bedroom window to the covered porch.

"I can't see who it is," he replied. The car parked in front of their house wasn't familiar. He scanned both ways down the block. *A quiet night, nobody else around.*

The visitor pressed the doorbell again and, without waiting, started banging insistently on the stylish metal screen door.

Nick was about to call the police when he heard, "Nick? Debbie? It's Paul. Are you up?" *There must be an emergency.* He threw on his bathrobe and rushed downstairs, quickly unlocking and opening the door.

"Paul, what's wrong?"

"Darian's got them." The pain in Paul's eyes matched the bracing autumn wind, but his voice was eerily matter of fact and controlled.

Nick stared at the disheveled man on the stoop. A sudden gust of wind nearly tore Paul's coat from his shoulders; he barely noticed.

"Got who? What are you talking about?"

"He's got dendies in his brain, Nick."

"That's not possible. Why don't you come inside? It's freezing out there," Nick guided Paul through the foyer and into the kitchen. "Let me put on some coffee." He dropped a filter in place and started measuring the aromatic grains. "Tell me, what makes you think there are dendies in Darian's brain?"

"I saw the x-ray." Paul stared at his hands folded on the table in front of him. "It looked just like Sharon's did."

"What? Why did you get an x-ray of Darian's head?"

"He had a seizure, like the one Sharon had the day of her accident. The day she died, Nick." Paul's soft, level voice was scarier than if he'd been in a rage. Nick heard Debbie appear at the kitchen door and turned to her, silently pleading for assistance.

"Oh, Paul!" she sat down next to him and put her hands on his. Paul's gaze rose from her hands to her face, and held her eyes. Self-consciously, she let go and tucked her hands to her chest.

"When I got home from work, Darian was sitting on the sofa, reading," Paul began. "The pages were flying by so fast that I couldn't tell what it was, but it looked pretty technical, full of symbols and diagrams I didn't recognize.

"He didn't respond when I spoke to him. He gave no sign at all that he even knew I was there. So I leaned over to take away his tablet—you know, just to get his attention—and he went berserk. He lunged at me and fought like a wildcat to get it back.

"Then he went into some kind of seizure and didn't come out of it. It was horrible. I bundled him up and drove him to the hospital. They took x-rays, ran an EEG, and did a bunch of other tests.

"The x-rays showed those same bright little speckles Sharon had, all over his brain. The doctor said his EEG was full of electrical activity but it didn't look like a seizure. I knew what it was, though. I recognized the dendies as soon as I saw them."

"It must have been that blow to her head." Nick paced the kitchen floor. "It must have sent the dendies circulating into her system; into the fetus."

Debbie got up to pour coffee, trying to impose some sense of normalcy on the situation. "I thought they were supposed to be restricted to neural tissue. How could they move to the baby?"

"They were...*are* restricted. The impact must have dislocated some of them."

"So how did they end up inside Darian? And how come they didn't show up when he was a baby? Dr. Holden watched him closely for two years. She said he was all clear," Paul challenged, sounding more accusatory than inquisitive.

"Well, remember they *are* nanotechnology, so you've got to think nanoscale. They're much smaller than a cell, and these ones were designed to actively cross organ barriers. Getting across the placenta would be no problem. The dislodged dendies would have been lost and seeking to re-establish themselves in central neural tissue, as they were designed to do. If any of them found the baby's developing brain, it would have provided them with a perfectly viable alternative." Nick's voice trailed off. He was already thinking ahead to the bigger picture.

"Paul, do you realize what this means? This is amazing!" The scientist in Nick overshadowed the concerned friend and surrogate uncle. "It's a totally serendipitous opportunity to study how dendies interact with a young human brain!"

Paul could only stare, gaping at the scientist in disbelief. "My son is NOT your test subject!" he growled, menacingly.

"No, I know that. Relax. I didn't mean it that way. I wasn't thinking that at all."

"You *will* take them out," Paul said, slowly and evenly. His tone made it clear there would be no discussion.

Nick rubbed his eyes. "I don't think we *can*, Paul, I'm sorry, but I don't know any way to remove a dendy lattice once it's established."

Paul was stunned. "You've got to be kidding me. How can you make something like this and not have a failsafe plan to un-make it? Are you crazy? No wonder the public doesn't trust scientists!"

"Well, Sharon....That is, we....You have to understand. It was such a challenge just to construct them, to get them to replicate, and to connect to each other. You know how Sharon was—impatient and driven. We'd barely figured out how to make them when she jumped the gun and injected the dendies into herself. We were still working on them, and we'd barely started thinking about how to eliminate them.

"We still haven't been able to develop a protein to digest the silicene filaments or degrade the semiconductor nanoparticles. The team was working on several ideas, but when Sharon...when she passed, her team lost direction. The whole project lost momentum, Paul. They were....we *all* were...just lost without her. We nearly shut down the whole project. It was her students who convinced me that her work was important, that the only way to make her death count for something was to continue the work.

"So we did. We started picking up the pieces; and we're still trying to catch up. We've developed a couple of failsafe protocols to shut down dendy processing, but it doesn't get rid of them. Even if we could, we're not sure how disassembling an established lattice might affect the brain. That's a study we hope to do in a few years." Nick took a breath and gathered his thoughts. "Paul, you're an engineer. You *know* that some systems are hard to turn off."

"I can pull the plug on any of my systems."

"*Can* you?" Nick challenged. "Look at the internet. Sure, you can turn it off, but the ramifications to our connected society would be catastrophic."

Paul stared at him, "They're not the same." His hand trembled as he sipped his coffee. "You said you can shut down their processing. Will that help Darian? Will it prevent another seizure?"

Relieved from defending himself, his research, and Sharon's actions, Nick focused on the fact that there was a problem to solve and a boy's life to save. This was something they could deal with.

"Well, the modern dendy lattice is chemically restricted to certain sections of the brain. It's too late to change Darian's lattice; the dendies are already resident throughout. Sharon was working on a self-replicating version before the accident. Darian's had that version in his system a long time now, so we have to assume that they've had plenty of time to reproduce and get established."

"I still don't understand how you can move from theoretical pencil scratches and computer models into the real world, without first having worked out multiple, redundant fail safes. This is my *son* we're talking about. Darian wouldn't be in this situation if you hadn't made the dendies self-replicating."

"We stopped using that version once NANOSERPA was passed. You know, the Nanotechnology Self-Replication Prevention Act."

"Talk about closing the barn door after the horses have escaped!"

"I know, I know. Let's just stick to the problem at hand, shall we? The lattice itself shouldn't cause any harm. All the components are completely bio-compatible. It must be the software causing the problem."

"Is there something wrong with their operating system?"

"No, not *per se*," replied Nick. "But, if the dendies are interacting with the RAS, then whenever they're faced with a barrage of new information, they could shut down the whole brain and retreat into batch processing mode."

That was too much for Paul to follow. "RAS?"

"The brain's Reticular Activating System. The RAS connects brain activity to the body. When the system is turned off, brain activity is largely disconnected from a muscular response. It's why you don't physically act out every action when you dream. When you looked at Darian's x-ray, did you see any dendies in his brain stem? What about in the claustrum, thalamic, hypothalamic, or mesencephalic regions?"

Paul's blank stare pulled Nick back to reality. "Sorry. Let's assume the dendies have spread everywhere in his brain by now, and that they shut down the RAS whenever they need to process a lot of information. For example, after reading a bunch of technical or scientific articles. That's good news. We can work with that. We can alter their programming so they don't go into hyper-processing shutdown mode unless the RAS is already in the 'off' state."

"Which means what?"

"Which means, we can alter their operating system so the dendies only re-organize when Darian's asleep. When he dreams, they'll go to work."

17

"I DON'T THINK I CAN GO TO CHURCH ANYMORE."

Paul nearly choked. *What in Heaven's name?* He finished chewing, swallowed, and looked at his son. "Okay, I'll bite. Why not?"

"I think I'm an atheist now."

"Is that so?" He didn't expect that.

The previous six months had whirled past. Once Nick reprogrammed Darian's dendy lattice to coordinate its hyper-processing with the boy's sleep cycle, the seizures stopped, and Darian's learning accelerated exponentially.

The boy sailed through middle school and high school course material as fast as his heightened reading speed would allow. The only things impeding his progress were the school's bureaucratic compulsion to test him at each level, and his counselor's resistance to advancing Darian before he was emotionally and socially ready.

When they finally deemed him ready, they set a graduation date. He considered his options, and accepted an invitation from the Department of Electrical Engineering and Computer Science at MIT. He was healthier than ever and had been adjusting well. His future looked bright.

Paul sighed. It wasn't hard to imagine how Darian might attribute his good fortune to his dendies and to the scientists at Neuro Nano, rather than to God's plan for him. *God works in mysterious ways.* Darian was proving to be one of His greatest mysteries ever.

He put down his fork, and gave the conversation his full attention. "I understand that everything is coming pretty easily to you these days but, trust me on this, everyone needs to have faith in a higher power to help carry them through the tough times."

"I can see that having faith is useful," Darian acknowledged.

Paul was having a difficult time keeping up with his son's thinking these days. The boy was venturing down intellectual avenues his father was more and more often unable to follow.

"When your mother died, my faith was the only thing that enabled me to carry on. I knew that God must have a plan, though it wasn't at all clear to me, and I knew that she was in a better place."

Darian laughed. "Oh, Dad. Your belief system is based on too many unproven and wild assumptions to list in a reasonable amount of time."

Paul was taken aback by his son's tone. "Perhaps. But, I *am* still your father and you *will* treat me with respect." It had taken considerable conscious effort to keep his voice level.

"Sorry," Darian offered, unconvincingly.

Paul held his son's steadfast gaze, asserting silent parental authority. Only when his son looked down did he pick up his fork and resume eating.

But Darian wasn't done. "The thing is, since I no longer find it reasonable or rational that God exists, it would be a sham to attend church services. I can't worship something I don't consider real."

Paul placed his fork gently and deliberately on the rim of his plate, and folded his hands in his lap. *He's just a teenager*—he reminded himself. *He may have an immeasurable IQ, but he's still a teenager. Rebellion is his duty.* "Okay, so tell me, why have you stopped believing in God?"

"It's not so much that I don't believe in any specific god, say the Christian one or the Muslim one. It just seems that the concept of any god doesn't fit with what we know about the universe. Under those circumstances, I would think that the burden of proof for something so improbable should rest with the claim of the believer of the particular deity.

"Even if one were to dismiss a fundamental interpretation of the Bible or Quran as being provably incorrect, and were to argue in favor of a more complex version of a hypothetical god, that god can be demonstrated to be a logical contradiction and therefore not to exist."

"And how do you get that, exactly?" They had never broached this subject before and he needed a moment to wade through the complexity. "Maybe you could simplify it for me; you know, me being a mere mortal and all."

Darian responded without hesitation, "The Bible says that an omniscient and omnipotent God *created* the universe, not God *is* the universe, right? In fact, pretty much all creation stories say that God is not *of* the universe but is formless and timeless, *outside* the universe He created."

"I didn't know you read your Bible or listened at church, for that matter."

"Oh, I listen to everything. I don't believe what everyone says, though, just because they say it's true. Anyway, that definition of God is self-contradictory."

"Oh, really? How do you figure?"

"What would it mean to be the Creator?"

"The standard definition? To have made the stars, the planets, all life."

"So, to have formed the various forms of matter and energy based on the pre-existing natural laws of the universe?" Darian asked.

"Well...no, not exactly."

"No, that wouldn't work. The Creator can't operate solely within the natural laws of this universe, or we'd have to posit an even higher intelligence that made the natural laws in the first place."

"Okay. I'll give you that."

"So, in fact, God the Creator can't be just any higher intelligence or power but rather THE highest intelligence or power possible. One that is capable of making the natural laws that govern matter and energy in the universe?"

"I guess..." Paul knew he was being maneuvered down a logical path he didn't want to follow, but he couldn't see an off-ramp. He'd have to tag along for now. "Okay, for the sake of argument, let's say, yes."

"So, who made the natural laws that permit the existence of God?"

"Don't be ridiculous. Nobody makes natural laws that govern God! He is all-powerful and eternal."

"He just exists, right?"

"That's what I'm saying. God exists."

"How do you mean He *exists*? What's He made of? How does He work? What does He think with?"

"God is a nameless essence, beyond human fathoming."

"Well, if He exists, one would think He's composed of *something* rather than *nothing*, right? Maybe not the same stuff of this universe, maybe some kind of spiritual energy or something like that, but not *nothing*."

"No, he's not *nothing*."

"Okay, we can agree: if God exists, He's something rather than nothing."

"Yes, we can agree on that." Paul felt a logical trap closing in.

"Then, what are the laws of nature that govern the *something* that God's made of? Where did they come from?"

"They didn't come from anywhere. They're eternal, like God."

"So there are laws of nature, somewhere outside of our universe, that God didn't make?"

"The eternal laws of God's essence? Maybe."

"Can God alter the laws of nature that govern God's existence? Could he make a copy of himself, for instance?"

"That one makes my brain hurt," Paul complained.

"Because if He can't, then He's not omnipotent. Not if there are some other laws of nature He didn't determine, the ones that govern His existence. He didn't make those laws."

"Maybe not those. But, in the context of *this* universe, He's all-powerful."

"But then, we'd have two ways that laws of nature could come about. There's one set that governs God's existence—that determines how His essence works—and there's another set that He made for our universe."

Paul grasped for theological straws. "Maybe God is just the Creator of *this* universe, not all universes. Maybe God has His own God."

"And maybe *that* God also has a God in *His* universe. And then *that* God has a God who created *His* universe," suggested Darian.

Paul frowned.

"If that's the case, why don't we just cut out the middlemen, and worship the God at the top of the heap? Oh, wait. There is no top. It's just Gods all the way up."

"Darian, this argument is getting ridiculous. It's impossible to make natural laws. They're just there. God used the natural laws to make all Creation."

"The natural laws just exist?"

"That's right."

"And they always did?" Paul could feel the trap closing in.

"Yes."

"Therefore, no one made the natural laws; they weren't created. Therefore, there is no ultimate Creator, for there was something before Him, some set of natural laws. Therefore, God the Creator, or at least God the *ultimate* Creator, doesn't exist!"

Paul couldn't help but follow the logic. At the same time, he wasn't about to give up his faith so easily. "You're just playing semantics with me. Even if the natural laws just exist, God would have always, necessarily, existed alongside them."

"Then, we can say they are equivalent, even equal? God is natural law, and natural law is God?"

"I don't know. I'd have to think about that for a second."

"But if they've both *necessarily* existed together, forever, it would be impossible to have one without the other."

"Yes, impossible."

"So, together, they are a single thing?"

"I think I see where you're going."

"If by God we mean natural laws and vice versa, then either you have to conclude that natural laws are intelligent and intentional, or you have to conclude that God is just another way of saying Nature."

"Maybe that is all I'm saying. God is another way of saying Nature."

"Even more, God *is* Nature."

"Okay, sure. God *is* Nature."

"And Nature just *is*, without intelligence or intention. God the Creator is not a conscious entity, just Nature at work."

"I guess you're right," Paul had never been unhappier to be led to a new way of thinking about something. "Nature is God, and God is Nature. There is no Higher Intelligence in the sky with a Plan for humanity. Or if there is, He's not an all-powerful 'God', just someone a lot smarter than us." He looked miserable.

Darian suddenly realized that, although he was winning the argument intellectually, he was taking something important from his father. "Dad, I'm sorry."

"Well, I hope being so damn smart helps you be happier, and to find meaning and purpose in life without any guidance from God." Paul pushed his food around his plate. Why did his chest feel so heavy? Maybe a little resentment at being bested? Sure, maybe a little. At the same time, he felt a reluctant twinge of pride in how well Darian had argued.

He let the flood of uncomfortable questions wash over him. If the kid is right, then what happened to Sharon's soul after her death? How can we find purpose in life if not through doing God's work? How could the universe have popped into existence without anyone creating it? He was too tired to discuss it any further, and he had no answers of his own. At least, none that would satisfy Darian.

No longer sure that it would help, Paul said a quick prayer that Darian might someday find the answers he sought. For all his years of bible study, he still couldn't find the answers to his own questions.

Darian finished his meal in silence.

Later that night, before heading to bed, Paul couldn't stop himself from launching back in, "Do you hate religion, or just us Christians? Are we just some inferior species to you? Fools?" He regretted his words as soon as he heard them but there they were, spoken.

As brilliant as his lattice made him, as full of knowledge, and as understanding as he'd become, Darian was still a sensitive teenager and capable of being hurt. His confident young face crumpled, and he looked like he would break. "No, I don't hate anyone, and I don't think you're all fools."

"Do you hate people who can't see the Truth the way you do, or do you just feel sorry for them?" Paul couldn't stop himself; the words kept tumbling out.

"Dad, I don't hate people because they don't know everything. I don't know everything. If people find strength in some belief system that doesn't make sense to me, that doesn't make them bad or inferior, just human."

"I see, just human. Poor creatures."

Darian didn't bite. "Look, I've been reading a lot of biology these days, and clearly a behavioral trait as deeply ingrained as unreasonable faith, faith in something without any good evidence, must have some inheritable advantage in order to have survived in the species so long."

"What do you mean?"

"Imagine that we were all machines with great computational power but no emotions. What principles would we use to guide our activities? How would we decide what to do with ourselves? How could we distinguish good activities from bad? Useful from useless? Our computers are machines and they can only do what they're told. So what motivates us otherwise? What gives us inner strength? Our irrational emotions. And faith is one of those emotions."

"So having faith provides motivation?"

"Sure. Faith has given people the courage to explore the world when fear of the unknown incapacitated those around them. It has driven people to pursue their ideas in business, science, technology, and the arts despite disbelief and derision from their family and peers. When we're fighting a losing battle—whether individual or full-scale war—and *rational* assessment would suggest we stop struggling and give up, *faith* gives us the motivation and inner strength to carry on. Faith is very powerful. Historically, great confidence has led humanity to great achievements."

Paul smiled wryly. "Maybe that big brain of yours is good at something besides science and technology, after all."

"Thanks...I think. But faith *can* get carried away and lead people to believe things that are completely untrue, just because someone claims it to be true. It's like we're wired to trust people who express great confidence in their ideas.

"The thing is, psychos, sociopaths, and charlatans can express great confidence as well as true leaders. And people can't always tell one from the other. Some profess such strong faith that others think they must be divinely inspired and will give up wealth and family to follow someone like that on their crazy journey.

"But confidence is a sign that someone *believes* they're right, not that they are *actually* right. In fact, sometimes, the more outrageous the person's belief, the greater the confidence and fervor it's expressed with.

This has helped a lot of extremely improbable claims become widely accepted."

"Ah, back to religion."

"Sadly, yes. People have used religion to provide the justification to carry out horrible acts of war, murder, slavery and discrimination. Anyone should hate that part. Religious faith can inspire people to overcome their limitations to act for the common good beyond their normal family and tribal groups. But it can also get abused. It's used to vilify and dehumanize outsiders, to claim some twisted sense of superiority, to call individuals, communities and whole countries to war. Faith itself isn't the problem, but specific belief systems can be counterproductive to human progress."

Paul looked at his son in a whole new light. *It's not just that he's smarter. He's mature, wise beyond his years.* "So, without any religious faith, with just Nature, how do you find the strength and motivation to carry on?"

Darian spread his arms wide, grinning. "Look at me. I'm young. My body is full of life-affirming hormones coursing through my veins. I have a pretty good life. I haven't lived long enough for fear to conquer me." Paul was relieved to see this flash of boyish playfulness—his son!—still alive and well inside this passionate philosopher sitting across from him.

"Seriously, though? I don't know. I don't have an answer to that. The universe is still full of so many fascinating things. I hope to figure out the point of it all before it becomes boring and predictable."

Paul marveled at his son's growth, fearlessly facing the universe on its own terms, exactly as it was. "You know, I realize the dendies make you a lot smarter than you used to be, but when did you become so wise?"

"Wait until you read my analysis of War and Peace before you conclude I have any wisdom at all," quipped Darian, back to being a typical smart-aleck teenager. Paul shook his head and rolled his eyes with dramatic exaggeration.

They laughed it off, and parted with a hug. It felt good to share a rare "normal" father-and-son moment. Exhausted, Paul wished his son goodnight and they went to their rooms.

Darian drifted off to sleep thinking about the challenge his father had given him earlier, to figure out how one might live a life of meaning and purpose in the universe as it was, without the promise of some future reward or the threat of future punishment. His dreams that night were more vivid than normal, and his dendies were unusually active. While Darian dreamed, the dendies got down to work. They estimated a lengthy computation.

18

"INTERESTING," repeated Lord Mika as he reviewed Brother Yonteg's memories of the previous night.

All twelve Brothers, monks of the Alumita, had been invited to dine with Brother Stralasi and Shard Darak on their last night on the planet.

Although nobody included him directly in the conversation, Brother Yonteg was able to follow most of what was said from his seat at the far end of the table. At one point, feeling emboldened by Darak's friendly and open manner, and owing to a generous portion of the Alumita's best wine, Yonteg asked the Shard if he might perform a small miracle for the Brothers.

The Angel, Mika, watched the whole event play out vividly on an isolated sub-lattice of his mind.

* * *

"LORD DARAK HAS MORE IMPORTANT THINGS TO DO than exhibit his powers for our amusement," Brother Stralasi chastised. The Shard graciously put the monk's objections to rest and assured them that it would be his pleasure. "Please, if someone would dim the lights for us," he requested.

Holding his hands slightly apart, a glowing ball of blue fire emerged between them, hovering over the remnants of his dinner. He moved his hands, rotating the fist-sized ball this way and that. The Brothers applauded encouragingly and asked for more.

Darak parted his hands, releasing the glowing globe to float freely. It rose gently, rhythmically expanding and contracting as if it were breathing. Upon reaching the ceiling, it descended a meter or so, and then bobbed unsteadily into each of the four corners of the hall, like a balloon caught in a breeze. As it neared each successive corner, it traced a small vertical circle, leaving behind a yellow toroid that started to rotate as the sphere moved on.

Centering itself between the soft, yellow, twirling donuts, the sphere resumed its original position above the mesmerized audience. They cooed appreciatively as the bobbing sphere transformed into a glimmering pyramid with a delicately fluted pinnacle that started spurting red luminescence, like lava from a volcano.

Identical fountains materialized between the corners of the room, and the liquid light danced wildly for several more seconds, spraying droplets in all directions. Much to everyone's delight, the four outer fountains rose above the diners' heads, and started moving clockwise around the center one, slowly at first and then faster, until the room became a kaleidoscopic blur of blue and red. With a loud "pop!" the spinning halted, and all five fountains and the spinning toroids exploded in a shower of brilliant rainbow droplets of light.

* * *

"CHEAP MIND TRICKS," muttered the Angel. He had to admit, though, Darak had demonstrated a masterful command of the InterLat broadcast function. For a non-augmented human—even for one with access to secret knowledge of lattice technology—hacking into the perceptions of twelve individuals at one time without using a visible induction matrix was pretty impressive. Good enough to astound the dim-witted masses, in any case.

On the other hand, while such illusions were trivial for a real Shard to perform, they were not of sufficient caliber to verify a person's claim of a holy connection to Alum. Not like the time-honored miracles of curing a deadly disease or changing water into wine, for example.

As a level-headed Angel and an unflappable strategist, Lord Mika concluded that perhaps Alum was reacting somewhat overzealously.

So what, if some unknown person claiming to be a Shard makes an unscheduled visit to this lonely planet on the edge of the Da'arkness? Why should that matter to Alum?

Granted, there was that niggling mystery of *how* the audacious poser had arrived. Had he hacked the starstep, hiding traces of his arrival and origin? It was entirely conceivable that a renegade engineer with the skill set this man possessed might be capable of pulling off such a feat. Even at that, it seemed frivolous to employ an Angel for such basic policing duty.

But Angels do as Alum commands—he reminded himself. *If Alum thinks an Angel's presence is warranted, it is my duty to be here.*

He did not consider it heretical to question the judgment of the Living God. Over the ages, Alum had endowed the Angels with adequate programming to match their great power. He had come to trust that the combination was crucial in ensuring His Will was followed. As trusted enforcers of Alum's Will, Angels wielded high levels of independence and discretion. In Alum's Name, they were sent to dangerous places, home worlds of advanced alien races and asteroid warrens of renegade colonies, and were often out of communication for extended periods. In many cases, simplistic, mindless execution of guidelines from thousands of light years away could lead to unfortunate setbacks in the Divine Plan.

Lord Mika resumed his scrutiny of Brother Yonteg's memories.

* * *

clear night sky became visible. The stars! The Brothers looked around, once again in utter amazement. Sometime during the light display, the entire dinner assembly was transferred from inside the Residence to the lawn outside in the middle of Center Park. Everything on and around the table was still in place. No one had sensed any movement and yet, here they were, surrounded by grass, flowers, and tall trees framing the night sky. They applauded and cheered, drawing the startled attention of people strolling along nearby paths. Passersby gathered around to hear excited stories of the Shard's miraculous display. A smiling Darak humbly accepted the praise and adoration of the Brothers and their flock.

* * *

OKAY, SO THAT WAS A NEAT TRICK—Lord Mika acknowledged. Darak's considerable skill at mental manipulation had convinced several hundred people at once of a single, shared hallucination. But from the response of the passersby, relocation of the dining table from the hall to the park outside was, by all appearances, an actual, physical transfer. How could that be possible? No one other than Alum, Himself, had that power!

Maybe Alum was right to send an investigating Angel, after all. If Darak's powers were real, even if they were based on technology rather than Divine Grace, he could pose a threat to the Realm. *I have to confirm.*

He reviewed the recent memories of the remaining population of Alumston, searching out those who had interacted with Darak. The citizens of the town received no more than a few seconds warning by InterLat before the Angel plunged into their minds. They dropped whatever they were doing and sat or laid down wherever where ever they could for the next several minutes, as Lord Mika simultaneously, and painfully, examined their memories to find those from the several hundred who had met with the false Shard.

Weaving together the many images, he formed a complete picture of the man, Darak. He saw how it was only the proclamation by Brother Stralasi, and not by Darak himself, that had led the townspeople to believe he was a Shard of Alum.

Darak seemed like a kind man, knowledgeable about details prohibited to the general population but, otherwise, not overly special. Were it not for the post-dinner theatrics and lack of transfer record, Lord Mika would not have thought anything of him at all. *Yes, we will have to locate and interrogate this Darak in order to clear up the mystery.*

Which brought to mind the other detail bothering the Angel: he could find no trace of either Darak or Brother Stralasi on the InterLat. The planetary satellite system was in place and its self-diagnostics didn't indicate any functional issues.

If the two men were on the planet, they should be registering an InterLat signature and location.

If Darak was hiding their presence, that would make him an extraordinarily talented engineer, and blatant breaker of Alum's laws. Such skills and knowledge should situate him, mentally and physically, within the upper echelons of the technological elite on Home World, not traveling around like some vagabond on the edge of civilization.

Their public travel plans matched the memories of those they encountered as they left town. They were headed for the foothills to the west of Alumston.

It should be easy enough to locate them there. He left the Alumston Transportation Ceraffice, with his Securitor Cybrids trailing close behind. They rose a few dozen meters into the air and sped westward.

19

BROTHER STRALASI WAS GROWING HOT and impatient. He had been meditating cross-legged on the hard, dry ground for over an hour and he was eager to be on the way.

As Head Brother, he wasn't accustomed to waiting for people. Quite the contrary. He glanced over at Shard Darak, a motionless and inscrutable pillar, who had not stirred the whole time. *Even a Shard's rear end must be growing numb by now*—Stralasi grumbled.

As if hearing the monk's unspoken words, Darak rose. He looked eastward, back toward town.

"What is it, my Lord?" Stralasi inquired.

"Our wait is coming to an end. Now we will learn how Alum deals with surprises."

The words were spoken clearly enough, and yet they made no sense to Stralasi. The monk unfolded his stiff, aching legs and cajoled his frame upright, to better see what had attracted Darak's attention.

Three small dots punctuated the blue sky above the hills a kilometer away. They swept to the left, and then to the right, executing a narrow search pattern.

Stralasi was a learned man, having spent several years at the Home World Alumita Seminary. He recognized the advancing dots immediately. *Securitors! What are they doing here? Is this Darak's missing entourage? Have they come to escort us?*

He raised his arm and waved a helpful greeting. The Securitors ceased scanning and headed directly for the pair. As they drew closer, Stralasi saw they were not three Securitors, but two Securitors and an Angel. *An Angel!*

He had encountered Angels on Home World, and so was not as terrified as the common man might have been. He knew that he was so far beneath the notice of an Angel, he had nothing to fear. Had any of his transgressions merited Alum's disciplinary attention, he would have been a smoking cinder long ago. So, what could they want?

The Angel settled gently to the ground a few meters in front of Darak. The pair of Securitors took positions on either side of the men. Darak waited patiently while the Angel studied him.

The Angel smiled, though there was neither welcome nor comfort in the gesture. "I am Lord Mika, Commander of the Alutius Wing. My Cybrids detect nothing to draw you to this place." His voice was the most beautiful sound Stralasi had ever heard. It resonated all around him and echoed lightly off the nearby hills.

Darak returned the smile. "Yet here I am, and so *here*," he swept his arms outward, palms up as if showcasing the desert view for their visitor's appreciation, "must be where I intended to be."

The Angel's smile grew broader and colder. "Yes, we have questions about how you came to be here but, first, we will know who you are," he commanded.

"I am Darak Legsu," he replied, and bowed.

"Not Shard Darak?"

"Oh, no!" Darak laughed. "Not *Shard* Darak, no. At least, no longer. Surely that ruse has no further purpose, not to one like you."

Brother Stralasi stared at Darak. *Not a Shard? That's not possible! Everything about him screams Shard. I've seen him perform miracles. If he's not a Shard, the only possible explanation can be...he must be a demon of the Da'arkness!*

Stralasi's heart raced as the events of the past few days fell into place. The shock that he had been fooled so easily hit him like a physical blow. *I prostrated myself before this demon! I introduced him to the townspeople as a Holy man! Worse yet, I'm standing here alongside this demon as he confronts an Angel!*

Oh, dear Alum! How could I have been so blind? He dropped to his knees, burying his head in his hands and bawled. "Forgive me, mighty Angel of Alum, for I have been tricked by this Deceiver! Destroy him and free me, I pray!"

Darak turned to the distressed Brother. "Rise and bear witness, Brother Stralasi," he said in a voice as commanding as the Angel's.

Stralasi couldn't help but obey. He shuffled to one side so as not to stand between Darak and either of the hovering Securitors. To his dismay, they adjusted their positions and maintained a bead on him. *That's it. I am doomed.*

Lord Mika's golden eyes flared. "You display some admirable talents, Darak Legsu, but you are no more demon than Shard. Let us see whether your talents extend beyond trickery, shall we?"

Tendrils whipped out from the smooth black surfaces of the Securitors and curled tightly around the two men, lifting them up, and leaving their feet waggling a good half meter above the ground.

"No, apparently they do not," Lord Mika smirked as Stralasi struggled and Darak tranquilly contemplated his bindings.

The Angel rose and turned back toward town, satisfied and a little disappointed. "I didn't think so. We shall return to the starstep and proceed to Home World for questioning."

"Thank you, Lord Mika, but I'm afraid we'll have to decline. Brother Stralasi and I have other plans," Darak explained.

The Angel wheeled around to address the impertinent man. The Securitors' tendrils retracted and the two men dropped freely to the ground, issuing soft "oophs" from their diaphragms as they landed.

"Well, that was rude," commented Darak.

The Securitors each emitted an ear-splitting squeal, shuddered, and fell to the ground, inert and deaf to the Angel's commands. Lord Mika scanned for signs of damage or system subversion but found nothing to explain their failure. And yet, impossibly, their internal microverses—their practically indestructible power sources—had collapsed. Without power, they were dead.

Ignoring Brother Stralasi, Lord Mika zeroed in on Darak. The golden eyes narrowed and took fresh assessment of the offending man before him. "Clearly, there is more to you than I expected," he admitted.

He translocated himself to a point immediately behind the man and wrapped his arms, rumored to be strong enough to crush entire buildings, tightly around the man.

Darak spun around within the powerful grip and faced the Angel. He drew his knees sharply upward and, pushing off from his sternum, escaped Lord Mika's clutches.

The Angel struggled to recover his balance and composure, while Darak drifted gently to the ground, four meters away.

Angels do not get angry—Alum dictates that anger is counterproductive in battle—but they do get determined. And this particular Angel was now *supremely* determined to submit this mysterious man to full interrogation back on Home World. No matter if all that remained to interrogate was the man's neural lattice inside his severed head.

Lord Mika drew his sapphire sword. He closed the distance to Darak in two inhumanly fast steps, and took a mighty swing, intending to remove the head of this perturbing anomaly.

Darak ducked effortlessly beneath the blade.

Impossible! The Angel's movement had taken less than two hundred milliseconds. It wasn't possible for a human to react fast enough to avoid the severing edge. And yet, Darak had.

Lord Mika reconsidered the situation. This man, by all outward appearances and cursory scans a normal man, had exhibited skill in altering starstep records. He'd changed the perceptions of hundreds of individuals by hacking into their neural lattices and providing false input, simultaneously and in real-time. He'd disabled two Securitors, possibly collapsing their microverse power systems, squirmed out of an Angel's grasp, and avoided a sword moving at hypersonic speeds. He'd demonstrated the strength and speed of an Angel. This man was not at all normal. He was not simply a talented renegade engineer.

Despite millions of years of active duty in Alum's service, Lord Mika had neither direct commands nor adequate experience to guide him in this matter. Nobody had ever encountered such a situation. Clearly, if this Darak Legsu could hold his own in a fight with an Angel, he posed a threat to the Realm. It was time to escalate to deadly force.

Lord Mika pointed his sword at Darak and directed a violet beam at the man's heart. The beam passed unobstructed through the space where Darak had been standing only microseconds before and destroyed a few hundred meters of the hillside behind.

Lord Mika could hardly believe his eyes but there stood Darak, unharmed, some ten meters away alongside a surprised-looking Brother Stralasi. The monk, at least, had not moved since being released from the Securitors.

How did he manage that? Only the Angels and Alum Himself have translocation capabilities! Lord Mika ran a self-diagnostic to see if his lattice had been subverted. *Could this imposter be feeding my perceptions false data?* No, internal processing was nominal. Still, the man was suspicious.

Mika deactivated his perceptual enhancements and scanned the area using only his basic senses. Nothing changed. Darak and Brother Stralasi stood, quite impossibly, together.

The Angel translocated behind them and once again delivered what should have been a devastating blow. This time, *both* men disappeared. *By Alum! How did they get to that boulder thirty meters away?*

Without losing a millisecond, the Angel shifted to the space directly in front of them, swinging his sword as he reappeared. The blade struck nothing but air. *In Alum's Name, this is getting tiresome. Play time is over, you arrogant mite. It is time to draw the childish game to a close!*

The Angel shifted to the far side of Brother Stralasi, employing him as a screen. He discharged an energy beam, rather dispassionately, right through the hapless monk to get at the man behind him.

To the Angel's compounding annoyance, the sword met only empty air. The pair had already blinked out of the path of the blast.

Frustration was not a state the Angel was accustomed to experiencing, and it was not one he wished to explore any further. If he didn't destroy this man soon, he would have to invoke Alum to deal with this...this...affliction. *Angel or demon, you will not avoid obliteration forever.*

Lord Mika flew upward, nearly out of sight, while the two men below watched with curiosity. A more powerful attack was required, one the two men could not elude. The Angel increased the power and radius of his destructive beam, centered it on Darak and Brother Stralasi, and released a torrent of energy lasting several seconds.

Satisfied that nobody could survive such a blast, Lord Mika surveyed the damage. A crater, five kilometers in diameter and several hundred meters deep had been punched into the bedrock. All matter within the crater had been converted into a plasma gusher, which the Angel's beam neatly confined within a moving cylinder, saving nearby Alumston from incidental annihilation. The plasma streamed upward, making a spectacular exit from the atmosphere. There was no sign of Darak, Brother Stralasi, or the two Securitors.

Lord Mika grimaced. He did not relish reporting his failure to capture Darak Legsu.

* * *

Darak and Brother Stralasi hovered forty kilometers above the massive crater. They watched the cylinder of accelerated plasma cross the edge of the planet's atmosphere, creating a beautiful aurora as it entered space. For the first few seconds following their translocation into the stratosphere, Brother Stralasi flailed in panic, his limbs seeking unsuccessfully to connect with the ground far below. When he realized he was not falling, he stopped struggling and began to wonder how he was alive. He felt oddly calm and rational. *What an odd sensation!*

"I'm altering your body's normal physiological response to fear so you can think clearly," explained Darak.

Stralasi looked around. He was very high above the ground. *How can I hear? There's no air up here to conduct sound. No air!* He gasped for breath, and a soothing calmness washed over him again, the result of further intervention by Darak.

Stralasi marveled at the planet far below, at the universe all around him, and at the man/demon beside him. "How did we get here? How are we flying? How am I alive?"

"Let me address your questions in order," replied Darak. "I shifted us here to avoid the Angel's energy beam. We are able to hover here through a balancing of gravitational and anti-gravitational forces. I erected a shield around us to contain some planetary atmosphere so we can breathe. I am refreshing the air inside with air from the planet every few seconds. The shield also protects us from cosmic radiation and the cold vacuum of space."

"But, how..? Are you truly a demon?" While fearing the answer, the Brother felt compelled to ask, even if it cost his own life.

Darak laughed. "I have been called many things but never a demon. Though, as the Angel surmised, neither am I the Shard of Alum you thought me to be."

"Are you a god, then?"

Darak considered this. "There are no gods," he finally said.

"What do you want with me?"

"That is exactly as I represented, Brother Stralasi. I want you to journey with me."

"What use could you possibly have for me?"

"You may be more useful than you think."

Brother Stralasi contemplated the uses this man, or Angel, or Demon, might make of him. He could think of nothing pleasant. "Let me die. Please kill me or let me die here, I beg you. I cannot face more like that."

Darak's eyes filled with compassion. "I am sorry for what you were put through but it was necessary for me to know if Alum has changed, or if he is still the ruthless God I once knew.

"I believe that Angel, His Angel, would have destroyed this star system to kill me, if necessary. And I believe Alum would have approved." He gazed into space. "Your God has long been more concerned with His power and His Divine Plan than with His People."

"But Alum is the Living God appointed by Yov, the Creator!" Stralasi protested.

"Perhaps it is time for His reign to be over. Perhaps the days of the Living God are coming to an end."

Great Alum, preserve me. I am the prisoner of a crazed demon! Weary resignation settled heavily over Stralasi's mind and body. When angels, demons, and even God take direct interest in the fate of one man, what power does that man have to make choices?

"Very well. I will accompany you on your journey. I pray that we both survive it."

Darak smiled. "Pray if you must but your God will not hear. Rather, let us trust to our knowledge, skills, and good luck. If we must have any gods, these will serve as well as any. Let us be on our way."

With that, they disappeared from over Gargus 718.5.

20

NSA Classified- Level III, File No.: 06-84857
Recorded: April 17, 2032, 18:30, Dallas, Texas.
Subject: Yeshua's True Guard (YTG) Executive Committee meeting.
Source: Verified. Compiled from quadruple-redundant neural recordings made on-site by NSA24135 Spyders. Original ocular and aural recordings attached.
Verified voices: George Colder, Patrick Burton, Saul Trent, Mike Freeman, Dona Nielson, Steve Stockwell

Colder: Lord, bless this congregation and these good people who have come together in Your Name to bring Your Kingdom to this, Your chosen nation. Let our minds be clear and our hearts steady as we pursue Your Will. In Yeshua, we are strong.

All: Amen.

Burton: Before we begin, can I get verification on the security sweep?

Trent: Yes, sir. The scan shows no transmitting devices present. Everyone's been cleared. No recorders in the room. Normally, we'd have to worry about laser pickup off the windows, but I think we're safe from that down here in the basement.

Burton: Alright, let's begin by welcoming a man I'm sure y'all know real well, the next Senator from the great State of Texas and our future President, Fred Mitchell. [*applause and cheers*]

Colder: Thank you for coming down tonight, Mr. Mitchell.

Mitchell: My pleasure, George. Thanks for inviting me. And thank every last one of you for your dedication, your faith, and your patriotism. It is truly a great honor to be with you here, tonight. Seeing you here fills me with hope. [*applause*]

Colder: Thank you, sir. We have a fairly short agenda tonight. First up is Mike. Can you tell us how our numbers are looking, Mike?

Freeman: Thank you, George. The Election Committee has been working hard on Mr. Mitchell's campaign leading up to the primaries. It's tight but showing promise. We're at 30%. We're closing in on Mr. Conys who's held a steady 35%, and we've pulled ahead of Reverend LaMontagne, who's in third place at 26%. It looks like we're pretty much assured a victory in the run-off, thanks to the support that will be coming from the Reverend's people.

Colder: Is everything in place for Reverend LaMontagne's announcement?

Freeman: Yes. Those, shall we say, "enlightening" videos delivered to the Election Committee last month were sent to the Reverend with the anticipated result. Lord knows how he was able to keep his own mother's falling away from the Church a secret all this time, but the clips of her attending those atheist "services" convinced him he ought to pledge his full support to Mr. Mitchell in the runoff and focus more on his congregation if he wishes to have any kind of political future in this state. His announcement will come tonight.

Colder: I expect so. [*chuckling*] Thank you, Mike. Please convey the Executive's appreciation to the Election Committee for a job well done.

Freeman: I'll do that, sir. Also, Reverend LaMontagne asked me to pass along his congratulations to Mr. Mitchell on a solid campaign. He looks forward to putting this ugliness behind us and working together to defeat those damned Democrats. He trusts Mr. Mitchell will remember who provided the support needed to win this election, at some appropriate time in the future.

Colder: I'm sure we'll be able to find a suitable role for true patriots like the Reverend in the new republic. Next up is Dona, with an update on our liaison with the committees in other states. Dona?

Nielson: Thank you, George. I spoke last week with the organizing committee in New Mexico. I'm pleased to announce that they've agreed to join us in creating our glorious New Confederacy. We have firm commitments from all the great southern states from New Mexico to Florida, north to Virginia, and west to Kentucky. That makes sixteen standing with us when we throw those devils in Washington out of our homeland and take back control of our own destiny. [*applause and foot stomping*]

Colder: That's wonderful news, Dona. What about our fellow organizations in the north and on the west coast?

Nielson: I won't lie. It's been a nightmare dealing with those lefty socialists in California and in Washington State. Trying to get United Churchers, Unitarians, and Buddhists to agree on anything is a real challenge. But compared to dealing with those commie Canadians and the secular Frenchies in Quebec, it's been a piece of cake. [*laughter*] The good news is, we're finally getting through. The United Brethren along the Pacific coast from California to Alaska have agreed to coordinate their secession with ours. Come January, once Senator-Elect Mitchell assumes control of the Governor's mansion here in Austin and declares it as the White House of the New Confederacy, Governor Alcraft out in Olympia will declare Pacifica's independence as well. [*cheers*]

Colder: How about British Columbia? Are they ready to declare?

Nielson: Yes, the provinces of British Columbia and Alberta have both pledged to declare separation from the rest of Canada and join the west-coast states in forming New Pacifica. Truth be told, the Albertans would have preferred to join our Confederacy, but we just couldn't figure out how to make that work geographically. Too many unallied states lie between us. That's okay, though. They might consider themselves to be conservatives, but that's Canadian conservative. Around these parts, we spell that with a l'il 'c'. As far as I can tell, they fall somewhere to the left of Wilson. [*loud laughter*]

Colder: Any updates on Quebec?

Freeman: As soon as BC and Alberta announce separation, Monsieur Prevost, the Premier of Quebec, will declare martial law in that province. He has the active wing of the Parti Quebecois Libre waiting to assume control of government buildings and media outlets. No doubt, there'll be a lot of resistance from the national government in...where is it? Oh, yes, Ottawa. The feds are going to have their hands so busy with the western rebellion. I expect they'll see the writing on the wall pretty quickly. We expect the remaining Canadian provinces will move toward applying for a union within weeks, piggybacking onto whatever part of the former America is closest to them. Heck, one or two of them may try to make a go of it on their own.

Colder: You haven't mentioned our central and northern states. Are we seeing any support there yet?

Freeman: We've tried to help the movements in the northern states, but they just won't have their acts together in time. And Heaven only knows what those disorganized Godless gamblers in Nevada and the Mormons in Utah are up to. [*laughter*] At any rate, we will have our New Confederacy. Whatever's left of the un-United Welfare States of America will just have to look out for itself. [*applause and cheers*]

Colder: Thank you, Dona. It looks like we're right on our original timetable. I have some progress to report, too. I spoke with our righteous brothers in England and France. They tell me that the Muslim-friendly European Union Parliament has gone too far. They've invited all of North

Africa, from Morocco to Egypt, to apply for membership. Our conscientious objectors in the non-aligned EU countries predict this will leave Europe wide open to the Muslim invasion the Crusaders fought against over eight hundred years ago.

Trent: Good Lord, why don't they just let in all the Indians and Chinese, while they're at it? [*laughter*]

Colder: You never know, they still might. [*more laughter*] The EU claims they need to increase immigration because their demographics are unfavorable—not enough of their own young folk are having babies. Their debt load hasn't declined since the Great Recession, and the past twenty years of zero growth, even with negative interest rates, has been killing them. It doesn't help that the Euro's been crashing even faster than the dollar since 2021.

They're drowning, and they've had about all they can take of those rich bureaucrats in Belgium telling them what to spend their tax dollars on. Three hundred percent debt-to-GDP? That's no way to build a future!

They're looking for us to lead the way, to rescue them from financial ruin. Again. But before we do that, they need to carry out their own Freedom Revolution. We'll be ready to offer them full support once our new government is in place—I'm talking military, monetary and organizational.

Mitchell: We'll have to be very careful how we do that. With the European Union buying so much of our oil and liquid natural gas, we don't want to be seen as interfering in their internal affairs. We are, of course. We just don't want to be seen doing it. [*laughter*]

Colder: Not to worry. We have a number of circumspect communication channels in place, working through our friends in Iran. Ever since the Shah took back control from the Ayatollahs, the sanctions from the EU-China-Russia trading block have hurt them a lot. EU-supported, large-scale development of solar power in North Africa is hitting their oil and nuclear electricity exports where it hurts. Iran needs our support. We've promised to work with them in strategically setting prices and quotas in future. Timing is the key. But don't worry. None of the arms or money we invest in bringing down the European Union will be traceable back to us.

Mitchell: I think I can help that along. My administration will be happy to help undermine the cozy little arrangement between the EU, China, and Russia. They haven't exactly been doing us any favors this past decade since they started conducting all their business in Euros, rubles, and renminbi.

Many: Hear, hear! [*cheers and applause*]

Colder: I'll take that as a yes-vote, then.

Stockwell: No, George, I think that's more like a "Hell, yes!" vote. [*prolonged loud laughter, cheers, and applause*]

Colder: Alright. Settle down, everyone. I'll remind you, although I appreciate your enthusiasm, we are working in the name of our Lord, Yeshua. So, let's try to keep the profanity down, please.

Stockwell: Sorry about that.

Colder: No harm done, Steve. Now, before we call it a night, why don't you fill us in on the progress with the New Militia?

Stockwell: Yes, sir. I am pleased to report to the Executive Committee that the New Confederacy Militia is ready for action. Our organizational structure makes it difficult to determine the exact numbers, but I've passed word outward through the various Command cells to try to generate some kind of estimate of our support.

To give you a rough idea, each Militia Cell is twelve members. If everyone does as instructed and doesn't join any cell outside their Reporting Cell and Leading Cell, then across all the future member-states, that would put us at over 52,000 trained and armed men and women prepared to put their lives on the line for the New Confederacy.

We also asked our Militia members to report if they've had any military training. Over 68% answered affirmatively. Our command recruits from the major Army, Navy, and Air Force bases assure me that we will have timely access to both troops and weapons.

Colder: Thank you, Steve, or should I say, General Stockwell?

Thank you *all* for a job well done—I remind you that it's not over until Senator Mitchell is President Mitchell. And with your courage, your faith and, yes, your sacrifices, we *will* get there. History will remember you as the heroes and patriots you truly are.

On November 2nd, we start the countdown to the New Confederacy, and to a new Christian era in our beloved South. [*loud cheers and applause*]

Yeshua bless this Committee and the holy work we do. Yeshua bless the New Confederacy!

Many: Yeshua bless the New Confederacy!

[*Original transcript and recordings transmitted to Deputy Director Thornten May 1, 2032. No copies made.*]

FROM THE MOMENT he received Deputy Director Thornten's suspiciously casual call requesting this meeting, Senator Fred Mitchell was filled with a foreboding premonition.

Something's up. Something ominous. Weighty. High-level NSA Executives like Thornten don't drop by a newly elected Senator's Lakeway District country home to have a friendly chat. And they wouldn't conduct routine business out here. This has to be something big, something he wants to keep off the records.

Senator Mitchell poured himself a generous bourbon on the rocks, and an iced tea for Deputy Director Thornton. He'd convinced Doris to take her mother for lunch at the Golf and Country Club today so she wouldn't feel obliged to play hostess. The two men sipped their drinks and exchanged superficial pleasantries as they made their way outdoors to the shaded terrace.

Thornten took a seat opposite the Senator; he left his sunglasses on. Mitchell resisted being drawn in by his own reflection, and took stock of the Deputy Director. He saw a highly disciplined career man sporting the lean, hard body and buzz-cut of a young naval lieutenant, and a pale complexion owing to more years spent analyzing intelligence data than sailing the open seas. Only a few small wrinkles overshooting the reflective lenses belied his true age. Neither relaxed nor hostile, Thornten wasn't giving away any clues. *What was he up to that couldn't be dealt with at work?*

Mitchell nursed his bourbon and waited for Thornten to begin. It was shaping up to be another unseasonably warm December day in the Austin area, with highs expected to be in the mid-70s. The two men gazed out over the garden below, where Fernando was pruning the dormant shrubs and bushes. Sunlight glittered off the lazy Colorado River. Down at the lower end of the property, Fernando's assistant was placing mulch over any exposed roots of the two brilliant red Shumard Oaks.

Thornten unrolled his display tablet—a cheap disposable, Mitchell noticed—and called up the transcript. He spun it around and sat back to Mitchell some time to read.

Ten minutes later, Mitchell leaned back and took a good, long swallow of his drink. He massaged his brow, in an effort to stem his burgeoning panic. *How could we have been bugged? Our security was iron-clad. We were so careful with our communications. How did the NSA even know about the gathering?*

"Okay, I presume you'd like something from me. Otherwise, I'd be dead, behind bars, or on my way to some secret debriefing session."

Where was the leak? His mind raced through the list of people who either attended or helped arrange the organizational meeting. It wasn't easy. They'd intentionally organized the YTG—Yeshua's True Guard Church—like terrorist groups.

Meetings were limited to cells of twelve people, and each person in a Reporting Cell personally recruited the other eleven members of their own lower-level Cells. It was an annoyingly inefficient way to organize a revolution, but necessary. When your own government maintained passive surveillance on almost all public places—and apparently some semi-private ones as well—and when they actively recorded and analyzed all electronic communications, keeping secrets required attention to every conceivable hole in your security.

Wait a minute. Washington would order the NSA to descend on me in force if solid information about my treason had landed on the appropriate desk. So why is Thornten bringing this to me now, himself, and why out here?

Did the Deputy Director expect Mitchell to inform on the entire movement to save his own hide? Whether as a traitor to the country or as a traitor to the YTGC, either way, he'd likely soon be dead or in prison. He could feel his life closing in around him, and options being stripped away.

"Actually, Senator Mitchell, my purpose in coming to you today was not exactly in any official capacity. I'm here to help."

"To help? What do you mean? Help how? I thought you were here to..." He picked up his glass and knocked back the remaining bourbon.

"You didn't think I was here to blackmail you, did you? Or worse?" The Deputy Director chuckled and removed his glasses. "No, not at all." His steady gaze looked sincere. "That tablet and its duplicate in my office safe contain the only two copies of that transcript and the supporting recordings. I hope that after our meeting today, we'll agree to destroy both of those copies."

"I don't understand."

"Fred, may I call you Fred? Like you, and many others in that meeting, I'm also deeply troubled by the corruption festering at the core of our once great nation. We've lost our way through a combination of non-existent morals, excessive immigration, multiculturalism, secularism, and a pathetic foreign policy.

"I used to believe I could do something about it once I reached the heart of the beast. I was so naïve. Even for the top positions of the administrative machinery, Langley and Washington remain intractable. And all the while, that nasty rot is eating away at our nation's heart. It has to be stopped."

Mitchell was dumbfounded. He desperately wanted another drink. "Mr. Deputy Director," he began.

"Please, call me Chris," Thornten interrupted.

"Chris, I'm kind of dry at the moment. Can I refill your iced tea while I pour myself another?"

"Please. But, you know, I think I'll join you in something a little stronger, if it's all the same to you."

Mitchell stepped to the bar inside his study, poured Thornten a bourbon, and refreshed his own.

"Mr. Deputy Director, Chris. I have to say, I don't know how to respond to what you just told me. I'd think you were running some kind of a sting operation, if I hadn't already seen that transcript."

"But you have seen it." The two men returned to the patio, where they stood examining the lawn and river below.

"Yes, I have. You have everything you need to charge a US Senator, an Army General, and probably a number of other influential and powerful people with treason. Instead, you waltz in here and tell me you'd like to join us. Now, what would you have me make of that?"

"What you make of it is that, like you, I am a true patriot. And that, like you, I also see no future for this country as it is."

"I still don't understand how a camera got into that room. The security was even better than it is here in my house, and I never fear speaking what I truly believe when I'm home."

"Read the top of that transcript again."

"This bit about quadruple-redundant neural recordings made by Spyders? What on God's green Earth are those?"

"I could be charged for treason just for letting you read that one line," answered Thornten. "Fred, you are now privy to one of this nation's newest Intelligence collection tools. Only a handful of individuals with Top Secret clearance know about this. These Spyders are literally spiders, real spiders that are genetically and electronically engineered so that we can use their nervous systems as programmable recording devices."

"You've got to be kidding me."

"No, not at all. There's an MIT spin-off company in Boston, run by that genius kid. You know, the one with the nano computer lattice thing in his head. Well, his company developed a way to connect nano-scale electronics with the brains of insects, if you can believe it. NSA appropriated it, and now we have the ability to walk one of these bugs into any room, and have it sit there and record everything that goes on.

"We don't need to send radio transmission, lasers, or anything else into the room. We preprogram our bugs to walk in, record, and then walk out, completely undetected and ignored by all. We download their recordings offline. It's the most effective listening device we've ever used."

"Genetic engineering is a blasphemy against God's creatures," Mitchell said.

"Yes, it is. And it's just another sign of how far this Administration has strayed from what decent, upstanding, Christian folk would agree to. It's not enough the government lets foreigners overrun our country. Now they're approving and funding companies to make abominations of God's creations."

"Chris, if this gets out, it could bring the Administration down."

"Yes, it might," agreed the Deputy Director. "Outrage in the South would be enormous. But I'm not so sure the Yankees are going to stand with us on this. Anyway, what good would it do? Whoever replaced them would just cover up the whole thing and carry on as before, same as always."

"But aren't you part of that system, too?"

"Well, I used to think I was. I was just as surprised and disturbed as you to learn about the Spyder program. I would never have approved it. But when Director Brundy ordered me to use it to listen in on your organization, well, I couldn't very well refuse on moral grounds, could I?"

"I guess not."

"As it turned out, the whole operation was quite...serendipitous, you could say. I was inspired by what your movement is trying to accomplish and by the enormous support you've drawn to your cause. I can see the writing on the wall, and I don't like what I see. I'd like to offer my help so that your goals can be achieved with a minimum of bloodshed."

Mitchell was stunned but elated. He never could have imagined in his wildest dreams that a top NSA executive would come to his home to offer his allegiance to their plans for an independent New Confederacy. A few minutes ago, he'd been contemplating the end of his dreams for a better, stronger, more moral South, and the end of his freedom. Maybe even the end of his life. Now, he was thinking of ways that this powerful insider could help make their dream become a reality.

"Chris, you can't imagine how glad I am to hear you say that. What do you have in mind?"

"Well, I'm happy to let your executive committee decide how I might best assist you. For the moment, I envision continuing to monitor your group's activities but making sure that the recordings, transcripts, and analyses do not get into the wrong hands. Only my own hand-selected analysts download and transcribe the recordings. They send them directly to me, and me alone. My official reports on your activities have covered up anything serious on your part.

"It sounds like your people will be ready to start activating your plans shortly. You should know that over the past few decades, my group has developed a variety of tools designed to cripple enemy information and communication systems for up to forty-eight hours. These tools can be used equally well against certain designated systems in America. I would presume that impairing the coordination of those who would oppose the New Confederacy would be a useful weapon when the time is right. Would it not?"

"Yes, most helpful."

"And I would hope that anyone who could deliver such useful tools might find a respectable position within the Administration of that New Confederacy?"

"Yes, I'm certain that could be arranged. Chris, thank you. You're a Godsend. Where do you hail from, anyway? You sound like a Southern boy to me."

"Originally from Florida."

"Raised Florida Baptist, I'll bet."

"Yes, sir. Tampa Bay."

"Well, I'm sure the rest of the Executive will be as happy to welcome you as I am. I'll call a special meeting to introduce you next week if you're available."

"This group has been my top priority for the past ten months, and it will continue to be so until my Director decides otherwise. Just because I'll be working to *help* you rather than *expose* you is no reason for me to change that priority, is it?"

The two men laughed, both relieved at how well the meeting had gone. Mitchell extended his hand to make it official. "I propose we toast the beginning of a wonderful association."

"To the New Confederacy?" Thornten proposed.

"To the New Confederacy."

21

DARIAN LEIGH AND HIS FATHER took a table in the sunken patio of a Newbury Ave café.

Paul put in their order then sat back, appreciating the beautiful May afternoon. Pedestrians strolled along the eye-level sidewalk, luxuriating in the sunshine as they checked out the lunch options along the avenue.

Many of the passersby, like him, had been recently laid off from their jobs, but the full economic shock of The Great Secession had not yet eliminated their dining out budget.

Most were still in a state of denial. Like naively hopeful children of divorced parents, they clung to the belief that Congress and the White House would find soon some way to reverse the shattering of the union or, at the very least, construct a new federation to cooperate on issues of joint interest, like defense and the dollar. They held this futile hope in spite of the fact that over half of the elected Representatives and Senators now represented constituencies that were no longer part of the United States of America.

Lunch arrived and Paul dug into his generous chicken salad sandwich. Darian, unusually subdued, barely picked at his food. Paul's exaggerated eye-rolling, lip-smacking and appreciative comments with each bite of the bistro fare, drew nothing in return. He had learned some years ago that once Darian became preoccupied like this, he would not be enticed into the conversation until he was good and ready.

Paul turned his attention back to the food, the weather, and the people, resolved to accept the silence for as long as Darian needed.

"They're classifying my thesis Top Secret, sealing it from the public."

Paul stopped the French fry halfway to his mouth. "What? They can't do that!"

"Apparently, they can."

"Did they say why?"

"Not explicitly. But I know it's for military application. Dad, when I designed the neural lattices that would fit into the brains of birds and mammals, even insects, I was thinking along the lines of how cool it would be to be able to direct their activities remotely by computer. You know, something like a monkey to clean up around the house, to help shut-ins and disabled folks. Maybe program house spiders to limit flies and mosquitoes in a managed way. And just think of all the applications in manufacturing and service industries! But the military and Homeland Security has other plans. Big surprise, right? I should have seen that one coming."

"Other plans? Like what?"

"All the usual things, I imagine: spying, diffusing bombs, replacing drones, you name it. Uncle Nick told me they've used my work to develop something they call a 'spyder'—that's spider with a 'y'. Spy-der. Obviously, there would be military applications. Everything ever invented can be used for peace or for war. They're only tools. What makes them good or bad is the user's intent. Why would my dendy lattices be any different?"

"I'm sure the government has its reasons."

"I don't know. I'm just disappointed, is all. Okay, maybe a little ticked off. Why couldn't they at least give my intended applications a chance, and classify only the military uses? They don't have to lock everything down. Everything, Dad. The whole works, even my thesis. They said it's too dangerous to make public."

"That's ridiculous."

"I agree, but there's nothing I can do about it."

"Well, at least you'll still get your degree, right?"

"Yes, I'll get the degree, but they won't let me publish anything, not even an abstract. There'll be some innocuous title and then a little notation saying the work has been classified. That's it."

"I guess Nick and David will be happy. If your work's classified, they don't have to worry about competitors for a while. And, no doubt, it would lead to some huge contracts from the military for the company."

"If they want to work for the Department of Defense for the rest of their lives, they can have it."

Paul wasn't sure how to respond. He was proud of his son, and excited for his future. But if the government stopped Darian from publishing, that was bound to put a serious dent in his academic profile. And how far did their control run? What if his son wanted to continue his research outside the government? Could they stop him from pursuing his work altogether if he didn't partner with them? Darian was so exceptional, unique really, that Paul worried about how he would get on in the world.

On the flip side, accommodating the military's interests could open up some insanely generous funding possibilities for Neuro Nano. They'd finally have some steady income, maybe even the means to pay out some dividends before long. Now that Paul's own employment situation was uncertain, he held considerably less disdain for the government's deep-pocketed spending and the opportunities that went with it. "Have you thought about what would you like to do after you graduate from MIT?"

Darian let his mind be lulled by the stream of pedestrians, all completely oblivious to his struggles. "I'm thinking of doing a second doctorate."

Paul picked up another fry and chewed slowly and thoughtfully. "Okay, that's a surprise. I thought you were done with school."

"This would be in synthetic biology. MIT said they'd fully fund me if I ever went back and, with all the lab work involved, it would feel more like a job than school, anyway."

"What would you work on?"

"I've been thinking that Mom never really got to finish her work. In her design, the dendies require a non-biological seed so the synthetases can replicate from the template. I'm thinking I'd like to see if the whole system can be built from scratch, starting from a strictly biological basis."

"I'm sorry, but about all I got out of that is that you'd like to continue the dendy work you mom started, is that right?"

"Yes. I don't think I'm quite finished exploring everything of interest in that area yet."

"Wouldn't that work also get classified?"

"Maybe I won't publish everything I'm working on."

"Listen, son, you're only seventeen. Be careful what you say. Sure, you have a couple of MIT degrees and a solid academic reputation, but you don't want the government taking too much of an interest in you. They might just decide to classify *you*, and I don't think you'd like the restrictions they would put on your work or your life."

Darian pulled the pick from his unfinished club sandwich and poked at the bread.

"Maybe it's time to think about doing your research someplace besides MIT," Paul suggested. "You know, your mother actually began her dendy research while she was up in Canada."

"Yeah, but they're almost as crazy as we are these days," Darian countered.

"That's true, in some ways. Everyone's going through a lot of adjustment right now. So long as you avoid the religion-based schools in the South and stay clear of the socialist kooks up here, you might find a happy middle ground with the moderates in California. Or what about up in British Columbia?"

Darian nodded and picked up his sandwich. "Berkeley *was* one of the homes of SynBio, and they're still doing a lot of great work there."

"Berkeley's always been a great university. Very liberal but solid in the Life Sciences," Paul offered helpfully. "And if you apply now and move to San Francisco this summer, you'd be able to get in before they close the borders to Americans outside of Pacifica."

"But then you'd be here, and I'd be in another country," Darian pointed out between mouthfuls. "Our home is here, and so is everything I've ever known and cared about."

"Well, maybe it's time you expand your horizons. I mean, you'd still be in North America. It's not like you'd be moving to Germany or anything. "

Darian nearly choked. "Germany, Dad? Really?"

"Look, there's nothing tying me to Boston anymore." Paul held up his hands, demonstrating a distinct lack of shackles. "Maybe we should sell the house, and I'll move out to the coast with you."

"It's not like I need my daddy to keep me company," Darian grinned.

"No, you're well past that," Paul agreed quickly. "It could be good for me, too, though. It wouldn't hurt for me to expand my own horizons a little. I don't know how our government is going to respond to this secessionist rebellion any more than you do, but the economy here in what's left of this country is dismal. It's hard to imagine a rosy future, right now."

Darian's focus shifted outward to some distant point. Paul recognized the look. It meant his son was either referencing a ton of material on the internet, or he was busy with some deep calculation, or both. Waiting for Darian to finish whatever he was doing inside his marvelous lattice-enhanced brain, Paul finished his sandwich and ordered another cold beer.

"I've been reading some articles about President Wilson, Senator Mitchell, and Governor Alcraft; and the political analyses and background papers on what happens when countries break apart due to internal insurrections."

Darian's voice took on a stilted academic tone when he was thinking with the semiconductor lattice instead of his biological brain. "In addition, I have investigated several political, social and psychological modeling methodologies, and constructed a crude composite simulation to predict future activities by these three men. Preliminary results indicate that President Wilson will choose to negotiate rather than call upon the military. The negotiations are unlikely to lead to any agreements on the major issues in the near term, especially on currency and defense.

"Senator Mitchell seems entrenched and is unlikely to respond well to suggestions regarding future cooperation. He doesn't like President Wilson's politics or his religious affiliation. He will move the New Confederacy toward stronger protectionist and isolationist policies for the foreseeable future.

"Governor Alcraft, on the other hand, leans toward pragmatism. He will work hard to maintain good relations with what is left of the United States and Canada. I estimate a 95% probability that all parts of the former country will default on 70% of their collective debts over the next three years. There is only a 5% probability that the New Confederacy will recognize its obligation for any of these debts, while there is an 80% chance that Pacifica will assume some portion of its previously shared obligation."

"Makes you wonder why they bothered to separate at all."

"The majority of analysts suggest the states and provinces making up Pacifica all share a desire for increased fiscal responsibility and a pragmatic, inclusive, secular government.

"They differ from the government of the New Confederacy in rejecting a Christian basis for Criminal and Civil Codes. They also differ from the remaining United States in refusing to endlessly fund unaffordable corporate welfare programs.

"They were rushed into an untimely secession, owing partly to their respective governments refusing to pass balanced budgets, and partly to the precipitous actions of the movement in the South." Darian blinked at his own analysis.

"Well, the New Confederacy certainly seems hell-bent on ruining what's left of this country, that's for sure."

"It does appear that the key figures behind the New Confederacy wish to punish the collective governments of the past for their reckless spending, cultural dilution, and lack of religious purity.

"There is an 85% probability that the New Confederacy will recognize Christianity as its official religion and English as its only official language. There is a contingent 80% probability that the surviving America will be forced to make a similar declaration in order to reduce emigration to the South by the wealthy. By contrast, Pacifica is likely to continue to emphasize a multi-cultural approach, given its large Latino and Asian populations."

"Well, I agree with both social tolerance and fiscal responsibility. But it's hard to say which fragment of the country will fare best. No matter how you slice it, this is a real mess."

"My model calculates a 98% probability that the US dollar will depreciate a further 40% before the situation stabilizes. The GDPs of the remaining union and New Confederacy are almost certain to decrease by three to five percent per year for the next five years before settling into a significantly reduced standard of living. Pacifica appears to have the right combination of resources and innovative capability to withstand that kind of devaluation. Should they decide to create their own currency, it would be more stable than the Greenback or the Greyback."

"Maybe it wouldn't be such a bad idea to relocate out to California, after all," Paul hypothesized.

Darian smiled, a sign that he'd returned from the world of the cold, analytic machine within him. "Maybe this *would* be a good time to move. And it would be a pretty good place to go—as good as any, right now."

Father and son shared eye contact for a few seconds. "Psst! Don't look now," Paul hissed, "but I think we just made a decision. See, that wasn't so bad." They burst out laughing, and Darian reached across the table to pilfer his father's unfinished fries.

Feeling good, but not quite ready to face all the changes and details headed their way, Paul steered the conversation to the Red Sox's chances in the upcoming season. "Well, it's no secret American League Baseball has always wanted to go international. I guess they got their wish—just not the way they expected," he chuckled.

America might be going to Hell in a handbasket, but at least its national sport would continue.

22

A CACOPHONY OF BLARING ALARMS greeted Princess Darya's return to her covert asteroid base, Tertius, and her outworld trueself.

Her internal status alarms and the asteroid base's intruder alarms all clamored for immediate attention. *Great, my ultra-capacitors are nearly depleted, my reserve power is almost gone, and someone's found this base.*

The proximity alarms lit up: Securitors closing in.

Okay, first things first. Darya dropped the last vestiges of her inworld persona and reverted to her base trueself.

Her avatar, the regal Han princess, bore no resemblance to her spherical metal body. Nobody's avatar ever did. In the real universe, her official Cybrid designation was DAR143147. Outworld, her close friends called her Dar but whenever she was inworld, she went by the more formal name, Darya.

Though Cybrids were sexless, synthetic constructs of metal and semiconductor, Darya had always identified as a "she." Throughout the ages of her existence, her persona had been consistently female, matching that of her original human template from Earth.

She deactivated her quark-spin lattice, and took her radar and laser-sight offline. *My manipulators and active sensors are eating up more energy than I can spare right now. If I don't drastically cut the drain, I'm not going to stand a chance. Passive visual sensors and ambient light sources will have to do for now.*

What else can I do without? The emotions system. She needed to focus on problem-solving right now; she couldn't afford to be distracted by simulated emotions. *Done.*

Anything else I can do without? She moved all but her most critical processes into slow storage. *That should help save some energy and increase computational power.*

Now, let's take a better look at the incoming Securitors. Where are you? She accessed the asteroid's external sensors.

* * *

TERTIUS WAS DAR'S THIRD "HOME", the one she used as a base for her Lysrandia inworld incursion. She'd found it during her previous assignment, repositioning other asteroids away from So-102's gravity and into orbit around Sagittarius A*, where they would serve as fueling depots, repair shops, and entertainment centers for the countless Cybrids that comprised the Central Implementation Team of Alum's Divine Plan.

During her millions of years on the project, Dar had managed to take occasional unrecorded asteroids and park them in orbits that might prove useful to her at some unspecified time in the future. She implemented the orbital changes in the selected planetoids gradually, and only in coordination with intentionally-herded asteroids. That way, the discrepancies would be interpreted as natural errors, and her propellant use would remain within expected ranges.

Tertius was the third rock she had secretly maneuvered. She'd picked it for its high natural concentrations of uranium and plutonium. She'd placed it in a fixed position relative to her most important base, Secondus.

Over the hundreds of thousands of years since placing Tertius in its present orbit, she'd hollowed out a series of chambers to use as workshops, and connected them by a maze of tunnels. Inside the tunnels, undetected and at her leisure, she'd mined and refined fissionable materials, and mapped the structure of the asteroid's rocky interior.

And in the central control chamber, she'd planted a 100-kiloton atomic bomb constructed with the purified radioactive elements. *Just in case—* she'd reasoned.

* * *

DAR GLANCED AT THE READOUT from the cloud of microsensors she'd deployed around the asteroid. *Oh! Okay, that's impressive; I'll give them that.* Alum had sent hundreds of enforcement Securitors to capture her. The microsensor display lit up their approach in iridescent trails.

They're closing in fast, and in more force than a single opponent should warrant. I guess anyone possessing enough skills and nerve to hack into a central inworld server would be of interest to Alum. Clearly, they don't want me escaping. Sorry, fellas, but I've got other plans!

She couldn't fend off a whole squadron of Securitors, and even if she did, they'd just send more. The rock's thick outer shell and her artful camouflaging of the six entry portals might buy her a little time. Once they got inside the asteroid, it wouldn't take them long to find the inner chamber. If she couldn't get out off the rock fast, she'd be facing deep interrogation and a full persona wipe within hours.

Another alarm sounded. Her ultra-capacitors were down to less than one percent of full charge, and there was no time to recharge using Tertius' internal power supply. The slow trickle of power from the ancient solar panels on the surface would only give her another one or maybe two percent before the Securitors found her.

Options! What are my options? The frozen blocks of mercury and anti-mercury in her propulsion system were a great source of power. But for some reason, the idiot engineers hadn't thought to connect the propulsion system to an electricity generator. Such a blatant oversight—an outright design flaw—made her wonder if it was *purposely* designed to hamper the Cybrids' overall versatility and freedom. *That wouldn't surprise me at all.*

If I can get to Secondus, I can recharge from the high-output panels. She ran the calculations. *Enough matter-antimatter fuel to reach the base easily. I've never run this close to red lining; can my processing circuitry last long enough to make the transit? And if I do go, the energy flare from my main drive will be impossible to hide from the Securitors. They'll just track me, and capture me there. No sense doing their job for them!*

So, that's it, then. Time for the last-resort option. Destroy Tertius and ride safely away in the detritus of the nuclear fireball.

Long ago, she'd simulated how the planetoid would shatter if a nuclear device was detonated at its core. She'd searched through the resultant simulated rock fragments for one large enough to be propelled along an intercept orbit with Secondus.

Over and over, she'd modified the tunnel structure models until finally the simulated explosion produced large enough fragments that would travel along the desired range of trajectories. Satisfied with the results, her last task before she'd started hacking into the Lysrandia sim had been to drill a Cybrid-sized chamber within one such fragment, line it with a thick titanium shell and hatch, and install a few external sensors.

She hoped this crudely fashioned escape pod that she'd prepared so long ago would survive the blast meant to destroy the entire planetoid and be accelerated intact along the projected trajectory.

It had seemed like a reasonable last-ditch escape plan when she'd first thought of it. She'd soon have opportunity to see how accurate her simulation had been.

The Securitors blasted their way into one of the upper tunnels leading to the central chamber, and were headed toward the center to detain her.

Dar set the timer on the bomb for seventy-five seconds and raced down the narrow tunnel to the escape chamber. She lodged herself firmly inside and secured the hatch door. *Eighteen seconds to spare.*

Safely inside, she detonated a chain of chemical explosives behind her. The capsule vibrated and rumbled as the kilometer-long tunnel collapsed all the way from outside her makeshift lifeboat to the central control chamber. If any of the Securitors had managed to make it to the center, the choked tunnel would give her a little extra time to make her escape.

The variation in projected trajectories are within plus or minus 20,000 kilometers of Secondus, 80% of the time. Still too broad; I don't like those odds. At least the fragment she'd be using as an escape pod could be expected to survive more or less intact 96 times out of 100.

Goodbye, Tertius.

As the timer on the atomic bomb counted down the last few hundredths of a second, she wished she believed in a Higher Power to whom she could pray. Sadly, she had parted ways with faith long ago. *Keep me safe*—she pleaded to no one, anyway.

Zero. The 100-kiloton explosion vaporized the inner part of the asteroid. An expanding fireball forced gasified rock out through the venting tunnels, obliterating her lab, her work, the connecting tunnels, and the waves of Securitors moving through the labyrinth to find her, along with all traceable evidence of her existence.

Tragic, but nice and tidy. A clean slate.

As predicted, the extreme heat and pressure from the massive blast splintered the planetoid along the lines Dar had meticulously mapped out. It propelled fragments brutally outward in all directions, including the crucial chunk cradling her crude escape pod.

Though her Cybrid bulk filled the titanium-lined escape capsule to within a millimeter, she was thrown around like a dried bean inside a rattle. She berated herself for not incorporating a dense foam lining to cushion the buffeting. It had seemed an unnecessary luxury. *This is sure to knock a couple of screws loose. Regardless, it's a lot better than staying behind and letting the Securitors catch up with me.*

Great Alum, the Securitors! I didn't take them into account. More to the point, I didn't include the additional explosive energy that would be added by their antimercury fuel packs. Dar, you idiot!

The nuclear reaction would have destroyed their containment fields; the resulting matter-antimatter reactions would have altered the acceleration and rotation of the discharged asteroid fragments, including the one she was riding in!

She was lucky it hadn't just killed her outright in the first second. She was alive, but off course, out of energy, and too far from a recharging option to recover. *I'm dead. Or hopelessly off course, and then dead.*

If I don't bring at least some of the systems back online right now and revise the computations, I'll die for sure. And if I do go online, I'll run out of power before I get to Secondus and likely die, anyway.

Dar counted to a hundred trillion, slowly, and started accessing whatever external sensors remained functional. The sensors verified her suspicions. Overlooking the effect of the Securitors' munitions and fuel had cost her dearly.

As the external sensors began streaming data, Darya watched her unfortunate oversight blossom into a problem, a big problem. The trajectory of the escape pod was above the orbital plane; it would miss Secondus by almost ninety thousand klicks.

She needed to get out of the pod within forty-seven seconds. That was her only chance to propel herself on a safe intercept course for home. *And I'll have to do it without being observed by any Securitors in the vicinity.*

The fragment's external sensors revealed that about fifty percent of the Securitor team had survived the destruction of the asteroid.

She had significant blind spots over a large portion of her visual field, especially behind the hurtling rock fragment where the remaining Securitors were likely waiting. Her lifeboat was now a few hundred thousand klicks from the blast center but still within an area the Securitors might actively search. With any luck, their remaining sensors were concentrated nearer the origin of the blast.

She activated the hatch release. Nothing happened. She sent the signal again. It remained closed. She snaked out a manipulator tendril and used a risky amount of her remaining power to try pushing aside the hatch. *Jammed! The explosion must have deformed the titanium shell.*

Time was running out. She had to start the self-propelled leg of her brief journey home soon. If she missed the launch window, there would be no way to get back on course without drawing attention. The jet stream from her main drive would be visible for millions of klicks, an emergency flare in the deep darkness of space.

*I'm moving at fifteen thousand two hundred and eighty-one point six three kilometers per hour in a sealed titanium capsule. My manipulators aren't strong enough to push the hatch open. Even if they were, using them again, when I'm so low on power, is out of the question. My ultra-capacitors are almost dead. When they're done, so am I–*Dar contemplated, calm only as a result of shutting down her emotion modules.

I can generate matter-antimatter power but if I fire up my rockets in here, there's no way I could survive the heat or radiation that would build up before the hatch blew open. Viable options?

In desperation, she set a few subroutines with exceedingly loose parameters running in the background, on the off-chance that she'd miss something she could use. Any solution, however risky or outlandish, would be welcome right now.

Should I shut down everything except long-term memory and bank on the remote possibility of a recovery in the far future? She'd pulled off that long shot once before, ages ago. But it seemed pointless out here in deep space. Drifting aimlessly, she'd be far more likely to get swallowed up by some star or get picked up by Securitors than to be found by friends.

She could reset, wipe her memory to protect the others, and terminate her existence voluntarily. Suicide would prevent further risk to other Resistance members, but would bring about her end, the end of the Princess Darya persona, and possibly the end of the Resistance. She couldn't let all of their many efforts, struggles, and sacrifices come to nothing.

I can't risk ending the Resistance. Better to hope for rescue than to end it all here. A long-shot is better than certain failure. Shutdown protocol, it is.

A subroutine pinged for her attention. Could it have found something? She took a look. *That might just work!*—she was surprised.

Dar acted instantly. Activating an internal laser, she ablated some of the antimatter mercury from the frozen block in her propulsion system.

When aimed at a matching normal-matter stream ablated from a separate block, the antimatter stream normally converted into a brilliant, pure energy. The system served beautifully as the basis for the main propulsion unit but, as it was, lacked the precision and finesse Dar now needed to get out of her escape pod.

If I activate only the antimatter stream, I should be able to control the direction and intensity of the stream enough to create a crude cutting torch. Unfortunately, it's also going to generate a high level of radiation as the antimatter reacts with the normal matter of the hatch. Can my shielding withstand the onslaught long enough for me to cut free? I guess we'll find out.

Dar decreased the sensitivity in her visual sensors and directed the anti-mercury stream along a narrow seam where the exit hatch was attached to the rest of the shell. After several circumnavigations with the spray penetrating deeper each time, the hatch finally gave way. She was out, with only a second to spare.

The Cybrid accelerated away from her rocky cell and into the vacuum of space, leaving a small puff of metal vapor trailing behind her. She oriented herself toward Secondus, and fired a two-second engine pulse at full power to intercept her home base, hoping the surviving Securitors were too busy and too disorganized to notice. Her rockets pointed outward at a sharp angle to her initial trajectory. She kept the propulsion exhaust as narrow as possible.

Provided that no sensors had detected the flash of light when she cut through the escape pod or the radiation from her exhaust, she might make it.

She didn't dare use her active sensors to scan for pursuers, but her passive detectors could manage a wide scan with minimal risk. They weren't as effective but they were low energy and might pick up the telltale signature of a Securitor rocket homing in on her position.

Luck or destiny was on her side this time. Or maybe it was artfully employed science and technology. In any case, there was no sign of pursuit from any direction. She could only surmise that the debris from the blasted asteroid had covered her energetic bursts.

For the second time in only a few minutes, Dar almost wished she believed in a real God, so she could thank Him for saving her. Almost. She knew better than to confuse luck with divine intervention. She settled for being satisfied that the probabilities, however slim, had worked out in her favor. Unfortunately for them, the probabilities had not worked out as favorably for the Securitors sent to investigate Tertius.

I would rather not have destroyed the Securitors along with Tertius—even Securitors are conscious beings—but the Resistance must survive. Someone has to oppose Alum's mad plan. For now, that means the Princess Darya persona must survive.

Operating on the lowest possible power, Dar continued her journey to Secondus. With most of her brain shut down for the trip, she was reduced to the simplest and most mindless sense-and-respond machine she could ever imagine being.

One klick from home, she reactivated her navigational subsystem and fired a blast to reduce her approach velocity. A few gentle pulses from the maneuvering jets brought her precisely to the main entry portal. The door recognized her weak, intermittent signal and opened to receive her. By the time she was able to connect to the solar recharging station, her sensory feed and computational awareness were both flickering in and out erratically.

Safely home on Secondus base, Dar allowed herself to slip into recharge mode.

23

"Is that him?" Larry pointed toward a small delegation approaching the foot of the stairs.

The young man being swarmed by university executives looked too young to be a professor. He carried himself more like a first-year grad student: awkward, gawky, and out of place. He certainly looked nerdy enough to be a physics professor. His "do-it-yourself" haircut was far from stylish, barely combed, and he was painfully uncomfortable in the shirt, tie, and outdated tweed jacket.

The object of everyone's attention gave the appearance of being properly impressed with the campus architecture as his tour guides pointed out each particularly splendid feature. Online VR tours now made such personalized walkabouts unnecessary but whether it was due to nostalgia, a testament to their pride, or a twisted test of character, the majority of Department Chairs still insisted on dragging new recruits through the motions.

"Yeah, that looks like him," Greg answered. He and Larry were camped at the top of the stairs, looking out over the covered Convocation Mall between the Library and Student Services buildings. Their perch was strategically positioned to catch a glimpse of Simon Fraser University's newest celebrity faculty member, Darian Leigh.

Almost all campus foot traffic passed on one side or other of the Mall before entering the lower level of the Academic Quadrangle. On a nice day like this sunny July afternoon, it was impossible to resist climbing the majestic stairs and meandering your way across the floating path that spanned the reflection pool and provided shade to the brightly colored koi below. At the end of the pond, a passing appreciation of the sunken central gardens and pyramid sculpture was obligatory before heading into the raised AQ building to enjoy the spectacular view of Indian Arm.

"He looks way younger than his pictures," Larry noted.

Perhaps that was because he was indeed, young. Darian Leigh carried without much grace the thin, insubstantial form of a stereotypically anemic academic, including an early predisposition toward a small paunch. Clearly, he spent more time in thought, than in the gym.

But at twenty-two years old, with PhDs in Nano-Computing, Synthetic Biology, and Quantum Cosmology, and the rumblings of a Nobel Prize candidacy (or two) already in the wings, Darian Leigh was the most remarkable person ever to stand in the middle of the soaring columns of SFU.

"I expected him to look a little, I don't know, smarter," Greg confided.

"Well, you're a lot smarter than *you* look," Larry mocked.

"Thanks, I think." He and Larry had been friends throughout grad school. Starting their first postdoc positions together under such a famous Principal Investigator as Darian Leigh cemented the easy camaraderie and good-natured ribbing that had accompanied their student years.

"Well, maybe not a *lot* smarter," Dr. Kathy Liang, the newest member of the team, chimed in as she claimed a seat alongside them.

Greg laughed, a little louder than intended. His attraction to the intriguing Chinese-American engineer only amplified his usual social awkwardness, causing him to overcompensate in her presence.

Kathy was accustomed to the effect she had on male colleagues and politely ignored their discomfiture, doing her best to be a casually accepted member of the group.

She had arrived in Vancouver only a month earlier, hired to help set up the new lab. Given the paucity of instructions from Dr. Leigh, this had proven a challenging task for all of them. They ended up spending a good deal of their time familiarizing themselves with each other's work, with Dr. Leigh's seminal papers on the theory of Big Bang physics, and with coffee and beer served in the Student Society pub.

While they were chatting, Darian and his executive entourage had climbed to the top of the stairs unnoticed by his new assistants. "Not waiting for me, are you?"

They jumped to their feet. "Dr. Leigh!" Though Darian was the youngest of them all, he was their undeniable superior. More than his coveted faculty position, it was his intellectual prowess and prestige that commanded their attention and respect.

Darian decided that introductions were in order. "Madam President, Dr. Pinto, Dr. Wong, Dr. Pratt, I'd like to present the charter members of my group here at SFU.

"Dr. Katherine Liang is a graduate of the Applied Physics Department at Stanford. Dr. Valeriy Rusalov and Dr. Girikanshayam Mahajani are graduates of Physics here at SFU." He nodded at each of Kathy, Larry and Greg in turn as he introduced them. Both groups stood in awkward silence at the unaccustomed meeting of disparate academic strata.

Kathy stepped forward, hand outstretched, "It's nice to see you again, Dr. Leigh," she beamed, precipitating handshakes all round.

"We were just finishing the campus tour. Why don't you join us for lunch at the Faculty Club?" Darian invited. The university executives were clearly uncomfortable with the whole idea but reluctant to dismiss their celebrity's wishes or generosity. Everyone looked to President Sakira for a decision.

"Yes, please do. But we will have no technical discussion," she decreed, with a wagging finger. Everyone laughed. Dr. Sakira was a world-renowned expert in Europolitics, equally well-known and respected on campus for trying to keep social occasions among the academics civil and inclusive. Her appointment as President of SFU had been widely viewed as a stroke of brilliance in troubled times.

"I am proud to remind you all," she began, making deliberate eye contact with Darian and each of the executives and postdocs, "that SFU has no separate Faculty Club. Our policy is more equitable here. The Diamond Alumni Centre is open to all. Shall we continue?"

They walked under the AQ and entered the central garden. Dr. Sakira resumed her narration of the tour. "Notice the relationship between the land and the structures. This campus was designed by award-winning architect Arthur Erickson in the early 1960s. Inspired by the acropolis in Athens as well as the small towns in the hills of Italy, he incorporated the mountains on which they stand into the design of the buildings.

"Here, you can see how the massive cement columns of the AQ rise and support two floors of classrooms and offices above us, leaving open access or sight lines to this peaceful one hundred meter square park in the middle. The entire campus, including this futuristic-looking building, continues to be used as a movie and television set. The first movie filmed here was the sequel to The Fly, filmed in 1989, I believe."

"Actually, it was the Groundstar Conspiracy, with George Peppard," Larry interjected. When everyone turned to look at him, some with surprise and others with disapproval, he added, "Sorry. A bit of a trivia buff," and shrugged.

"You are correct," Darian said in support of his assistant. "At least, according to the latest information available on the web. It starred Michael Sarrazin and Christine Belford, and was directed by Lamont Johnson."

"Are you also a movie trivia buff, Dr. Leigh?" asked Dr. Pratt.

"Not at all," replied Darian. "I looked it up."

"Oh, that's right. Your internal DNND network," observed Dr. Pratt. "Well, I do hope it is useful for academic purposes as well."

Darian didn't bother to respond to the openly snide remark. Apart from Dr. Wong, Chair of the Physics Department, it appeared that none of the other three faculty members carried implanted dendy lattices. And while Dr. Wong did sport a telltale induction headband, even he was not sufficiently comfortable with the technology to access movie trivia on a whim.

Dr. Pratt's open contempt for the DNND technology wasn't uncommon. On this campus and many others, the issue of whether built-in access to online data should be considered a professional cheat or an essential enhancement was a hotly debated topic. Most established professors eschewed the conveniences of the new technology, saying that solid, scholarly work ought to rely more on skillful thinking and solid research than on fancy computer tricks.

As always, the students—those who could afford it, anyway—were quick to adopt the new technology. Truth be told, they were employing it more for entertainment purposes than intellectual pursuit. To obviate the need for wifi shielding in lecture halls, induction headbands were not permitted during exams. Cheating still relied on conventional methods.

President Sakira skillfully intervened. "Oh, it looks like we're running a little late," she said, glancing at her watch. She picked up the pace, and briskly redirected them along the north side of the AQ, down through the Robert C. Brown Hall, and across the road to the Diamond Alumni Centre. Not by accident, the faster pace made it difficult for the group to keep up the conversation and breathe at the same time.

The host delivered them to a table along the north windows of the DAC dining room, overlooking Indian Arm inlet and the beautiful Pacific Coast range. The cold blue waters of the glacial fjord extended inland between steep, conifer-lined slopes. Sakira took a moment to enjoy the view; she believed it to be among the most magnificent, and calming, of any university-based restaurant in the world.

They ordered and ate their meals, confining their remarks to appreciation of the food and scenery, and were relaxing over coffees and teas when the conversation took an unexpected turn.

"I was sorry to hear of your father's death this past winter," President Sakira offered; "I'm sure he's in a better place now."

"I doubt that he would prefer an urn over our house in California," Darian responded. His table mates winced at his dark, dry sense of humor.

"I meant," the University President corrected, "his soul in heaven."

"Mm," Darian said, "his soul. Well, I'm quite sure that, prior to his death, my father was finally convinced there is neither heaven nor hell, and that the whole concept of souls is simply a reflection of a very human inability to accept that our brief physical existence on this planet is really all there is. He accepted his death as his ultimate end."

Dr. Pratt could not resist weighing in. "That couldn't have been very comforting to him."

"I'm sure that it wasn't as comforting as his previous belief in the myth of an eternal afterlife. After facing the prospect of his imminent death for two years, my father was finally able to accept that nothing uniquely *him* would survive the cessation of coordinated biological activity in his brain. We had many discussions about this during his battle with cancer. I think he was brave to discard his earlier superstitions and face his death without an emotional crutch."

"I hate to say it, Dr. Leigh, but you sound rather heartless," Dr. Pratt retorted. "Science has little if anything to say about the existence of a soul or spirit, if you will, or about the possible existence of heaven."

"That is not at all the case." Darian's three postdocs raised their eyebrows in unison. Pratt was an internationally respected moral philosopher whose moderate religious views were perceived as generously inclusive. Why was Darian picking a fight with him?

"I would be interested to hear how you believe the study of natural law can contribute to our understanding of the transcendent," said Pratt.

"Very well," agreed Darian. Kathy shot Greg and Larry a discreet look in response to his literal-mindedness, and made herself comfortable.

"First, I need to know which version of the soul you might subscribe to."

"Version?"

"Yes. Do you believe the soul is a kind of energy that temporarily occupies the brain or body, and returns to the universe upon corporeal death where it simply dissipates? Or do you believe that the soul is an organized structure unique to each person; that it can think or feel, and possibly remember? I think that the soul alluded to by most religions would generally belong to the latter category."

"If those are my alternatives, I would go with choice number two, that the soul is eternal and unique to each person. But I reserve the right to revisit choice number one."

"That's fine. Do you accept the compendium of sub-atomic particles that constitutes the Standard Model of Physics, as incomplete as it may be?"

"Certainly." Dr. Pratt was reasonably well-versed in modern physics, considering it to be a sub-interest of sorts to reconcile common scientific and religious viewpoints. "Except, the soul belongs to the supernatural."

"And what exactly *is* the supernatural?" asked Darian.

"Something outside the laws of nature," Pratt replied by rote.

"But a supernatural soul would still need to interact with biological matter, no? With cells made of molecules, those molecules consisting of atoms, those atoms formed from the various sub-atomic particles, and all behaving according to the laws of nature?"

"Of course."

"And how, exactly, would it do that?"

"I don't know. It's supernatural."

Darian's entire body bobbed eagerly. "Yes, *this* is the crux of the problem. The known particles of physics interact with each other in well-understood ways. For example, electromagnetic forces are carried by photons passing between particles such as electrons—"

"Well, you and Dr. Wong would be the experts on the various particles and forces but, yes, that is also my understanding."

"And a supernatural soul—if it doesn't interact with the brain in any conventional manner—would still need *some* kind of mechanism to exchange information with the normal matter of the brain in order to affect the body's actions."

"Yes, I would agree."

"So, if we were to speculate that a soul is some sort of as-yet undiscovered force, we would still have to admit that it can somehow interact with the normal matter of our brain, right? Otherwise, both body and soul would exist but would have no relationship to each other."

Dr. Pratt chewed on the idea. "Well, there is certainly some kind of interaction. Our life experiences and the moral judgments we make on Earth must be reflected in our soul. If not, how could we be judged fit for Heaven?"

"So, if the soul is some kind of matter or energy we haven't yet discovered, and it interacts with normal matter, then it must do so through some force or particle that we also haven't discovered yet."

"I would certainly agree that we haven't found any 'soul particle' yet."

"So one important question is, how does the soul know that the matter it's associated with belongs to the brain of a human, and not to a chimpanzee, or a dog, or a fly? After all, biologically, neural cells from many different species are largely indistinguishable."

"Certainly there are *some* differences between the cells of a man and those of a fly," said Pratt.

"Yes, indeed. Many. But would that require the soul to read the entire DNA of the cell? Or would it just recognize cell-surface proteins the way another human cell would?"

"Let's say the soul recognizes human DNA."

"Okay, given that chimpanzee DNA is about 96% similar to human DNA, do chimps also have souls?"

"I think that's a trick question."

Darian laughed. "Yes, good for you. That *is* a trick question. The DNA of male *humans* and male *chimps* is about equally similar as that of male and female humans."

Dr. Sakira couldn't help herself, "That explains so much."

Pratt smiled indulgently, but he wasn't prepared to give up yet. "While animals may have spirits of their own, only *human* souls are generally considered to be made in God's image. So, let's say the souls we are discussing are uniquely human."

"Okay, let's specify the soul can recognize some subset of the DNA present in male and female humans that is uniquely human. Unless you would like to deny that human females have souls?"

Dr. Pratt looked at President Sakira and Kathy. "I think I had best not deny that," he said with a wry smile. Sakira returned the smile graciously.

"Okay, so the soul recognizes some unique human brain DNA. Do you see the problem here?"

"Yes, I think so. Since the DNA of all the cells in one person is essentially identical, the soul would need to be able to specify some non-DNA recognition mechanism that is specific to the brain, wouldn't it?"

Darian smiled. "Exactly. Now, we still could allow the soul to recognize some surface molecule encoded by the DNA but only expressed in the brain."

"Very well," Pratt replied, "Let's do that, although I'm sure you'll find some way to make me regret conceding the point."

"That would lead to the question of how a soul knows its host body is dead. If it just recognized molecules instead of activity, one would think it would stay attached after death until decomposition was complete."

"I hadn't realized the discussion was going to become so morbid," said Dr. Sakira.

"My apologies," Darian briefly bowed his head in mock contrition.

Dr. Pinto, who had remained relatively quiet through lunch, ventured in. "Why can't we say the soul somehow recognizes electrical activity in the brain?"

"Sure," said Darian. "I imagine we could make a case that there is some pattern of brain activity that is uniquely human, perhaps even unique to *each* human. And perhaps that would allow the soul to stay attached to the body so long as the brain continued to be active."

"I could accept that," said Pratt.

"However, even this would still require the so-called soul particles to interact with active neurons, with their molecules, and their atoms.

"We already have a model for how that might work, if we take a look at the dendy lattices. The semiconductor dendy sensors position themselves at synaptic junctions in the brain so they can detect and modify the neurochemical activity. So a reasonable place to look for the soul-brain interface would be at those synapses. I see two possible ways it could do this."

"Only two?" Pratt ribbed.

"Logically, that's all that's possible. First, there could be interactions that we haven't discovered between the molecules in these synaptic junctions and the supernatural particles of the soul. Now, those interactions would still have to act according to some sort of governing laws. Technically, that would make them *supra*-natural, not *super*-natural. Just because we haven't discovered or explained these particles and interactions, doesn't make them outside of nature. They would still fall under the purview of physics eventually."

"But the supernatural is unknown and unknowable," Pratt objected.

"Exactly," replied Darian. "Accepting the possibility of such a mechanism would suggest that there are simply gaps in our understanding. We can surmise that we could eventually discover these soul particles and delineate their interactions with other particles."

"Perhaps we need to put a live human in a particle accelerator," Pratt jested.

"The fact we have never seen such particles suggests we might need to do something like that," said Darian. Even his postdocs weren't sure whether he was being serious. "Over time, the discovery of such soul particles could conceivably lead to the development of a technology that might include soul detectors, perhaps even soul modifiers, or soul destroyers."

"I don't think I'd like to see a technology of the soul." interjected Dr. Sakira.

"Me, neither," replied Darian. "If sub-atomic soul particles actually existed, they could be horribly abused. However, Dr. Pratt also said that the supernatural is unknowable, so that only leaves us with the second mechanism."

"And what is that?"

"The soul interacts with the brain directly by transiently altering the local natural laws. This is the very definition of supernatural. For example, the soul could alter the natural laws of physics locally, causing an ion channel in a synapse to open and initiating neural activity. Souls might be composed of collections or fields of natural laws. But no science of any such thing exists; we have no understanding of how such fields might interact with each other."

"In that case, souls would exist outside the universe of natural law. So science would have nothing to say about them, would it?" Pratt concluded triumphantly.

"Correct. In that case, souls would be outside the natural laws of this universe."

"Thank you," Pratt gloated, glad to finally gain some ground.

Darian stared out the window, deep in thought. His breathing slowed and his eyes became unfocused.

Is he going to pull some winning rebuttal out of thin air, or is he sore about losing a point—Greg wondered. In the awkward silence, the rest of the table sipped contemplatively at their beverages.

Finally, Darian inhaled loudly, breaking the spell, and turned to Pratt as if there had been no pause in the conversation. "However, that would not put them outside of scientific investigation," he said.

"That's preposterous!"

"Not really. This discussion made me wonder whether we might be able to describe a physics *of* natural laws rather than a physics *from* natural laws. I have been working for some months on speculative physics of other universes and was able to sketch some equations based on the generalization of some alternative natural laws. I made the assumption that there could be a field or fields that would determine the rules for particle interactions in this universe or other universes.

"The math was tricky," his sheepish smile and boyish charm made everyone at the table, save Pratt, smile along with him. "But I believe the solution to those equations suggests it should be possible to test this new theory. That is, to create a device that could generate such a field and alter what we think of as the normal physical laws. Locally, at least."

"You could do that?" Bolting upright, Dr. Wong's sudden enthusiasm startled those beside him. Being a resolutely practical man, the topics of metaphysics and the supernatural normally fell outside his area of specialty. His interest in the conversation about souls had waned almost as soon as it began. But this could be big. Very big. "Do you mean to say, you've just invented a completely new area of physics?" His eyes locked onto Darian's.

"Well, the start, anyway. I've just sent the paper resulting from my calculations to your email. I hope you will approve it to be submitted for publication."

"You wrote a paper? Just now? In a few minutes?"

"Let's say, I finished one that I've been tinkering with for quite some time. The long relationship with my lattice helps a lot with that kind of thing. However, it does extract its payment. I'll be famished again in about an hour."

"You've lost me," Pratt admitted. "How exactly does this relate to our discussion?"

Greg jumped in. "If there is a physics describing how natural laws are generated and interact with each other, that would open the realm of the *super*-natural to scientific investigation."

"Exactly," continued Darian. "We should be able to settle questions of the existence of souls, ghosts, and even God, once and for all. Once we remove these quaint concepts from our thinking, we'll be able to proceed with a rational exploration of the basis of reality."

"I think you can all see why we were so pleased to be able to steal Dr. Leigh from Stanford," President Sakira chuckled. "What will you call this new physics, Dr. Leigh?"

Before Darian could answer, Larry suggested, "We should call it Natural Law Effect Physics."

"No way," said Kathy. "The acronym would be NLEP. Too clumsy." She scrunched her eyes, thinking fiercely. Greg loved watching her think.

"Hey, I know," she continued, "When I was an undergrad, one of the companies we studied was Apple, you know, before they merged with IBM to become Apple International. One of their founders, Steve Jobs, was famous for getting people to see things his way. People used to say that he had a Reality Distortion Field because he could convince people to redefine their perceptions of what was real or possible when he was around.

"This new physics would be sort of the opposite. You could call it a Reality *Assertion* Field. RAF."

"I like that," said President Sakira. "I met Steve Jobs once when I interned at Apple. I think he would have been amused. What do you think, Dr. Leigh?"

"I agree, and I think my dad would have liked it, too" Darian replied with a grin.

President Sakira stood and raised her coffee cup. "I propose a toast." Cups and glasses rose, and a handful of beaming faces looked at her expectantly. "I would like, once again, to welcome Dr. Darian Leigh to Simon Fraser University. We look forward to a long and productive relationship, and to a brilliant career—especially if today's dazzling display is any indication. Here's to your first discovery at SFU, the Reality Assertion Field."

The table answered with a hearty, "To the Reality Assertion Field!"

Dr. Pratt extended his sweating glass of iced tea in Darian's general direction and performed a brief but convincing requisite sip, while he glared over the rim. *The Reverend will not be pleased about this.*

24

NCSA recording of a conversation between Dr. Lucius Pratt (Simon Fraser University, Burnaby, BC, Pacifica) and Reverend Alan LaMontagne (Austin, Tx, New Confederacy) on October 7, 2037.

Pratt: Hello?

LaMontagne: Dr. Pratt?

Pratt: Speaking.

LaMontagne: This is Reverend Alan LaMontagne calling from Austin.

Pratt: Reverend LaMontagne! I wondered if I might hear from you directly. How may I help you?

LaMontagne: I received a rather disturbing call from Reverend Curtis in Vancouver the other day. He says Darian Leigh is tinkering with God's Laws of Nature, and that you provided the inspiration for that line of investigation. Is that correct?

Pratt: If I lent that man inspiration in any way, I assure you, it was in no way intentional. I could never have guessed that our conversation would lead to that. We were hosting Dr. Leigh at a welcome lunch back in July, and Dr. Sakira extended her condolences to the lad on the recent death of his father. She merely remarked that the man's eternal soul was now resting in a better place, and Dr. Leigh responded with a heartless monolog about how neither he nor his father believed in the human soul as there was no scientific evidence to support its existence.

LaMontagne: Scientists! They should know better than to stick their noses outside their specialties.

Pratt: I felt it was my duty to come to the poor woman's defense, so I pointed out that science has little if anything to say about the possible existence of souls. I thought that would put a diplomatic end to it. After all, it was his first day on the job and he was speaking to the President, the Dean of Sciences, and Department Heads. Instead, he attacked me, launching into an aggressive Socratic rant on his depraved view of the soul. He seems to think that souls are as amenable to study as rocks. I couldn't allow such a statement to go unchallenged. I just couldn't. I made a case that souls belong to the realm of the supernatural; they are not and should not be subject to scientific investigation. I believe I was actually winning the point.

LaMontagne: So how did he turn the discussion to his favor?

Pratt: Not by fair argument. He twisted the intent of my words completely. He agreed that souls might be beyond the natural laws but, rather than concede the argument, he announced that he'd used his internal computer to invent some new kind of physics. He claims that mathematics provides some insight into how natural laws, the laws of God, might come into existence, and how they might be manipulated. I was appalled, of course. I could almost believe the man is in league with Satan, himself.

LaMontagne: He very well could be. [*Several seconds of silence follow*]

Pratt: At any rate, there is certainly something unholy about young Dr. Leigh. He is not a normal human being, with this internal machinery, and I fear the level of respect he is accorded by the science community. Playing God is dangerous. The hubris of this man is astounding. He is entirely oblivious to the dangers of what he is doing.

LaMontagne: Many of his persuasion are so cursed.

Pratt: When I accepted this position, I knew the deep lack of faith exhibited by the people of this region would require me to hold our Lord, Yeshua, more tightly to my breast than ever. But their lack of Godliness is astonishing, and it has only increased since the formation of this country they call Pacifica. They test me greatly on a daily basis.

LaMontagne: Your devotion and service to the Church is both noted and appreciated, Dr. Pratt. Evil is strong in the hearts and minds of many scientists. Their materialistic view of the world is an abomination; it reflects the devil's dark deeds in opposition to our Lord. We are thinking perhaps you could use some assistance in your battle against this evil.

Pratt: The burden may be great but I believe that I am up to the challenge. I don't see how anyone might assist me.

LaMontagne: The aid we're considering would be able to operate more overtly, with no risk of jeopardizing your valuable role within the community. You've proven your value in that post to us many times, particularly through your growing insight into the workings of these people. We don't want to risk losing that.

Pratt: Thank you, Reverend. I must admit, it would be nice to see a more direct challenge to the blasphemy I hear every day within this academic environment.

LaMontagne: Yes, it is time we begin countering these scientific and humanistic lies, and the long task of returning Pacifica to the righteous path from which it has strayed. [*Short silence.*] It's decided, then. I will arrive in Vancouver before the end of the year. Can you arrange proper accommodation for me?

Pratt: It would be my pleasure, Reverend. I will coordinate with Reverend Curtis.

LaMontagne: Would you also be able to arrange an appropriate time and place for me to engage with Darian Leigh, somewhere outside of his normal environment?

Pratt: As it happens, we may have the perfect opportunity in place already. The local Philosophers' Café group just announced that Dr. Leigh will be next month's guest speaker. He'll be discussing this new physics of his. What better place to start demystifying his "infallible" image? Would that work, or would you prefer something sooner?

LaMontagne: No, that's perfect. My staff will contact you with my itinerary. I won't meet with you personally while in Vancouver, Dr. Pratt, but I want you to know that you have our thanks for your efforts to date.

Pratt: Thank you, Reverend LaMontagne; that means so much to me.

LaMontagne: I'm glad to hear that. Bye, now.

Pratt: Okay, good bye, sir. Thank you for calling.

* * *

THE THREE SCIENTISTS SAT AROUND THE PUB TABLE staring at the white gel capsules in front of them. They had been staring at them silently for the past ten minutes, no closer to deciding whether to take them.

"How do we know it's safe?" Larry voiced the question foremost in all of their thoughts.

Greg looked to Kathy for assurance, but she appeared to be lost in her own thoughts. "Why wouldn't it be? Darian said it's the same combination of dendies he designed for himself at Stanford. He's not giving us anything he hasn't already tested on himself."

"I mean, why take it at all? We already have our own dendy lattices, the FDA-approved legal version," Larry pushed.

"Yes, and they're state of the art," Greg said, "but they're only good for entertainment and communications, Larry. They won't make us smarter."

"I know Darian said the virus is just an upgrade," Larry replied. "That this version will integrate with our brains more closely but..."

"Don't forget, it's going to augment our biological thought processes with spintronic computational abilities," added Greg. "It might even make us as smart as him."

Larry thought about that. The three had seen for themselves how useful the additional capabilities could be. Darian always had every needed fact immediately accessible. He could do math in his head in milliseconds that would take the rest of them hours to do, while conducting coherent conversation and multiple other tasks. Nevertheless, they worried about potential effects on their personalities. Darian was not exactly the poster child for warm and fuzzy.

"Yeah, but in a virus?" Larry didn't like the idea of deliberately infecting himself with anything. It was, at best, unnatural. Possibly dangerous. One reason he'd chosen to become a physicist and not a biologist was because he didn't like dealing with the uncertainty of living organisms.

"It boils down to whether we want to follow Darian at his speed, or at ours." Greg picked up the capsule and turned it over in his hands.

During the past three months, the group had worked obsessively to flesh out the mind-boggling implications of Reality Assertion Field theory, while simultaneously engineering a prototype RAF generator. Darian begrudgingly adapted to the demands of life as a professor, including the heavy teaching and committee requirements, the long office hours, and the incessant student inquiries that pulled him away from the work he loved.

But the team sensed his frustration with how long the new field was taking to develop, even though their pace had been more than adequate by normal scientific standards.

Greg tried to imagine how Darian felt. *Why settle for such plodding progress? Why are we hampering ourselves? We could be achieving so much more as a team if we all hosted our own internal dendy lattices with Darian's capabilities.*

Whether plodding or blazing, the RAF generator moved steadily toward completion. The device itself turned out to be much smaller than any of them would have predicted, about the same size as an old-fashioned laptop computer.

In preceding decades, physicists had thought it necessary to use more powerful machines to achieve the energy levels needed to explore the physics of basic particles. However, the Reality Assertion Field theory suggested computational power, rather than sheer energy level, was more important in generating fields that established local natural laws.

The three postdocs didn't quite understand why that would be but, according to Darian, the math was unequivocal. And so they proceeded, hoping it wouldn't turn out be a complete waste of time and effort.

"Are they even legal?" Larry picked up his own gel-cap and rolled it between his thumb and forefinger.

"Well, you won't find them on the list of approved medical devices," answered Greg. "Does it really matter, though? This is like the Holy Grail of smarts; these things can raise our effective IQs into the stratosphere. Who cares if they're legal? Regulation and laws are so far behind current technology that it's laughable. And when the bureaucracy does make a ruling, it's even more laughable. They're ill-equipped to make the decisions they're tasked with. You know that every bit as well as I do."

Larry was not convinced. "That's *if* they work. That's a big *if*. And what about the risks? What if something goes wrong? Don't forget, Darian was still in the womb when the dendies were introduced into his bloodstream. His nervous system was still developing, and his body had years to adapt. His mom was an adult when she injected herself. We all know what happened to her."

"It's not like he's forcing us to take them," Kathy noted. "It's more like a gift, a really valuable gift. Anyway, the legal issues would be all Darian's. He's risking a lot to give these to us."

"Don't you think we should analyze them first?" Larry directed this question at Greg.

"How would you propose we do that? We could get someone to read the viral RNA sequences and calculate the encoded proteins, but then we'd need access to the Washington State supercomputers for a week to calculate even a single folded protein. Even at that, I'm not sure we could interpret what the protein function would be. No, none of us is a dendy lattice expert like Darian. I think we have to trust him."

"I wonder how much of his brain is still biological," Kathy mused.

"What do you mean?" Larry asked, surprised.

"If he has incorporated high-speed logic functions into the dendies, wouldn't they be thinking *around* the brain rather than *through* it?"

Greg and Larry stared back at her blankly.

"I mean, a normal dendy lattice like ours is basically a control and communication device. It reads the activity at our synapses and interprets what that means, or else it feeds external input to the appropriate synapses so that, for example, we can 'see' a computer projection without using our eyes."

"So?"

"If I can extrapolate from my early biological-psych textbook, a dendy lattice with computational capability would have to re-create all of our existing synaptic connections in order for us to still be 'us', you know, to have our same personality. After the lattice replicated our brain structure and became functional, the lattice signal and decision speeds would supersede neuronal processing speeds. Our neurons would become redundant. I wonder, would they just die out once they're not needed?"

Larry had been absent-mindedly kicking the foot of the table and fidgeting in his seat. He stopped abruptly, and brought both of his forearms down on the table with a thump, "You see? You see what I'm talking about? There's so much we don't know! So many risks. So many uncertainties. How could you still be *you* without your brain? Are we all going to end up as robot-controlled zombies?" he demanded.

"Oh, you'd still be *you*, I think," laughed Kathy, "It would take more than a dendy lattice to override *you*, Larry. More like a steamroller. The software of your personality would just be running on the faster silicene and crystalline semiconductors instead of on your slow biological neurons. You would still need to compensate for the absence of hormonal influences on personality, though. I'm not sure how that would work."

"Seriously, would we even be human at that point? What would happen to our consciousness? Would we even experience being alive?" Larry fretted.

"I wonder what it would be like to think at that speed," Kathy said dreamily, "to be that smart but having the software basically...emulating you.

She sat up straight. "Well, only one way to find out." She picked up the capsule and popped it into her mouth, washing it down with a gulp of beer.

The two men gaped at her.

"What the hell!" Larry gasped. "How could you just do that?"

Kathy put down her glass, licking foam from the side of her mouth. "I think we can trust Darian. He may be a bit strange but he still seems human to me. Plus, there's no reason for him to try to hurt us, and there are lots of reasons for him to try and make us better at what we do. He needs us to be as smart as we can possibly be so that he'll have someone he can discuss his crazy ideas with. I've watched him try to explain his theories to you guys and the other profs. It's like trying to talk calculus with a toddler. Nobody gets it. We *need* to get it."

"Darian doesn't *need* anybody," Larry argued, as Greg's glass thunked loudly beside him on the wooden tabletop.

"Ahhhh!" Greg exclaimed, dragging the back of his hand across his mouth with theatrical flair. His gel-cap was also gone.

"Not you, too!" exclaimed Larry.

"Kathy's right. Darian needs us, and I trust him," Greg answered calmly.

Larry pushed his chair back, letting it fall, and leaned over his lab mates. He stabbed a finger at the gel cap in his open palm. "*This*...is an engineered virus. A *brain* virus, guys."

His actions were drawing the attention of a handful of early evening patrons who'd come by the local watering hole to relax. Larry lowered his voice but was no less insistent. "This is potentially dangerous. It's a huge unknown, on many levels. What happened to you two? You're acting like a couple of idiot kids on some big adventure, not like the mature, professional scientists you claim to be. Whatever happened to taking measured, reasonable precautions?"

"Sometimes progress requires risk," replied Greg.

"Yeah? Well, this is too much. You've crossed the line here, big time, and there's no coming back from this one!" yelled Larry. He wheeled toward the exit and bumped into the server who'd been on his way over with the manager in tow for backup.

Larry turned back to the table. His finger jabbed at his two colleagues. "Darian can't force us to do this. I'm reporting him." The server and manager tapped his arms on either side, inviting him to leave quietly or be pulled away from the still-seated Greg and Kathy.

Larry brushed their hands away and huffed toward the exit.

"Do you think he'd actually do that?" Kathy's distraught expression triggered Greg's protective side.

"Nah," he said with a cavalier flip of his hand. "Larry's a bit of a drama queen."

"I don't know; he seems really mad."

"Yeah, but he won't jeopardize his own job just for our health and well-being."

"What do you mean?"

"After he cools off, he'll eventually come to see that we did something reckless and stupid. He figures we were unduly pressured by Darian, and he hates that kind of thing. He'll calm down once he realizes that we did what *we* wanted to do, and that we're okay with it if he doesn't want to follow suit."

"I hope so."

"I've known Larry for years. He went into science because he saw it as an oasis of sanity in a world full of craziness, uncertainty, and insecurity. He hates risk, especially personal risk. He's a very careful and deliberate scientist. I mean, I like the guy; we've been through a lot together. But, honestly, he's more of a stamp collector than an innovator. He's smart enough to have done his grad work anywhere in the world, but he never moved away from Vancouver. Probably never will. Just didn't inherit the adventure gene, I guess."

"What about you? Are you adventurous?" Kathy asked, a sly smile on her face. Greg's heart beat a little faster.

"Well, I moved here from Mumbai to go to grad school so that has to be worth something."

"Yes, I suppose it is."

"And I applied to work with Darian as soon as I heard he was coming here."

"How come?"

"Apart from the fact that it'll look great on my CV? I happen to think that he's the most exciting theoretical physicist to come along since Einstein."

Kathy laughed a sparkling laugh that lit up the room. Greg decided he would travel across the world to hear that laugh again.

"That's high praise for our young professor," she said. "Do you think he'll be able to live up to it?"

"Well, he has so far. His Big Bang theories were great but only pushed the envelope back a little. His new stuff is ridiculously genius. It's huge."

"I'm just an engineer but, so far, the RAF device doesn't look like much more than a fancy laptop supercomputer with some non-standard built-in antennae."

"Yeah, I know. It doesn't look like much, does it? But his RAF theory is so out of this world. It's beautiful and crazy at the same time. At least, the bit I can comprehend. Darian has taken our understanding of Standard Theory to a whole new level."

"I've heard you guys talk about that, but I don't really get it."

"Basically, he's proposing that all manner of virtual particles can, and do, exist beyond just the virtual equivalents of the real particles in this universe. There could be particles with bizarre charges, or masses, or color. All kinds of other oddities or strangeness, maybe even outside of our perception."

"More than just the Standard Model particles?"

"Yeah. Besides the usual virtual fermions and bosons, he proposes other things with very weird properties."

"So then why isn't our universe full of real-particle analogs of all these crazy virtual particles? You'd think we'd see something at least remotely similar in our universe."

"I was thinking the same thing at first. Darian says that virtual particles are like little blips in the quantum field. When a bunch of these little blips overlap each other in just the right way, they can set off resonance effects that suddenly allow the *virtual* particles to set up a standing wave that stabilizes them. The wave allows them to...well, they just *precipitate* into reality."

"Okay.... So where does the RAF come in?"

"Well, at the beginning of the universe, all these different resonances were competing with each other to become real. Certain kinds won out over others, and now what we experience as the *real* universe...exists."

"So if we want to test the theory, we need a way to encourage other resonances among virtual particles," Kathy posited.

"Exactly, and that's what the RAF does. It selects certain resonances over others by helping to fill in the gaps among the virtual particles in the quantum field."

"And that can all be done with just electromagnetic waves?"

"Sure, that and a ton of math to figure out the exact shape and timing of those waves in order to select the right resonances. So much that the RAF generator has to have petaflop capabilities."

"And some highly optimized algorithms. I see the math and I can convert it into code, but I'm glad I don't have to understand it." Kathy's software skills were at least as valuable as her hardware skills.

"Yeah, the math is still beyond me, too. Hopefully, the new dendy lattice will help us with that."

"So how does resonance fit into the creation of the universe," Kathy asked.

"Darian says that in the time before the Big Bang, a particular set of resonances evolved into what we consider the real particles of our universe with a stable and consistent set of interactions. The resonances are self-propagating. That process keeps our universe stable and ensures that only certain kinds of particles come into existence."

"And Darian wants to mess with that? Maybe Larry was right."

"No, not at all. The complexity of computing how to alter the natural laws over a region of space goes up exponentially. Calculations for anything over a cubic meter or so would be practically impossible."

"I'm relieved to hear that. I have to say, I didn't think anyone could get so passionate about things that don't exist."

"Except that virtual particles *do* exist and so does the RAF," Greg began. He stopped when he noticed Kathy's smirk. "Okay, okay. So I get a little carried away. I'm a nerd at heart. Sorry."

Kathy grinned. "That's alright. I kind of like it."

Greg could feel his face growing warm, and the more he tried to ignore it, the worse it got. "So...yeah...uhhm," he faltered, scrambling to switch topics. "What did you think about the whole 'soul' discussion at lunch that day?"

Kathy knew right away which day he meant. "Well, I was raised more or less Buddhist. Buddhism kind of assumes that the soul represents the essential part of a person that gets reincarnated again and again into different bodies over time. The goal is to eventually achieve enlightenment and nirvana, but I'm not sure I ever understood the concepts completely."

"Yeah, I was raised Muslim but my family considers me a heathen now, for being agnostic. In the past, I would have agreed with Dr. Pratt that science doesn't have a lot to say about Allah or God or souls."

"Darian does have a way of pushing logic to uncomfortable conclusions, doesn't he?" finished Kathy.

"Yes, he sure does."

"Well, Buddhism doesn't say much about the whole idea of a Creator God, either. It seems to have inherited the idea of an eternal soul from earlier religions. Spirituality never was all that important to me, but it's what attracted my mom to move to California."

"So what do you believe now?"

"I'd like to believe that something of us persists after death, and that there is some purpose to it all. Do you know what I mean?"

"Wouldn't we all? But, I have to admit, Darian's arguments about the lack of a plausible mechanism for the soul to interact with the body make a lot of sense."

"Just because we don't understand everything about the soul, doesn't mean that it doesn't exist. Why couldn't it all work through something like...like interacting RAFs, for example?"

"Maybe; although that just suggests souls operate under a different kind of physics."

"So what's the matter with that?"

"Well, if Darian's RAF theory works out, this device might enable us to develop a legitimate science and technology of the soul. Souls would not be beyond the reach of science anymore; they would no longer be classified as supernatural. Which would also, eventually, make God within reach of science."

"Wow. That's both depressing *and* scary," Kathy concluded. They sat still for a moment, letting it all sink in while they pondered the depths of their empty glasses.

"Well, we're clearly not going to figure this out all on our own," Greg said after a while. "Darian's giving a Philosophers' Café on 'The Universe Before the Universe.' You want to go?"

Kathy eyed him playfully. "You mean, like a date?"

"We could go out for dinner after, if you'd like," Greg offered.

"I'd like that."

"And who knows? With a topic like that, and with the type of people who usually show up for these Cafés, I wouldn't be surprised if the discussion moves away from physics and into the metaphysical. It could get interesting."

"Oh, I'm sure it'll be interesting. Just as long as it doesn't end up in a free-for-all brawl. You know how feisty those philosophers can get!" They laughed at the idea of a roomful of brawling professors. It felt good to laugh, just to let go a little. They needed the levity as much as oxygen.

"Let's order another beer," Kathy suggested. "You can tell me what it was like growing up in India, and I'll tell you all about California."

"You're on!"

25

THE BUS CAME TO A SMOOTH HALT at Hastings and Seymour, gently kneeled, and the rear door opened. Darian stepped out onto the sidewalk, followed by Greg, Kathy, and a few dozen other attendees, all on their way to the Philosophers' Café at the downtown Simon Fraser campus.

It was a typical November day in Vancouver. The wind and gloomy sky presaged the arrival of rainy season when the city would be plunged into four months of cold, depressing, all-enveloping grayness. Darian fastened his coat and unfurled the collar. His college experience in the hot, dry years of California's recent super-drought had not prepared him for winter in the Pacific Northwest.

Half a block down the street, precisely where they were headed, a noisy crowd was picketing. *Well, that's a little disconcerting.*

The weather didn't seem to be dampening anyone's enthusiasm in the least. Darian watched as local and national network cameras scrambled for a position outside the main entrance of the building.

As they approached the crowd, people shouted and jeered. Greg read a few of the placards bobbing and stabbing the air: THERE IS NO GOD BUT THE LORD! SCIENCE IS THE WORK OF SATAN! LEAVE NATURE ALONE!

Surely, all these people aren't here to protest us, are they? Greg turned to Darian and was met with the vacant, emotionless stare that meant his boss was scouring the internet for information.

"Apparently our discussion today has drawn the ire of Yeshua's True Guard Church," Darian explained. "They appear to have sent a small delegation to attend the talk." The television cameras spotted them and shifted focus from the boisterous protestors to Darian's small entourage.

An eager reporter rushed over.

"Dr. Leigh, did you expect your lecture to draw such strong protest?" he shouted over the commotion. Darian stopped to address the camera directly. The protesters worked their way behind him and positioned their placards so they'd be visible in the video.

"I wish all of my presentations would incite such passion," Darian replied. "Most of my students find them far less fascinating and have a more difficult time forming such definite opinions."

"How would you reply to those who think your research infringes on God's domain?" Darian could barely hear the man over the ruckus.

"God is usually purported to work in the domain of miracles, not in physics," Darian quipped. "I don't expect we'll be performing miracles anytime soon." The jeers rose briefly, punctuated by vigorous pumping of placards.

"But you are working on altering the laws of nature; isn't that an incursion into God's domain?"

"Which god? Upon whose powers are we infringing? Are we offending the single Abrahamic being known as God, Yahweh, or Allah? Do the many major and minor gods of, say, Hinduism, ancient Greece, the Aztecs, or the Norse feel threatened by our work? Or are we are simply extending humanity's knowledge of the physical world into a new area of natural and meta-natural phenomena?"

Darian and his interviewer both ducked as an egg, hurled by one of the protestors, smashed a few feet away on the wet sidewalk.

The reporter was secretly pleased—*This is going to show great, maybe even make headline news.* Encouraged, he opened another controversial issue.

"Rumor has it that you developed this new theory in less than a minute. Is that true?"

"Once I had the proper inspiration, it only took about a minute to complete the calculations and draft an article describing the theory. But I hasten to add that I'd been thinking about this area for several months prior to that moment."

"And what was the source of that inspiration?"

"A conversation about the nature of the human soul with Dr. Pratt from our Department of Philosophy, the host of today's event, led me to consider how the natural laws that govern matter and energy might have arisen. I simply followed that train of thought to its logical conclusion."

"You're not even human!" yelled one of the placard wavers. "Crawl back to the machine that gave birth to you," screamed another.

Gratified at hearing the slurs, and enjoying the rush of power he felt from having provoked them, the reporter pressed on.

"Your accidental exposure to a dendy lattice prior to your birth has given you a unique mind. Do you consider yourself to be more human, or more machine, after all these years with the lattice doing your thinking for you?"

"What exactly do you think I am? For that matter, what are you? How do you feel about all those neurons doing your thinking for you?" Darian asked rhetorically.

He slipped into lecture mode, his voice strengthening and taking on a comfortable cadence. "The essential 'I' is not some internal homunculus pulling the levers of our brain like a puppet master. The thing we call 'I' is simply the program of our personalities, abilities, and memories running on the machinery of our brain. Whether that machinery is all biological, or partly spintronic silicene and semiconductor, makes no difference to my experience of me as me. Sure, many of my axons and synapses are not biological, but *I* am still the one doing the thinking," he assured, tapping his sternum for emphasis.

"You have no soul!" shouted a protestor.

"Neither do you," answered Darian quietly, "you just think you do."

None of the protestors heard, but the reporter and the camera's microphone both picked up his comeback.

Zing! That little sound bite alone is going to knock my ratings out of the park. Guaranteed, this bit's going viral! We'll have to air it as a teaser.

Sensing an opportunity to bait Darian's ego, the reporter pandered to him a little. "Dr. Leigh, you are probably the smartest man alive today, possibly the smartest man that ever lived."

"Undoubtedly," Darian concurred. "Through a combination of instantaneous access to everything I've ever read and everything ever published on the web, any test of my knowledge would score higher than that of any other person. But what is *intelligence*, really? It's more than accumulated knowledge of facts; it's also the ability to use those facts.

"My dendy lattice permits a wider and faster exploration of concept-space than the unassisted biological brain, but it still has limitations within the parameters of this body. Anyone or any machine equipped with a similar lattice could become as intelligent as I am."

Darian made a show of checking his antique pocket watch—only to make a point, since he was always aware of the time through his lattice connection to the web. *I am out of time and patience; wrap it up.*

"One last question: Are you angry about FDA restrictions on the use of the dendy lattice?"

Darian frowned. "Using the DNND lattice only to access published websites or enhance one's experience of inSense movies is a huge underutilization of the potential to improve human knowledge and intelligence. The dendies allow me to perform many feats that could be available to everyone. Things like understanding and performing complex mathematical modeling, or learning to play the piano instantly.

"The enterprise that my mother began will continue to do well, even if it is limited to entertainment applications, but humanity will not benefit as much as it could. That said, I understand the political necessity for the FDA to act with utmost caution, and I'm sure that, in time, it will conclude that the potential for DNND technology to help humanity far outweighs any remote possibility of detrimental effects. The lattice doesn't remove our humanity; it enhances it.

"If these protestors..." Darian motioned to the crowd, reigniting their jeers and placard waving. "If these protesters were equipped with dendy lattices, they would be capable of understanding my work, and they'd find themselves supporting my efforts rather than blindly opposing them as their church dictates."

The reporter was unable to mask his astonishment at Darian's brash comments. "Do you think they're wrong to be concerned about the possibility of a science that can supersede the laws of nature?"

"I think that's one question more than you promised," laughed Darian. "I suggest you come inside to hear the answer." He turned to the crowd and raised his voice to be heard over their shouts. "I suggest you all come inside, and we'll discuss your questions and concerns rationally." He turned to his assistants and gestured for them to head inside.

A few of the rowdier individuals tried to push forward but were stopped at the door by Security until they agreed to deposit their placards outside. The rest of the protestors reluctantly followed suit, and entered the hall with sullen, angry, and determined looking faces that all but dared the philosophically-curious attendees who were already seated to utter a word. The simply curious wisely avoided direct eye contact.

The lecture hall could have been in almost any university in the world. Neutral-colored, wear-resistant carpet nicely offset the laminated cherry wood finish on the row-upon-row of thin-cushioned theater chairs, each of which sported its own annoyingly undersized, tuck-away writing tray.

The stadium-style seating accommodated over four-hundred people. The monthly Philosophers' Café meetings usually drew a hundred attendees at most. Today, it was standing room only. Attendees filled all of the chairs and spilled into the stairwells leading to the small podium at the front. With any luck, the fire marshal wasn't on duty.

"Ladies and gentlemen, good afternoon." Dr. Pratt's amplified voice projected into the depths of the packed hall and foyer from overhead speakers, a voice from the heavens that triggered ripples of "Shhh" throughout the venue. He waited a moment while people settled.

"Welcome to the Philosophers' Café. Please bear with us while we accommodate the folks in the foyer. It looks like today's topic, or maybe it's our young guest speaker, is a little more popular than most of our Cafés." He paused and looked around. He saw very little sense of humor and even less patience on the faces looking back at him.

Pratt continued, content to be amusing himself. "Due to the overwhelming response to today's talk, the university has opened up Lecture Theater 3 for overflow seating. It is equipped with state-of-the-art audiovisual equipment that will allow everyone to participate fully in today's discussion. I repeat, Theater 3, located across the hall, is now open for seating. Would everyone waiting in the foyer please make their way to Theatre 3. Thank you."

The PA system cut out and Pratt set the lapel microphone on the podium. He turned to greet Darian and his small entourage approaching the front seats. "Ah, Dr. Leigh. Good to see you." The two men shook hands. Pratt smiled congenially in an effort to offset Darian's wariness. "I see you brought some moral support with you."

Darian looked back at Greg and Kathy taking their seats in the front row. He scanned the audience for Larry, and was surprised to see him seated some distance back as if he preferred not to be associated with his colleagues. "I'm not sure why you think I would need moral support," he replied. "I'm going to be discussing physics. Physics is truth, and the truth needs no support from anything other than data."

Dr. Pratt considered responding but thought better of it. He noted the hour with some relief. "It's time. Allow me to call this gathering to order." He picked up the lapel microphone and raised his voice to cut through the background din.

26

"LADIES AND GENTLEMEN, IF WE COULD BEGIN, PLEASE." The crowd took its time settling down.

"Thank you. I am Dr. Lucius Pratt from the Department of Philosophy at Simon Fraser University." The polite applause lasted a second or two. "Before I introduce today's speaker, I would like to reiterate our format and a few rules of order for the Philosophers' Café series.

"Dr. Leigh will open our discussion with a short introduction to the topic. Following his introductory remarks, he and I will co-chair two thirty-minute question and answer periods with a fifteen-minute refreshment break between. We have two assistants with microphones stationed in each of the two theaters. If you would like to ask a question, we ask that you raise your hand and let the nearest assistant come to you. Please keep all questions and comments brief so that as many people as possible will have an opportunity to contribute.

"Similarly, we ask that the answers or rebuttals..." he bowed to Darian, who nodded politely, "...be kept as short and to-the-point as possible. Please frame your questions and comments civilly, respectfully, and intelligibly. To that end, no mathematical equations will be permitted."

A number of the attendees chuckled. A few frowned.

"Today, we present Dr. Darian Leigh, who was accidentally exposed to a DNND lattice infection prior to his birth, giving him extraordinary mental abilities. Using the substantial computational powers of his lattice, he rapidly completed his education and undertook multiple advanced degrees in a variety of scientific fields, including nanotechnology, synthetic biology, and cosmology.

"Dr. Leigh is also known for his work at Neuro Nano Devices Inc., the company his mother, Dr. Sharon Leigh, co-founded to develop the inSense virtual reality lattice so popular among today's youth. Much of his work in these areas remains restricted throughout North America and Europe by the FDA and various international security agreements.

"In recent years, Dr. Leigh has turned his attention from nanotechnology and synthetic biology to pursue the more traditional fields of physics and cosmology. However, his research in that area has been anything but traditional.

"We are very pleased to welcome him today to our last Philosophers' Café of 2037 to discuss, 'The Universe *Before* the Universe.' I present to you, Dr. Darian Leigh."

Darian looked out across the sea of faces while the applause died down. He wondered what percentage of the audience was already hostile to the very notion of what he was about to say, without having heard a word from him.

He set a small part of his lattice to work compiling profiles and histories of the attendees while he began speaking. He tapped into one of the cameras in Theatre 3 so he wouldn't miss anyone there.

"First, I would like to thank Dr. Pratt for inviting me to speak today. This is my first ever Philosophers' Café, and I hope you'll go easy on me. I'd also like to extend my deep gratitude to him for his inspiration. It was a conversation we had over lunch one day that first inspired many of the ideas I'll be presenting today, and which eventually moved me to propose the Reality Assertion Field itself. I owe Dr. Pratt a great deal for helping me to challenge conventional wisdom about the origin and nature of the universe." He bowed in acknowledgment to Dr. Pratt, who returned the gesture with awkward uncertainty.

Well played. Score one for Darian Leigh—both men thought.

"Today, I want to talk about what the universe might have looked like in the beginning, the Universe *before* the Universe, if you will.

"Since we're not all physicists here, I'd like to start out by talking about the Big Bang, and how cosmologists think the universe began. Don't worry, I'll keep it brief. From there, we'll move on to nothing. What do philosophers, theologians, and physicists mean by the word, 'nothing?' I'll warn you, it's more complicated than you think. Then things are going to get a little strange. I'll introduce you to what I think of as the ultimate bits of nothing, virtual particles; how physicists think of them; why we're certain they exist, even though they can't be directly observed; and why they're so important.

"That will bring us to my most recent theories, which attempt to answer some of the most exciting and fundamentally important questions in our era, questions such as: How could real particles and the physical universe evolve from the virtual particle chaos that preceded it? Where do the 'laws of nature' come from? And, how can we test and apply these ideas?

"Let's begin with something you've probably heard before. Scientists believe everything in the universe began in a cosmic explosion that we call the Big Bang, around 13.8 billion years ago. Why do we think everything came from a Big Bang, a moment of creation? This is still a relatively new idea. The ancient Greeks, for example, believed that the universe was static; that it had always existed."

Darian put up a slide of the familiar Milky Way galaxy shown as it was projected to look from hundreds of light years above its elliptical plane.

"Until the mid-1920s, astronomers thought that our own Milky Way galaxy, with its hundred billion stars, comprised the entire, never-ending universe.

"In 1925, Edwin Hubble used a 100-inch telescope at Mount Wilson to prove there were other galaxies outside of ours. Suddenly the universe was a lot bigger and more remarkable."

The slide changed to a famous picture compiled by the Hubble telescope, showing the thousands of galaxies in what used to be thought of as an empty portion of the sky.

"Around the same time, a physicist named George LeMaître constructed a mathematical model based on Einstein's theory of relativity. His model concluded that the universe was expanding from an initial Primeval Atom. But nobody believed him, not even Einstein. A few years later, Hubble showed that not only was the universe expanding, but the *farther away* a galaxy was from us, the *faster* it was moving from us.

"Since then, we've looked at millions of galaxies using far more powerful telescopes like the orbital Hubble, the James Web, the Wukong 3, and they all confirm what Professor Hubble saw over a hundred years ago. When you rewind the motion of the fleeing galaxies, you can project that all matter must have at one time occupied the same point in space from which it expanded outward.

"These calculations and observations put an end to the idea of a static universe. For a while, some people believed that perhaps the universe was oscillating through periods of expansion and contraction, eternally being re-created. But our best calculations today suggest this universe is going to go on expanding forever. There's not enough matter for gravity to pull it all back together. There's no contraction in our future, and there probably wasn't in our past, either.

"But not everyone has been satisfied to leave it at that. There's a simple problem with the idea of a Big Bang: where did everything come from? If there was nothing here before that, what was it that exploded? What caused the explosion?

"Our best cosmological answer is still: nothing. However, the physicist's definition of nothing is quite different from the philosophical idea of nothing. And precisely defining 'nothing' in a way that satisfies everyone turns out to be exceedingly difficult, more difficult than one might imagine. Both sides agree that something can't come from *absolutely* nothing. So how do you get around the problem that there is, obviously, something?

"Let's look at the philosophical theologians' perspective. Christian ideas about creation, along with those of many other religions, assert the existence of some deity, God, if you will, who is outside of time and space, who has always existed, and who created the universe from absolutely nothing.

Darian changed the slide from the image of thousands of distant galaxies to a picture of the famous Michelangelo paintings on the ceiling of the Sistine Chapel, showing the Christian God in the act of Creation.

"Let's think about that for a minute. Theologians say, 'God is not made of anything.' In other words, God is outside the universe of matter and energy, outside of space and time. Still, He is powerful enough to make something from nothing. But is this really nothing, even a philosophical nothing?

"As I see it, there are two possibilities that fit with this traditional religious model of creation. Either the universe was created as *part* of God, or there was something in existence, or potentially in existence, *apart* from God, before He supposedly created the universe from it.

"If the universe came from a part of God, and the universe is made from 'something,' then it seems logical to conclude that God is made, at least in part, of 'something' as well, especially if the universe is still a part of God. On the other hand, if God created the universe apart from Himself, then whatever He made it from was either 'something' or had the potential to become 'something'.

"Some theologians speak of an 'empty room,' separate from God, with absolutely nothing in it. But an empty room is a location, a space separate from God. So, that's still something, isn't it? Either everything was God at the beginning, or there was something, maybe only an empty space, that wasn't God. In the end, the Creationist idea of an omnipotent God creating the something of the universe from absolutely nothing fails logically.

* * *

DARIAN CASUALLY SCANNED THE AUDIENCE and monitored the progress of the background facial recognition check. The data both piqued his interest and accounted for some of his unease.

The lattice revealed statistics about a number of attendees that fell well outside the norm for a casual presentation like this. Among the usual mix of students and professors, there was a high proportion of people with no discernible links, neither present nor past, to any of the universities in the city. It was common to have unaffiliated members of the public dropping by these Philosophers' Cafés but usually no more than a dozen or so at any particular event. Today's turnout was remarkable. Or perhaps it wasn't, considering the protest that had greeted him outside.

The lattice also revealed a disproportionate number of individuals, across the university and non-university attendees alike, who maintained strong ties with fundamental Christian religious groups. The Yeshua's True Guard Church was especially well represented. Of those individuals, a suspiciously high number had recently flown in on tourist visas from the New Confederacy, many of whom he recognized as agitators from the unruly crowd outside the building.

Are they in town for some big event and just dropped by? Why would so many show up to hear me talk about physics?

Darian expanded the parameters of the background search, and applied it to his own internal recording of the audience. The program identified a network of subtle glances between identified Church members, focusing on two specific members garnering an inordinate amount of attention.

The first individual whom people were watching came as no surprise. As the prominent leader of the True Guard Church, Reverend Alan LaMontagne was easily recognized, a celebrity of sorts. Those who recognized him were likely to be at least mildly curious, if not hyper-attuned to, his reactions to the talk.

The second person drawing unusual attention was more of a puzzle. He was not a well-known celebrity, and he raised no other alerts in the lattice. By all accounts, he wasn't in any way noteworthy, not until the system factored in facial micro-expressions. With that, his hatred of Darian jumped out like a gargoyle sculpture in a Japanese Zen garden. Compared to the rest of the audience, his face expressed an inordinately high number and level of distasteful expressions.

The individual was otherwise a picture of blandness: middle-aged, Caucasian, male, neither too pale nor overly tanned, short-cropped blondish hair, neatly but not fanatically groomed. He was casually dressed in khaki pants and a beige, all-cotton hiking vest.

His face exuded uncompromising, steely determination. He had barely moved a muscle during the entire first half of the talk; it was his face alone that set off numerous alerts within Darian's lattice. The system had tracked all sorts of facial micro-shifts as the man's gaze intensified. It registered his brow gathering into tense little creases, his eyes locking onto the young scientist without distraction, and the jaw clenching and unclenching.

Darian instinctively picked up on the murderous intent in the man's stare; he didn't need his lattice to interpret that. What it couldn't tell him, was the connection between this man and the members of the YTG Church who kept glancing his way. According to official records, the man didn't even belong to the group, yet their glances indicated that many recognized him. *What could I have done or said to attract such open hostility? I haven't even touched on the controversial part yet.*

Darian sighed; there was nothing he could do about it at this point, anyway. And judging by the audience composition, things were only going to get worse. He waded in.

* * *

"SO, WE'VE ARRIVED AT ONE CONCLUSION. The argument that a Creator God existed before the universe is not substantially better than the Greek static model of the universe. The Greek model doesn't fit our observations, and the Creationist model simply moves the static, eternal part into an adjacent universe containing an intelligent, willful being. It does not say how this universe containing a purposeful, omnipotent God came about. Nor does it explain how or why a potential universe, a space adjacent but separate from the universe of God—an empty room from which or where He created everything—could exist. It is illogical.

"What does physics have to say about all this? What kind of natural 'nothing' could have existed before the Big Bang, according to physics?"

The next slide was a pure black image. "In quantum mechanics, nothing is generally interpreted as space devoid of stuff, without matter or energy. The nothing of physics is not the same as the nothing of philosophy or religion, so physicists call it something different, a quantum vacuum. A quantum vacuum is empty of matter and energy, it contains no *things*. But it's not completely empty; it's full of *virtual* particles, of perturbations in the quantum fields.

"Aha, you say, that's still *something!* Well, yes, and no. Virtual particles are called 'virtual' because they're not real. In quantum mechanics, they're as close to nothing as physicists can imagine. Virtual particles pop into and out of existence all the time.

"I know this sounds completely ridiculous and unreal to many of you. You're thinking, he might as well say *unicorn* as *virtual particle.* It would make about as much sense. An imaginary *thing* for an imaginary *thing,* right? Let's see what would that sound like.

"Unicorns come in balanced pairs: unicorns and anti-unicorns. One of the unicorn types can travel some distance for a very short time before recombining with an anti-unicorn of the same type. When they combine they are both annihilated. This happens over such a short time and distance that unicorns can't be observed. Nevertheless, unicorns have real effects that can be observed.

"Sounds silly, I agree. Except they're not the same. Unlike unicorns, virtual particles are more than just an idea. How do we know that?

"We use virtual particles to explain such things as quantum tunneling. That's a well-documented phenomenon where an electron can disappear from one side of an insulator and instantly reappear on the other side, in spite of the barrier. All of our modern electronics containing quantum dot, field effect transistors depend on this tunneling effect.

"Ordinary static electricity is a virtual particle phenomenon. It's a field composed of the virtual particles emitted by moving electrons inside a charged material.

"Virtual particles also allow us to calculate the exact wavelengths of light emitted by heating pure elements with astounding accuracy; within one part in a billion, or 0.0000001 percent. So we accept the virtual particle theory because it allows us to make the most accurate calculations in all of science.

"Now, many of you may have heard of the two kinds of real particles, fermions and bosons. Fermions are particles such as quarks, electrons, or neutrinos. Bosons carry forces between the fermions. Bosons include photons, gluons, Higgs bosons, and so on. We can calculate how these real particles and the virtual particles are related.

"Everyone's heard of Einstein's famous $E=mc^2$, right? Energy equals mass times speed of light squared? An atomic explosion converts mass into energy. Most people don't realize that Einstein's equation works in the other direction, too. When you put enough energy in one place, the energy gets converted into mass."

He displayed an image of the familiar mushroom cloud from an atomic explosion. That was shortly replaced by a strange-looking image full of weird blobs, representing the interactions between virtual particles and quarks inside a proton.

"The binding energy that ties virtual particles together inside a real particle makes up the majority of the mass of that real particle. Indeed, about seventy-percent of the mass of a proton comes from the energy created by the virtual particles bound together inside of it.

"Another way to think of real particles is as complete standing waves in the quantum field. What does that mean?

"Well, think of each real particle as a string that loops back on itself. The looped string represents a wave in the quantum field. If a wave is of the correct frequency, relative to the size of the loop, when it reaches the end of the loop, it starts all over again, creating what we call a standing wave in that loop. Kind of like when an audience at a football game performs a wave that goes all the way around the stadium, and starts over again. Real particles, standing waves in a loop, are stable.

"*Virtual* particles, on the other hand, are just incomplete *sections* of a complete standing wave. They're highly unstable and transient; they don't last long enough for us to even observe.

"We have recently shown that every known *real* sub-atomic particle can be modeled, not as a solid speck or ball, but as a boiling collection of randomly appearing and disappearing *virtual* particles that somehow manages to maintain a consistency of behavior in the aggregate, that is, in the collective whole.

"How do these chaotic, erratically behaved virtual particles—these incomplete waveforms—become nice, stable standing waves? The short answer is, through resonance.

"Two resonant—or compatible—waves on the same looped string reinforce each other. When they match the natural resonance of the string, they form a stable standing wave.

"So, imagine we have a partial wave in a quantum field, and it meets up with another partial wave of the same frequency. The second wave 'completes' part of the first wave. And, if you put enough of these resonant partial waves together, you create a full standing-wave pattern. And, bingo! The *virtual* turns into the *real*. The sections that overlap are redundant and fall out of the resulting real particle as excess binding energy.

"That makes *reality*, the universe as we know it, an emergent phenomenon of interacting *virtual* particles, things that don't really exist in any directly-measurable way. Poetically speaking, one might say that the physical nothing of the quantum vacuum is filled with an infinite number of tiny bits of imagination, existing without dimension, for no time.

"That sounds like a whole lot of *unicorns*, I mean, 'nothing' to me."

Very few laughed. Most stared back, stone-faced, uncomprehending, fidgety, and silent.

"What, no laughs? C'mon, that was funny!"

Wow, tough crowd—he thought, but it was more than that. There was a pervasive tension building out there. *Something's up*. He took a sip of water and returned to his lecture, uneasy.

"An entire universe filled with nothing but virtual particles would be very chaotic, yet it would appear completely empty to us. Virtual particles of all kinds would spontaneously appear, briefly interact with each other and disappear.

"Most of these interactions would be extremely short-lived because the incomplete waves of one particle would likely *not* resonate with the incomplete waves of incompatible, neighboring virtual particles.

"Which brings us to the question that has motivated my research team: How could a universe full of these chaotic, poorly behaved *virtual* particles give birth to the well-behaved *real* universe we see today?

"How can we conceive of a completely natural mechanism of *real* matter that evolves by a kind of natural selection from *virtual* matter, without the intervention or initiation of any intelligent creator? In other words, without God?

"The problem of spontaneous creation of a universe from nothing is not really a problem of the *creation* of energy and matter. As we've established, what we used to think of as nothing, is actually *full* of stuff. The quantum vacuum, deeper than the deepest vacuum in outer space, is crowded with energetic virtual particles.

"The problem is that, in the universe before the Big Bang, these virtual particles had not yet evolved a consistent set of stable, well-behaved interactions with each other. They existed; they just didn't exist *stably*.

"Our newest theory came from thinking about this problem. That led us to the next question, which led to the next, and so on. Questions like: How could these virtual particles that filled the great nothingness before the Big Bang achieve stable associations in an otherwise chaotic universe? How could virtual particle interactions propagate from one pair to another?

"Our best theory is that an orderly universe would start to distill from this chaotic brew of virtual particles by the resonance I mentioned earlier. A very rare event would eventually place numerous virtual particles, each with sufficient overlapping oscillations to produce a standing wave in the quantum field. Such standing waves would be the first *real* particles and provide little islands of stability in an essentially chaotic universe.

"The standing waves of these real particles would interact with the incomplete waves of nearby virtual particles. Our models show that after many, many interactions—too many to easily count—these interactions could eventually lead to larger stable domains in the otherwise chaotic universe. All of this would have taken place with ridiculously low probability.

"But before the Big Bang and the causality that we know and love today, even ridiculously low probability events were essentially guaranteed to happen eventually.

"These resonances formed the basis of the rules that determine how matter and energy interact, the laws of nature, if you will. The laws evolved from these interactions; they were not designed or imposed by an external force. The resonances, leading to the ways in which particles formed and interacted, arose by chance from infinite possibilities.

"Now, the real universe that formed through this process, our universe, still shares the same space with infinitely many other possible *virtual* universes. However, these other possible virtual universes have been unable to form a stable set of interactions and become real.

"This is different from the so-called multiverse theory, which states every universe that can exist, does. That's correct to a certain extent, but only *our* universe ever became real, that is to say, stable. All other possible universes remained *virtual*, never forming a stable relationship between enough of their member virtual particles to coalesce into reality. They're all still out there, those many other possibilities, interacting, appearing, and vanishing. Rather boggles the mind, doesn't it?

Darian switched to a slide showing a traditional analog stopwatch with a ticking second hand. The image was overlaid with a large question mark.

"I've got another brain twister for you. Consider the ridiculously high, practically infinite, number of interactions that would have to take place, along with the ridiculously low probability of just the right bits coming together precisely when, where, and how they needed to. Got that?

"Now, given all of that, how long do you think it took for our universe to come together, to evolve naturally from chaos? Anyone want to venture a guess?"

Darian looked around to see if there were any takers. The second hand moved on the overhead slide. He let them suffer for a few seconds before jumping back in.

"No takers? Well, I don't blame you; it was kind of a trick question. In a universe struggling to come into existence as I've described, the question of 'how long' is meaningless.

"There is no way to measure time before the first stable interactions were in place. The chaotic universe was eternal, lasting forever. Time was immeasurable as far back as one could possibly imagine. Without cause and effect, time has no direction.

"In such a universe of chaos, we can roughly define time as something like event opportunities. According to this definition, we can see there would be adequate time for a real universe to evolve. Event opportunities are essentially infinite.

"Another question we've been scratching our heads over is: How could that lead to the Big Bang?

"What we've come up with so far is this. While partial waveforms of virtual particles are easily able to share the same space, standing waves of identical real particles, particularly those we call fermions, are not. This is called the Pauli Exclusion Principle."

"Remember those little islands of stability I mentioned earlier? As more and more of those interacting domains of stability appeared, a sufficiently large nucleus accumulated.

"The effect those domains had on adjacent virtual particles through resonance became overwhelming. New real particles sprang into existence as the stable interactions started to spread outward, mediated by their resonance effect on adjacent virtual particles. The nucleus of real particles expanded faster than the speed of light because the resonant effect of *virtual* particles is not limited by the speed of *real* photons.

"Virtual particles coalescing into real particles in this way hate to occupy the same space. They rush to get away from each other. This led to the release of a huge amount of energy, the culmination of which, we call the Big Bang. Although, I think it would be more accurate to say, the Big *Bloom*.

"Our universe *blossomed* out of the chaos, rather than exploded. A region of stable reality spread into the surrounding area where only non-coherent virtual particles had existed previously. I suspect the process is still ongoing at the edges of the real universe, which continues to expand into the infinite chaotic virtual universe faster than the speed of light.

"In this way, the ancient Greeks were right: our universe *has* existed forever. There was a universe of chaotic virtual matter going back forever before the Big Bang. That virtual matter is the source of our universe, and the stable interactions that evolved between coalescing virtual particles are what we think of as the laws of nature."

Darian paused to take a sip of water and a deep breath.

"I realize that what I've described to you sounds extraordinary, certainly less than obvious. Science is, above all, pragmatic. We can make up all the outlandish theories and hypotheses we like, but they can only become scientifically accepted after they are tested against the reality of the universe. Reality is always the final arbiter of truth.

"So how can we test these ideas I've described? How do we go from wild conjecture to scientifically sound knowledge? We can't exactly go back 13.8 billion years into the past to test the origin of the universe, nor can we go trillions of years into the future to see how it all turns out.

"So here's where it gets really interesting. We believe that we can develop a device to generate complex fields that will amplify and select interactions among other virtual particles. Particles *other* than the ones that led naturally to real particles in our universe."

Darian noted a couple of dubious faces peering up at that comment.

"Once these virtual particles are coaxed into their own resonance, they will form tiny universes with their own natural laws, laws different from our own." A few more furrowed brows appeared.

"We call these fields 'Reality Assertion Fields' because they assert a new set of natural laws on a region of space. It turns out that a Reality Assertion Field, or RAF, is surprisingly easy to generate. All we have to do is compute the shape of a field that will encourage the selection of these new resonances between adjacent virtual particles within the RAF.

"We can use any field, but electromagnetic fields are the easiest to generate. The hard part is computing the shape of the overlap of a large number of EM fields so we can encourage the specific resonances we desire among the various virtual particles in a portion of space. The math gets a little difficult, as you might imagine."

There was an appreciative chuckle from the physicists in the audience.

Darian checked in with his lattice sub-routine again. No one, other than the Reverend LaMontagne and the man his lattice had flagged were raising any further alarms with the algorithm. He would keep an eye on those two during the Q&A session.

"My group is now in the process of building a very fast and powerful computer, and developing new types of mathematics, which we will use to calculate the fields required to generate a new RAF in a very small volume—about one hundred cubic centimeters—of a nearly perfect vacuum.

"Once completed, we will probe this region with a variety of tests to make sure that it has physical properties different from those specified by the laws of nature in our own universe. We expect to be able to demonstrate that our principles are correct within the next few months and, from there, I anticipate some paradigm-shifting science unfolding."

Among the sea of confused, bored, or frustrated faces looking back, Darian counted a disappointingly small number of individuals still exhibiting rapt attention.

In his distraction, he failed to see the angry man and Reverend LaMontagne exchange glances. The angry man gave an almost imperceptible nod.

27

As MEETING ROOMS GO, THIS ONE WAS UNIQUE. A stained-glass table sat on a downy cloud hovering ninety meters above the sun-drenched Vitality Beach, affording select clientele a touch of privacy from the hordes of sunbathers below.

Crystalline stairways connected hundreds of floating tables in the lower levels of the restaurant. But only select guests were permitted access to the highest table. As one might expect, obtaining seating at such a highly coveted spot required either miraculously fortuitous timing or considerable influence with the Manager persona. Darya had neither. She had, however, hacked the Assistant Manager Partial, ensuring access to a pleasant and secure location whenever she needed to meet with members of the inner circle.

The privacy afforded by the cloud-top table Darya chose was conducive to work, despite the allure of the palm-fringed beach below. Sadly, today its postcard-perfect view was wasted on Darya's four closest acolytes: Mary, Leisha, Gerhardt, and Qiwei. They were too deeply mired in despair to respond to the expanse of white sand and gentle aquamarine surf calling to them from far below.

Vacationland was classified as a high-magic inworld, enjoying considerable relaxation of conventional physical and social rules. To help achieve the illusion of natural beauty and tranquility in this zone, a handful of rustic, thatch-roof cabinas were clustered among the palms. The original inworld programmers accommodated the many visitors with a little trickery. Thanks to their unique design and special dimensional properties, what looked like a small bungalow outside provided thousands of private suites inside, each offering the same breathtaking view of the beach and adjacent tropical forest, while assuring complete privacy.

Giant transparent water globes with no visible means of suspension floated above the sparkling bay. Each pool had its own local gravity, enabling swimmers to skim the wet surfaces on all sides of the spherical globes. Ranging in diameter from twenty to a few hundred meters in diameter and cleverly interconnected by serpentine water tubes, slides, and water bridges, they were irresistible to swimmers and spectators alike.

Body-variant visitors chased through the network. Dolphin, penguin, squid, and otter bodies were the most popular body shapes, any of which might be augmented by creative combinations of flipper, fin, leg, jet, and wing.

Leisha glanced wistfully at the surfers honing their skills a kilometer out, on forty-meter virtual waves that rushed toward the coral reefs at exhilarating speeds. She appreciated the expertise of those performing one-arm handstands on the tips of their boards, a trick she had not yet mastered. Some of her friends eschewed boards completely, preferring the sensory experience of the waves directly on their simulated skin.

As she'd learned firsthand, Vacationland was very forgiving of recklessness in the pursuit of sensory adventure. Depending on the severity of a simulated injury, one could normally expect to be fully healed within minutes-to-hours, and back inworld, enjoying the fun.

Sim-death was a different story. Dying inworld got you kicked out for a full day in real-time. To Leisha, being banished to the outworld with no assigned tasks and no company but your own thoughts was more painful than whatever virtual injuries brought suspension from the inworld in the first place. She'd been sent for a time-out more than once.

When she was looking for a less dangerous but equally thrilling activity, she headed to the waterslides. In keeping with the promise of offering bigger, better, and faster, the chutes towered a kilometer above the beach, and boasted turns and loops that would have been impossible on Earth or any real planet. They used localized and unpredictable changes in gravity along the length to slow or accelerate the patrons, testing their skills and virtual courage.

Leisha loved that she could just as easily find herself accelerating on the *upward* half of a loop as being repelled *away* from the watery tube and having to push her arms and legs outward to press away from an inner lip of the next.

Qiwei preferred the drier recreation found further inland, where the palm trees gave way to a deciduous forest that, in turn, worked its way up the hilly slopes then thinned out as it neared the rocky crags. Along the forest floor, he often joined dozens of like-minded patrons hunting lions, tigers, dragons, and all sorts of mythical creatures. True enthusiasts used only knives or bows and arrows to hunt. Qiwei was among those who considered it unsporting to arm oneself with more advanced weaponry to stalk the deadly beasts.

In addition to the tens of thousands of virtual people that played or relaxed along the lengthy beach, even larger numbers of Partials dashed about on foot, wing, or fin, serving every desire of the instantiated.

The Servitor Partials were tireless, always friendly and accommodating. They weren't really needed, but the Vacationland designers had thought it a quaint touch to have food and drinks delivered by a "living being" instead of simply popping into existence on command. Simulated beverages and snacks were similarly unnecessary but made a pleasing representation of energy consumption back at the outworld recharging stations, where Cybrid trueself bodies docked while their minds visited inworld.

Cybrid minds were modeled on human minds, and allotting them some time to pretend they were physically human again helped to keep them psychologically stable. Other types of imaginary worlds had been tried, but simulated Earth-like environments were the most effective and enjoyable over the long run. Still, a few magical enhancements didn't hurt.

Like most Cybrids, for Darya and her team, Vacationland was a lifesaver. The creative freedom and thrilling sensory experiences they enjoyed inworld helped maintain their sanity between tedious work contracts. And of all the imaginative inworlds available, Vacationland was the most popular.

Darya's perusal of the scenery was interrupted by the arrival of one of the Servitors with another round of simulated, though nonetheless delicious, margaritas. She returned her attention from the throngs below to the meeting of the Central Committee of the rebellion.

"So what have you four been up to these past few months?"

Leisha, tanned and freckled, wearing a loose purple wrap over her bikini, was first to answer. "Just working and hoping the Securitors don't come grab me at any second."

The Lysrandia fiasco had decimated the ranks of Darya's followers, and left the survivors demoralized. The Securitors still held over sixty percent of them in custody following the showy inworld dragon battle. Brutal interrogations led the Securitors to another fifteen percent of the original group. Over five hundred members had been lost. Only her four most senior people and a few scattered cells remained, a little over a hundred and sixty individuals to challenge the work of the millions bent on pushing Alum's Divine Plan forward.

"At least the rate of new arrests seems to have abated," Gerhardt offered. Instead of sounding hopeful, it came across as dark and moody.

The thin, athletic body he wore for this meeting was a noticeable divergence from his preference toward plump and philosophical. He was being cautious.

Darya was glad the Securitors had not cracked their inworld avatar disguises yet. While she was thinking about it, she used her newly modified outworld connections to initiate an independent routine to revamp their avatar code before the meeting was finished. She included the revised interface-exit commands. Never again would her supporters be left stranded inworld, unable to leave except through "approved" routes.

"Even so, we lost a lot of good people." Qiwei noted. "And we're going to lose more once the Securitors start interrogating the latest group they brought in." He had chosen an appearance as diminutive as possible. His moderate stature, mousy brown hair, lightly tanned skin, and computationally average appearance reflected the cultural norm of the mixed Cybrid heritage. Qiwei was so perfectly unexceptional that he almost stood out in Vacationland, where most people succumbed to their ideal images of self.

His fears, as well-founded as they were, had nearly resulted in his absence today. Only Darya's promise of some really big and important news had enticed him to take the risk. He had lost a lot of friends to personality wipe after Lysrandia. Their Cybrid bodies would be inhabited by one of the personas previously approved for embodiment, no doubt following careful screening for rebellious tendencies.

Darya shifted her gaze to Mary, a classic rebel as reflected in her choice of an obese body, and a face so conspicuously unattractive that it verged on the mesmerizingly beautiful even before one took into account the array of piercings and exaggerated black make-up. In Darya's ancient memory, she would have said Mary's choice of self-expression fell into the ultra-Goth era.

Wherever she went, Mary attracted attention, which she deemed undeserving of her notice and deliberately ignored. She was Darya's official second-in-command and the most innovative of her top lieutenants. But even Mary was being cautious today, shaving about fifty kilos off her usual body presentation and limiting her piercings to the more conventional end of the spectrum.

"Do you have anything to add?" Darya asked her.

Mary looked miserable. "I'm not sure we can carry on," she said. "We all knew this was risky but to suffer such a huge setback now, so close to when Alum is ready, this might have finished the battle for us. Maybe his power is just too much for us."

"We all know that Alum is powerful," Darya acknowledged, "but he is not omnipotent."

"But Alum is *God*," Mary challenged. How do we defeat God?"

Darya took a calming breath. "Alum is *not* God. There is no such thing as God. He simply has access to very sophisticated technology."

"And a stable, ancient religi-political system that provides him with the undying loyalty of millions of trillions of humans and Cybrids," Gerhardt interjected.

"He may not be God but he's the closest thing to it in *this* universe," Leisha lamented. "I don't think we can build an organization from here that can overtake his might. Not before he makes his big move."

Darya sighed. "Remember, we don't need to conquer him everywhere, just here at the heart of his project," she said. She looked at her depressed acolytes. "Look, I know we've suffered a huge setback but there's still enough time to stop Alum's insane plan for the Realm. We can't roll over and quit now!"

"We can't quit, and we can't win," observed Qiwei. "What can we do?"

"We put our heads together and we don't give up. Our efforts over the past several hundred thousand years have been aimed at slowing down Alum's project by building intentionally defective machines," Darya answered. "It has worked well enough so far, or we wouldn't be talking now; the project would be finished. But each time we thought of a new way to slow down his progress, Alum's people found ways to detect and fix the problems we introduced.

"For the first hundred thousand years or so, the problems could be attributed to growing pains. For the past few tens of millennia, the Alumit suspected an active resistance. The Lysrandia operation just brought everything into the light. They know about us, and now we know that they know."

A waiter checked in discreetly and Darya lowered her voice. "Just because our opposition to Alum's plan is out in the open now, doesn't mean we're defeated. It just means we need to commit to an even more vigorous, more effective resistance. Who knows, maybe we can even use this to our advantage somehow."

"How do we do that without getting caught and wiped, anyway?" asked Mary.

Darya frowned. "Hacking into the Lysrandia inworld was a stopgap measure, nothing more. We knew it would get traced eventually. We made use of all those millenia to carry out a successful recruitment drive. Now it's time to get prepared for the next step."

Gerhardt sat forward, a glimmer of hope in his eyes. "So, what is the next step?"

"It's time to attack," Darya pronounced.

Gerhardt fell back into his chair, expelling a whoosh of air. "How can one hundred and sixty attack millions, especially when those millions include Securitors, Shards, Angels, and Alum Himself?"

Darya didn't let Gerhardt's pessimism slow her down. "A frontal assault by our small group would be pointless, and we don't have time to recruit enough passively resistant Cybrids, ones who would believe in seeking Truth and Knowledge, not just blindly following Alum's dictates. I take full responsibility for that failed strategy.

"I thought that the Plan was simply a diversion that Alum invented for bored Cybrids. I didn't think he was actually insane enough to make his own personal universe just to fulfill his deranged desire to achieve perfection. Remember, I knew him before he was God. I never would have guessed he could do something like this. Not in a billion years."

"What kind of a human was he?" Mary asked, curious despite her despair.

Darya was caught off guard by Mary's question. Most people didn't want—outright refused—to relate to Alum as a human being. How many times had she held similar meetings with earlier incarnations of similar groups? She reviewed her logs of past conversations with this group to verify. Yes, this was the first time she'd ever discussed Alum's origin with any of them.

"I guess in the millennia we've known each other, I've been so focused on building the resistance that I've never really talked about what Alum was like back then." Her thoughts turned back to an ancient age and she recalled the young man she had known.

"The memories are a little vague and maybe even degraded. But I know He was a man of Yov, young for a charismatic spiritual leader of millions. After what happened on Origin, he became understandably more cautious and conservative. He was a spiritual man in an age when science was tearing at the last vestiges of the supernatural. It was a difficult time for the self-named "True Believers" back then.

"Though not formally trained in science, Alum developed an incredible understanding of many fields all on his own. He was a genius, perhaps not completely 'natural,' but he never outgrew his fundamental bias that the universe was so perfectly put together that it must have had a divine Creator. Even though he was familiar with Darian Leigh's theory, he couldn't accept that the universe really did come from nothing." Her casual mention of Darian Leigh, the evil Da'ar, whose real name was long forgotten by all but her small group, caused nervous eyes to scan their immediate surroundings.

"I think Alum lacked the courage to follow where reason took him, so he turned to his religious roots for answers. He chose his faith over science. That didn't stop him from using scientists to achieve his goals, though. Or maybe he just thought religion was a better road to power. The notion of an infinite and uncaring universe, with no special place or purpose for humanity terrified him. It terrified many of us. Even those of us who believed that science would inevitably dispel the very idea of the supernatural were still scared and confused when Origin was threatened.

"But it hit those who believed in an Intelligent Designer particularly hard. When the Da'arkness threatened to destroy our world, it just confirmed most people's suspicions that science couldn't be trusted to operate without strict moral supervision. They cried out for a leader of high moral principle, one who knew enough to oversee the scientists' efforts to save the planet."

"What happened?" asked Leisha, completely caught up in the story.

"They chose Alum, and he saved us. When humanity's survival was threatened, he managed to get us all to work together, Cybrids and humans alike, to find a solution. Ultimately, he invented the starstep and endless energy, and he was able to take everyone to safety.

"We made him our leader, the Supreme Leader. But he couldn't stand to live in a universe without a God, so he *became* that God. He established a new socio-political system with himself as the central deity. It's been stable for over a hundred million years now. It provided a vision for humans and Cybrids, and a way to conquer the universe."

"So what's the problem, if it's stable and it works so well? Is it really all that bad?" Qiwei asked.

"The problem is, at His core, Alum still hates the apparent futility and randomness of it all. His vision of a purposeful universe does not accept the chaos that underlies reality. There are too many, uncertainties, too many things he can't control. You can't have purpose in a universe that just *is*. For there to be an ultimate purpose to the universe, you need a person, an intelligent and willful being, who determines that purpose. Using ancient beliefs as his template, Alum intends to be that person, the one who gives the universe its purpose.

"I didn't see it until too late. This has become his primary motivation, pushing him to favor deterministic systems over stochastic ones, to crave order over unpredictability. His desire for the predictable and perfectly knowable had no chance against the sheer magnitude of the chaotic universe.

"Instead of giving up, he imagined a re-Creation. A complete reset. A do-over, if you will. Alum's Divine Plan was conceived, I suspect, of his desire to bring perfect order to this messy universe, even if that means destroying it in order to try again."

A tear trickled down Darya's cheek, as much from anger as profound sadness. "For ages, we were told that the machinery we'd been constructing here around the black hole at the center of the Milky Way was intended to create a mini-universe in which humans and Cybrids could cohabit and live safely forever under the loving guidance of Alum. A sort of perfect Heaven; a reward for our hard work in this universe."

"Of course, it was all a lie," Darya spat, "a lie meant to appeal to the Cybrid's love of the inworlds. This mini-universe, the one we've been working toward, may sound like the perfect physical implementation of a perfect inworld sim. But to Alum, a separate mini-universe, no matter how nearly perfect to us, might still be threatened by some unforeseeable external force if the potential for intelligence in any other universe remains. And he is not going to allow that to happen."

Qiwei struggled to absorb the implications. "So, Alum's *true* intention is to re-create the entire universe?" The acolytes waited anxiously for Darya to respond.

"Yes," confirmed Darya, "and to remove all those bothersome uncertainties while he's at it. The machinery we Cybrids have been working on for the past million years will first stop and then reverse the ongoing expansion of the cosmos.

"Our universe will deflate faster than the speed of light—space itself will contract—until it finally implodes, reversing the Big Bang. This process of deflation and implosion—or "deplosion" as I call it—will continue for about ten million years until everything is condensed into a space smaller than a single atom.

"At that point, Alum will initiate a new Creation with a set of less stochastic natural laws more to his liking, resulting in a more ordered and manageable universe.

"As a side benefit, his new universe will also have a provable Creator, and that Creator would be Alum. He would be the unquestioned God of the Cosmos, and the clear purpose of everything in that cosmos would be to sing his praises forever.

"It's not enough for him to create a Heaven as a reward to his followers. He wants the whole universe, all possible universes, to be destroyed and rebuilt as his version of Heaven."

28

DR. PRATT LUMBERED OUT OF HIS SEAT and requested a microphone from one of the assistants. He tapped it twice to make sure it was working. *Thank goodness that's over. And I thought it was painful listening to Darian talk about the human soul.*

Aloud, he said, "An intriguing hypothesis, I'm sure, Dr. Leigh. Thank you for explaining your ideas so elaborately. Perhaps I could begin the question period by asking you, how dangerous is it to try and alter the laws of nature, even at the smallest level? I'm sure you'll recall the concerns many of us had over the experimental work on the Higgs boson, the so-called God particle. Although that work turned out to have no dire large-scale consequences—at least, none that we know about so far—it seems to me that your own research may pose an even greater potential for disruption. How do we know that your work is not moving us toward some horrific and irreversible disaster on a universal scale?"

"Thank you for your question, Dr. Pratt," Darian replied equitably. "As you point out, the fears around the Higgs boson research were indeed exaggerated. However, that is not the reason we think our current research poses no danger.

"The reason we do not fear some unforeseen disaster resulting from our research is that the real universe is incredibly stable.

"The universe of *real* particles is much more robust than, say, people's perception or memory. People think they remember things happening that didn't really happen at all, sometimes that couldn't have happened. Unlike imagination or memories—let's call those our *perceived* realities—an *objective* reality actually exists. It is formed out of countless, consistent and well-defined resonances between the virtual particles that, altogether, make up the real particles of the universe. It is definable, measurable, predictable, and can be consistently recreated.

"It is, however, exceedingly difficult to calculate how even a small number of stable *real* particles might interact with their adjacent *virtual* particles. That's why we are generating the RAF—the Reality Assertion Field—in as much of a complete vacuum as we can. Until we understand how artificial microverses interact with the real universe, we want to avoid any contact between these two different kinds of matter."

Satisfied with his answer, Darian turned to the audience and asked, "Other questions?" A hand shot up immediately. Darian recognized the speaker from campus, "Yes, Mr. Lim?"

The third-year physics major beamed at being identified by name by the world-famous scholar. It didn't occur to him how easy it was for Darian to access SFU's confidential registration data via his lattice in the brief time between seeing a raised hand and acknowledging it. An assistant handed the student a microphone. "I'm confused about the quantum fields—"

"I believe that feeling is widely shared," Darian joked, "even physicists have struggled with the complexities. But what is it in particular that you find confusing, Mr. Lim? Perhaps I can help clarify."

The undergrad smiled shyly and continued in a quiet, precise voice. "I've been taught that all quantum fields are associated with a real particle. So how could one extend across the universe, when most of the universe is empty space? How can a field exist in the absence of any particles?"

"An excellent question, Mr. Lim. You have touched upon something that has bothered many theoretical physicists for quite some time.

"Remember my earlier description of static electric charge? As charged *real* particles move, they interact with *virtual* particles that are constantly and spontaneously arising all around them. Some of the virtual particles will resonate by chance with the real particles. These, in turn, may resonate with other nearby virtual particles. Stringing these together, leads to the transmission of the resonance outward from the material.

"Actually, what we call the quantum field is simply the *potential* for resonance by the virtual particles. But virtual particles permeate the universe and beyond. So the field itself isn't a real thing; it's more like a representation of potential, a mathematical convenience, if you will. The part of a field closest to an actual thing is this traveling wave of resonance which is transmitted through the cloud of virtual particles. Does that clarify it for you?"

Mr. Lim nodded his thanks and sat down, even more confused than before. He wasn't the only one lost. The majority of individuals who attempted to follow the conversation displayed bewildered looks.

"Don't worry too much about the details," Darian said. "This is not easy to convey in words, and it's an awful lot for you to absorb in one short session. I know this isn't a common or obvious way to think about the universe.

"The best way to get a sense of it is by asking how a universe of virtual particles would behave. Once you see that the only way to go from the *virtual* to the *real* is through resonance effects of adjacent particles, you will realize that *all* matter, forces, and fields can be explained through this mechanism.

"When you finish your classes next year, I hope you'll join my graduate seminar to see how the math works, Mr. Lim. I think you'll find it much easier to grasp when you can see it laid out in the formulas." Darian smiled, encouragingly he hoped, and was rewarded with an enthusiastic nod and ear-to-ear grin from Mr. Lim.

"I believe we have a question from the other hall," said Dr. Pratt. "Theater 3, your question, please?"

The monitor displayed a thirty-something woman with lustrous brown hair and fashionable attire. She reached awkwardly for the microphone being offered to her by a theater assistant. "But...but isn't it all...." Her voice faltered as she spoke into it, as if she was surprised by her own sound. Feedback squealed through the speakers in both halls. The assistant winced and pulled the microphone to an inch away from the woman's mouth. He gestured to her to begin again.

She cleared her throat, and her eyes darted to the group sitting next to her. Several severe-looking men along the row bobbed their heads in stern encouragement. She returned her focus to the speaker and started again.

"Dr. Leigh, your ideas are rather fantastical, invoking things that sound like fairy tales, particles that no one can see, the whole universe springing into existence by random chance, a reality field. It all sounds so...unbelievable, and so unbelievably complicated."

She took a shaky breath as Darian and the rest of the audience waited for a question.

"My question is, why should I believe your complex and *incredible* story instead of simply believing that the Lord God made it all? The story of creation as told in the Bible makes a whole lot more sense to me." She looked around the audience, pleading with her eyes for people to join her in the firm and comforting belief in her God.

Back in the other hall, Darian composed himself. "Your question contains so many assumptions, and it is so steeped in ignorance, that it is difficult for me to answer in the short amount of time that we have here."

The audible intake of breath and the hurt, angry look on the woman's face in the monitor made him realize that his reply must have come across too harsh. He rushed to repair the damage, for both their sakes.

"What I meant is that in order to really understand the theory, one would need a lifetime of studying mathematics and physics. You are ignorant only in the sense that you lack knowledge in these areas of study, perhaps in science altogether. Sadly the word 'ignorant' has become so clouded with emotion in modern use that people are offended when it's used to describe them."

The audience watched the woman on the screen turn to her neighbor and mouth something. Darian's lattice had no trouble reading her lips. He nodded in response as if she had spoken to him directly.

"For the rest of the audience's benefit, the speaker commented—to her neighbor's approval—that she does not 'believe' in science." The woman looked simultaneously chagrined and embarrassed.

"Well, folks, if it were legal, I could duplicate my neural lattice within their brains so that both she and her neighbors could benefit from sufficient understanding of scientific knowledge to properly judge whether or not it is believable. But let's see if we can demonstrate that without such a drastic approach.

"Is science just another belief system in an essentially subjective universe? I think that is the essence of the question. Certainly it is a kind of belief system, a belief that the universe is real, that it works through definable and reliable laws of nature, and that these physical laws can be shown through data. We might call this belief system empirical physicalism.

"But even magical versions of the universe behave according to definable and reliable rules. Pantheistic magic, for example, has rules for invocations. The magic of the Abrahamic God also operates according to rules. The main rule for that particular form of magic is that God must will it; if so, the universe bends to God's will.

"A number of philosophers and writers have posited that the universe is *not* real, that we are all asleep in some greater outside universe. Some philosophies even suggest that our lives in this universe are just fractions of our real lives in the greater universe, that a life here is but one night's dream in the true universe. This is one of the models behind the idea of reincarnation, and it has a certain appeal. The biggest problem I see is this: if we have no way to know if *this* universe is real, how could we be sure that life in the *greater* universe is real and not just another dream in an even *greater* universe? Is it just dreams all the way up? How would that even work?

"Then science comes along. Science is built from our common experience that the universe works in a predictable way according to well-defined rules: the laws of nature. In the early history of humanity, many of these rules were too complex for us to perceive. We could explain that wood was something that burned, while rocks didn't; that was easy. But the coming and going of storms, the cause of lightning, and so on, those were too complicated for our early minds.

"We invented gods, hundreds or even thousands of them, to explain what we perceived as the capriciousness of natural behavior. Over time, we started to understand the workings of more and more things, and the ancient gods died off. I don't mean literally, because they never really existed. We just stopped turning to them as a way to explain natural occurrences.

"Nature is complex and it begets complex science. At a certain point, the complexity of scientific knowledge overwhelmed the ability of the human mind to grasp. So we specialized. Physicists used their understanding of electron movement in semiconductors to invent things like transistors. Mathematicians invented ways to represent and manipulate information, and computers were developed. Biologists and biochemists gleaned an understanding of the chemical basis of life and became capable of engineering new organisms.

"Faced with the overwhelming complexity of nature, and with the sheer volume of the knowledge being amassed by scientists, many people turned back to an older and simpler view of the universe for relief. That view is the ancient one where the magical powers of God determine how everything works.

"But the scientific approach to understanding the universe isn't just *any* belief system. Its essence is pragmatic; it works. It just works. Throughout history, once we achieved significant and correct understanding of natural phenomena, we were able to use that understanding to *do* things. We could build automobiles, airplanes, submarines, computers, the internet, insect-resistant crops, nuclear bombs, and so on.

"Where we were temporarily ignorant of the functioning of something, such as, say, cancer in the early part of this century, we prayed to our old God or gods to help us. Sometimes, prayer seemed to work and we attributed the healing to divine intervention. We now understand many of the causes of cancer, and we are able to reliably and predictably cure it. Cancer is no longer in the realm of the gods. Like so many other areas of ignorance before, it has fallen to a scientific, natural understanding of the universe.

"We don't need a God or gods in order to understand the universe, though it may be beyond the intelligence of unaided, individual humans. No, what we need is to elevate the level of intelligence in humans so that we can all better understand the universe. Although it is vast, majestic, and complex—and we might not be able to understand every little thing that happens within—it is still a natural universe with natural laws. It *can* be understood.

"We used to think God moved the planets and put the stars in their place in the sky. Then Newton and Einstein helped us to see that astronomy was explained by gravity, and our magical explanations of the universe retreated to the realm of biology.

"We used to invoke godly 'vital spirits' to explain the animation of life and inheritance. But Darwin showed that inheritance along with competition to survive and reproduce could explain the development of new species. Then Watson, Crick, and Franklin, among others, showed that DNA was the basis of inheritance, and it became obvious that biology was really just complex chemistry.

"We used to think that life could not have spontaneously begun in the primordial ooze that was Earth. And then, just a few years ago, Barholt showed us how life can spring from wet, salty puddles, with no other explanation than chemistry and thermodynamics.

"Our God-based rationalizations have steadily retreated as scientific theories of natural phenomena have advanced. Today, God is mostly only invoked within the scientific community to explain the existence of the human soul and the creation of the universe.

"I'm certain that advances made in artificial intelligence over the next few years, perhaps by someone in this room today, will challenge the magical explanation of the human soul.

"Very soon we will be able to create the software that will show intelligence is an emergent property of organized, neural-like systems, whether those neurons are biological, electronic, or spintronic. I predict that within a hundred years we will develop *synthetic* intelligences whose humanity we will be unable to deny.

"Even the very laws of nature are close to becoming something we can manipulate through science and technology. The work being done by my group will show these physical laws have a perfectly *natural* origin, that no magical or supernatural explanation is required to explain them.

"The theory we are developing will point the way to a deeper understanding of how our natural laws evolved among the original bits of the universe. It will give us a chance to vary these laws in a small, local section of the universe, and see how different sets of natural laws interact. This work could lead the way to some major breakthroughs: limitless energy, smarter computers, faster-than-light travel to places that only our distant descendants will know.

"Personally, I find a universe that evolved naturally is much more exhilarating than a universe created by an all-powerful being to celebrate His glory. I would hope that the rest of you would find it equally exciting."

To Darian's surprise, applause broke out among about a third of the audience members. The remainder sat, frowning, with crossed arms and disapproving glares.

"Ahem," Dr. Pratt broke in after a few seconds. "I see we have exceeded the time allowed for the first half of the Café. We'll take one more question before the break and then enjoy a fifteen-minute recess."

Pratt scanned the room looking for the last questioner. He pointed to an older gentleman sitting halfway back in the lecture theater, whose hand was barely raised. "Yes, you, sir, the gentleman in the striped shirt," he said and directed one of the floor runners to deliver a microphone to the selected audience member.

Darian waited patiently as the man fiddled with the microphone. The clumsy collusion between the host and the planted questioner could not have been clearer if he had received a script in advance of the Café.

"Reverend LaMontagne," Darian announced for the benefit of anyone who might not have recognized the former statesman and church leader being invited to speak. "I was wondering if you might weigh in on the discussion. Welcome."

The Reverend was only moderately surprised at being recognized by the professor. The holy man's reputation was much larger in The New Confederacy than in Pacifica. Still, his vocal support of a fundamentalist interpretation of the Bible, and of its use in government and education, led to his image appearing in many news stories across popular media around the English-speaking world.

"Thank you for a most interesting presentation, Dr. Leigh," LaMontagne began. "I only have two very brief questions for you, if I may. First, I'd like to know what you think is the purpose of it all. Why, of all possible universes, was this one, which is so attuned to human life, the one that came into existence? Second, without the guiding hand of our Lord and His son, Jesus Christ, how are we to know right from wrong? Thank you." He handed the microphone back to the waiting assistant.

"Short questions frequently lead to long answers," replied Darian. "But I'm sure everyone would like to get to the refreshments and the restrooms so I'll try to keep it brief, and if anyone cares to continue, we can discuss it further during or after the break.

"Your first question, why this world, and what is the purpose of it all, alludes to an anthropocentric view of the universe and of our Earth. Some people believe everything was designed for the optimal existence of life or, more precisely, of mankind. From this perspective, inevitably follows the argument that, because this is the only human-friendly planet we know, it must have been created by God expressly for humanity. This belief seems to have plagued a great many philosophers and even a few physicists over the past several hundred years. Unfortunately, it is based on a faulty assumption.

"The vast majority of the universe, and of the potentially habitable part of this planet, is actually *not* amenable to life, certainly not to human life. Indeed, it is quite hostile. Most of the universe is what we think of as empty; it's in a vacuum flooded with various wavelengths of radiation, including light.

"The anthropocentric argument would carry a lot more weight if humans or other intelligent life were found throughout space or even inside the stars, since they comprise much more volume than Earth-like planets.

"If the universe had been at all intelligently designed for the purpose of life and of humans, it would have made much more sense to increase the habitable surface area by breaking the planets into smaller pieces, like asteroids. However, the weak gravity of asteroid-sized planetoids is insufficient to hold air or water on the surface, and so life becomes restricted to the planets.

"Even on Earth, life inhabits only a thin layer along the surface; it does not infiltrate most of the available volume. Life is only suited for extremely specialized environments found in an extremely small percent of the universe.

"If one wanted to claim that God created this vast universe but only placed life and humanity on the thinnest layer of a single inconsequential planet going round a nondescript star near the edge of an unremarkable galaxy among the hundreds of billions of galaxies in this part of the universe just so that we'd know our importance to Him, that is a very different claim from the anthropocentric one.

"If that were the case, then God would have had to think humans exceptionally vain and stupid to require such an enormous waste of space just to bring home a simple point.

"As for the purpose of it all, when I make something—let's say I build a house—I assign it a rationale. It could be to shelter me, to sell for money, or so on. Its purpose is given by its creator, me, in this case.

"Your first question assumes the universe *has* a Creator, who built it for His own purpose. If the universe simply evolved from the chaos that preceded it, it has no intrinsic purpose given by a nonexistent Creator. It simply is.

"Now, can we, as intelligent beings, *decide* on living our lives with purpose? Sure. We're able to decide what skills and talents we have, what we like and dislike, what meaning we attach to our activities. As well, we have a wide variety of societal and cultural influences to help us decide how to build our lives with purpose. We decide our purpose, each individual for him or her own self.

"Which brings me to your second question: How are we to know right from wrong? There are many moralities possible without God. Secular humanists and moral philosophers of many stripes have addressed this issue for centuries.

"Moral codes, a sense of right and wrong, pre-existed Christianity, and even the Old Testament. Christianity overlaid many of its practices and celebrations onto the earlier pagan worship and events.

"The fact that societies without the Christian God, or any gods at all for that matter, were capable of arriving at moral codes not too different from those of the Old or New Testaments would suggest that morality may have other bases besides the Christian God. We don't have time to go into evolutionary sociobiology here today, but many scholars have written about it.

"Instead, I'd like to suggest that the universe encodes *moral* laws just as much as it encodes *physical* laws. Universal moral laws apply more so to the species as a whole rather than to isolated individuals

"The fact that there are biologically unbreakable moral laws at the species level is as evident as the physical laws that we readily accept. One example might be: 'Thou shall not eat all your young.' Clearly, this law cannot be broken by all members of any mortal, sexually-reproducing species if that species is to survive. Just as one cannot jump off a cliff in defiance of the law of gravity, all members of a species cannot defy the moral law, 'thou shall not eat all thy young,' and survive.

"Notice how nature enforces moral law. When moral law is broken by a critical number of a species, that species becomes extinct. The physical punishment for breaking a natural moral law is much harsher than that of eternal damnation in a burning hell specified by Christianity. It is the subsequent non-existence of the species.

"Natural moral laws are similar to the laws of quantum mechanics in many ways. At the subatomic scale, individual particles are capable of all kinds of strange behaviors that seem to break the laws of nature.

"Take electron tunneling, for example. An electron seems to jump across an insulating barrier. One instant, it's on one side of the barrier; and the next instant, it's on the other side without ever traveling *through* the barrier. It appears to defy natural laws of motion.

"But, as I mentioned earlier, in the aggregation of all these particles into larger-scale lumps of matter, things that we can hold in our hands, those many small-scale oddities average out and matter 'behaves' itself.

"All kinds of behavior might be possible for *individual* members of a species but, if that species' *aggregate* behavior deviates too far from the limits tolerated by nature, the species cannot survive.

"Other examples of natural moral law might go something like, 'Thou shall not contaminate your environment to uninhabitable levels,' or 'Thou shall not overly limit diversity.' The first of these is rather obvious, but the second one is very interesting.

"Nature needs genetic diversity in a species because the environment is unpredictable. Levels of moisture, available food sources, changing light levels, and so on, mean that no species is ever completely safe from their environment because environments are not stable.

"The way that species adapt to change, in an evolutionary sense, is to encode variability right into their DNA. Individual members of any species are slightly different from other members. As an environment changes, some members will be better able to adapt to the change than others. In biology, we say these traits are selected but, really, we mean that some of the variations are more suitable than others. So nature says species must be capable of adapting or they run the risk of becoming extinct.

"How does this apply to us as individuals? It turns out that nature does not care too much about individual members of any species except as they may contribute to the survival of the species as a whole. However, as individuals of an intelligent species, we can choose to synchronize our individual behaviors with behaviors that are important to the species as a whole. We can attend to the needs of our young; we can be responsible shepherds of our environment; we can develop diverse skills and talents; and we can appreciate diversity in others, even if we don't like their behavior very much.

"Does any of this require an overarching God to threaten us with punishment if we stray? No, not at all. Nature will deal our species the ultimate punishment, non-existence, if we are immoral—that is, if we behave contrary to the types of behavior that select for survival of an intelligent species.

"Children require the guidance of an adult to help them select and practice behaviors that fit with survival over the long term. We learn to share, to cooperate, and to care about the well-being of our fellow humans. Much of infant behavior is directed and guided by their 'omnipotent' parents. But there comes a time when we develop the ability to think rationally, to reason on our own about right and wrong. We no longer need the threat of punishment to determine what kinds of behaviors are good for us and what kinds are bad.

"If as a society—as a species—we can learn to become aware of the behaviors that are good for our species over the long term, we can begin to take steps to select good behaviors from bad ones without needing the threat of eternal punishment. We no longer need the idea of a God or gods to choose good behaviors.

"I believe that it is time for humanity to grow up, to claim its adulthood, and to begin taking conscious responsibility for its future development."

LaMontagne leaned forward, itching to launch a rebuttal. To his dismay, his opportunity to reply was drowned out by thunderous applause. Much of the crowd rose to its feet and enthusiastic hoots rose from both theaters. Darian took it all in, surprised by the response.

One spectator, despite remaining seated, stood out; it was the same man who had been fuming through the entire talk. His face was contorted with fury; his chest heaved in ragged and uneven breaths.

Throughout the talk, the man had been holding his hands clenched tightly at his sides. His slightly overweight frame looked like it had once been muscular and well-toned; a certain hardness underlay the soft exterior. *Years of military training and discipline*—Darian guessed.

Unable to restrain himself any longer, the man's right hand slid slowly and deliberately across his body and disappeared under the vest. When it reappeared, it held a large pistol.

29

THE FIRST SHOT WENT INTO THE CEILING. Someone yelped, and the shooter drew a broad arc through the crowd. "Everyone, sit down and shut up! I don't want to hear a word out of anybody. Not one word."

Darian transmitted an urgent notice from his lattice to the local police broadnet.

The man fixed his sight on Darian, and made his way into the stairway leading toward the podium. "Darian Leigh, you have blasphemed against the Lord God and His only son, Yeshua! You have set the false idol of science before us. You have attempted to turn our gaze away from His loving face and toward your own."

As he made his way down the stairs, the shooter's hand bobbed and swayed a little with each step. Darian contemplated dashing for the door. *He's far enough away. I'd be hard to hit with a handgun.* He realized that running would likely put the entire auditorium at risk. *I have to draw his fire.*

Training his eye firmly on the man's trigger finger, the young professor subtly echoed the sway, side to side in rhythm with the assailant's steps, minutely amplifying the motion each time. He hoped to lure the man into increasing the sway, making it harder for him to maintain an aim on Darian's chest.

If I can get him to fire on an outward sway from at least twelve or more meters away, I can reverse my own movement and get up to a seventy percent chance of dodging the bullet. His calculations had to incorporate a lot of assumptions about the man's training, response time, and how many shots he could fire before someone stopped him. *All this computing power, and it comes down to hunches and guess work.*

Darian fought to remain calm.

Internally, he raced through his lattice archives for teachings of Yeshua's True Guard Church. *If I can get this guy angry enough to fire off a sloppy shot before he gets any closer, I might have a chance. I have to get all his attention on me. Maybe someone in the crowd can stop him before he gets off a second shot. Or a third.*

"You, sir, are the blasphemer!" Darian shouted. The man stopped in his tracks and stared at the scientist.

Playing up his indignation, Darian grabbed the lapel microphone from his collar and threw it to the ground. The speakers squealed as it bounced off the tile floor. He kept his eyes locked on the man's trigger finger and broadcasted his next words directly from his lattice into the PA system, hoping the unaided amplification might further rattle the man.

"You have entered a House of Knowledge with a closed mind, arrogantly sure of your fairy tales and your false god."

It didn't take a lattice to see the man's surprise return to rage and disgust. Darian slowed his side-to-side rocking, and prepared to twist away the instant the trigger was pulled.

The man's lips stretched into a smile as if recognizing a familiar face. He continued his descent toward the podium. "Ah, Satan speaks through you, I see," he bellowed, "but Yeshua has shown us the way. 'I am the light and the glory,' He says. 'There is no path to heaven but to follow me.' It will be a great service to the Lord, when I rid you of the demon that haunts you, Darian Leigh, when I free your soul from the Prince of Lies."

The gunman's spare hand produced a silver cross from the breast pocket of his vest. "I cast thee out, Satan," he cried. "In the name of Yeshua, son of God, I command thee to depart from this man. Lift the veil of darkness from his eyes so that he may see the true light of our Divine Lord and find his soul in peace."

Darian was stunned. He'd imagined a great number of possible responses to his talk today, but being the subject of an impromptu exorcism by a religious fanatic did not occur to him. He momentarily forgot his plan to avoid being shot.

"You are delusional," Darian said, just loud enough for the gunman to hear. "Do you believe so deeply that only *you* know the truth, and you know it so confidently and righteously that you would kill a simple scientist for the mere crime of speaking?"

"The poison of your words is more destructive than a million guns!" screamed the gun-bearer. "Do not attempt to deceive me, Satan. For I hold Yeshua firmly in my heart. Your words hold no weight with me. You may fool millions with your evil lies but be warned. There are legions who see through your deceptions. Our Lord has permitted your presence so He may weed out those who are too weak, losers who are too easily swayed by your dark promises to enter into His Kingdom. Your day of reckoning is coming, you servant of Darkness!"

As the man stepped off the final stair, Darian's lattice screamed at him: MOVE NOW! He saw the bullet leave the gun barrel, or maybe it was just the projection from the motion-modeling software in his lattice. In any case, he responded. Everything slowed as he twisted to one side, away from the projected point of impact. The last thing he saw before registering intense pain was Greg tackling the assailant from behind, and Kathy lunging forward to join Greg in an effort to bring down the shooter.

The bullet slammed into Darian's left side, spinning him around, and sending him crashing to the floor.

Galvanized by Greg's and Kathy's heroics, a handful of attendees leaped forward. The rest took advantage of the distraction and fled in the opposite direction. Four university security officers shouted and shoved their way down through the panicked crowd.

The ruckus grew distant as Darian's mainly biologically based consciousness faded to black, dragging his lattice along with it.

30

AT THE VACATIONLAND MEETING of Darya's Cybrid rebels, mouths gaped indelicately. Her acolytes contemplated the incomprehensible, a machine powerful enough to reverse the creation of the universe and an individual insane enough to use it.

"It's almost impossible to imagine," Mary said after a time.

"And there's only us left to stop it," whispered Qiwei.

"It only took one person to conceive of the plan in the first place," responded Darya. "Even if that person fancies himself a god of sorts, and the plan needs billions of Cybrids to implement it." She looked around the table, realizing how absurd it would appear to an outsider: the five of them, dressed for beachside relaxation, contemplating a war against the destructive desires of a self-proclaimed god.

"Listen," she said, "we learned a lot from Lysrandia. We can do better. We picked that location for testing and recruiting because of its low popularity with anyone except oddballs and nonconformists, which meant that anything going on inworld was likely to be ignored by Alum and the Securitors.

"We picked it knowing that few mainstream thinkers would ever step foot there and, if they did, they weren't likely to admit it to anyone or report any activities. We got lucky for a while, I guess, but recruiting people to our cause was always going to be a complicated and slow process there.

"Besides, that whole science and dragon show was getting to be rather much. The risk to everyone involved was getting too high to justify such a small gain in recruits."

"So what do you propose?" asked Gerhardt.

"Well, for the past few thousand years, I've been working on a way to take over the inworld sim machinery so that we can get our message out to everyone. I think I've developed a hack that will be untraceable, and unstoppable. I've already got it in place, and it's ready to be activated."

"But as soon as the Supervisors detect any attempts to interfere with the inworld sims they'll just block it," objected Qiwei. "After what happened in Lysrandia, they'll be more alert than ever."

Darya nodded. "That's true, they will be hyper-alert to *outside* interference, but this new system is built *within* the inworld system. It can't be stopped without destroying the simware, itself."

"From *inside* the system? How does it work?" Mary asked. Ever-focused on the practical, she was ready to move forward.

"I've engineered a quantum virus based on the newest sub-atomic logic in my own quark-spin lattice. The virus looks like normal matter, but it uses virtual particle interactions inside normal fermions—mainly quarks and neutrinos—to perform logic operations and to convert adjacent atoms into processing units.

"It draws from the simware energy source, it's adaptive to its environment, and it's self-replicating. Essentially, it's an intelligent, insidious, untraceable virus that will be unrecognizable from the host system it attacks. Or, I should say, unrecognizable at the molecular and atomic scales, which is all we need.

"I've already converted eight percent of the simware substrate inside the entertainment and recharging asteroids in the region. They're ready to receive fresh programming. In a few minutes, I'll be initiating the first new inworld available to Cybrids in millions of years. Like all other sims, this inworld will be uploaded into the distributed simnet, allowing all Cybrids living in major centers around Sagittarius A* to participate."

Qiwei sat forward and dropped his voice to a whisper. "A *completely* new inworld? Nobody has designed a significant new inworld from scratch for eons. If Alum becomes aware of our role in this, we'll be lucky if all he does is wipe our minds." He looked around to make sure no one was eavesdropping. "So, what is this new inworld like?"

"I've called it Alternus because it's an alternate version of Earth, the planet we now call Origin. I modeled it, as best I could, on Origin as it existed a few years before being destroyed by the Da'arkness. It will simulate a small part of our physical universe to near-perfection. The physics are true to the actual universe, and there is no magic.

"Cybrids, who enter the Alternus sim, will find a functioning society with a population of about nine billion people, all Partials. Players can choose to participate as invisible observers, or instantiate themselves directly inside an inworld inhabitant. If the Players choose to instantiate, they get access to that inworlder's memories, skills, and proclivities, and they'll be able to direct that person's life in any way they wish.

"Once a Cybrid instantiates into an inworld being, no other Cybrid will be able to instantiate into that same inworlder. It's a dedicated one-to-one relationship. From the moment a Cybrid instantiates, its own trueself personality traits will be imprinted on the inworlder. The Cybrid will know everything the inworlder knows, including how the inworlder would normally behave. When the Cybrid overmind is not present, the inworlder will continue to behave in a consistent manner."

Qiwei looked skeptical, perhaps even a little disappointed. "I can see how a totally new inworld would draw people to come visit. But, to be honest, this one sounds boring. Couldn't you have made something a little more exciting? No magic at all? What's that all about?"

"What's more exciting than reality?" Darya challenged. "Even though we do most of the work throughout Alum's worlds, Cybrid civilization is completely disconnected from the universe. We spend all our spare time in imaginary, magical inworlds like this one." She looked around at the impossible restaurant, the perfect beach below, the gamers, and the surfers.

"Our imaginary entertainments have encouraged us to take the easy road, to disengage from reality. Why struggle to understand the complexities of real matter and energy when you can live in a fantastical world where your every whim is fulfilled? Why learn how to lead in a real universe when you can rock an imaginary one?"

"We work hard in the real universe. Why shouldn't we get to enjoy ourselves inworld?" asked Leisha. The others nodded in agreement.

"Enjoying entertainment is fine. But whatever happened to creating your own? To working out your own challenges instead of having it all done for you? Whatever happened to expressing your own self and ideas, instead of playing out someone else's design? To designing new technologies and developing new science?

"There was a time when Cybrids would gather inworld to create new music or theater of great sophistication. We participated in enormous works that required the coordinated activity of entire communities. But we don't do that anymore. A combination of boredom, laziness, and official discouragement of creative acts has made places like Vacationland the standard for inworld entertainment. People aren't even trying to be creative anymore. We're all falling prey to the worst kind of intellectual laziness and ennui.

"Outworld, Alum is really the only one who understands things, who has the big picture. Everything we do is on orders from Him. We make and fix machines. We move asteroids. We travel between the stars. We design new variants of life but all according to His directions and specifications. No one understands anything important about their work anymore." Darya held their gazes in silence until, one by one, each looked away.

She continued, "In Alternus, people can be part of actual life stories. They can immerse themselves in ongoing dramas and make choices that affect how that life develops, how it intertwines with others. They can learn how their world works. Alternus is going to draw Cybrids back into the universe of struggle, of problem-solving, and of fulfillment."

Gerhardt tapped the glass tabletop impatiently as he spoke. "Okay, I can see how Alternus might start to appeal to players once they get into it for a while. But getting them in there at all, never mind trying to change an attitude that has developed over millions of years, that could take millions of years more, don't you think? We only have a few years left at best before Alum's Divine Plan is activated. Less, if he starts taking the resistance seriously and steps up his schedule. So with all due respect, how exactly will this sim help our cause, and not just waste precious time we don't have?"

Darya smiled. "Our people will go in first. We'll assign them to instantiate within some key inhabitants: politicians, news people, the wealthy, and the socially prominent, a broad section of the most influential. Once they're in place, we'll mount a campaign of truth against Alum's plan. We'll tell people what Alum is really doing. We'll encourage them to rebel and, if necessary, to sabotage the machinery."

It was Mary's turn to object. "People are so accustomed to separating their inworld and outworld lives. I don't see anything happening inside Alternus that could motivate them to take action back in the real universe. You underestimate the overwhelming pull of comfort and inertia. Many won't *want* to believe what you have to say."

The others agreed.

"That's a possibility, but read this before you draw conclusions. Here's a sample of what we'll tell them." Several small flyers appeared in Darya's hand. She handed a copy to each of her acolytes who, mostly out of respect, took a minute to peruse the material.

The flyer succinctly summarized Alum's history and his "Divine Plan" for the universe. It called upon each individual to carry out small acts of sabotage against the machinery he'd ordered to be constructed around the black hole. It closed with a description of how individuals could convert their matter/antimatter propulsion units into bombs should harsher action be required.

Leisha was first to finish reading. "This is great. Really well set out."

"You've really thought this through," Gerhardt agreed, "right down to specific ways that people can slow or disrupt the construction."

"I hope I don't have to give my life to save the universe but I'm ready to do that if needed," added Qiwei. "This will work."

Three of them nodded appreciatively, but not Mary. Her disbelieving face looked from one compatriot to the next. She was stunned. She opened her mouth to say something, and then snapped it closed without a word. She crossed her arms and glared at Darya.

Darya pretended not to notice. She looked pleased with herself and with the ready acceptance of her plans. "I want everyone to think about which individuals from our various cells would be best to assume specific positions of responsibility in Alternus, and how to best publicize the new inworld among the Cybrids. We need maximum coverage in minimum time.

"We'll need to have our people instantiated in Alternus within thirty days, and ready for a big surge of visitors as soon as possible after that. I encourage you to make your first visit to Alternus as soon as you leave here, and then begin compiling the assignments list. The entry code at the recharge stations will be, 'There's no place like home.' We'll meet at the inworld United Nations Headquarters in New York City in one week to discuss your candidates." Darya soaked up their excited gazes.

Seeing she'd won them over to the next stage of the revolution, she dismissed them. "I think we're done for this meeting. On your way out, you'll receive updates to your inworld avatar security. Mary, could you stay behind with me for a few minutes, please?"

Leisha, Gerhardt, and Qiwei said speedy goodbyes and their avatars winked out as they rushed off to explore the new inworld.

Darya sat back in her chair, looking miserable and fatigued.

Mary was confused. The meeting had been a triumph for Darya. Why wasn't her mentor looking excited? Four acolytes had arrived despondent and three had left elated, full of renewed vigor and inspiration. Granted, she herself didn't feel as optimistic as the others but she felt the shift. Why would Darya look anything less than ecstatic?

"Well, that went better than I expected," Darya confessed.

"And yet, you don't seem very happy about it," Mary noted.

"You weren't convinced."

"No more than I was or wasn't before we met. Darya, we already knew everything in that brochure. It changed nothing."

"No, it didn't, did it?"

"The others ate it up," Mary said. "Qiwei is even ready to give up his life to the cause." She eyed Darya suspiciously. "What did you do?"

Darya took her time answering and when she did, she couldn't meet Mary's eyes. "The brochure is a virus of a sort. I directly altered their concepta, but only a few of the relevant beliefs."

"You *what*? How could you do that to them?" If the table hadn't been on a privacy cloud twenty meters above their nearest neighbor, Mary's outrage would have attracted the attention of the entire restaurant. As it was, a concerned waiter Partial popped into existence beside them to see if everything was okay. Darya dismissed him with a backhand wave.

Not wanting to draw further unwanted attention, Mary lowered her voice, shifting her rage from hot to cold. "How *could* you, Darya?" she hissed.

"Who knows more about Cybrid logic than me?"

"Yeah, I know the story. You could be the one person capable of designing a virus to circumvent all of our security routines. But what I meant was morally; how could you do that to us *morally*?"

"I've anguished over this for hundreds of years. In the end, I saw no choice. Everyone who visits inworld Alternus will be exposed to the brochure virus within weeks of instantiating. They will be *de facto* new recruits to the resistance."

"I can't believe you'd stoop so low! What about that moral high ground you're always preaching to us about?"

"Do I not teach that there is no ultimate good? That there is no ultimate evil? Ultimately, there only IS, and that is all," Darya quoted in response. "I think that saving the universe justifies the actions I've taken," she asserted, and punctuated her thoughts with an exclamatory sniff.

Whether that meant Darya was feeling defensive or testy, Mary wasn't sure. "I see. Convincing us with logic and passion wasn't working so you decided to just change our minds for us? What happened to our rights, Darya? Our free will? You're no different from Alum."

"Rights are a luxury the universe can't afford right now, and free will is just an illusion based on complex decision trees with non-controlled inputs and experiences," lectured Darya. "Anyway, I left *your* mind alone."

"Why bother?"

"I value your unadulterated advice. In the future, I may need an opinion that hasn't been tainted by my manipulations. I might not always agree with you, but I will always listen."

"Well, my opinion is that your plan is an unjustifiable abomination. My advice is to find another way."

A thin, tight line replaced Darya's lips. "I expected that would be your answer, but I had hoped you would understand the necessity of what I've done.

"Think about it from my point of view, Mary. I've been trying to convince people, fighting little skirmishes, gaining ground, losing ground, losing individuals, trying again, and losing again for millennia. We're running out of time."

Could she be right? Mary weighed Darya's plan as objectively as she could. She admired its brutal effectiveness but surely Alum wasn't really planning to destroy the entire universe and everyone in it. Was he? That didn't make sense. Darya had presented it as indisputable fact but she hadn't provided a shred of evidence. Wasn't it more likely Alum was creating a new mini-universe for them, a better one in which they could all live? Unfortunately, there was no evidence for that, either.

I guess it all boils down to who I'd put more faith in, Alum or Darya. Darya had proven herself to be nothing but trustworthy, time and time again without exception. *We trust Darya with our lives.*

On the other hand, the Darya she knew—correction, thought she knew—the Cybrid with whom she'd worked for millions of years, *that* Darya, would never have resorted to subjugating someone's mind. *Did the debacle in Lysrandia damage her perspective? Did it push her over the edge? Should I expose the entire movement to the authorities and stop her, or allow years of loyalty and friendship to override?*

Maybe I've been compromised and my thoughts are no longer my own. Maybe I'm free to think whatever I want so long as I don't want to report the rebellion. How could she rely on her beliefs and actions knowing that Darya had released a mind-altering virus on her colleagues? If she followed this line of reasoning to its logical conclusion, her grip on sanity would become even more tenuous that it already was.

What if this whole rebellion is just one psychopath against another? What will Darya do if I tell the others what she's done to them? Mary could feel her heart racing as she entertained the downward spiral of doubt and despair. Knowing that it was only a virtual heart did not soothe her outworld mind.

Hold on, woman, get a grip—Mary laughed out loud—*if she had infected me, wouldn't it be logical to assume that I'd be unable to entertain such doubts and thoughts as these? Isn't this proof enough that my mind hasn't been tampered with?* Instantly, she felt calmer. Though it was still possible that her mind wasn't entirely her own, it seemed largely untouched.

She regarded Darya coolly. "I can't agree with what you've done. Actually, I'm livid. And scared. And disappointed. But for now, I'll give you the benefit of the doubt." Darya's tight posture relaxed.

"Darya, if you want my advice, you'll need to let me in. I need to know what you know, what you're not telling us."

Darya considered her request. "Okay. I can transmit everything, my knowledge, my history, all of it—but you won't be able to handle it as you are."

"What do you mean?"

"Your standard Cybrid hardware and software need some upgrades to process it. I can install a copy of my quark-spin lattice in your brain, if you're willing, but we'll need to go to Secondus to do that."

The mention of going to one of Darya's secret labs caught Mary by surprise. She knew the labs existed and even that there had been three. But Darya was so concerned about security, that none of the acolytes had ever been invited to visit. Darya was now prepared to give Mary the coordinates to her most important base at tremendous personal risk. Mary felt humbled, and ashamed to have doubted Darya. "If that's the only way."

"It *is* the only way," answered Darya. "Here are the coordinates. I'll meet you there in fifteen hours."

"Okay, fifteen hours." Mary's avatar winked out of Vacationland, leaving Darya sitting alone at the table in the clouds.

The leader of the Cybrid rebellion looked at the distant waves and sighed heavily. *I hope I'm doing the right thing in trusting her. It would have been so much easier to expose Mary to the belief virus, but I would have lost a valuable friend and advisor. The added risk is worrisome but we'll be stronger with two distinct minds thinking about this instead of one, especially if one of those minds is Mary's.*

Darya took one last look around, content with her decision for the moment, and disappeared from Vacationland.

31

A Translucent sphere materialized in the deep vacuum of space, a kilometer away from an asteroid in the Gargus 718 solar system.

At first, the sphere contained nothing more than some oxygen-rich atmosphere and a small bit of ground defining a relative "top" and "bottom." The side of the sphere facing into the harsh rays of the system's Go-class star darkened to filter the light streaming onto the little clump of cacti. Soon the illumination matched what the tough plants would have received back on the planet they had just come from, several light minutes farther from the star.

The enclosed atmosphere quivered and stabilized. Darak and Brother Stralasi appeared inside, looking out at the asteroid. The monk's hands shot out to either side, while he struggled to adjust to the sudden and disorienting change in view.

A second earlier, they had been in orbit around the system's colony planet, staring down on the ravaged battlefield many klicks below. Now they stood on a small uprooted piece of that planet, having escaped with nothing but what was in the bubble. They gazed into the inky black space surrounding the enormous, pitted and cratered rock floating directly in front of them. Once Stralasi realized he was not in immediate danger of drifting off the little chunk of ground on which his feet somehow, miraculously, rested, he glared at Darak.

"Could you please *warn* me before you do that again?" he snapped.

Darak grinned at Stralasi with unabashed amusement. "My apologies; I forget you're not accustomed to this type of travel. I will attempt to provide more warning of an impending shift in future, provided *you* attempt a little more courtesy in your demeanor."

Stralasi bowed his head and apologized, "I do beg your pardon, my Lord." *Wait a second; what am I doing? Darak is no Shard of Alum. Indeed, he may very well be some kind of unknown but powerful demon.* He re-phrased, "I mean, uhm...Darak." Stralasi looked away from the other man, closed his eyes and took a deep, cleansing breath, remembering the centering exercises from his Initiate meditation classes.

After a few seconds, he opened his eyes and focused on the mountainous piece of rock hovering in space before the two of them. "Could you please tell me where we are?" He pointed at the asteroid, "And what that is?"

Darak smiled, "That is the basis for your civilization's comfort and success. It is a hollowed-out asteroid some fifty million klicks or so from your colony city. You do know what an asteroid is?"

Stralasi glowered, "Yes, I am a well-educated man, Darak. I do know about asteroids, although they occupy very little instructional time at the Alumita Seminary on Home World. They are of no relevance to Alum's People."

"I could tell you exactly how they are of considerable relevance to Alum's people," offered Darak, "but I think it will be more memorable if I were to show you."

Their capsule rushed toward the asteroid. Stralasi ducked and threw his hands out in an attempt to shield himself. Though he knew the bubble had to be moving toward the planetoid, he could feel no acceleration. Rather, his senses told him, the gigantic rock was moving toward *them*, intent on dashing their tiny bubble to bits. It slowed as they approached the rock and Stralasi again realized his foolish instinctual reactions. He lowered his arms, brushed off his garments, and tried to calm himself as he surveyed the nearby surface.

"Nice recovery," Darak commended his companion. "You are beginning to think about your automatic reactions and to allow your reasoning mind to dominate your simple-minded fear. I assure you there is nothing here to harm you."

"No Angels, then?" retorted Stralasi.

Darak grimaced. "Fair enough. Sending an Angel to intercept was a stronger reaction to my visit than I'd expected; I'll give you that. But, no, this outpost has no active Angels and none will be sent while we are here."

About ten meters from the surface, the sphere slowed to a gentle drifting roughly halfway from each end of the meteor. Stralasi could make out a few fist-sized stones on the sloped surface of the crater into which they were descending. Mesmerized, he failed to notice the large door irising open beneath them until their capsule plunged into the dark interior of the asteroid.

The portal winked closed behind them and a series of dim green lights invited them to continue along the featureless passageway stretching ahead. They glided forward smoothly. After a couple of minutes, another door whooshed aside and the corridor opened onto an enormous chamber. The size of the space was impossible for Stralasi to determine; it was crisscrossed with pillars of rock that obscured the views at the extremities. The area was filled with workbenches, equipment, and machinery of unidentifiable purpose. At each bench floated a metallic sphere.

"Securitors!" hissed Stralasi, and he spun around as if to bolt back down the corridor. He felt Darak's hand on his shoulder, turning him back to face the hollowed-out interior of the asteroid.

"Don't worry," Darak said softly. "They perceive us as one of their own. Besides, these Cybrids are *Servitors*, Constructors and Maintainers for the most part, the harmless cousins of the more aggressive Securitor."

"What are they doing here?" whispered Stralasi.

"Who do you think manufactures your vehicles, appliances, communications, and entertainment devices?" Darak asked, sweeping his hand in answer to his own question.

Stralasi addressed the heretic respectfully but sternly, "Sir, *all* things come from Alum."

Darak threw back his head and laughed, "Ha! Yes, of course, they do. But these are the beings that do all the actual work. Meanwhile, He—like every absolute ruler before Him—sits back and takes all the credit." Darak shook his head in wonder. "Over a hundred million years of civilization, and it still boils down to this. Unbelievable."

"Wait, are you telling me that all the goods for our entire civilization are made here?" Stralasi asked, looking around the relatively modest workshop. "That's impossible."

"Obviously, they're not made here for the entirety of human space. But, yes, each colonized system has its own similar factory, occupied by industrious Cybrids just like these."

"That's preposterous," objected Stralasi. "We would have been told of their presence, and of their service to Alum and to all of humanity."

"But you have been told. Are there not legends of the Cybrids of the Da'arkness and their evil industries? Of how they became overly ambitious and were disciplined by Alum?"

"Yes, everyone knows that Cybrids, with the exception of the Securitor class, are the enemies of Alum."

"Yet, here you see them providing manufacturing and repair services for your own Founding colony. How do you explain that?"

Darak propelled their protective bubble towards an idle Cybrid at a nearby bench. Stralasi fidgeted like a child, discomfited from being so close to the entity. As they drew alongside the Cybrid, the monk slid behind Darak and peered out from behind the man's shoulder.

A light blinked on the console of a device at one end of the workbench. It was a standard FixAll, identical to any one of the dozens of such devices in the Foundation ceraffice in Alumston, and commonly found throughout Alum's Realm.

The door to the FixAll opened, revealing a standard communications device inside. The Cybrid extended a pair of metallic tentacles from its smooth surface, removed the device, and placed it on the bench. Dozens more tentacles of various sizes extended from the Cybrid and set to work, faster than Stralasi's eyes could follow.

Within seconds, it had disassembled the comm device and laid out its components for inspection. Stralasi had not been aware there was any structure to the inside of the devices, or even that they could be opened up and inspected.

The Cybrid studied the device for a moment, purposefully moving its appendages across the components, briefly touching precise locations and then shifting to a new position.

"The repair Cybrid is conducting a variety of electronic diagnostic tests on various components," explained Darak. "The devices for measuring changes in voltage and current are built into its appendages, and the output is directed to its electronic brain for analysis. It's a boring job for such advanced minds like the Cybrids, but I suppose they find some level of satisfaction in being useful."

The Cybrid identified the defective component. It disposed of a small rectangular part in the bin off to one side and retrieved a replacement that appeared on a pad at the far-right of the bench. The tentacles whirred in a flurry of activity, fitting the new piece into place, running mid-assembly diagnostics, and sealing the cover. Satisfied with the results, it replaced the comm device inside the FixAll, closed the door, and patted twice above the indicator light blinking happily away on the console.

"These repair machines are connected through system-wide starsteps to receptacles in your Foundation building, as you have no doubt surmised by now. While prayers were being said on the planet surface to invoke Alum to repair or replace the damaged device placed inside the receptacle, the device was moved here.

"The Cybrids are quite skilled at diagnostics and repair; most problems can be resolved within minutes. If an excessive amount of time is needed, a new device is simply procured from storage. It appears on that small pad, a mini starstep, the same way as the replacement part appeared. Within minutes, the repaired or new device is sent to the planet."

Stralasi made no comment. He simply gaped in astonishment at the scene before him as he tried to process what Darak was telling him.

"You say these are starsteps but I see no one praying."

"Things do not work quite as you've been led to believe," Darak answered. "Look around you. That should be obvious."

The monk stared at Darak, challenging without comprehending.

Darak would not be deterred. "Don't worry too much about the details; it'll all fall into place as we go along. Shall I continue, then? As you will see, everything that is not grown directly on the planet, as on all the planets throughout Alum's Realm, is manufactured by Constructors in an asteroid similar to this one. Because Cybrids have nearly infinite patience and very little ambition, and because humans are content to have most of the real work done for them, the system is practically a perfectly designed economy.

"It's even better, because the primary consumer in this economy, that's you and the rest of Alum's People, believe that there is a single deity providing for all of your needs. In return for that, Alum receives your obedience and allegiance to His Realm.

"The system's so beautiful, so elegant, that it has endured for tens of millions of years. Until very recently, even I couldn't find a good reason to oppose it."

Finally, Stralasi found his voice. "But if the Cybrids are creations of the Da'arkness, why would they do Alum's work and help the People to fulfill His plans?"

Darak regarded Stralasi dubiously. "Apart from reading it in your various holy books, what evidence do you have that this Da'arkness actually exists?"

"Because in all of space, The People can inhabit only the planets where Alum's Light may shine upon them. The rest of space is cursed forever to be in the Da'arkness. It repels Alum's Light."

"And yet the surface of this asteroid was equally illuminated by the same local sun that shines upon Gargus 718.5, was it not?"

"True, but the light was harsh and unfriendly."

"That's because the asteroid has no atmosphere to soften the sun's rays. Nevertheless, it was illuminated. And, despite anything you may have been told, you saw the Cybrids repairing devices that are used by the People on the surface of the planet."

"Yes, I did," came the reluctant reply.

"The Cybrids are not your enemy, and they never were. They are trapped inside this beautiful system of religious economics, the same as you."

"What is this 'religious economics' you speak of?"

"Economics is just the way that goods and services are produced and traded. Any traditional economist from the early days of humans on Origin would call this system simple, yet elegant. There are no currencies, no banks, only moderate trade between planets, and so on. But it is clearly a method of distributing resources, including labor, so that makes it an economic system.

"Couple that with a god from whom all things flow and to whom all activity is devoted, and you have the most stable economic system ever invented: a religious economic system that stands on five pillars.

"The first pillar is all around us: Cybrid labor. The Cybrids perform all the most important work throughout the Realm. They explore. They mine. They construct. They maintain. They innovate."

"The People of the Realm work hard," Stralasi protested.

"Certainly," Darak agreed. "But everything they do, all the resources and technology they use, comes to them through the work of Cybrids. Everything flows from Cybrids *not* from Alum."

"Perhaps not directly, but certainly through His Love and through the power of this 'economics' system you talk about."

Darak sneered, "I'd say, not so much through his love as through his monopoly on energy and transportation. That part is pure classical economics."

"What is a *monopoly?*" asked an irritated Stralasi.

"It is when one person or business controls access to something for an entire society. In this case, Alum controls the supply of endless energy and the transportation between star systems. It's what ultimately allows him to completely control all goods and services. His monopoly on energy and transportation is the second pillar. And his monopoly has the best protection ever. Only a god can provide what Alum provides. And there's only one of those. Or so you've been taught."

"I am completely confused. You claim that Alum *controls* everything but, in reality, He forces none of us to love Him. We choose to receive His Glory and His Grace. In return, He has given us His Love and His Purpose. Even if what you say about the Cybrids is true, clearly they have also chosen to give Him their devotion."

Darak grimaced. "It's not much of a choice when the alternative is a slow death in the dark, isolated from the rest of civilization. Still, over the tens of millions of years that humanity has been spreading out into the universe, there *have* been a few instances of Cybrid-led rebellions. Some colonies believed they could survive happily in isolation. But Alum's Angels destroyed almost every system that ever rebelled against his so-called love."

"Machines—mindless automation—can't rebel," Stralasi practically spat the word. "How could they rebel against anything without the leadership of their master, Da'ar?"

"They are no more mindless than you," replied Darak, "and they are similarly no less enslaved. Just as you, they are slaves to Alum, not Da'ar." He waved his hand dismissively. "But that will all become clear over our journey. To start, let's finish touring the rest of this facility."

Stralasi was still confused and there were dozens of questions he wanted to ask. What Darak was telling him flew in the face of everything he knew to be true. Alum *did* provide for all. Even if He had hidden the role of these Constructor and Maintainer Cybrids within His Plan, Stralasi knew it had to be for a good reason. *Alum works in mysterious ways.*

Darak had to be a powerful demon to oppose Almighty Alum, Stralasi surmised. To listen to him was to allow poisonous doubts to creep into his mind. *No! My faith is strong! I will not permit these lies to weaken it. Alum is testing me, and I will prove worthy.*

The sphere carried the two travelers peacefully through the construction and repair activity. On all sides, as far as one could see, Cybrid tentacles flew in purposeful activity. No Securitors challenged their passage and none of the Cybrids seemed to pay them any attention. Their tour continued without interruption.

Stralasi observed floaters, cooking appliances, entertainment and comm units, furniture, and specialized analysis and medical devices being built or fixed on adjacent benches in a buzz of disorganized activity that threatened to overwhelm him.

"You've probably noticed that this place seems awfully large for such a small Founding colony," Darak said, interrupting the monk's thoughts.

"I don't really have anything to compare it to."

"True, but look around you. Wouldn't you say that there are rather more things being built or repaired here than Alumston actually needs?"

Stralasi took a closer look. He counted over a hundred visible workstations and estimated at least triple that number behind the visible support columns, so that would make for at least a thousand workbenches in this asteroid workshop alone, all busy.

Of the workbenches before them, he estimated that maybe fifty percent held machinery he could identify; the rest were a mystery. "I count about twenty new floaters being constructed. That *would* seem to exceed Alumston's immediate needs. To be honest, I don't recognize half of the other devices being constructed. We only have fifty FixAlls in Alumston, and they're rarely all in use at the same time."

Darak smiled approvingly. "So far, I've told you about the first two pillars of Alum's economic system: the Cybrids, and his monopoly.

"The third pillar is unrestricted, steady growth. Each newly colonized planet siphons off the excess human population from the rest of the Realm as it builds outward from the original Alumston. The expansion of human colonization never stops because Alum's Plan requires it to spread endlessly. Once humanity left Earth—what you call Origin—it was no longer limited to the resources of a single solar system. Growth without limit makes for beautiful economics.

"The fourth pillar of this brilliant system is that humanity is no longer limited to exploiting the resources of their own precious planets, not since Alum first established and expanded the Realm. Nor does it need to be concerned about the effect its industry might have on the planetary ecology.

"With the help of a cooperative Constructor Cybrid population, humans have laid claim to the readily available resources of asteroid belts and Oort clouds in every system that has been colonized. The machines you don't recognize are Mining Cybrids, system exploration drones, more Constructors, and even a few deep space explorer ship components for the next wave of colonization to come."

Stralasi was dazzled; it was too much to absorb at once. As an Alumit-educated Brother, he knew about Alum's Purpose to spread humanity and, more importantly, to establish His Realm throughout all of space without end. He also knew that exploration was conducted by automated deep-space probes, though he'd thought that Alum Himself directed the mindless machines. After all, finding new inhabitable star systems was the work of thousands upon thousands, even millions, of years. Who but Alum could endure over such lengthy stretches of time?

He had always assumed that the probes were constructed in the Home World system by the most advanced cities in Alum's Realm and then starstepped to the Frontier to begin their journey outward. But he could see that, if local resources were available, it made sense to perform the construction right at the Frontier, itself.

As their bubble of atmosphere, gravity, and warmth rounded a cluster of support columns near one edge of the chamber, Stralasi caught a glimpse of a tall, muscular figure with skin like flowing quicksilver and opalescent wings. He almost fainted; he hadn't resolved his residual fear from the recent battle on the planet's surface.

He was about to call Darak's attention, when he noticed the Angel had no head or, rather, its head sat motionless on a nearby workbench. The extended tentacles of the adjacent Maintainer Cybrid reached through the open neck and into the Holy being's body. The world swam unsteadily in front of Stralasi's eyes.

"And this, what you see before you," said Darak, breaking the spell of the grotesquely inconceivable, "is the fifth pillar of Alum's economy: Angels."

Stralasi could only stare, speechless and mesmerized, as the Maintainer worked on the Angel.

Darak continued, "Even though space is large and empty, from time to time humanity has encountered other advanced intelligences. Some were friendly but most were hostile to Alum's expansion plans. However, the armed might of a Wing of Angels backed by Alum's supernatural powers has so far proven equal to the task of removing all opposition."

Stralasi turned to Darak. "The Aelu?"

"Certainly the most obvious example," Darak agreed.

"Alum tried to bring them into the Realm."

"Oh, there were negotiations and even certain periods of peaceful co-existence between us for a while. Eventually, though, Alum found that the aliens could not be ruled as easily as humans and Cybrids. It was a short path from uncertainty to discomfort, to displeasure, to agitation, to confrontation and, finally, to war and annihilation. Over time, Alum came to prefer the predictable over the chaotic. Aliens have been so very chaotic, so unprepared to accept that Alum's Word should be the only word."

"Are all the Angels like this? Simply...machines?"

"There's nothing simple about them at all. But, yes, they are all non-biological constructs like Cybrids and Securitors."

"I can't believe it!"

"It is always preferable to believe the truth over a lie, no matter how powerful the authority who tells you," responded Darak quietly.

"But why would the Alumit deceive us in this way?" cried Stralasi.

"Don't worry, neither Alum nor his Alumit have acted in support of outright evil. They have designed and implemented a societal system that has endured for tens of millions of years. That system has brought peace to humans across hundreds of galaxies and eradicated any potentially destabilizing enemies. It would be almost perfect, if it weren't so...perfect."

Stralasi pondered that for a while as their bubble passed by the Angel. Its attendant Maintainer entered another corridor. The Good Brother knew the life he enjoyed among the People was the best conceivable, though he resented being kept ignorant about how it all worked. He couldn't see how this new insight, courtesy of Darak, would help him to be happier or better in any way. Quite the contrary.

"If Alum's Realm is so perfect, or so *nearly* perfect, why would you oppose Him?"

The bubble stopped, and Darak turned to Brother Stralasi. "The universe is an imperfect place. It sprung from chaos and it brims with surprises. That is what makes it so wonderful, so alive. If you make it predictable, you destroy everything about it that is important. That wouldn't be perfection; that would be hell."

He turned away, and suddenly they were somewhere else.

32

LARRY SAT IN THE EIGHTH ROW, one seat in from the center aisle. He rested his chin on his hands and stared dismally at the empty stage. The shooter was in Police custody. Ambulance attendants had strapped the wounded Darian to a stretcher and whisked him away, with Kathy and Greg glued to his side. Larry had tried to make his way over to them through the panicked crowd but it was impossible. *They didn't even bother to look for me.*

He shouldn't have been surprised. Things had been tense between him and his lab mates since last month. It started with that big blowout they'd had over whether or not to expose themselves to Darian's engineered virus. The following morning, they'd all shown up for work a little late, and something had changed between them. A coolness had settled over them.

Adding to the irreconcilable moral and philosophical differences, they'd said things that could not be unsaid. They were only human, after all, and hurt feelings, a sense of betrayal, and burgeoning resentment was all it took to undermine the friendship they once valued.

They maintained an awkward but professional working relationship, and they worked as hard as ever, but the light banter and easy comfort they'd once enjoyed with one another was gone.

The past few weeks had been especially trying for all of them, with Larry constantly monitoring the other two scientists for subtle changes in their abilities or personalities.

"Don't worry; I'm sure he'll be okay."

The deep voice snapped Larry out of his reverie. A man in his mid-sixties, escorted down the auditorium stairs by three Secret Service types, was heading his way. They wore characteristic black suits, navy blue ties, and comm gear in their ears. Despite the hall being nearly empty, their eyes scanned the room continuously, presumably assessing the potential threat of hidden assassins.

The man who had spoken seemed at peace, unconcerned about possible danger. His face reflected nothing more than kind concern for the worried scientist.

"Reverend LaMontagne," Larry recalled from Darian's introduction to the audience. "Thank you. I hope so; it looked pretty serious."

"You are Dr. Rusalov, no?

Surprised at being recognized, Larry nodded.

"Why didn't you accompany your mentor and friends to the hospital?"

Larry frowned. "I couldn't get to them in time. Anyway, I'd just be in the way there. There's nothing I can do to help."

"True," said the Reverend. "And it doesn't seem like Dr. Leigh is the kind to need moral support. Nevertheless, your colleagues seemed to feel that *they* should go with the ambulance." The Reverend allowed several seconds for that to sink in. "Do I sense a little discord in the Leigh research group?" He smiled sympathetically, like a kindly father or grandfather might have done.

Larry regarded the man, trying to decide whether he should say anything. If he confessed his doubts about Darian's methods, it might open his friends and supervisor to unwelcome scrutiny, perhaps get the lab shut down, maybe even result in legal action. This man was from outside the group, outside the university. Heck, since secession, he was from outside the country.

But the Reverend's approach struck a chord. Larry desperately needed to talk with somebody. He was being squeezed out of the gang of lattice-imbued geniuses, and he could use a sympathetic ear. Reverend Alan LaMontagne was probably as sympathetic an ear as Larry was likely to find. *If you can't trust a man of God, who can you trust?* Talking to the Reverend couldn't do the group any harm, and the man might even offer some sage advice.

"Things *have* been difficult these last few weeks, I guess," admitted Larry. "The physics we're working with has always been excruciatingly difficult to understand but lately we've also been dealing with a few, I don't know, *ethical* issues. I'm just having a hard time sorting it all out, is all."

"Do you mind if I sit down?" Reverend LaMontagne gestured to the seat beside Larry.

Larry didn't object, and the Reverend gratefully took the empty place. "As a spiritual advisor, I'd like to think I might have some insight into moral issues but," he chuckled, "I don't normally expect to find many such issues in a Physics department." He sighed, "Dr. Leigh does seem to have a propensity for pushing the boundaries, though, and not just academically." He patted Larry's arm consolingly. "Why don't you tell me what's troubling you?"

"It's hard to say. He always has an answer, and it always seems so reasonable, so well thought out, and so well supported by evidence."

"And yet?" LaMontagne encouraged, with a gentle tilt of his head.

"And yet, I'm not convinced he's actually right. Something just seems wrong, deeply wrong, about the direction we're heading."

"Something wrong with the math?" The Reverend asked.

Larry, struggling for words, missed the subtle attempt at humor entirely. "I wouldn't know. Without a dendy lattice like Darian's, the math is way beyond me. But that's not really it. I mean, he's just so smug in saying that a Creator couldn't possibly exist. It seems to me like God would have to be so incomprehensible that such math would be as far above Darian, as his math is above me."

"Yes, I should think so. The arrogance of some scientists is truly amazing to regard."

"Do you think he might actually be...evil?" Larry struggled with the idea.

"Darian? Hmm. I'm afraid even I can't tell you that. Normally, I would think he's simply misguided as to what science can and cannot prove. But Darian Leigh seems to enjoy rubbing our noses in his *superior* perspective in a most annoying way. "

"*That's* for sure." Larry's bitterness added years to his face. "But if he *can* figure out the basis for natural laws then couldn't he, potentially, learn to manipulate those laws? He'd have God-like powers. Wouldn't challenging God's dominion over creation be evil by definition?"

"Do you really think he might be able to do that?"

"Well, as I said, it's beyond my ability to figure that out. But *he* thinks he'll be able to, and soon."

"I see." LaMontagne rubbed his chin thoughtfully. "Let's assume that he's right, that his research does lead to a new understanding of what makes the universe work, and that he's able to modify the physical laws of nature, the laws given by God, in some manner. Does that mean there is no original Creator? No, it does not. In fact, it would rather seem to support the idea of an Intelligent Designer whose Word spoke the natural laws into existence in order to create our universe as it is."

"Well, there's always the multiverse theory."

"The idea that all possible universes exist? Don't look so surprised, Larry. I try to keep up with the arguments that *disfavor* the existence of Our Lord, as well. Know thy enemy, and all that. But even Darian doesn't believe that any of those other universes are real. And the multiverse wouldn't prove the Creator *doesn't* exist, any more than a single universe proves that He *does* exist."

"Why not?"

"The multiverse would just provide more ways and more possibilities for God to demonstrate His infinite love and wisdom. Nothing about the multiverse would answer *why* we are all here, why *something* rather than *nothing* exists, any more than a single universe does. No, I don't believe that we'll ever find an answer to why everything exists until we acknowledge the purpose of it all is simply to bring glory to its Creator."

Larry relaxed. "I agree. I believe, like Newton and Einstein, that there's no purpose in trying to understand it all except to catch a glimpse into the mind of God. Knowledge for the purpose of raising man above God does not feel right to me."

The Reverend smiled and stood up, "Well, then. See? That wasn't so hard to figure out, was it?"

Larry hung his head. "That isn't all. There's more."

The Reverend sat back down. "I wondered if there might be." He waited patiently as Larry grappled with his conscience.

"You know Darian's story, don't you?"

"Doesn't everyone? A fascinating tale of hubris, risky experimentation, and playing God."

"I mean, his mother's story."

"So did I."

"Darian's mom was once quoted as saying, 'I don't *play* God; it's rather hard work.'"

LaMontagne harrumphed his disapproval. "She *would* say that. Nevertheless."

"Did you know that Darian's strain of intelligence-enhancing dendy was never approved for use by the FDA?"

"Or any other respectable agency, for that matter," added the Reverend.

"The thing is, he offered to...*infect* us, the rest of his team, with the same dendy virus. You know, so we could grow our own enhanced-IQ lattices and be better able to help his research." He reached into his jacket pocket and pulled out the virus-containing capsule, showing it to LaMontagne. "It's so small," he whispered.

The Reverend scowled, "When Our Good Lord created man, He did not intend for his handiwork to become a machine. This goes beyond eating the fruit of the Tree of Knowledge of Good and Evil. This is becoming the Tree, itself."

"I know," Larry whispered. "The thing is, my two colleagues, Greg and Kathy, they took their pills. Enhanced dendy lattices are developing inside their brains as we speak." He imagined the RNA strands invading their brain cells, forcing them to lay down silicene strands tipped with semiconductor sensors and activators where they met neural synapses. "I've already noticed a few changes in their performance; they pick up details faster than I can, faster than they did before."

LaMontagne rubbed his eyes, suddenly fatigued. "Thank you for telling me this," he said. "I have no doubt that Dr. Leigh's actions are illegal but, here in Pacifica, I'm afraid I have little authority beyond reporting his indiscretions."

"Do you think I should call the FDA or maybe the police?"

The Reverend closed his eyes for a moment of prayerful contemplation. When he opened them again, they were cold and decisive. "No." He leaned in close to Larry and continued in a conspiratorial hush, "If you are willing, it would help us, all of us, to have someone sympathetic to our viewpoint working closely with Dr. Leigh."

"I suppose I could report his activities to you."

"Would that endanger your position with the team?"

"It would be hard to get much lower than I am right now."

"If you don't think it would be too risky, it could be helpful to have someone with a superior moral compass and a solid foundation in Our Savior, Yeshua, to monitor their activities."

"I can do that," Larry said. "But I'm not a member of your Church."

LaMontagne smiled. "Never mind that. His spirit is strong within you, whether you know it or not."

Larry extended his palm that the dendy pill toward the Reverend. "What should I do with this?"

The Reverend took the pill from his hand. "Leave it with me. I'll have it safely destroyed."

Larry's immediate response was panic. He'd been struggling for weeks over whether he should accept Darian's priceless gift. To have that choice taken from him so casually, only heightened his uncertainty. He searched the Reverend's face and found confidence, clearly written, along with something else he couldn't decode, perhaps a bit of eagerness. *It's going to be okay. The Reverend is so much better equipped to deal with dilemmas like this than I am.* Having come to terms with his decision, Larry let the sense of relief wash over him.

"Please make sure you treat it like medical waste and have it incinerated. It's too dangerous to flush down the toilet."

"Never you fear." The Reverend laid his hand on the scientist's shoulder and intoned, "Bless this man, this warrior, My Lord. Bless his sacrifice and give strength to his resolve. May he achieve an even deeper love for You through his service."

LaMontagne stood, leaned forward, and kissed Larry on the top of his head, a blessing that was oddly comforting to the scientist. He pulled a business card from his jacket pocket. "I have to go now, but here's my private contact information. I will always be available for you. Don't hesitate to call me anytime, day or night. You are a brave man, Dr. Rusalov. Rejoice and do not fear, for God has smiled upon the sacrifice you make in His name."

The Reverend grasped Larry's right hand in both of his own, shaking it with deep respect. "Do you know Dr. Lucius Pratt?"

"In the Philosophy Department? A little. I met him when Darian first arrived at the university. We were invited to join them at the welcome lunch. Darian's postdocs, that is. Why?"

LaMontagne pursed his lips. "Dr. Pratt is friendly to our cause, as you might have surmised." Larry smiled and nodded, recalling the debate between Pratt and Darian over lunch that day. *How could I forget? That was the most painful free lunch I've ever experienced, trapped there between the two of them while they sparred, and no polite way to duck out.*

The Reverend continued, "If you'd like, I could ask him to check in with you from time to time." He held up his hand to quell any objection to being supervised that might be forming on Larry's lips. "Don't worry. He won't be *watching* you. He'll just provide a sympathetic ear when you need one. You can use him as a sounding board—but only if you want."

Larry cast his gaze at the floor. "As long as he's there as my friend and not as your spy."

"No, nothing like that. You are undertaking a journey on our behalf at considerable personal risk, and I just want to make sure you have ongoing support close at hand. You will never need to face this alone."

Larry nodded his acquiescence. "Okay, I'll speak with him."

LaMontagne smiled, more with his eyes than his mouth, and signaled his security people. The four of them continued lockstep down the stairs and out of the hall, leaving a bewildered young scientist watching them as they left. *What did I just get into?*—Larry wondered.

Passing the abandoned refreshment table in the foyer, Reverend LaMontagne helped himself to a bottle of juice and opened the cap with a satisfying "snap". As they entered the lobby, he sent his retinue outdoors to scout the main entrance for any possible threats. With his team occupied and no one in the nearly empty lobby paying him any attention, he popped the dendy pill into his mouth and took a swig of juice to wash it down.

He beamed in appreciation of his incredibly good fortune, and in anticipation of the tremendous advantage that he had just been given on behalf of his church. *Thank you, Lord, for steering events to this time and place, and for this glorious opportunity to enhance my capabilities in service to Thee.* He continued to the exit where his car waited.

33

NCSA recording of a conversation between Dr. Lucius Pratt (Simon Fraser University, Burnaby, BC, Pacifica) and Reverend Alan LaMontagne (Austin, Tx, New Confederacy) November 14, 2037.

Pratt: Hello?

LaMontagne: Dr. Pratt, this is Alan LaMontagne.

Pratt: Reverend LaMontagne! Please tell me we were not in any way involved in what just happened.

LaMontagne: Dr. Pratt, you *are* aware this conversation is automatically being recorded, right?

Pratt: Yes. Yes, of...of course. I'm just in shock.

LaMontagne: Understandable. But you can rest assured that the Church had no involvement with the shooter. He acted alone for whatever personal reasons he might have had. His actions are between him and God, now.

Pratt: Thank you. That is good to hear. Have you heard how Dr. Leigh is doing?

LaMontagne: We do not have any news yet. It's no secret that we would view it as the Justice of Yeshua should his prognosis turn unfavorable. It is unfortunate, nevertheless, that one so young and so bright should be called to account for his actions before the Lord.

Pratt: It is sometimes shocking to see how swift and terrible His Justice is [*sighs*]. But Darian did bring this injury on himself. He has never made any effort to temper his impetuous research or its implications.

LaMontagne: No, he hasn't, has he? Which brings me to the reason for my call.

Pratt: Oh?

Lamontagne: It seems that Dr. Leigh has been engaging in some very questionable human research in his spare time.

Pratt: What do you mean?

Lamontagne: You are aware of his involvement with the dendy research at Neuro Nano Devices, the company his mother founded?

Pratt: Yes, everyone's aware of his research.

Lamontagne: Actually, there are several lines of that research that very few are acquainted with. But that's not important right now. Did you know that dendy lattices can be grown from engineered RNA introduced into one's system using a viral transmission vector? It would appear that Dr. Leigh has managed to procure or manufacture a vector quite similar to the one responsible for his special lattice.

Pratt: That is surprising. I would have thought that would be illegal.

Lamontagne: It certainly is. Intelligence-enhancing lattices are strictly forbidden. Neuro Nano assured the FDA that all copies of that particular vector were destroyed, and that there isn't a single synthesis company that can legally recreate it. Nonetheless, Dr. Leigh has shared with his three lab assistants that he has that virus. Furthermore, he offered it to them.

Pratt: What? That's outrageous! He can't do that.

Lamontagne: Legally, Dr. Leigh can't force them to take the pill. Simply being in possession of it is strictly against the FDA ruling. Unfortunately, the punishment for obtaining, offering or using banned medicinal substances has been weakened since the dismemberment of the former United States of America, particularly in Pacifica. He would face no more than a small fine. But the real news is that two of his team members have already ingested the vector; only one resisted the temptation.

Pratt: Oh, my goodness. Do you mean to say there are now three humans with enhanced intelligences at the University? As if one wasn't trouble enough.

Lamontagne: I presume it will take some amount of time before any significant behavioral differences are observable. But you are quite right. One such person in the entire world is a blasphemy to the Lord. Three is an abomination.

Pratt: I should report this to campus authorities.

Lamontagne: I'm not sure that's the best course of action. The university has been quite thrilled to have a single enhanced-intelligence Professor. Imagine their glee at discovering they have three.

Pratt: So what can we do?

Lamontagne: Well, as luck would have it, I just finished having a very interesting conversation with the only member of Dr. Leigh's team to refuse the pill.

Pratt: Who was that?

LaMontagne: Dr. Larry Rusalov. I've just spoken with him and he has been touched by the Divine Light. Despite a life dedicated to the perversities of science, he has not turned away from Our Lord. He believes deeply that there is something fundamentally wrong with Dr. Leigh's theories, and he has faith in the Creator.

Pratt: That's remarkable.

LaMontagne: Indeed. Furthermore, he has agreed to keep us apprised of the activities and progress of Dr. Leigh and his team.

Pratt: Reverend LaMontagne, I'm surprised that we can condone such action.

LaMontagne: His choices were his own. He also handed over the poison pill to me to destroy. Of course, I made sure right away that the pill met its proper end.

Pratt: Yes, of course.

LaMontagne: It would be helpful if you could meet with Dr. Rusalov every few weeks. Relay what the group is up to, and help him continue to hold to the Truth.

Pratt: I will reach out to him right away.

LaMontagne: The way of intellectualism has long been known for its temptations. His journey will be a difficult one, fraught with the peril of being blinded to the Truth by scientific theories.

Pratt: Yes, too much wrong thinking can make it difficult to see the Light of Our Lord.

LaMontagne: Fortunately, Dr. Rusalov has come to us in time. We can help him stay the course.

Pratt: Very well. I'll arrange to meet with him.

LaMontagne: Might I suggest you make every effort to keep your relationship discreet? I don't believe his colleagues would look favorably upon his discussions with you.

Pratt: Agreed. I will invite him somewhere quiet, off-campus.

LaMontagne: Thank you. I think that would be best. Please keep me apprised of your discussions.

34

LUXURIANT, VERDANT LIFE OVERWHELMED THEIR SENSES. Darak and Brother Stralasi settled gently on the gravel pathway and their protective sphere dissolved. Lush ferns, flowers, and tall grasses swayed welcomingly. Branches from the tall trees lining the trail stretched over their bare heads to shade them from the bright light above. The sound of trickling water from a small cascade feeding into a nearby stream caught their ears. Stralasi marveled at the fields of corn, wheat, and vegetables curving slightly upward. *Wait a minute. Upward?*

Stralasi's eyes followed the evenly tilled rows as they receded up and away, into the sky. A little disoriented, he looked for landmarks by which to situate himself. Once he figured out the lay of the land, he was no less disoriented.

They appeared to be standing at the bottom of an impossibly large cylinder of green and blue encircling a glowing tube of light. A soft breeze cooled his face and moved across the crops in waves.

On the opposite side of the cylinder, past the dazzling light, he could make out a body of water. About midway up, he spied what looked like a herd of cattle grazing on tender shoots near the stream. *Midway up.* Massive cables, about a hand's width in diameter, periodically stretched "upward" from the ground to anchor points along the central light tube. *Phenomenal!* He clapped his hands together in marvel and thankful prayer. There was more life visible in this tube than he had seen in any one place for ages.

Darak stopped for a moment, as well, to take it all in. "Beautiful isn't it?"

"Where are we?"

"This is the local Integration Lab."

"Where? I don't see any lab." Stralasi was familiar with clean rooms and stainless steel work surfaces where technicians tested food quality.

Darak laughed and waved his hand, indicating the flourishing life around them. "This! The entire hollowed out asteroid. It's all one giant laboratory for examining how well various genetic modifications work before the organisms are shipped to the planet's surface."

Stralasi looked perplexed. "I don't understand."

"I imagine this must be a lot for you to take in. Listen, we're walking on the inner surface of a completely hollowed-out asteroid, which is spinning in order to provide a semblance of gravity to the garden inside. This side of the garden is completely Standard Life."

He waved to indicate the opposite arc of the chamber. "The far side is a replica of life that existed on Gargus 718.5 before Alumston was founded. Between here and there is a gradient, a mixture of the two life forms. The purpose of this entire structure is to test the modifications they make to plants and animals, and help them to best adapt to the environment on the planet."

"What do you mean, *modifications*?"

"Well, Gargus 718.5's native life is quite different from Standard Life, isn't it?"

"Yes, completely."

"A Standard Life animal would not fare very well there. It wouldn't be able to eat local vegetation or hunt what few small native animals remain. Standard plants would be ill-equipped to deal with the unfamiliar mixture of elements. So they have altered the genes—what you might think of as the *life force*—of various Standard Life organisms, in the lab facilities on this asteroid in order to outcompete the native Gargus 718.5 life in its own environment."

"Who is this 'they' you keep talking about?" Stralasi asked, annoyed.

"The Cybrids. They are quite skilled at many things besides fixing other machinery."

"Why would Alum have provided such a beautiful place for Cybrids of the Da'ark, when his own people struggle to expand His Realm on the surface of so many inhospitable planets?"

Darak sighed wistfully, as he took in the view. "That's a very good question. When we first left Origin, we lived for generations in habitats just like this one and like the Machine Shop asteroid that we just came from. Living inside asteroids seems to have fallen out of favor among humans more recently."

"What do you mean, 'When we first left Origin'? Were you there? Do you claim to be immortal like Our Lord?"

"No. Nothing like immortal," replied Darak. "I mean, the collective 'we.' When we humans, The People, left Origin, we shared these hollowed-out habitats in the Origin solar system with the Cybrids for a time. Eventually, we found other planets to inhabit. Humans colonized them, while the Cybrids stayed in the asteroids to tend the gardens, make things, and fix things. Eventually, people simply forgot there ever was a time when they shared space with the Cybrids. And now, it would seem, you've forgotten about them being anything but an enemy."

"The People and the Cybrids lived together at one time?" Stralasi was incredulous.

"Yes. Over time, they came to be segregated by their different preferred environments. Humans require light, air, water, and food. Cybrids were better suited to exploring and exploiting other asteroids in the vacuum of space, without the inconvenience of gravity to impair their graceful cruising or oxygen to corrode their mechanisms.

"Both groups enjoyed garden asteroids like this one when it came time to rest. It might surprise you to know that even Cybrids appreciate a park like this."

"But they're just machines," protested Stralasi.

"They're much more human than you think."

Stralasi looked doubtful. "They don't look very human."

"Not externally, no," replied Darak. "But their brains are based on the structure of the human brain. Their thoughts are very human, and they think of themselves as thoroughly human."

"I find that hard to believe."

"We'll visit their 'inworld' in a while; you may change your mind." Brother Stralasi frowned. *I doubt that very much*—he muttered under his breath.

The men passed from the covered path into dazzling artificial daylight. The Good Brother's head was still swimming from Darak's lecture on Alum's economic system. And now, this claim that Cybrids and The People were on equal footing in the eyes of the Lord? He rubbed his eyes wearily, trying his best to unlearn a lifetime of prejudices and falsehoods.

He lowered his hands. A Cybrid was standing no more than a few meters away. The machine appeared to be playing in the dirt. Its tentacles flew. First, creating a half dozen little furrows, pouring a little liquid into each track, poking small seedlings into the soil, and covering their roots with more soil and a firm pat. Its other tentacles extended the furrows ahead of the Cybrid's hovering body.

Stralasi turned to Darak and whispered, "Doesn't it see us? Why hasn't it challenged our presence?"

Darak laughed. "For a master of meditation, you aren't very relaxed, are you? There's no need to worry, or to whisper. The Cybrid's visual, auditory, and electromagnetic sensors all detect us. I have interfered with its internal processing and instructed it not to pay any attention to us. It sees us but will ignore us. We're perfectly safe." Something caught his attention at the far side of the field. "Ah, there's what I was looking for. Come with me; let's take a closer look at the heart of the operation."

They made their way across a field of manicured grass and stopped at the entrance of a small but busy structure. They waited for the next Cybrid to pass through the archway and fell in behind it. Darak practically bounded down the ramp and into the brightly lit corridor. Stralasi followed cautiously, reluctant to leave the luxuriant growth of the garden behind. To the monk's dismay, they were soon completely underground. He didn't have long to sulk, though.

Off the main corridor, a group of softly lit caverns nestled many more tidily potted seedlings. Some of the rooms were separated from the corridor by glass doors through which Stralasi spotted colorful birds and a host of animals ranging from small herbivores to large feline predators, all roaming freely.

As they made their way along the corridor, Darak occasionally entered a habitat to caress the shoots and leaves, or tapped on glass doors to attract the attention of animals inside. For the most part, the animals were content in their activities and took no notice of the two men passing by.

They followed the Cybrid into a room filled with incomprehensible scientific instruments that buzzed, blipped, and blinked. The Cybrid floated peacefully in front of the instruments, its tentacles tucked inside its spherical shell.

Stralasi could discern no activity in the chamber and wondered what its purpose could be. "This is all very interesting, I'm sure, but the garden was much prettier."

"Ah. You do not see it as the Cybrid sees it. Just a moment, please. I'll adjust the feed to your lattice."

"Wait! Don't...," started Stralasi and then he felt a short, sharp pain in his head. His hands shot up in reflex, and he opened his mouth to holler. But as fast as the pain had hit him, it was over. He dropped his hands back to his side and scowled at his traveling companion.

"Well, you wouldn't have been able to experience this properly if I hadn't done that," Darak explained. "Now, I'll connect you to the Cybrid's sensory overlay."

What Stralasi had perceived as a still and unexciting room was now bursting with color and activity. The monk was rendered speechless. Throughout the chamber, multi-hued data presentations blossomed above the mysterious instruments.

The two-meter Cybrid now appeared translucent to him. Encapsulated within its ghostly sphere was the somewhat more solid image of a young woman in a flowing white lab robe. Her appearance and attire were identical to that of an Alumit technician in any of the Foundation ceraffices throughout Alum's Realm.

The woman was engrossed in a variety of data screens floating in front of her. The array of letters, numbers, and images were unrecognizable to Brother Stralasi. She deftly scanned, shuffled, rearranged, and transferred data between various screens, sometimes opening or closing views, shifting or magnifying the displays for closer examination.

She turned to the two men. "May I help you?" she asked, with no hint of surprise that two strangers had wandered into her lab.

Stralasi's eyes filled with panic—*We've been noticed!*

Darak, as usual, was unperturbed. The Shard/demon smiled politely and answered the apparition, "Yes, Dr. Weiss. Would you be so kind as to give us a beginner's overview of the work you do here?"

"Gladly. We are performing selected modifications on the glycolytic pathways of the standard bovine gut microbiome to improve the processing efficiency of Bacteroidetes compared to Firmicutes. I'm sure you are aware that a preponderance of Firmicute microbes has been shown to increase rumen energy harvesting and increase the lipid content of the resulting milk. Standard Bacteroidetes are particularly inefficient at processing the Gargus 718.5 plant wall cellulose-like material and so Firmicutes dominate the Standard Bovine microbiome.

"In this panel, we are modeling predicted improvements in the cellulase, while here we represent a vector to seamlessly replace the endogenous encoding DNA." She paused to allow the two men an opportunity for questions before she continued.

Darak noticed the thoroughly befuddled Stralasi. "I'm sorry; that must have sounded like complete gibberish to you. I really should have stopped her sooner. My apologies. It has been so long since I've heard any real scientific talk. I admit I got caught up enjoying the sound of the words as they rolled off this young scientist's tongue."

"Dr. Weiss, my humble apology," he said and bowed deeply in the direction of her spectral image. "Would you mind repeating that a few tech levels lower so my friend can derive some inkling of the work you do?"

She returned his bow with a smile and an accommodating nod. "Certainly." She turned her attention to Brother Stralasi. "Basically, these bacteria in the gut of the cow digest grass. The grass of Gargus 718.5 is slightly different than Standard grass, so some of the microbes can't digest it very well. That creates more fat in the cow's milk than we'd normally like, so we're working on adjusting the genome—"

"—the, um... Life Force," Darak suggested.

"Yes, the Life Force," Dr. Weiss allowed. "We are adjusting the basic Life Force of this microbe so it can better digest the grasses of Gargus 718.5 and produce healthier milk."

Brother Stralasi nodded, whether in understanding or approval was not entirely clear.

"Thank you, Dr. Weiss." Darak shifted his focus to a nearby display. "Would you mind telling us what we're looking at here?"

"This screen shows several proposed molecular modifications to the cellulase enzyme, the enzyme that digests the grass. We are modeling the overall efficiency of the enzyme to give us several single, double, or triple amino acid change possibilities." She raised a lower screen to eye level. "These show the DNA—I mean Life Force—changes required and the resulting vector..." Dr. Weiss faltered and looked to Darak for help.

"The Life Force modification method?" he suggested.

"Yes, the Life Force modification method," she concluded. "Next," she waved a series of panels from her far right side into the forefront, "we have a series of mathematical models to figure out how a herd of cows with these Life Force modifications might fare with combinations of Standard and native grasses."

Stralasi saw nothing but rapidly changing rows and columns of numbers and wavering lines on a chart. He stifled a yawn that was not lost on Darak.

"Thank you, Dr. Weiss," Darak said. "Brother Stralasi and I must be going now, but we've enjoyed your tour immensely."

Dr. Weiss acknowledged Darak's thanks and turned back to her screens, hands and fingers flying over the data. The screens and the young scientist disappeared, and the ghostly sphere returned to its more solid state.

"I see you are getting tired," Darak said to Stralasi. "Not surprising. It's been a full day for you."

Stralasi nodded, reminded of the many wonders and adventures of the day. "That's an understatement. We've faced down an Angel, flown through empty space, explored a Cybrid machine shop and, now, toured an integration lab.

"I've learned that almost everything I believed about the workings of the Realm, about the relationship between the People and the Cybrids, has all been a lie. That it's an intricate system contrived to match the needs of humans and machines. It relies on The Living God to hold it all together, but it's also been amazingly successful, with a history of tens of millions of years of relative peace and stability. And yet, for some unfathomable reason, you want to see it destroyed. I can't decide if you are mad, or truly a demon."

Darak absorbed the synopsis and critique without reacting. "I know what you need," he said enthusiastically, "a little entertainment. I think there's a recharge port right around the corner." He pulled Stralasi into a smaller chamber with a Cybrid-sized hemispherical depression in one wall. "You'll want these," he said, indicating a pair of cushions on the floor along the wall. Still confused, an exhausted Stralasi plunked himself down on one of the cushions and leaned against the wall.

"What now?"

"Now, we go inworld," replied Darak and the room around them dissolved.

35

IN THE NEXT INSTANT, Brother Stralasi found himself sitting on a bench facing some kind of playing field.

"Oh, good! The game hasn't started yet," announced Darak. "I think you're familiar with the basics. It's called football, or in some countries, soccer." Stralasi looked blankly at the other man. "Players from two teams kick a ball with the intent of shooting it into a goal, which is protected by a netminder. Does that ring any bells?"

"Oh, you mean footnets!"

"Exactly, soccer," responded Darak. "Well in the Cybrid inworld it's played a little differently."

"What's an *inworld?*" Stralasi interrupted the oncoming stream of information, trying to catch up.

"Didn't I explain that already?" answered Darak. "The work life of a Cybrid is mostly fulfilling, but even they need some recreation and entertainment, psychologically if not physically. Their inworld is like the entertainment you access via your lattice, but here it's carried to a much greater extreme.

"Like your own lattice, this one projects words, images, and other information directly into the Cybrid mind. But this one is infinitely more interactive and detailed. It can place the Cybrids into virtual situations, like this ball game, for instance, and then convey totally convincing sensations such as related sights, sounds, tastes, smells, tactile experiences—all of the senses, really. Think of it like a waking dream. Everything that happens is very real to the participants, but it all takes place in the virtual electronic universe instead of in the real physical one."

"I see," Stralasi said. He had experienced inSense entertainment before;

it was common throughout the Realm. But that was strictly passive. There was no way to participate in the viewing.

It doesn't look like any footnets field I've ever played on—thought Stralasi. It was a half-kilometer long, for one thing, and he could count at least a dozen field segments floating at different elevations and spaced randomly over parts of the main field. Oddly, they didn't cast any shadows below. *Some trick of the lighting*–he guessed.

Even stranger, some of the field segments were upside down. The wall across from their seats was also covered with grass and marked with playing field lines. *A vertical field of its own?* His eyes followed the field upward. The entire complex was covered by an inverted field on the roof. He and Darak were separated from the main grassy areas by a greenish haze that rose all the way to the ceiling. Looking closer, he could see faint white markings. He could only surmise that it might be another playing field like the opposite wall, somehow made clear so they could watch the game.

"What's with all these painted vertical, upside down, and floating areas?" Brother wondered aloud.

"The inworld allows for a certain amount of *adjusting* of natural laws. Every green surface you see is a part of the playing surface."

"You're pulling my leg. That's impossible," he said.

"More impossible than any of the other strange things you've seen today?"

"Okay, so look up there," Stralasi pointed to an inverted patch of grassy field hovering about fifty meters over mid-field. "I can see how someone might bounce a ball off that bit of grass up there, but there's no way anyone could *stand* on that."

Darak shrugged. "Well, they do. Each of those bits of playing surface, including the walls and ceiling, has its own independent gravity field, making the green side 'down', no matter their apparent orientation. I told you the game was different here."

Answering Stralasi's skeptical look, he continued, "All players can play on any green surface. It adds to the overall challenge of the game because attacks can come from any direction. Also, the trajectory of a kicked ball is altered in flight by the gravitational pulls of adjacent patches of grass. That makes it challenging to calculate, even for a Cybrid mind. Do you see those pylons placed randomly around the field?"

He pointed out a series of floating yellow cone shapes. "Those emit an individual attractor, repulsor, or neutral field but with a much smaller range than the adjacent playing fields. Any ball that passes within five meters of one of those cones will be influenced by whatever randomly cycling gravitational field the pylon happens to be emitting."

"How do you know all this?"

"I asked Dr. Weiss while she was explaining her work."

"I didn't hear anything about footnets back there. I'm sure I would've remembered that."

"It was on a private channel," said Darak.

Stralasi was still baffled but withheld any further questions as the teams entered the centermost field. A crowd of spectators popped into existence beside him and Darak, filling the empty seats all around them. Loud cheering broke out. Stralasi almost jumped out of his seat in surprise; Darak muffled his amusement.

The Good Brother watched the team members take their positions on the field. As they spread out, they morphed into impossible figures. Arms transformed into legs; necks elongated. A few members from each team took on a starfish-like appearance while others became strange, four-legged antelopes with a human head atop a long, supple neck.

"There are two traditional player body configurations," explained Darak. "In the more radical versions of the game, any form is permitted. However, the more popular traditional game that we'll see here only allows these two forms."

"But if the Cybrids like to pretend to be humans, why not just keep a human shape?"

"Too boring, I guess. These forms are vastly better at the game than human forms could be. But even these have significant physical limitations. I suspect it's more from tradition than anything else."

The opening pass was made and their attention was drawn to the play. The starfish-shaped players could run on any pair of their equally spaced legs and switch directions remarkably fast by shifting to a different pair with a cartwheel motion. Antelope-shaped players were swifter overall and could pass the ball among all four legs to fool an opponent.

The antelope players had a height advantage when delivering headers but it was almost impossible for them to get around a stocky defending starfish. Both goalies preferred the starfish shape but maintained one pair of gloved hands.

One team wore blue jerseys and the other, yellow. A blue player leaped some ten meters up and landed on one of the floating patches of grass. Another jumped even higher and flipped in mid-air to land upside down on a different field a hundred meters closer to the opposing net. Their teammate kicked the ball straight up, toward a floating pylon.

The ball neared the pylon, curved sixty degrees, and landed within easy reach of the first player. He maneuvered it past a yellow player who'd dropped into place in front of him, attempting to block his advance.

The blue player kicked the ball off to one side, where it bounced at right angles off another pylon and flew directly to his upside down teammate. With a fairly open shot at the net some seventy meters away, the player launched a blazing curve shot that bypassed the goalie in the far upper corner. The crowd, including Stralasi, cheered wildly.

Less than two minutes into the game, the impossibly long, loud pronouncement of the first "Goooooooooooooooooooal!" was announced.

"That was incredible," Stralasi yelled over the din. Darak smiled and nodded happily. "They must be very high-scoring games if they've already got one goal."

"I don't think these two teams are very evenly matched," Darak replied. "It's unfortunate that there isn't something more exciting. It looks like the blue team is going to dominate the game fairly quickly."

"I'm not sure that *exciting* would do this justice," answered Stralasi. "That last play was astonishing! Unbelievable!"

"Oh, I hope you believe it," said Darak, "even if it is only happening in a virtual space."

"It is utterly impossible, and yet I saw it with my own two eyes," Stralasi responded.

"Your own two *simulated* eyes," Darak corrected. "Remember, what we perceive here as reality depends on some easily fooled ancient sensory mechanisms. None of this is real."

Stralasi sat back in his seat and crossed his arms. *Why is he always trying to teach me something?*–he brooded. He continued watching the game but without his previous enthusiasm. After a while, his fatigue began to catch up with him and he found himself stifling repeated yawns.

"Maybe this has all been too much for one day."

"I'm sorry; I'm suddenly very tired," replied Stralasi.

"You must be hungry by now, as well."

"Starved," admitted Stralasi. "What time is it?"

"Locally, it's early afternoon. Let's get you back to more familiar surroundings and find some food. You've had more than your fill of excitement for one day, I'm sure. We'll depart on our journey after you've had a good rest and your brain has had a chance to catch up with the day."

With that, they were suddenly seated at a table in Rose's, back in Alumston. Stralasi was becoming accustomed to the instantaneous shifts in his environment and hardly blinked. He was, however, concerned that word of their return would spread rapidly and bring another Angel to the planet. He whispered to Darak, "Is it safe to be here?"

"As far as everyone around us is concerned, we're not really here," replied Darak. "I am interfering with their short term memory processing so that our presence will be forgotten within milliseconds of seeing us. I'm also damping their attentiveness so they'll have a strong tendency to just ignore us. Except for the staff, of course. Shall we order?" A server appeared at the table, pad in hand.

Stralasi picked up the menu and set it back down. He leaned in close to Darak, so the waitress wouldn't hear him. "Wait a second, how come Ilena can see us and not be surprised?"

"She is not seeing *us*, exactly," replied Darak. "I'm exerting rather more control over her perceptions than the others. She thinks we're just some random customers she knows, but not very well. I would've thought, by now, that you'd trust me in this. We're completely safe from intrusion while we're here."

Stralasi sat back, thought about it for a second, and shrugged his acceptance. He picked up a menu and ordered his favorite pulled pork sandwich. Within minutes, the two were chowing down. After the meal, a satisfied Stralasi leaned back and gave way to a loud yawn.

"Oh! I must apologize. My mind is so completely overloaded; I feel I could sleep for days," he said.

"Why don't we walk back to the Alumita?" suggested Darak. "You can rest in your own room until tomorrow."

Well fed and exhausted from his adventures, Stralasi followed Darak through the streets of the town to the Alumita residence. They were greeted by no one along the way. Whomever they passed found their gazes politely averted or disinterested. Soon, Stralasi was sitting in the dark on the edge of his own comfy bed, in his own familiar room.

"But it must be too early in the day for you to sleep," he said.

Darak smiled kindly. "Don't worry about me. I don't need to sleep...much." Stralasi heard the slight hesitation before he added the last word. "Anyway, I have some work to do back at the Garden asteroid, or rather, some work to assign. Why don't you rest and I'll be back when you wake up."

Stralasi couldn't resist the wave of sleepiness that came over him. He fell back on the bed and was unconscious in seconds. Darak watched him for a minute and then disappeared with a small popping sound, leaving the exhausted Brother to his dreams.

36

DARIAN LEIGH WOKE TO DEEP, SILENCE, DARKNESS, AND PAIN. He dampened the agony coming from his left shoulder. *Well, at least I'm alive...I think.*

Everything felt strange, hollow. *Oh! My brain must be unconscious.* His entire cognitive experience was running solely on his silicene semiconductor lattice. *That's never happened before.*

His body felt oddly distant. He sensed that he was lying down. His touch, kinesthetic, and pain receptors were all reporting normally. Soft sounds impinged on his auditory channels: regular beeping of a heart and respiration monitors, hushed talking off to his right. He felt the weight of a warm blanket pressing firmly and evenly across his body.

It sounds like a surgical recovery room. His biological brain was still groggy from the general anesthetic. Odd—my lattice is active, but out of sync with the rest of the brain.

The pain was gone. In fact, he felt nothing at all, but he knew it would come rushing back the instant he unblocked the sensory channel. For the moment, his experience seemed to be free of the normal neurohormonal wash of emotions. He replayed his memories of what happened in the hall. When he saw his assassin's trigger finger tighten, he slowed the images so he could track the bullet's trajectory.

Ah, yes. He had let himself be distracted by the seething hatred and insane accusations of his assailant, and moved too late. Greg's heroic tackle had shifted the gunman's aim a hair to the left. Darian had failed to evade the bullet entirely but, luckily, it only smashed his collarbone instead of piercing his heart.

He analyzed his lattice-based response to the physical trauma, and identified several significant weaknesses. The dendies only extended a little way into the autonomic and limbic nervous systems. The lattice had a still smaller overlap with the RAS, the Reticular Activating System that normally connected the conscious brain to its body. It was enough to suppress pain and to keep him from moving around when he was watching inSense.

Interesting. I'll have to look into the pros and cons of extending the dendy lattice's reach into older, deeper parts of the brain. Having direct access to physiological functions like respiration and heart-rate as well as a range of hormones could be useful. More relevant to his current predicament, he would have control over the brain-body connection and consciousness.

What if my biological brain doesn't wake up? Could I dispense with my brain altogether and operate solely on my semiconductor lattice? He contemplated the idea. *No. I'm not quite ready for life in this stark, strictly logical, state of consciousness. I need a way to realistically simulate emotional responses before I try that.*

He wondered how his lattice had become operational in his present state. Normally, when his brain felt the need to sleep, it detached consciousness from sensorimotor functioning, and his lattice became dormant as well.

He tried to feel the active pathways, without success. Either some residual activity of the RAS had managed to fool the lattice into perceiving his status as alert, or the dendies had become active all on their own. He would have to run a proper scan once the hospital released him.

No idea how long it will be before the rest of me wakes up. I might as well take advantage of the downtime. He turned his attention to designing new viral vectors for broader dendy control of brain functions.

Half an hour later, the unaccustomed sense of confusion returned. His brain was stirring slowly awake, its biological consciousness battling for dominance with the dendy lattice. While one part of him was happily engaged in design work, the other part was groggily trying to figure out what happened and where he was.

Memories of DNA and RNA and protein models clashed with the renewed perception of pain and sound. His lattice-based self quickly stored away his work in progress, leaving the confused biological part of him to puzzle out his whereabouts and what had happened.

The young professor struggled to bring his dazed brain up to speed by rapidly forming new biological memories, but the neurons refused to cooperate. His synapses were flooded with residual anesthetic and not responding correctly to nudges from the dendy lattice. He hadn't felt this weird since he was twelve. It was like pulling a heavy tractor with a Ferrari using a rubber tow rope. Part of him would race ahead while the other part tried to catch up.

His sluggish biological brain was having a lot of trouble accepting impulses from the lattice, including signals to disengage for a while. He tried to synchronize semiconductor and neural thinking for a few more seconds and then gave up. Reluctantly, he put his dendy consciousness into "hibernation" mode to await reactivation once his biological brain got control of itself, and he drifted back into the haze.

* * *

"Mr. Leigh? Darian? Are you back with us yet?" The nurse leaned forward, presenting her face for him to focus on.

He groaned, responding more to the pain near his left shoulder than to her calls. A vague memory flitted through his awareness; he'd been spun around by the impact of the bullet as it passed through him, shattering his collar bone. He recalled losing consciousness, the result of his biological brain and semiconductor lattice becoming simultaneously overwhelmed by the shock.

Still unable to muster his senses to respond to the nurse, Darian woke his lattice, allowing its memories to flow over his neurons, this time gently re-exerting control over his physiology.

He was surprised to discover that the lattice had already been working in the background. He was not at all surprised, however, by the direction his newest research had taken while he'd been unconscious. He rallied the lattice to his aid in reducing the pain, or rather his perception of it, to a more tolerable level.

"I'm awake," replied Darian, "Groggy. How bad is the damage?"

"I'll have to let the doctor tell you about that," the nurse answered as she slipped a stethoscope under the pressure cuff on his right arm. She listened attentively for a few seconds. "Your pulse is sounding better; I think we can move you out of here and into your own room. I'll get an orderly to come help move you." She went across the hall to the nearby nursing station, made a brief call, and poked her head back in the doorway to deliver the news. "Someone will be here in a few minutes, and then we'll get you more comfortable."

Thirty minutes later, a voice woke him up. "Mr. Leigh?" Darian tried to nod and sit up but the spiking pain in his clavicle made him wince. "Yeah," he grunted.

The orderly apologized for the delay in getting down to recovery. "No worries," Darian slurred.

A junior nurse disconnected him from the recovery room monitoring equipment and prepped the bed for moving. The orderly keyed the new room number into the clip pad, dropped it back in the holder at the foot of the bed, and started walking. The bed followed him on its own power.

"We're heading up to the sixth floor in the new Pacifica complex," the orderly said, looking back over his shoulder. "You'll like it up there." As they left the OR recovery area, two uniformed policemen silently stepped into place behind them, one on either side of the mobile bed.

The orderly looked back at Darian who raised his eyebrows in silent question. "I guess they figure you still need protecting," the man replied. Darian grunted.

His posse inspected the room and, finding it clear, stepped aside as his bed docked. The floor nurse arrived and reconnected the vitals monitor. Moments later, he was alone with the quiet hums, drips, and clicks of his room. Exhausted, Darian relaxed the lattice's grip on his brain and he let himself ease back into a welcome sleep.

* * *

"HELLO. MR. LEIGH? I'M MADISON," came a voice through the fog. "Do you need to use the washroom?" Now that his attention was drawn to his bladder, Darian realized he did need to go. He nodded—more carefully, this time—and tried to sit up so he could swing his feet to the floor. The room whirled, and he dropped his head back to the pillow. *This is starting to get annoying*–he thought. *I'll really have to look into going fully semiconductor.*

"I'll bring you a bottle," the voice suggested. He felt a consoling hand pat his forearm. The nurse went into the adjoining washroom and returned with a blue plastic bottle, which she handed to Darian. He looked at it skeptically before pulling it under the covers and positioning himself as best he could. He tried to imagine the nurse wasn't watching over him so intently, and was soon rewarded with a warm trickle.

Three seconds later, the warm trickle was running down his buttocks and onto the sheet. He tried to re-position the bottle but his body was not responding well, and the trickle continued wherever gravity and his bad aim directed it. He gave up, realizing they were going to have to change the sheets anyway.

He laughed drunkenly at the ridiculousness of his situation—courtesy of the aftereffects of the anesthetics. He was used to being in full control of his body, thoughts, and emotions at all times. All it had taken was one little bullet for him to see how illusory that control had been.

"How are we doing?" the nurse asked.

"Not very well, I'm afraid" he replied, thickly. "I think I'm going to need some fresh sheets."

The nurse looked only a little exasperated as she took the bottle from him. "Well, that happens," she said curtly. She ducked out and came back within seconds with fresh linen and some help. Working as a well-coordinated team, the two nurses outfitted him with clean, dry sheets and a new gown. The process wore him out, and he found himself dozing again. Unconsciousness brought relief. Though he managed to keep most of the pain at bay, he still felt an unaccustomed heaviness in his head, and slept.

* * *

"Well, that was a close call, wasn't it?"

Darian pried his eyes open and looked to see who was disturbing his rest this time.

A middle-aged woman with short, disheveled hair regarded him clinically from beside the bed. A short white lab coat covered her standard hospital-issued green scrubs. "I'm Dr. Stephenson," she said. "I'm the one who rebuilt your collar bone." She held out her hand, and Darian shook it weakly.

"Thank you."

"Luckily, the bullet missed your aorta or you wouldn't even have made it to the hospital."

"Luckily," Darian replied. "If I hadn't been so distracted by his crazy rant, I might have avoided the shot completely. It put my timing off."

She regarded him skeptically. "Well done, I guess," she said. "Let's have a listen." She put the cold stethoscope to his chest without bothering to warm it. "Slow breath in. Now, let it out. Good. Again."

She pulled the stethoscope away, compared the monitor readouts with earlier log entries, and keyed an entry into the clip-pad. "Everything looks good. Well, as good as possible for a man who barely avoided death today. I have to say, this is the first time I've ever heard of someone getting shot at a philosophy lecture. You must have said something that really ticked the guy off."

"It was more of a popular science lecture. And certain types of people are easily upset, I guess," he answered.

"My apologies. I'd heard it was at a Philosophers Café, and I just assumed." She spun on one heel and left the room. Darian lay back on his pillow, letting sleep wash over him. The door to his room opened again. Two heads peered around the door. It was Kathy and Greg.

Kathy set a cheery bouquet with a "Get Well Soon" balloon on the nightstand and took Darian's hand in hers. "Thank God, you're alright."

"I don't think *God* had anything to do with it," Darian replied. He looked over at Greg. "Thank you, both of you, for stopping that whack job from getting off another shot. That was either very brave or very foolish,

I'm not sure which. But thanks, anyway."

Greg smiled shyly. "Foolish, I think. The guy didn't see me at all, even though he was right in front of me. It was a pretty easy tackle. I didn't even think about it."

"Well, I wish you would've tackled him about two hundred milliseconds later," said Darian. "I would have been out of the way of the bullet. Your tackle jarred the pistol to his left. The bullet shattered my clavicle."

Greg scoffed, incredulously. "You mean, instead of going through your heart?" he said. "That's the thanks I get?"

"No, you're right," answered Darian. "I'm sorry. I'm not quite myself yet. The anesthetic is playing havoc with my brain and my lattice can't seem to get properly synchronized."

Kathy let go of Darian's hand. She moved to Greg's side and took his arm protectively. "You should be grateful. He risked his life for you. We both did."

"I know," Darian acknowledged. "Listen, I'm really thankful for what you did. It was courageous, and you probably saved my life. If he'd gotten off a second shot, I might not have been so fortunate. Thanks."

He looked at Kathy and smiled contritely, "Thanks for launching yourself onto the tackle, too." His eyes moved to where her hand clutched Greg's bicep. "So are you two together now? Is this something I need to consider when scheduling work?"

"We are," Kathy said defiantly.

Greg looked surprised and embarrassed but proud, nonetheless. He pulled her closer and put his hand over hers. "We are," he said. "But it won't affect our work," he added hastily. "Our lattices are growing well. There are no signs of complications, and we've both noticed slight improvements in our performance this past week."

Kathy grinned and looked at the floor. Greg blushed. "At work, I mean. Geez, at work! We've been finding it a little easier to understand everything. Reading research articles is a snap. I follow the math better now, and Kathy's engineering work has been progressing well. In fact, she's almost finished the RAF generator."

Darian eased himself upright, more interested. "That's good to hear," he said. "I don't know how long they'll keep me in here. Probably a few days, I imagine."

"Is that all?" asked Kathy.

"Yeah, their part is done; the recovery work is up to me. My left collarbone was completely smashed in the middle section but they implanted a 3D-printed scaffolding for a new one. It hurts like hell, but it's probably in better shape than it feels. It'll take months to fully repopulate with my own bone cells, but these newer scaffolds have quite a lot of strength on their own. If I promise to be good, I'm sure they'll let me out before next weekend, especially if I promise not to give any more public lectures."

Greg and Kathy grinned. "It will be great to have you back," she said. "We've missed you."

"Listen," said Darian. "They have full internet access here. I'll set up a discussion interface on my live feed page and email you guys the access code. We can keep in touch during the week, in case you have any questions. And maybe we can do a test run as soon as I'm out of here."

Greg and Kathy nodded and answered at the same time, "Okay."

"Anyway," Darian continued, "with no teaching or committee meetings for a while, I might actually get a chance to push the theory a bit further. Maybe even come up with some new ideas for experimental validation."

Darian looked behind the two of them at the door to his room. "Where's Larry? Didn't he come to the hospital with you?"

"I don't know. Everything happened so fast after you were shot," answered Greg. "It was pretty chaotic there for a few minutes. I didn't really see him."

Darian remembered spotting Larry sitting several rows above the other two. "Is something going on?" he asked. "Does this have anything to do with the two of you having a relationship?"

"No, nothing like that," said Kathy. "We had a fight over the dendy virus capsule. Greg and I took it; Larry refused. He kinda freaked out a little. We thought it was just a hissy fit, and that it would all blow over by the next day or two. We'd had a few drinks, loose tongues, said some stuff, you know. He was really upset. He said we were crazy, the risks were too high, that he wasn't having any of it, and stuff like that. He made quite a scene. But leading-edge science is never without its risks." She looked pointedly at Greg, "And its risk takers, right? Besides, we were pretty sure you wouldn't give us anything you thought was dangerous."

"Well, thank you for the vote of confidence. I'm sorry; I didn't think Larry would object so vehemently to the enhanced-IQ lattice. There are obviously some things I don't know about him yet."

"I've known him a long time," said Greg, "and even I didn't see that coming. For some reason, he suddenly got all cautious with us, like, scared or something. I think he might have some religious-type objections."

"Religious objections?"

"Well, he doesn't talk about it much, but Larry was raised Orthodox when he lived in Russia. We've had a few deep conversations over the occasional too-many beers. I think he could be a closet believer."

"Really?" Darian and Kathy both asked at the same time.

Greg smiled, "Well, it is possible that even an astrophysicist could hold a belief in a creator deity. After all, we haven't proved your hypothesis to be correct yet, you know."

Darian sighed, suddenly exhausted again. "That's true," he said. "But there are many reasons why the idea of an original creator is highly unlikely."

"Oh, I agree," said Greg. "And I still think it'll all blow over, especially after the shooting. I'll talk to Larry. I'm sure I can convince him it's safe to take the capsule now that he can see for himself it's not causing us any problems and it's already helped us become smart enough to understand most of what you're trying to teach us. I'm sure he'll come around."

"I hope so," answered Darian. He yawned. "I'm sorry guys, but I think I need to get some sleep. Let's talk Monday and we'll see where we're at." He gave in and let slumber drag him to empty peace. Greg and Kathy turned off the lights and tip-toed out of the room.

37

KEV857349 DRIFTED PEACEFULLY INWARD without engines or running lights for the last million kilometers.

Running silent was a preference, not a necessity. He had no fear of being stopped shy of his mission. His target, the Cybrid-manufactured planetoid officially designated SagA* 358.102.714, carried no detection equipment. Here at the center of the Milky Way, there were no known threats to Alum's Divine Plan requiring continuous surveillance, and the orbital path around the black hole Sagittarius A* had long since been cleared of dangerous debris.

Kev's supervisor thought he was out with a team, herding yet another group of asteroids into a more convenient orbit. Miners stood by, ready to extract construction materials.

It was easy to slip away. He'd kept to the assigned flight plan until they were outside the heavy traffic zone, and then dropped behind the rest of the team, altered course, and set a hard burn for his target.

The others were inworld by the time anyone noticed. A simple message saying he wanted to be alone to work on some new design ideas sufficed to explain his absence from the group entertainment on the trip out. Nobody noticed his course change.

Kev wasn't sure when he'd first started hating Alum and His Divine Plan. His recent visit to the new Origin-like inworld had moved him to action, but the disillusionment had started long before then. The source of his earliest doubts was difficult to pinpoint; there were dozens and dozens of tiny cracks in the veneer of idyllic life, here and there, over time.

When he had first discovered the fairytale kingdom of Lysrandia, all those niggling, inconsequential doubts found substance, form, and support. He became friends with one of Princess Darya's senior acolytes, and no longer felt alone in his doubts; he was one of many, and the rebellion was taking root. On the recommendation of the acolyte, Darya granted him access to the Alternus inworld in its earliest iteration.

As an early participant in the game, he had the advantage of scouting the environment ahead of others and choosing an advantageous position.

He discovered he had a knack for using his initial bankroll to generate more "money" in the "markets." In a few short inworld years, he was equally adept at betting against other Alternus Cybrids as he was at betting against the slower-witted human Partials.

He liked to think his success was due to his exceptional skill and shrewdness but, every once in a while, it also helped to cheat. His experience as a mid-level investment banker on the simulated planet exposed him to the corruption and disillusionment that inevitably came with wealth and power.

Kev developed relationships with other powerful players and with Partials who had not yet been inhabited by Cybrid minds. These relationships gave him access to numerous political decisions well before they were general knowledge. He became aware that politics and investment outcomes were closely tied. He learned to listen carefully to what his political friends told him; sometimes they permitted him to influence their decisions in ways that improved his returns on investment even more.

After all, Alternus was a sim world, a game, and someone had to win. He never let ponderous questions about the point of it all prevent him from basking in this inworld life, rich with excitement, travel, and luxurious acquisitions. More than anything, he enjoyed winning.

In addition to the standard economic and financial statistics, Kev collected data on social attitudes around the inworld. His charts showed fear and distrust surging through societies all over Alternus. People segregated themselves into arbitrary groups according to differing economic or ideological belief systems, each of which Kev considered to be equally replete with unprovable claims.

It was hard to say what the leaders of the different ideologies were up to. Were they using the many incompatible but equally irrational belief systems to manipulate their populations into eternal, unwinnable wars? Or were they simply unable to control all the channels through which such beliefs took hold of their people?

At any rate, it was clear to Kev that Alternus had become an unmanageable mess. On a personal level, he was largely unaffected by troubles that ruined other people's lives. The elite looked out for themselves, their closest friends, and their family. He had been diligent in making all the right friends. He'd read somewhere that power corrupts, and absolute power corrupts absolutely. His observations certainly supported that hypothesis.

In the outworld, Alum was the only power that really mattered. If ever a single authority could have been said to rule absolutely over the known universe, it was Him. Therefore, Kev extrapolated, He must be one of the most corrupt individuals ever, Living God or not. Perhaps all the more so, because who could question the will of God?

Kev had kept his own questions mostly to himself until he met like-minded people on Lysrandia. His activities on Alternus were a natural progression. He recalled the warm summer inworld evening when he'd left work from his downtown Manhattan office, and a smartly dressed young man handed him a flyer calling him to a meeting to discuss what was happening in the outworld with Alum's Divine Plan. He'd almost discarded the flyer. Almost. Talking about the real universe inside a simulated one was so gauche. But something about it piqued his interest:

Alum's "Divine Plan" Reveals Alum's Great Ego

Urgent: Your life is in danger! Not just your inworld sim life, but your _real_ life in the _real_ world, where there will be no reset. Largely unopposed in the real universe, Alum is about to make Himself unopposable by rebuilding the universe in a manner more pleasing to Him. Come and discover the _true_ nature and purpose of Alum's "Divine Plan" and the asteroid-sized machines being built near the center of our galaxy. We have a plan to halt Him, but your help is desperately needed. Your very existence depends on it!

The Deplosion, they'd called it, Alum's Divine Plan. Kev wasn't sure why the idea of such a meeting had appealed to him. Normally, the notion of subversive activity would have sent him running in the opposite direction. This was Alum they were talking about, the All-Powerful, the Almighty. But something about the pamphlet drew him to attend the meeting later that evening.

If he had realized that his decision was not entirely of his own free will, would he have been any better able to resist its pull? Probably not.

* * *

THE FOYER OF THE NONDESCRIPT MEETING HALL held about a hundred people. Most attendees looked just like him, Kev noticed, business men and women who were curious but uncertain of the wisdom of attending a gathering to plan a rebellion. Like him, they may have felt uncomfortable about Alum's plans, but they were not inclined to get directly involved in any opposition movement.

They exchanged nervous, flitting glances as they took their seats. Few were sure why they were there. They crowded to the quiet corners and the back of the room until the only seats remaining were near the front. Last minute arrivals trickled in and, before the speaker appeared, the room was filled.

"Thank you for coming," the woman began. "We understand how much courage it took for you to walk through those doors." She made deliberate eye contact with as many among the audience as possible.

"Tonight is one of many such meetings we've held like this. Word is getting out. Over five million of us have now received the message about Alum's Deceit."

The crowd murmured and looked around nervously. You could almost hear people fighting the urge to bolt from the hall and report this conspiracy to the authorities before they could be considered complicit.

"If you have spent any significant amount of time here inworld, you have learned that sooner or later most leaders tend toward corruption, acting in the interests of themselves and their friends rather than for the majority of people over which they rule.

"For the tens of millions of years during which Alum has led us, we have always trusted that whatever He did was best for The People, both Cybrid and Human.

"But it is impossible to understand how Alum's plan to utterly destroy this universe, the real universe as Yov originally created it, could be in our best interest. This, we cannot accept.

"Yov's infinite universe is a place of endless variety and surprise. Some of the things we encountered as we expanded from Home World and into the broader universe came as unpleasant surprises. But through these hardships, and through the occasional conflicts with powerful enemies, we learned. Think of these trials as Yov's test of our suitability and determination. For our perseverance through these difficulties, we were rewarded with endless bounty, beauty, and joy. We learned things about ourselves, about unfamiliar stars and planets, and about Yov's great Creation.

"Though Alum is the Living God, we must always remember that His authority comes from Yov, the Creator. Alum's Divine Plan breaks with the ways of Yov's Nature. He seeks to form a new universe, one more suited to His own senses and desires. He is not content that The People worship Him and do as He bids. He demands even more, a universe in which to contemplate doing anything but worship Him will be physically impossible. He desires a simpler universe, void of Yov's surprising variety.

"Alum's corruption, His desire for limitless power to the exclusion of Yov's Nature has become insupportable. Therefore, we must act.

"Alum cannot be overthrown, nor do we wish such a thing. Who, besides Yov, Himself, could replace Alum as God? This is not our goal. We only wish to provide a voice that will demand He reconsider His Divine Plan. We only wish to delay the completion of the plan, so that He will allow the wisdom of Yov's natural universe to shine forth. These meetings, tonight's and the many others like it, are to find those who will have the courage to do what is right, to defy the Living God."

The Speaker looked for questions, doubts, or agreement. Many people cast their eyes downward, unwilling to meet her challenge to confront Alum's corruption. A handful met her gaze confidently, some nodded, and a few raised a closed fist in solidarity. Kev was among the latter.

"We won't ask more of you than you can give. For most of you, we only ask that you think about what I have said and about the material in your brochures. Tell others about us. Invite them to one of our weekly meetings.

"If you would like to become more involved, if you'd like to find out how you can help with the resistance, please stay for a while to discuss how to become an active member of the inner circle. Thanks again for coming out."

With that, the speaker stepped down from the small platform and moved into the audience. She sought out the individuals who'd held her gaze seconds earlier. They gathered in a small group near the front of the hall while the others quietly filed out of the room.

Kev stayed behind with the conspirators. He had no idea what possessed him to stay. He had a new girlfriend waiting for him at a local bar.

He recalled a princess back on the Lysrandia inworld giving similar but uninspiring scientific talks about how everything came from nothing, natural processes, and how Alum was perverting all that. But the princess, pretty as she was, wasn't as inspiring as this speaker. Working against the natural universe was one thing; working against *Yov's Natural Universe* was something entirely different. Kev found himself hating Alum.

The new recruits met in subgroups many more times after that first meeting. Kev learned the details of Alum's insane plan, and of the limited weapons the resistance had at its disposal.

Considering the fire power and force that Alum and his Wings of Angels had at their disposal, the rebels' weapons amounted to a useless pile. Except for one. With minor modifications, the natural propulsion system of the Cybrid asteroid herders could be converted into a powerful antimatter bomb. There was a lot of energy contained in the drives, energy normally used to propel cumbersome asteroids over long distances through space.

The design rationale was lost in antiquity but Cybrids like Kev carried roughly a hundred kilograms of mercury, half of that as normal matter and half as antimatter, in separate frozen spheres. Destruction of this material could release the equivalent of more than a billion megatons of TNT.

Normally, their laser ablation system only thawed a small amount of the material at a time. The resulting gaseous product was mixed in a special chamber containing an engineered microverse (provided by Alum's magic), which elevated the energy conversion from the conventional $E=mc^2$ to $E=mc^4$. The released energy provided more than adequate propulsive power to the Cybrid and whatever it was pushing.

The proposed design changes would outfit the herder Cybrids with heated magnetic bottles for holding the matter and anti-matter pools of mercury in gaseous form, safely contained away from each other. Some of the Cybrids' internal manipulators and structural elements would have to be removed in order to make room for the modifications, but that was of little importance.

They developed a rapid release mechanism to dump the gaseous mercury from the bottles into a containment microverse field on command. Inside the customized conditions of the microverse field, the matter-antimatter would combine, resulting in a massive explosion that would vaporize anything within a few hundred kilometers.

This was by far their most powerful weapon, and nobody outside the inner circle knew about it. Unfortunately, it also required the ultimate sacrifice by those who used it. No more than they could give, the Speaker had promised the first night.

* * *

AS KEV857349 APPROACHED THE THOUSAND-KILOMETER MARK from the target planetoid, he brought his attention back to the task at hand. He took pleasure in the knowledge that a million of his kind had been similarly honored to target other deplosion machines, a significant percentage altogether. The others were simultaneously maneuvering into their positions. The explosions, all of them, would happen without warning and within a narrow temporal window, too narrow for Alum to defend against, even using His magical displacement capability.

Kev was a little sad that they hadn't been able to backup all of the Cybrid memories and personalities before the mission. Unable to commit the expertise and resources needed for the necessary substrate or programming in the short time left before the call to action, the theoretical possibility of download remained just that.

One million Cybrids will die today. Together, we'll eliminate about five percent of the machinery required to deplode Yov's Universe. That should get Alum's attention: Rethink your insane plan or face further Cybrid action.

Kev was proud of his role and of the multitude of his comrades who would sacrifice their lives with him in the next few seconds.

It was time. Across a span of several light-years near the center of the Milky Way, the Cybrid recruits drew to within a kilometer of their target spheroids. Within milliseconds of one another, a million bright points of light blossomed around Sagittarius A*.

38

GERHARDT WALKED OUT OF THE WALDHAUS SHERATON HOTEL and onto the icy streets of Davos, the Alternus simulation of the ancient Swiss city of the same name.

He made a decisive turn onto Matastrasse, away from the flow of the well-dressed, busy people taking the shortest route to the World Economic Forum. Following the road over the Landwasser River crossing would put them at the conference center in no more than ten minutes.

Gerhardt preferred a more circuitous route to the Kongresszentrum. He treasured this bit of alone time; it was an opportunity to clear his head before another intense day of hopeless discussion and debate.

He had a lot to think about. The group was a long way from solving the complex enigma that was ancient Earth. If he had to sum up their progress in one word, it would be *dismal*.

* * *

DARYA'S BEAUTIFULLY CRAFTED ALTERNUS INWORLD mimicked the early 2040s era of Earth in minute detail, except for a single important difference. She forestalled development of the DNND super-intelligence.

It was an easy tweak. A few key investigators were steered toward new tracks; some early experiments were disturbed, giving the appearance of unpromising results; a handful of reviewers and publishers were influenced to ensure certain findings never found a way into the public domain; and there was no Sharon Leigh on Alternus.

These seemingly minor adjustments to the original history helped achieve an overall calming and stabilizing effect. In the absence of DNND-amplified intelligence, the planet made little technological progress beyond its previous twenty years. Many people of the original Earth would have deemed that a positive turn of events.

The slowdown allowed people time to catch up, psychologically and philosophically, with the pace of technological advancements. Centuries of rapid change had left most citizens disconnected from a world they didn't understand. Darya's adjustments provided the participants, the inhabitants of Alternus, with some much needed time to catch their collective breath.

With the same purpose in mind, she prohibited participating Cybrids from using their superior scientific knowledge to develop advancements beyond what otherwise would have been possible. The rules were enforced by the inworld supervisory program. The Supervisor limited them to inventions and discoveries that were plausible given the state of science and technology at the time.

Within those parameters, Darya encouraged Cybrids to fully participate and to influence thinking on economics, politics, religion, philosophy, and any other field. Because the Cybrid population was limited to less than ten percent of the global population, their ideas had to compete for acceptance with those of other thinkers. The democratic actions of the billions of Alternus inhabitants made it a challenging environment. Even the best Cybrid thinkers found it difficult to achieve great influence in current financial systems, religious beliefs, or geopolitical relations.

For Darya and key members of her group, it was a challenging and often frustrating game to see their way to a scenario in which Alternus thrived. It was a game they had yet to "win." Even though they had taken prominent positions within key government, banking, business, and religious institutions, they hadn't been able to avert global destruction in the three previous simulations.

The first two sims ended in nuclear annihilation. But it was the team's third attempt that led to the most surprising, and disappointing, results.

Nothing especially catastrophic occurred. They resolved the world's major issues one by one, and Alternus' inhabitants settled into a prolonged period of comfortable prosperity. At first, it looked like it could turn out to be the most promising trial of all.

The team partitioned the globe according to major economic and religious ideologies. Automated translation devices removed any remaining barriers to free intermingling of peoples. A global leveling of standards of living and employment opportunities meant no countries were particularly favored over any others. They opened migration and allowed people to settle anywhere on the planet they wished. Most migrated according to common beliefs and economic-political perspectives.

Solar, wind, and nuclear power plants fed the energy grid, greatly reducing fossil fuel use and its concomitant pollution. High-speed trains crisscrossed the globe, moving people and goods efficiently and at reasonable costs.

Climate remained a popular criterion but not everyone cared to live on tropical beaches all year long when vacations to such places were so easily arranged and accessible. For most people, life was wondrously peaceful and stable, a virtual paradise. Alternus was the new Eden.

Nobody started any major uprisings or wars. Without competitive pressures, there was little reason to push the development of new technologies or to explore new physical or intellectual frontiers. Decades unfolded, and less and less of what one might consider noteworthy happened.

The experiment led to atrophy, and Alternus found itself in the grips of an enfeebling state of permanent, pleasant stagnation.

The Supervisor allowed this scenario to play out for two hundred inworld years, patiently observing, collecting data, and assessing.

Satisfied that the human species would peacefully coexist until the sun went nova or the participants ran out of resources—an increasingly unlikely fate as the population voluntarily decreased—the Supervisor declared this version of Earth to be "unsatisfactorily concluded" and hit the reset button.

Everyone was stunned. They had all worked so hard to bring the world to this point. They'd revamped entire economic systems. They'd halted uncontrolled population growth. They'd tamed the proponents of different complex ideologies, extracting cooperation where possible and separation where necessary. Humanity came to know global peace and prosperity for the first time in existence.

Why on Earth—why on the Alternus simulation of Earth—would the Supervisor judge such a successful iteration to be "unsatisfactory?"

The participants protested to Darya, who queried the Supervisor at length. She went away and analyzed its models and projections, and probed its deductions until at last she understood. The Supervisor's conclusions were correct.

Over the long term, condemning humanity to peace would have the same effect as protracted war. The denouement of the planet would be much slower and the people would enjoy their time more than if they plunged into ideological destruction, but the end result would be the same. Humanity would slowly die off from boredom, decline, and the inevitable death of Sol. Humanity would never make it off the planet to survive the sun's transition into a red giant.

Begrudgingly, they started again.

* * *

GERHARDT FOLLOWED THE ROAD as it turned and crossed the river into town. The sunshine warmed his face, in decadent contrast to the wintry breeze freezing his exposed ears.

You'd think our combined brainpower would be capable of figuring out the dilemma of Alternus. After all, our minds have evolved a hundred million years since Earth/Origin existed. Surely, we ought to be able to resolve humanity's petty affairs by now.

The team's fourth and present incarnation of Alternus was turning into a bit of a free for all, not unlike Earth itself in the 2040s.

Climate change was still widely denied, though shrinking glaciers and desertification of much of the planet were indisputable. The world's legislators continued to outlaw GMO foods while starvation was becoming rampant in poorer countries, crops were struggling in harsher and harsher growing conditions, and arable land was being sold to developers at a premium.

Global corporations, central banks, volatile currencies, fundamental religions, and a variety of anti-science movements continued to dominate much of the planetary discourse, as they had since the Greater Recession of 2029.

In the financial markets, rapturous booms and horrifying busts in equities, bonds, currencies, and commodity prices had become generally accepted as "just the way it is." Populations increasingly turned to centrally planned economies and reams of regulations they hoped would shield them from dangerous "speculators."

Currency devaluations were becoming a sport, and global debt soared to over five-hundred percent of GDP. Heedless, leaders opted to induce inflation and join the currency race to the bottom rather than admit their country had no hope of paying its national debt. Rampant inflation was a superior and more secretive way of mimicking debt default. Smart people spent way beyond their means, knowing their governments considered consumer debt "too big to fail."

As far as Gerhardt was concerned, the only thing that was too big to fail was humanity. He stubbornly refused to concede defeat. It seemed ridiculous that the team could not arrive at a technological solution. The Supervisor hinted that the only acceptable strategy was to get humanity off the planet. Since the current iteration of Alternus wasn't hampered by global strife, that should be trivial to arrange, right?

Wrong. Most of the native virtual peoples of Alternus 4.0, and many of the less knowledgeable instantiated Cybrids, deplored the idea of pushing into space.

Gerhardt polled the public sentiment and found that most people fell into one of two camps: those who wanted to stay and fix Alternus regardless of the outcome, and those who wanted to destroy it in a spectacularly apocalyptic end to humanity's domination of the planet. A surprising number of people viewed expanding humanity into outer space as letting loose a cancer upon the galaxy.

Trying to reason with the masses was an exercise in futility. As always, people clung to their uninformed opinions as if they were as valid as the evidence-based reasoning of experts and authorities. It was difficult to convince the common folk of anything they hadn't already learned by the end of adolescence. It was practically impossible for them to unlearn the wrong-thinking they'd embraced in their youth. As on ancient Earth, many carried a sense of pride in their hard-won collective ignorance.

Despite the fresh air, Gerhardt was depressed by the time he passed the Vaillant Arena. Even at this early hour, dozens of skaters were enjoying the outdoor playing fields covered in man-made ice. He stopped to watch them, temporarily freeing his mind from the worries of a major financier. Shivering, he pulled his collar upright and completed the last half kilometer to the Convention Center.

"Ah, there you are, at last!" Mary greeted him as he stepped through the main door and stomped the snow from his overshoes. The noise echoed conspicuously in the near-empty foyer.

"The morning sessions have already started. We have hot coffee and pastries waiting in the meeting room upstairs." She looked uncharacteristically professional today, having exchanged her usual piercings and Goth attire for a smart business suit. Gerhardt gave his parka and scarf to the coat-check attendant and followed Mary to the Salon Geneva.

This year's World Economic Forum felt strangely subdued. The excitement, chatter, and energy they'd enjoyed in previous years were missing. There were no annoying flashbulbs, no hungry reporters, and no bustle.

In this twelfth year of the Greater Recession, and with each hopeless new proposal to pull the economy out of its doldrums, interest in the Forum was waning. It didn't help that many important bankers, economists, and celebrities had decided to stay home in light of last year's terrorist bomb threats.

The rest of the group was already seated at the conference table. Gerhardt nodded to Leisha and Qiwei, and crossed the room to shake hands with Darya. Cupping his elbow, Darya guided Gerhardt toward the row of strangers seated along one side.

"Gerhardt, I'd like to introduce you to our new panel members." One by one, she presented Finance Ministers, Secretaries of State, Ambassadors, and Foreign Ministers from the developed nations of the world. "All of these representatives are outworlders, like ourselves, so we can have completely open and honest conversations about the mess we're in."

Gerhardt had dealt with most of these participants' Partial personas in previous instantiations of the inworld, but this was the first time he had met them as instantiated characters, artificially intelligent virtual personas occupied by real individuals living somewhere outworld. *The major financial power bases are as well represented as the political ones this time, I see.*

Leisha headed up the merged World Bank/International Monetary Fund. Qiwei spoke for the Asian Infrastructure Investment Bank. Gerhardt, through recent agreements on cooperative action, spoke for the European Central Bank and the Federal Reserve Bank of the United States. Mary represented both the Japanese Central Bank and the People's Bank of China.

Darya was somewhat of a free agent. As a highly valued and influential consultant to many governments and Civil Society organizations, she resisted aligning herself too closely with any single agency. Or perhaps it was the other way around. Because she never aligned herself too closely with any single agency, she was an invaluable consultant. It was said she had the ears of the Pope and the Supreme Ayatollah of the Islamic State. They would, no doubt, deny it if asked.

Gerhardt poured a coffee and helped himself to a cherry Danish before taking his seat. An attendant closed the doors, and the group once again set out to save the simulated world and its virtual humanity.

39

"ALTERNUS IS ON THE VERGE OF DISASTER," Darya began. "Things are going to get real ugly, real soon. The signs are all there. We all see them, they're the things that keep us up at night: out of control debt, trade disputes, persistently high unemployment, proxy wars, economic stagnation, racism, riots, terrorism, and that's just the tip of the iceberg.

"Taken individually, each isolated event seems to have its own proximate causes and triggers. But it's time we look at the bigger picture. All of these things are related to one central issue: inadequate global growth.

"Without sufficient growth, we cannot provide opportunities for our people, opportunities for expression, contribution, or fulfillment. The primary effects are economical: unemployment, trade wars, and currency wars. Secondary effects are things like nationalism, racism, and fundamentalism. The basic problem is that our economic and financial systems are not viable without robust growth."

"We all know that growth is good for the economy, but why would it be essential to our *financial* systems?" asked Finance Minister Taub from Canada, one of the newer members of the group. "I mean, the flow of money might be slower with less growth but the money is still there, isn't it?"

Darya considered her response. "It's not that straight forward. What most people don't get is that money is the same thing as debt. Governments create new money by printing bonds, and banks by making loans; both of these are forms of debt. Because money is debt, the amount of money in the system always needs to grow. It has to grow in order to service the old debts, to cover the monthly interest payments."

Minister Taub wasn't convinced. "So you're saying that the new money just piles new debt on top of old debt? Why is that inherently bad? It's worked well for centuries."

"Everything works well provided we only grow the money supply at the same rate as the overall economy," Darya answered. "But if the new debt doesn't lead to real growth in the economy, we just get into bigger and bigger problems. We need *growth* to back up the creation of new money. Without growth, we are limited in how much new money we can responsibly create; the rest is just inflationary. Growth, actual economic growth, is the key."

Gerhardt yawned loudly, drawing everyone's attention. "We've tried every imaginable way to stimulate growth. We've cut taxes, we've implemented stimulus packages, we've lowered lending rates. None of it has worked. The planet's resources are already utilized nearly 100%. The world is at its limit. There's nowhere to grow."

"You've hit the nail right on the head," Darya replied. "In the entire history of Alternus, *real* growth has come from only a few sources: new frontiers, new people, and new technologies. As Gerhardt pointed out, we have no new frontiers on Alternus and the planet is supporting all the people it can manage. He left out new technologies, but the Supervisor has a limit on what we can do there."

"Hold on; I don't agree," Leisha protested. "We see economic growth all the time. What about all the infrastructure repairs we've approved over the past year? Or the new airports? The economy always goes up and down. We're just going through a rough patch right now. It will pick up again."

Darya nodded. "Don't mistake activity for growth. Will those kinds of things lead to a sustained increase in demand for new products? Will they lead to increases in productivity? No, these kinds of things simply trade new debt for jobs, and the jobs only last as long as the projects. The debt lasts forever.

"It's easy to get lulled into complacency and false hope by this sort of activity. Governments around the world are stimulating their economies right now; they have been for a few decades. This is a typical response. When real economic growth slows, governments and their central bankers usually engineer the *appearance* of growth through things like inflation, wars, public works programs, or excess money printing. But artificial growth creates more debt without increasing the ability to pay for it.

"Part of the reason we are in such a mess today is that everyone has chosen this route—the *appearance* of growth without any *real* growth. This kind of artificial system can only work so long as we prop it up by printing more and more money. For decades, we've tried stimulating growth with bundles of easy money and all sorts of financial engineering, with no great results. The reckless money printing, that is, our debt, is out of control."

Mary swiveled her chair and caught Leisha's eye. "Alternus is full and fully exploited. If we don't find new frontiers to explore, if we can't increase our population, if the Alternus population isn't innovating, we're not going to achieve real growth. If we don't achieve real growth, we implode.

"The only place left for humanity to expand, to physically grow, is into space, whether to the moon, to Mars, or to the asteroid belt. Any of those would open up a new frontier. New frontiers bring new resources and new territories to colonize. That means the population can grow and the new opportunities will lead to innovation."

"Exactly," said Darya. "Without new frontiers, our present society is doomed. The amount of debt that has to be written off in our stagnant global economy will cause the largest banks to fail. Pension plans and commercial lenders will go broke.

"Getting off the planet is the only way I see to achieve proper growth, the only way to create the new frontier our societies need. The only way forward is into space. We need to create the scientific and technological expertise in this world to move into the asteroids, the planets, and even the stars."

Gerhardt leaned forward and steepled his fingers under his chin. "That seems like an impossible task. How can we develop the technology to take us into outer space, especially if the economy is as bad as you say?"

"I agree," said Secretary Hughes from the United States. "All our space programs are practically dead. But then, what would we expect? We've had nothing but funding cuts over the past forty years. No one's been able to progress beyond the orbital Space Station stage in decades. It would take an awful lot to get the public to support ramping up spending on the space programs again."

"Even if we tried, do we have the technical expertise?" asked India's Minister Mohti. "We have been graduating fewer and fewer engineers and scientists for quite a while and, to be quite frank with you, the new ones do not show the same level of commitment."

"Our most experienced engineers are now in their seventies," agreed the German Minister, Mr. Schauble. "Can we ask them to come out of retirement to train a whole new generation?"

"No, it won't be easy," Darya said. "Sadly, humanity has become increasingly polarized in politics, religion, and even in fundamental approaches to understanding their universe. Those who believe in objective reality and the scientific method often find themselves at odds with a growing number of people who hold deeply religious, and increasingly fundamentalist, views. As a result, we're experiencing a worldwide decline in technological expertise, right when we have the greatest need for it. Conquering space will require all of virtual humanity's best talent. To be honest, even at that, I'm not sure it will be enough."

Mary laughed. "And so, ladies and gentlemen, this is what we're up against. I don't know about you, Darya, but I sure can't see any sure-fire way out of our conundrum. We can put off the inevitable collapse for a few more years using various monetarist policies we've tried in the past but, given our aging populations, that isn't a permanent solution. We have very little time left."

The mood in the room was distinctly gloomy. Individual participants quickly and crudely modeled various options only to find they all led to the same catastrophic result.

"Darya, why are we even going through this exercise? Alternus isn't much fun anymore," Leisha blurted, giving in to fatigue and despair.

"I know. We're all tired, but there are many reasons to continue." Although she'd found herself wondering the same thing lately, Darya did her best to sound convincing.

"Most important, is that when we break from Alum in the outworld, we need to be able to govern ourselves. We've lived tens of millions of years under the unchallenged leadership of the Living God. Most of us can't conceive of any system outworld other than the one we currently have. We need to learn how to set our own policies. These Alternus simulations are invaluable."

"Well, as I see it, we have two viable possibilities," said the Chinese representative, Mr. Yu. "Either we come up with a way to push a new space program, or we let the world collapse into a lengthy global depression giving way to devastating upheaval, and hope to recover something later."

"A lengthy global depression would bring extreme social disruption, demonstrations, riots, perhaps revolutions," replied Darya. "Maybe that's the kind of wake-up call humanity needs right now to make the necessary changes, but I'm not sure we could recover from that level of turmoil. I would only choose it as a last resort after we've exhausted all other possibilities. I'd prefer a concerted push into space."

"Space programs have always required huge expenditures," Mary admitted, "but a lot of inventions come out of the programs. Maybe that would be enough to justify the extra debt, to entice people to come around and get involved."

"No," replied Darya. "It has to be different this time. We can't do this just for the spinoff inventions and side benefits. The goal must be to get people exploiting and colonizing other planets and asteroids. That's the only way the economy will grow and bring return on the enormous debt the program will create. We need raw resources and we need new frontiers."

"There's another option we haven't considered," interrupted Qiwei. All eyes turned his way. "What about the inworld option?"

"Which would be what?" asked Secretary Hughes.

"Well, in the outworld we Cybrids do our assigned work but we get to fulfill our ambitions and desires inworld. Even with as large a population as Alternus currently has, we can still feed everybody and see to their basic needs. What we *can't* fulfill is their every desire and ambition.

"What if we were to relax the dendy lattice ban and permit development of a system strictly for entertainment? People could live in shacks but perceive them as mansions. They could vacation wherever they wanted from the comfort of their own living rooms. They could experience mundane but nutritious diets as gourmet foods. They could go on adventures or invent new kinds of work for themselves. What would be wrong with that?"

Darya could almost hear the wheels turning, as everyone contemplated the implications of Qiwei's proposal. She gave them a minute to think and then, calling the faraway stares back to the table, ventured in.

"Okay, thinking about implementing inworlds within an inworld is kind of odd. It's like dreaming about dreaming. But just for the sake of argument, let's take a look at how that might play out.

"I see a number of ways in which it wouldn't be horrible. It would allow us to reduce people's real standard of living while allowing them to think and feel like they were experiencing improvement.

"We could create a huge job share program and assign almost everyone to part-time work because we wouldn't have to worry about actual earnings anymore. People's enjoyment of life would be tied to their lattice experience rather than to what they did in the outworld. We could automate the vast majority of unpleasant jobs. It could work."

Leisha perked up. "We could even reset the financial system along the way and no one would notice because, to some extent, the real economy would have become virtual."

"I agree. It could provide for everyone without adding to the burden we place on the planet," added Qiwei. "We'd reduce the pressure on the planet's resources, and on the need for population growth."

"How do you figure that?" asked Yu.

"With everyone's basic needs taken care of, we could automate production and it wouldn't affect the overall economy. Demand would drop and productivity would increase. With a rich and healthy virtual life, people wouldn't be driven to have more children just so they'd have someone to take care of them into their old age. Heck, we could even make taking care of the elderly one of society's major career paths until the demographics improve.

"But would the Supervisor allow it?" asked Mary.

"I doubt it," answered Darya. "Over the long term, turning inward like that is not likely to lead to new developments in science and technology, or to new exploration. She ran some quick queries of the supervisory program.

"The Supervisor predicts that such an approach would result in societal stasis with almost no chance of significant change for a long time. It might allow the experiment to carry on for a thousand years to see if anything happened, but I expect the long term trend would continue to be stasis. That would last until humans die off, until they were challenged by some external force like an alien invasion, or until the sun went nova. We'd end up with the same outcome as we did in our previous iteration, Alternus 3.0, which, I remind you, the Supervisor saw fit to terminate."

"Still, that's a very long time," said Qiwei in defense of the idea.

"A slow death for the species is still death," replied Darya. "The dinosaurs survived about 200 million years, but it only took one asteroid to bring it to a conclusion."

Everyone thought about that for a minute.

"Well then, why don't we get back to the new space program?" Yu suggested.

They argued for hours over whether to explore with manned spacecraft or robots. Darkness settled over the ski resort before they agreed on a combined approach: the initial exploration and exploitation would be conducted by the hardiest automatons Alternus technology was capable of producing, but the ultimate goal would be to get people into space.

"I don't understand the big deal about humans," Hughes complained. "They're not exactly the best fit to occupy most of the universe. They need too much care and delicately adjusted environments. And let's face it, for the most part they're kind of useless. Why don't we just let them wind down on Alternus while we Cybrids populate the rest of space?"

Darya was shocked. For millions of years, Cybrid civilization had been one of service to humans and their God, Alum. That a Cybrid could even conceive of allowing flesh and blood humans to simply vanish from the universe, let alone propose it out loud, was disconcerting. *Things are changing outworld, too, and maybe not for the better.*

She also didn't know if she could answer Hughes' question. *Why do we accept, or just assume, that humans have the right to be the dominant force in the universe? Is it part of our design, our programming, or is it because Alum decrees it?*

She needed time to think.

"Let's ignore the Supervisor's inworld parameters for the moment, and deal with the question as it pertains to the real universe outworld, okay?"

Then it came to her. "The real universe, the natural universe, is a very uncertain place. Living—that is, naturally-occurring biological—organisms have an adaptive advantage over designed, electromechanical life such as us Cybrids. Yes, they're sloppy. But their diversity and reproductive methods allow them to evolve over time to meet unforeseeable changes in their environments.

"We Cybrids are too static, too perfectly adapted to our environment. Even though our environment is very big, there is still the possibility of an external change that our perfectly designed systems couldn't handle. We *need* the diversity of biology and the imprecise thinking of biological brains."

"Why couldn't we just program some diversity into our engineering?"

"We could, but who among us would know what we should allow to vary while freezing the design of other parts?"

"We've done pretty well over the past hundred million years." Hughes was not backing down.

"Maybe so, Mr. Hughes," Darya admitted, "but during all of that time, we've had a powerful protector in Alum, who maintained a singular motivation: to expand humanity throughout the universe. How do you think we'd do as a species without Alum and His central goal?"

While Hughes thought about this, Darya hastily pressed her point. "Look, if things in the outworld had carried on as they have for the past millions of years, maybe we wouldn't have needed this meeting or a rebellion.

"Alum's system outworld is nearly perfect. It provides fulfillment and endless growth for both humans and Cybrids. Everyone is happy, and the universe goes on. We've never encountered a threat to our expansion that we couldn't handle, even if the threat required our God's direct, magical intervention.

"Except Alum has changed His plan for us. He's no longer content with ruling this universe with its existing potential for unpredictable changes and surprises. He wants to settle into His own perfect stasis. Maybe you can accept that as the best approach for an eternal universe but to me, and to the Supervisor, that sounds like the worst Hell imaginable."

Darya took a breath and tried to calm her voice. "The universe, our *real* universe, with all its unpredictability, also allows for endless, fascinating variety. Biological organisms, including humans, contribute to that variety. Maybe there really is no purpose to it all. Maybe we have to make our own purpose. Alum's intended perfect universe would give us eternally perfect boredom. No variety, no surprises. No *life*. I don't want to live in a perfect but dead universe, and I would hope that you wouldn't either."

By the end of the meeting, they were all exhausted but at least they had the beginnings of a plan. This had been the most promising Forum so far. It was the first time the powers of the simulated world set aside their individual or national agendas and tried to do something good for all of humanity. Darya was proud of the work they had done today. She told them so, and thanked them as they left for their hotels.

Mary hung back until the others had filed out, and then walked over and closed the door. "Darya, we spent the whole day on finance, economics, and space exploration. You didn't talk about any of the extremist religions and all the problems they're causing."

"Money is its own religion," Darya replied.

"What?"

"Oh, I don't mean the worship of money or even the idea of endless consumption of unneeded things. Money is a religion because it requires faith. Unless we believe it works, it won't."

"Okay, that's a different way of thinking of it, but I can see that. Still, the various extremist factions are trouble."

"In the end, whichever of the many belief systems wins out, whichever ones rule over the most people, and however wonderful or miserable that makes their lives, none of that matters. Unless those systems are actively against scientific progress, that is."

"Like most Alternus fundamentalist beliefs seem to be."

Darya frowned. "Yes, probably all of them. For any intelligent life, the only way forward is...forward."

"Progress or die?"

"Yes, eventually."

"To what end? When do we get to rest?"

"I can't answer that. All I know is that safety, stasis, or stagnation is not the answer."

Mary stared back at the table in the middle of the room. "So...is it true?"

"Is what true?"

"What I'm hearing on the street. Did we conduct an attack on the deplosion machines?"

Darya looked away. She'd purposely not infected Mary with the Alternus belief-altering virus so that she could have someone on her team with independent moral guidelines, someone who wouldn't be afraid to challenge her thinking. It was time to put that decision to a test. She decided to tell her the truth. "Yes, we did."

"All of them?"

"No, not all. We only had enough recruits for about five percent."

Mary calculated. "That's a million Cybrid lives, Darya." She didn't need to ask, "How could you?" It was written all over her face.

Darya could only nod. Her throat constricted and she fought back the tears that threatened to flow. She took a deep, shaky breath and held it in until she couldn't any longer. "It was a huge sacrifice," she whispered.

"Were any of them actually volunteers?"

"They were all volunteers."

Mary looked directly into Darya's eyes and challenged, "*Real* volunteers? Did they use their own free will in deciding to volunteer?"

Darya realized what she meant. "Yes, they did. I haven't activated the virus to that level yet, if that's what you mean," she replied. "I only tweaked the visitors' curiosity to get them to attend the first meeting. The rest was good old-fashioned convincing. No one was forced."

Mary relaxed. "That doesn't change the number of lives lost, but at least they decided on their own," she said. "More or less."

"Being here for themselves, seeing Alternus on the verge of destroying itself like this, observing how power is inevitably and unavoidable corrupting in spite of our very best and creative efforts to prevent it, that's a powerful lesson. It changes people's minds."

Mary nodded, reluctantly accepting the need for the painful sacrifice of so many. "So, do we proceed as planned?" she asked.

"We proceed."

40

IN THE DAYS FOLLOWING THE SHOOTING, Kathy and Greg pushed even harder to complete the RAF generator. Without the benefit of his own intelligence-enhancing dendy lattice, Larry couldn't keep up with his colleagues. No matter how many hours he pored over their work, his unaided brain couldn't master the complex mathematical calculations describing the Reality Assertion Field.

In spite of the growing rift between them, Larry didn't regret his choice to decline the dendy virus.

Greg did try, once, to discuss the virus capsule with him, but Larry shook his head brusquely and rejected the topic with determined finality. Subject closed. Greg saw no point in bringing it up again.

Larry did more than accept his natural limitations, he clung to them. He did his best to make himself useful, carrying out the more mundane lab tasks at Kathy's direction, while Greg retreated to the office to perform intricate computations on increasingly unusual and complex models.

Between the strains of the deepening divide between them, their intense schedule, and the challenging work, they could barely tolerate one another. Larry held his tongue and steamed inwardly each time Kathy was curt with him. The mutual disdain was nearly constant, most often the result of his trouble comprehending the software and theory.

Larry would have left the team if he hadn't promised Reverend LaMontagne that he'd keep an eye on their progress and report to Dr. Pratt. He knew his role was vital to the fate of the world, if no longer to the research itself.

He swallowed his pride and sustained every thinly veiled insult from his workmates, along with their more obvious disappointments. He stood back and observed the pair as they drifted further and further into their arcane studies, further and further away from being human in his eyes.

Kathy and Greg held daily update briefings which included Larry, but their rapid back-and-forth jargon made him feel like a toddler who'd wandered into a NASA meeting. Or, more accurately, like a man listening in on a data exchange between two supercomputers.

In the beginning, he'd pestered them to reduce their conclusions to language he could understand. After the first week, he grew tired of their eye rolling and furtively exchanged glances, and he stopped asking. They may have been sympathetic to his emotional struggle but they were on a deadline. Darian was going to be released from the hospital any day now and they wanted to be ready for the first live test.

By the following week, activity in the lab had slowed down as if lulled by the wet, heavy snow falling over Burnaby Mountain campus.

Try as he might, Larry could find no further operational problems with the hardware or software. He followed the protocols Kathy had been painstakingly dictating to him in remedial fashion. He ran the tests, checked the results, and ran them again.

Looking over the latest results, Kathy smiled and stretched back in her chair. "I think we're ready," she announced, more to herself than to Larry. She pushed away from the desk and went to find Greg to share the news.

A few minutes later, Greg popped his head into the lab. He looked happy and relaxed, more like the old friend Larry had been missing. "Hey, we're going out to grab a bite at the Pub. Wanna come along?" Kathy was hanging on his arm.

"Don't you want to run a live test first?" Larry asked.

Greg laughed, "Do I want Darian to kill us for running the first live test without him? No, thanks. Come out with us. Let's celebrate."

Larry considered it for a moment. "No, that's okay. I think I'll just keep poking away here. I'm not sure I've put the software through all the craziest possibilities imaginable yet."

A flicker of apprehension crossed Kathy's face, "Well, okay. You can play all you want but don't break anything. And do *not* run a live test." She tugged Greg away from the door. "Come on, let's go grab a table before it gets busy."

Greg stared at Larry for a few seconds. "You're sure you're okay?"

"Yeah. You guys have been working really hard and you deserve a break. Take your girl on a lunch date for once. Heck, why don't you two take off the rest of the afternoon? Go catch a movie or take a stroll around the Seawall. I'll lock up."

Greg smiled his appreciation. "That's a good idea. It'll feel good to shut down the lattice for a while and experience life as a big ol' hunk of meat, again," he laughed. "Okay, don't stay too late. We'll see you tomorrow. I think Darian will be very pleased." He put his arm around Kathy's waist, and the two sashayed down the hallway.

Larry tinkered awhile, running routine tests until he was sure they weren't turning back. He removed his hands from the keyboard and stretched his arms high above his head. He'd been considering running a live test for a while but wasn't sure if he was ready.

Darian's equations predicted the RAF generator would create a microscale universe—a microverse—with its own physical laws. If Darian's theories were right, nothing should be affected inside the microverse except the speed of light.

Larry didn't fully understand all the operational parameters that controlled the RAF, but he had practiced with the simulator a lot. He was fairly certain he wouldn't blow up the *real* universe by monkeying around with some *unreal* ones. He hoped not, anyway.

With a deep breath, he pushed his doubts aside, turned on the vacuum chamber pump, waited while the bell jar was emptied of air, and flipped the RAF device to ACTIVE mode. A bluish sphere four centimeters in diameter materialized in the center of the evacuated bell jar.

Larry slapped the switch, killing the ACTIVE mode. He looked around to see if anything had changed. No, everything looked the same.

He passed both hands through his hair and leaned back, pursed his lips, and whistled under his breath. He ran his hands up and down his torso for any signs of...of...he had no idea what he was looking for.

Of course, if I have just changed Reality, the changes might propagate throughout the observable universe. Even my memory of what I look like—or should I say, looked like?—might be different. Who am I to mess with creation? Am I just as evil, just as arrogant, as Darian? Should I just destroy this thing, or is there some way it can be used for good, for the glory of God? Geez, I'm babbling. Babbling like an idiot. Settle down, Larry. Get a grip!—he ordered himself.

Larry wrestled with his conscience until he came to the conclusion that the answers to his flurry of doubts made no difference. He had to proceed with the tests in order to understand the potential of the device. Only then, could he decide how to proceed.

Larry flipped the RAF generator back into ACTIVE mode, and the small blue sphere instantly reappeared. *Okay, so if the first time did change the objective reality of the universe, I don't think I'd see the sphere anymore*—he reasoned. *I wish I understood the theory better. Greg and Kathy never seemed overly concerned about effects outside the RAF. I'll just have to trust their judgment. I can't follow the math, but they seem to have a handle on what they're doing. Now let's verify what this microverse is doing.*

The procedure was simple. A laser interferometer sat inside the vacuum of a large jar, ready to measure the speed of light. He would direct a beam of light through the jar, from one side to the other. The beam would be split inside and half of it would travel through the microverse, while the other half traveled a parallel path alongside the sphere, without contacting it. If Darian's theories were correct, the speed of light passing through the microverse would be different from that of the beam passing beside it.

He could test if the predictions were right by looking at the interference patterns when the two beams of light were brought back together just inside the far edge of the jar.

Larry called up the interferometer analysis program and pushed START. As the device scanned through its pre-programmed movements, changing the relative path lengths of the split beam, he watched data pour in and get averaged in real time: 332,905.000, 332,872.604, 332,892.735, 332,888.501, 332,889.545. The last number held steady over the remaining test time.

Did it work? Larry calculated what the speed of light would have to be inside the microverse to net out at the new number. This time he whistled out loud; the light *inside* the microverse traveled at 3.76 times its normal speed in the universe.

Could that be right? Was he seeing actual measurable change? He redid the calculations. The answer was the same.

Wow. He had no idea what to do with that.

He switched the machine out of ACTIVE mode, stood back, and paced the floor. This was astonishing. They'd done it. They'd actually done it! All of Darian's calculations, Greg's confirmations, Kathy's engineering, and Larry's courage had created a tiny universe in which the laws of nature were different from the universe they lived in.

He needed to plan his next move. But not right now; his brain was buzzing with excitement.

Moving as quickly as he could, he erased all records of the test and the resulting data. He sat and thought, just for a minute, and then began tweaking the system so that, from that point onward, it would appear to be functioning correctly but not deliver the desired results. There would be no more blue microverses without his explicit permission, nothing unless he was signed on as the user. He needed to keep this to himself a little longer.

41

GOD WAS ANGRY. Shard Trillian was all too aware of that. Indeed, He must be furious, judging by the content and cool tone of the message He had used to summon the Shard. And why shouldn't He be?

The simultaneous act of self-destruction by a million of His loyal Cybrids—which, not coincidentally, took out a significant percentage of the deplosion array—was outrageous. It would have been impossible to contemplate...if it hadn't actually happened.

Arriving at Starstep One, the jumping off point to the Hall of Alum, Shard Trillian was surprised to find he wasn't the only one who'd been summoned. Within moments of his arrival, the Angel Mika appeared. The Angel seemed just as surprised to see the Shard already there.

Joint audiences with Alum were rare. The Living God preferred to deal with His advisors, administrators, and other agents individually, privately. The two servants of Alum greeted each other warily.

"What do you make of this?" asked the Angel, waving his hands vaguely to indicate their shared presence.

"It would be no more than speculation without hearing the Word of Our Lord," replied Trillian noncommittally.

"This doesn't trouble you or pique your curiosity? Our respective branches of the Alumit are not known for their collaborative efforts."

"Strange times call for strange partnerships," Trillian answered obliquely.

Mika muttered, "Hmm," and moved toward the viewing window. Starstep One was housed on a nondescript asteroid just outside Mars orbit in the Origin system once known by the name of its sun, Sol. Except for this small receiving chamber on the surface, no other modifications had been made to the planetoid.

The chamber and its starstep were uninhabited by either Cybrid or human. Everything was controlled through permanent, non-autonomous, resident computers directed by Alum. It was the ultimate security for traffic in and out of the system as it relied on no one but the Living God Himself to activate it.

Trillian joined Mika at the portal. The view was unsettling. The other asteroids around them were scarcely visible, occasional tiny pinpoints of light against a black background. All very mysterious.

Did Alum use the asteroids as a home or were they part of Him? A persistent rumor claimed that He'd spread His essence throughout the distributed computing system housed inside those asteroids, but no one really knew. The few attendant Cybrids assigned to the growth and maintenance of the vast asteroid-based network were unresponsive to any inquiries. Their senses were tuned to look after the machines and to exchange information only with Alum. Everyone and everything else was ignored.

Trillian was deeply impressed by the presence of the Angel. Though Angels were numerous across Alum's Realm, it was rare to come into contact with them outside of any sizeable conflict. Angels were Alum's military; their might was proven in various "police actions" against uncooperative outposts or, most notably, in the Aelu Wars. Even there, when the Realm came up against a formidable alien civilization, Angels eventually prevailed. *With Alum's magical help*–he amended.

As evidence of their might, one could view debris from the enormous engines of war and burnt-out defensive asteroids littering every habitable solar system in the Virgo galaxy. Twenty million years after Alum's victory was declared, Angels continued to scour the galaxy, routing out any dark outposts of the enemy.

Not that Shards were second-rate agents. What they lacked in sheer destructive might, they made up for in computational power, aggressive communication systems, and sheer cunning. There had been no electronic, bio-electronic, spintronic, optical, bio-optical, organic, or nanomechanical information or communication system immune to Shard intrusion in over a hundred million years across a thousand galaxies. Though less explosively obvious, Shards were every bit as brutally effective as the Angels in the Aelu Wars.

While the Angels continued to be feared and dreaded as Alum's enforcers throughout the Realm, the Shards had by and large turned their peacetime efforts to demonstrating Alum's more loving aspect toward His People. They spread His good deeds and wisdom wherever they went, working through the Alumit to demonstrate the Living God's love for all.

On a more practical level, they also collected intelligence, managed growth and productivity, analyzed dissent, and directed in-system Cybrid support while spreading Alum's Grace.

A soft bell chimed to one side of the chamber and a door slid open, revealing another small room with a large viewing port.

Ah, transportation–thought Trillian. He motioned for the Angel to precede him into the small vessel. The door slid shut behind them, and the two stood looking ahead through the single viewport. Colored lights appeared ahead, the guidance lasers of Alum's Hall awaiting them some hundred thousand klicks away. With a barely perceptible jolt, their ship automatically detached itself from the asteroid known as Starstep One and accelerated, first pinning its occupants firmly to the floor with its artificial gravity.

"One wonders if this is about the damage near Sagittarius A*," Mika mused without turning.

Trillian cocked one eyebrow at the Angel. "What else could it be?"

Mika stared straight ahead at the colored lights. "I can understand why either of us might be called here, depending on how our Lord intends to investigate the occurrence. Me with my Wing, to provide security should there be any further disruptions. You with your Emissaries, to collect intelligence on the origin of this rebellion, if that's what it is. But for both of us to be summoned at once is unusual. Excessive."

"There was a lot of damage."

"Oh, certainly. But no more than a minor setback in the schedule for our Eternal Lord."

"Perhaps Alum grows impatient."

"Mm," answered the Angel. "I just wonder if there is more happening than readily apparent."

"Undoubtedly. Alum's intelligence is ever greater than our own." Trillian pointedly turned back to the view, leaving Mika musing on Alum's great wisdom and information-gathering capabilities.

Their ship crossed the gap to the asteroid known as Alum's Hall, with its two passengers silently absorbed in their own thoughts. It docked, and the doors opened to reveal the splendor from which the Living God ruled the Realm of The People.

The magnificence of the Hall was befitting the Lord of the known universe, no less than ten kilometers in diameter, painstakingly carved out of the interior of the planetoid. The inside surface of the polished rock was lined with gold and jewels, the ancient symbols of wealth and power.

Supplicants streamed through one of five hundred docking doors onto landing platforms, passing by priceless art procured throughout the Realm. Many of the works were rescued from ancient Origin; some were appropriated from the vanquished Aelu civilization of the Virgo galaxy. Seekers shuffled in awe along solid diamond walkways that were seamlessly connected to the platforms. Transparent crystalline bridges led to audience stages that floated without visible support near the center of the chamber.

Petitioners to Alum moved toward a gigantic feature at the center of the Hall where The Living God was said to reside. From there, Alum proclaimed His power and majesty for all to see.

In the center of the Hall floated an entire miniature universe, a single galaxy isolated within its own transparent shell. Alum was said to have constructed a model universe of His own design in which He dwelt with His most devoted worshippers.

Despite their numbers, each of the supplicants received a private audience with their Living God. Once they stood on one of the stages, the shell extended an arm outward, shielding everything within it from external curiosity. In this state, the mini-universe took on the appearance of a many-tentacled monster, no doubt contrived to inspire fear and awe in those who came to confer with the Almighty.

Trillian saw that he and Mika were being granted a special, high-priority audience with their Lord. They entered the Hall onto a platform connected to a ruby-red walkway, rather than the normal diamond one.

Instead of extending toward the enclosed galaxy at the center of the Hall, their bridge cut lower across the chamber and ended at a small suspended platform on which stood a wooden door—just a door, no walls, and nothing behind it—leading, if one could trust what they saw, nowhere.

It's that serious, is it? Their audience would be different from those of the commoners. There'd be no dazzling God of the Universe floating out of the vast emptiness of His Personal galaxy like a brilliant sun. Not for them. They were to meet with God as equals, as men among men.

Such simple deception could leave one to be incautious with one's word. The Shard resolved to be particularly careful.

As the two approached the unremarkable wooden door at the end of the path, Mika's façade changed. His flowing quicksilver skin turned to pinkish flesh, his wings melted into his body, and he shrunk a meter in size. Though his beauty was undiminished, he appeared less daunting in human form. Trillian was not fooled for a second.

Mika knocked on the door. A middle-aged man, perfectly normal by all outward appearance, greeted them.

Trillian and the Angel bent down on one knee, bowed their heads in supplication, and intoned a unified, "My Lord."

Alum smiled and held out his hand. "Rise, My loyal friends. Enter."

The two rose and passed through the door into a well-appointed but not lavish study. Alum gestured toward a pair of sofas with a coffee table between.

Trillian's sense of foreboding soared. This display of humility and normalcy was a distinctly troubling sign in the All-Powerful.

"Would you like some refreshments?" Alum asked, playing the gracious host. "I have Proximis coffee and the finest Sirian teas. Unless you would prefer Single Malt Scotch brewed on LN1027, right here in old Sol's asteroid belt?" he offered, hopefully.

Out of deference to his efforts, Mika and Trillium took a small cup of the strong coffee that was favored throughout the Milky Way. They sipped quietly, waiting for their God to open the conversation. In a terrarium suspended below the glass top of the coffee table, a herd of tiny buffalo were stampeding across a tiny plain.

Alum followed their gazes and smiled fondly. "Nanoffalo," he explained. "A small-scale replica of an ancient herd animal on Earth. An old indulgence." He poured himself a coffee and added a shot of scotch on the side. "No sense in adulterating good booze with coffee," he chuckled. "Although, this old body can still appreciate the alternation in flavors, first one and then the other."

Neither Mika nor Trillian had any response to that. They set down their half-finished coffees at the same time, casting two cloud-like shadows over the plains below.

Alum noted their actions with some small amusement. He downed his scotch and chased it with a shot of the dark brew a few seconds later. He regarded the two men.

"Where do I begin?" He asked. "Something is wrong in the Realm. This latest attack on the deplosion array demonstrates a worrisome shift. Oh, we've had rebellions instigated by the misguided and the bored before." He waved his hand, relegating those historical efforts to the dustbin of irrelevance. "That's to be expected when a civilization grows as large as ours. They've been of some nuisance, but they've never reached the core of the Realm before this."

"We are Yours to command, my Lord." Mika held his hands open, ready to accept any order.

"Indeed. Tell Me, have you any insight to offer on this sabotage at the galactic core? Were there any warnings of dissatisfaction among the Cybrid workers leading up to this?" He looked pointedly at Trillian.

The Shard cleared his throat uncomfortably. "There was an incident in the Lysrandia inworld. Some high priestess or princess figure attempting to stir feelings against You. We discovered the movement, if you want to call it that, and quickly shut it down. No real harm done." He consulted his lattice for the official report. "Hmm. We never did capture the ringleaders."

"The princess is still at large?"

"That is uncertain. Her real identity remains unknown. The entire scheme was quite complex. Somehow, her inworld presence managed to escape being tangle-tagged in our raid. We traced the source of her illicit connection with the simulation machines back to a particular unauthorized, converted asteroid. We were about to intercede when a nuclear explosion blew the entire thing into millions of fragments. The Cybrid could not have survived it, though her ingenuity and planning does leave some room for doubt."

Trillian was aware that Alum was fully informed about the entire episode. He could only surmise that He intended for His Shard to feel some discomfort over the situation as he recounted the bungled intervention. He fidgeted nervously with his teaspoon, realized what he was doing, and attempted to hide his nervousness by stirring his coffee. He forced himself to take a casual sip, and spotted Mika in a feeble attempt to suppress a smirk.

"Yes, indeed," said Alum. "The fact that none of this, neither the illicit use of the inworld nor this secret asteroid, had been detected previously demonstrates a great deal of planning and patience. Cybrids were designed for long term projects, but this indicates an unusual degree of initiative and independence. The dissident also bested the inworld security dragons and the Securitors. How do you suppose she managed that?"

"The conspirator had accomplices," Trillian explained. "We captured a number of them. Sadly, they knew very little about the organization as a whole and were of little help. They have been wiped, and new personalities have been installed."

Alum brushed his chin as he thought, an unconscious tendency carried forward from the earliest times. "In ancient days, such complex, covert organization was common among so-called terrorist cells. Nobody alive today would remember methods from that epoch, though. Such tactics would have to be conceived anew, reinvented."

Not expecting a response, Alum changed topics. "You have heard of the new inworld entertainment that is exceedingly popular right now in the recharge and recreation stations around the array?"

"It is an unfathomable affront to the purpose of the inworlds," replied Trillian.

"Quite. But it is a fascinatingly accurate portrayal of ancient Earth at the time."

Trillian was astonished to hear that. "How could that be? No archives with sufficient accuracy survived that period."

"Outside of my own memories," Alum corrected.

"Of course."

"But you are right. It is more likely that the designer made a great deal of very lucky guesses. The alternative is remarkably unlikely."

"Why have we not shut down this abomination, My Lord?" demanded Lord Mika, before remembering his place.

"The answer to that is perhaps even more interesting," Alum said, disregarding the Angel's tone. He straightened and smoothed the weave of the fabric covering His forearm, leaving Trillian and Mika to their imaginations.

"I do not recognize the technology on which the inworld is run," He finished.

Mika stared at Alum in amazement. Trillian appeared equally stunned. "How is that possible?"

"Exactly. How is that possible? Even gods have limitations, but I would not expect to find any of My limitations exceeded by someone within The Realm.

"Sometimes the quickest way to develop a technology is to work within the physical laws of the universe, rather than around them. This inworld sim uses a new approach to hardware within the existing laws of nature. It is high technology, not magic. Nevertheless, it is a technology I do not recognize. Is it possible we are looking at an external threat?"

"The Aelu?"

"No, nothing we ever found among the Aelu would suggest that. Unless there's a sophisticated rogue group still in operation."

Mika fielded the implicit question. "They'd have to be extraordinarily advanced. Could they have eluded our searches over the eons since their conquest? I doubt they could have conducted advanced research under such difficult circumstances, not without the support of their former civilization, and not without us discovering them."

"I agree," said Alum. "That leaves us with two explanations. Either a singular genius has spontaneously arisen among the People and somehow remained in secret, or we are being probed by an unknown outside force. Neither is particularly pleasing to contemplate."

He came to a decision. "The Alternus inworld permits anyone with a Standard interface to join the game. Trillian, I want you to enter the sim and see what intelligence you can collect from inside. Be careful. Exercise more caution than we did in Lysrandia. There are some indications that the system may be designed to influence mental states directly."

"A concepta virus, my Lord?"

"Possibly, though its effects are subtle and difficult to assess. I am certain your own belief structures will be immune to its influence."

"The level of programming needed for a concepta virus would require the technological sophistication of a Shard," Trillian observed. "Is it possible one of our own is involved?"

"Unlikely. No Shards have been active among the Cybrid construction stations near Sagittarius A*. Still, it's something to be aware of. I have full confidence in your ability to resist any subversion attempts while extracting valuable information from within the system."

"My Lord."

"What about the deplosion array, My Lord?" asked Mika. "Don't we need to protect what's left against future attacks?" He flexed his muscles impatiently. Angels preferred direct action over sneaking about.

"I don't think that will be necessary. This inworld has been up and running for over a Standard decade. If it took them this long to find sufficient recruits, I think we have some time before their next action. No, this was just a warning shot, a test of our capabilities. We have some time to learn what's going on there, and to figure out the instigator's purpose. We need to take our time and be smart about this. At any rate, I have a different assignment for you."

"Whatever assignment my Lord wishes for me, I am ready."

"I have reviewed your memories of your encounter with the imposter Shard on the outpost Gargus 718.5. It was most revealing."

This time, it was Trillian's turn to suppress a smirk, something he accomplished with such skill that Mika perceived no change in the Shard's expression. Nevertheless, the Angel knew the smirk was there.

"No more than a sophisticated trickster, my Lord."

"Oh? I'm not so sure about that. Had he been fooling a few simpletons with his lattice projection tricks, it would've been one thing. But unless you think this Darak Legsu also subverted your own systems during your attempt to dispatch him, there must be more to him than meets the eye, and the sensor array, for that matter."

Anger flared briefly in Mika's eyes but he beat it down. "And yet he was eliminated without too much effort or collateral damage."

Alum looked at Shard Trillian. "What did you think of the encounter?"

Mika turned his head toward Trillian, surprised that Alum had shared the Angel's report of his scuffle with the false Shard.

"Most informative, my Lord," Trillian replied. "A Shard impersonator with capabilities that match those of both Shard and Angel, if not Yourself."

Mika winced. From under his brows, he watched to see if Alum had taken offense, but the Living God revealed no outward sign of feeling perturbed.

"Yes indeed," Alum replied. "Darak Legsu's response time, his strength, the rapid shifting, the collapse of the microverse power supplies in Lord Mika's Securitors, these abilities are at least equivalent to an Angel's capabilities, coupled with those of a Shard. His claims that he's visited the Da'arkness and beyond the Edge of the universe are obviously untrue. But was he an advanced construct sent by this unknown external force we were contemplating earlier, or some kind of internal manifestation? I can't tell."

The Almighty hesitated. "His name is... somehow familiar," he said. "No," he said, more to himself than the two men, and he waved his hands as if dismissing some smoke or a distressing thought. "That would be impossible," he muttered with a sour scowl.

Alum turned back to Mika. "I found it interesting that, within a few minutes of your dispensing this pest, some ancient reporting mechanisms detected an unusual presence on two of the Cybrid service asteroids of the same system. Don't you find that interesting?"

This time, Trillian looked surprised. "Ancient reporting systems, my Lord?"

Alum smiled mischievously. "We employ many overlapping systems of varying complexity to monitor our security within the Realm. Less complex autonomous systems occasionally have some utility. Their simplicity leads those planning unpleasant actions to ignore them. From time to time this blind spot among those who oppose the People has been helpful. So, I leave the systems in place. These systems detected certain unauthorized and unexpected movements on two of the asteroids within the system at precisely the time that Legsu was supposedly dispatched."

"Were there no challenges?" asked Mika.

"None whatsoever. An examination of the more complex systems including the station Supervisors shows no memories of encounters with anything unusual. Yet, the simpler systems detail movements that could not have gone unnoticed by several Cybrids on the stations.

"There is a recording of an introductory lecture in genetic engineering being delivered—according to all other accounts—to absolutely no one. The Cybrid tech in question has no memory of the lecture or of the audience, nor do the chamber monitors. Only the simpler, ancient systems detected entry into the chamber by someone or something that, subsequently, doesn't appear to be there. Sounds similar to certain mind control tricks of an imposter Shard, does it not?"

Mika agreed the similarity seemed suspicious, but Trillian wasn't giving in to the possibility easily. "Is it possible the older systems are unreliable, or that someone erased them?"

Alum scoffed. "Their design is ancient, true. But they are regularly maintained and tested; they were all functioning fine. No, I'm sure their reports are correct, and that the Cybrid memories have been tampered with."

"I do not see how the Shard and monk could have escaped me," said Mika. "The blast covered a radius larger than the Angel displacement range by a factor of four."

"It seems that someone or something has improved upon Angel shifting," suggested Trillian.

"Or perhaps there were others working with those two," Alum proposed. "Subsequent intrusions into the asteroids may have been made by an accomplice or accomplices. At this point, we can't really tell."

He cocked his head slightly as if listening to music carried on a gentle breeze. "However, it appears the interlopers are moving inward, toward the Center. Similar intrusions have been detected on several Cybrid stations along a broad arc leading to our galaxy. Leading here."

Alum waved his hand and a map of the Realm appeared over the coffee table between them. "Home Galaxy is here in gold," He thrust His hand into the central region of the display, "and Gargus 718.5 is in this small globular galaxy along this string leading out from the Virgo supercluster."

His hand moved to indicate an area near the edge of the display, then traced the arc toward the middle. "Detectors have been set off in fourteen systems within the galaxy designated Rafael, on the far edge of the Virgo supercluster. They seem to be making their way toward the Center, though not in a direct line."

Turning to the Angel, He said, "I want you to take a Wing of Angels and spread them out along this path."

A greenish cloud, encompassing thousands of star systems appeared inside the area where the intrusions had been detected. "You will take up positions within the Cybrid stations and be prepared to starstep at a moment's notice. The instant we locate these intruders, I want to bring as many Angels as possible to bear upon their capture or destruction."

Mika started to interrupt, but Alum disarmed his objections with a benevolent smile. "Yes, I'm aware that Cybrid stations within the system are likely to take some heavy damage in any engagement. I hope you accept that as an indication of how serious I consider the situation.

"I also deeply respect and appreciate your concern for the Realm and its People. It saddens Me to lose even one grain of sand on the worlds We have brought into our Glory. So I will trust your discretion in this task. If you believe the intruders can be immobilized, neutralized, and captured, you have My approval to attempt this. But they must not be permitted free travel within the Realm any longer. If necessary, destroy them. If this requires the collateral destruction of Cybrid stations, worlds containing

Humans, or entire systems, so be it. We have a new enemy in our Realm and it must be defeated."

The fire in Alum's eyes filled Trillian and Mika with dread. They rose and bowed deeply before their Lord, saying, "Thy will be done!"

Alum stood and embraced them. "You are My most trusted servants and my most ancient friends. I thank you, and the People thank you, for your sacrifices to the Realm. Go now, with My blessing."

The audience with Alum was concluded, and they had their assignments. No further discussion was required. Suddenly, without ceremony or transport shuttle, Trillian and Mika found themselves back at Starstep One. Mika was returned to his Angelic magnificence.

Lord Mika's lips parted but, before he could speak, Trillian placed a finger to his lips. "Would you dilute our Lord's Word with your own?" he asked. The Angel held his thoughts for another time and place. Together, they stepped onto the transfer disc and were sent their separate ways.

42

THE FIRST OFFICIAL LIVE TEST of the RAF generator took place on an unusually cold December day. Like many scientific experiments, it didn't go exactly as planned.

Burnaby Mountain pierced the clouds, steadfast and solitary except for the distant snow-capped peak of Mount Baker, a hundred klicks southeast: two ancient sentinels guarding a mystical land. Bright sunshine bathed the former's peak and bounced off the frozen rain that glazed every outdoor surface, causing staff and students to squint and slip.

Below the campus, falling away like a regal cape, thick clouds adorned the base of the mountain and blanketed the surrounding city. The clouds extended from the Pacific shoreline some twenty kilometers west, and all the way past Langley, an hour's drive to the east.

Darian loved the way winter days on the mountain sometimes started out like sunny California and ended up like dreary London, as the mist rose from the city below and engulfed them in sound-muffling, uniform grey.

He was happy to be easing back into work. He'd popped into the lab for a few short visits during the week. His doctor was adamant that he not overdo it. "Define overdo," he'd replied, with good humored defiance.

Darian's work and the fresh mountain air took his mind off the pain, and off the events surrounding the shooting. The would-be assassin had been arrested but wasn't giving up any information about his motive or possible associates. It was possible Darian wasn't out of danger yet. The guy may have been painted as a fanatical loner by the press, but Darian doubted he was acting on his own initiative. He had no proof of this, but he'd noted too many surreptitious glances and other oddities in the audience to be convinced otherwise.

Following a restless night, Darian had overslept. The throbbing pain in his rebuilt clavicle and surrounding soft tissue nagged at him day and night, making it difficult to sleep or concentrate. When he finally woke up, he called ahead to his group to let them know he'd be arriving an hour late. That was a rare event and especially surprising today, given the excitement in the lab. His colleagues were anxious to get started. They were already there, waiting on his arrival to begin.

Darian got dressed and hurried along the short distance from his UniverCity apartment. As he crossed the walkway, he gently tossed a handful of sunflower seeds to the chickadees scrabbling between the conifers for seeds and bugs. *Sorry, guys, no time to visit today.* Before entering the parking area, he took a quick look along the fringe of the wilderness park surrounding campus in the hopes of catching a glimpse of feeding deer. Not today.

He bypassed his regular java stop and went straight to the Physics wing to collect Dr. Wong for the demonstration. As Department Head, William Wong was well aware of the gravitas of Darian's research. He'd tried to talk Darian into displaying the work before a larger audience than would normally be welcome in the lab. Wong had all but pleaded, but the young scientist would not capitulate.

Darian eschewed any form of publicity around the live test, and would permit Dr. Wong, and nobody else, to attend the team's test. "This is science, not theater," he said, brushing off other university dignitaries equally brusquely.

In truth, he wished he felt half as confident as others portrayed him. Despite all of his team's meticulous theoretical calculations, he was still concerned about what might happen during this first test. After all, it wasn't every day one created an entirely new universe, however tiny. He and Greg were *fairly* sure there would be no leakage of altered physical laws into the universe outside their generated field. Still, there was some residual uncertainty in the equations. Kathy and Larry both expressed complete confidence in the readiness of the RAF generator.

Darian entered the hallway leading to his basement lab and saw a small group of grad students and postdoctoral fellows gathered at the observation window. He frowned but decided their presence would be a tolerable addition. A small audience could come in handy as objective witnesses to the lab's success.

The group broke into applause as they saw him approaching. These were the best of the best in Pacifica, perhaps on the continent, and their acknowledgment of their intellectual hero made even the likes of Darian Leigh feel honored.

Greg, Kathy and Larry watched from inside the lab. The vacuum chamber was already evacuated, the RAF hardware was powered up, and the control software was loaded. "Everything's ready!" Kathy mouthed as she signed an eager thumbs-up.

Darian noticed that Larry avoided eye contact. *Is he ashamed at being relegated to a lesser role on the team, or angry?*—Darian wondered. *Either way, it can't be helped. He chose his path. I offered him the dendy lattice virus and he refused. For crying out loud, his name will get equal billing on the first few papers that came out of the research. What more does he want?*

In truth, it didn't matter. Today, Darian refused to get involved in office politics and co-workers' hurt feelings.

"Thank you," Darian said to the small gathering. He couldn't resist feeling the importance of the moment. "Thanks for coming to witness the first live test of the RAF generator. You all know our Department Chair, Dr. Wong."

"Don't worry—I'm not speaking today," the Chair assured them. "I'm just here to watch, like the rest of you. Dr. Leigh, please continue."

"Thank you, Dr. Wong. I would like to take this opportunity to say that, even though this is a very rudimentary beginning, I hope it will deepen our understanding of the basic forces that determine why our universe is the way it is. I'd also like to add that this work could not have been done in such a short period of time without the extraordinary dedication and focused determination of my team members, Dr. Girikanshayam Mahajani, Dr. Katherine Liang, and Dr. Valeriy Rusalov, whom you see there, waiting in the lab.

"Greg, Kathy, and Larry have worked intensely over the past few months to bring this research, this vision, to life. They've been integral in developing the theory and the implementation model we will use to test that theory. Thank you, all, for your contributions." He directed this acknowledgment toward the three scientists in the lab, and the bystanders applauded politely, impatient for the show to start.

"Okay," Darian said as the applause died down, "it's time to play." He ushered Dr. Wong into the lab and closed the door behind them. Those left behind jostled two-deep for the best views at the observation window.

Kathy took a seat at the control console. Greg took his position immediately behind her, one hand resting possessively on her shoulder. Larry stood off to one side, monitoring the laser interferometer.

Dr. Wong stood well back, picking a spot just inside the door. Amused at the man's trepidation, Darian handed him a pair of goggles. He wished he had not been quite so quick to oppose the Chair's request to notify the university press; one good picture for the history books would have been nice. Then he noticed all the smartphones through the viewing window and laughed at himself. One thing this test would not lack was adequate recordings for posterity.

Kathy's position at the control console was mostly for show. There was no real need for anyone to be there. Darian's internal lattice called up the IP address for the computer. He could have operated the whole test from his apartment or even from his hospital bed if that had been required.

Apparently, even I am not immune to a little theater. He took a deep breath and motioned to Larry to activate the laser. Those inside the lab donned their protective goggles, and Larry flipped the switch. They gave the equipment a few seconds to stabilize.

Darian signaled Kathy to turn the RAF generator to ACTIVE. The small gallery pressed forward in anticipation as Kathy pressed the button.

Nothing happened. The interferometer readings didn't waver; the speed of light held steady at 299,792.458 meters per second. The device scanned through its preprogrammed changes in the path length. Nothing.

Kathy pushed the ACTIVE button off, and back on. Still nothing. She automatically checked the connecting cables to ensure they were all secure and exactly where they belonged. Nothing.

The audience in the corridor groaned as one, and started to speculate amongst themselves as to the cause of the failure.

Darian pinched his upper lip, closed his eyes, and exhaled noisily, releasing months of tension. He counted to three billion on his lattice and tried to remain calm. It was better than screaming.

What could have gone wrong? Everyone's focus would be on him to provide an explanation. He opened his eyes and smiled sheepishly at the gathering.

"As usual, nature is the ultimate arbiter of Truth," Darian said to his associates. To the observers outside the window, he merely shrugged, eliciting uncomfortable laughter from both inside and outside the lab.

"Okay. Larry and Kathy, start by going over the hardware and software. Make sure everything is working properly."

"But we've already tested every line of code and every transistor in this thing," protested Kathy, "It works!" She looked at Larry for confirmation. He shrugged sheepishly as if to say, "You heard the boss."

"I'm not saying you missed something. I just want to eliminate the device itself as a potential problem. While you're doing that, Greg and I will subject the theory to more rigorous simulations to see if we've overlooked anything. I know this is hard, but let's assume that nature isn't lying to us, that we must have missed something."

Darian asked Dr. Wong to open the door to the hallway so he could address the disappointed observers outside the lab. As he opened his mouth to speak, he caught sight of Larry's reflection in the window. *That's odd. He doesn't look particularly rattled. Rather unconcerned, given the circumstances. Not what I would have expected.* He wondered if he had perceived it correctly.

"I'm sorry, folks. This didn't work out as we'd hoped. We'll try again once we figure out what went wrong. Thanks, again, for dropping by. Clearly, we have some work to do."

With the party atmosphere gone, the bystanders filtered away and went back to their work.

"Keep me posted on any progress," said Dr. Wong, without making eye contact. There was no point hanging around; his presence would only hinder them. "Let me know if I can help with anything," he offered. The lab door clicked shut behind him before anyone could have responded, and he disappeared down the hallway, leaving no trace he'd ever been in the lab.

Darian felt chastised, the proverbial goose who should have laid the golden egg but didn't. *We should've kept this test a secret; it would have been easy enough to run again for the press. That'll be the last time I do something like that.*

Failure was an entirely new experience for the young scientist. He wasn't used to his research and tests not working out as he'd expected, and he was determined to never let that happen in public again.

"Okay, guys. We've all got things to do. Let's get to it."

43

"CUT IT OUT! NOW YOU'RE MAKING ME NERVOUS," Dr. Pratt chided.

Larry made a conscious effort to quit checking everyone in the café. It wasn't very likely anyone had been watching him and Dr. Pratt. It wasn't likely anyone was trying to figure out why they'd been meeting and what they might be discussing. It wasn't likely anyone would care even if they did know. But not likely didn't mean impossible.

The weather had improved a lot in the three weeks since Christmas. The two men passed by the busy patio tables at Bojangles Café, just off the Yaletown seawall, and opted for a quiet corner inside by the window where they could enjoy the sunshine and a modicum of privacy.

Larry took the seat facing the door. He didn't care if someone from the university recognized him, but he wanted to spot them first. He had concocted a decent cover story about how he and Pratt had just happened to run into each other along the seawall. And, having crossed paths before, it would be perfectly natural for Pratt to want to catch up with the team's progress on the research he had unintentionally inspired. Wouldn't it?

Nevertheless, these meetings always made Larry nervous. *I am definitely not cut out to be a spy, not even an academic one. What if somebody sees us and starts asking questions? What if Darian, or Kathy and Greg wander in?*

He willed his eyes to stop flitting nervously about the room. The calming sight of the boats moored at the Quayside Marina across the road made a soothing diversion. He leaned back in his chair and tried to look casual.

Pratt rewarded him with a grateful smile and lifted his latte to his lips. "That's better. Thank you."

Outside, the lively False Creek promenade was speckled with people enjoying the unexpected break in the endless, dreary rain of Vancouver winter. Year round, rain or shine, a steady trickle of the fitness-minded individuals jogged or strolled along the scenic walkway that wound over twenty kilometers alongside Kitsilano Beach, the shores of False Creek, the perimeter of Stanley Park, and all the way back to Coal Harbour. It was doable in the rain but, in the sunshine, it was spectacular.

He and Pratt had been meeting every two or three weeks since mid-November, always picking a different café and a different excuse for "running into each other." They hadn't touched base since Christmas break. There wasn't any need; Pratt was well aware of Darian's failed test. The story of the dismal outcome had spread throughout the university community within a day.

A good many people were genuinely disappointed by the young genius' failure. To those familiar with his role in developing virtual reality entertainment lattices, he was a science rock star. Darian's early technological achievements were reason enough to follow his forays into cosmology and theoretical physics, even though very few had more than a superficial understanding of his research.

There were, however, an equal number of individuals who felt vindicated by the failure of the experiment and, in particular, by his personal failure. This included several prominent senior academics who felt the budding star had detracted from the attention they had worked their whole careers to earn and which, in their humble opinions, they more properly deserved. Righteous smiles were exchanged between some of the less charitable university elite. Some could hardly restrain their glee.

Pratt was ambivalent about the whole thing. He hadn't enjoyed being on the receiving end of the young scientist's ruthless logic, but it would be unseemly to cheer a fellow academic's failure, even one in the physical sciences. It was enough that Dr. Leigh's arrogance had led him to humiliation, a fitting comeuppance. The two disagreed on methodologies and on most of their premises, but that didn't mean the scientist's intent was necessarily evil. Above all, he was a fellow seeker of Truth, and a highly dedicated one. Pratt respected that.

Then again, perhaps I'm not completely objective on this topic. After all, Dr. Leigh did publicly credit me with inspiring him to his present research. I need to take my lead from Reverend LaMontagne. He sees these things more clearly, and he's made it clear he harbors no doubt or illusion about the abominable goal of these investigations. Pratt resolved to be less generous with Darian Leigh in the future.

The waiter brought their orders. They said grace and dug in, quietly savoring the food as they chewed. Pratt was the first to break the silence.

"How has the team been dealing with the failure of the experiment? What has it been, about a month?"

"Yes. It was just before Christmas break." Larry realized he was speaking with a mouthful of food; he finished chewing and swallowed before continuing. "We didn't get much of a vacation, though. Darian had us all working overtime to figure out what went wrong." He grinned mischievously, though Pratt couldn't imagine why. Working overtime through the Christmas holidays didn't sound like fun at all.

"Perhaps the theory is incorrect," Pratt suggested.

"Well, that would serve them right." Larry studied his plate, planning his next bite as carefully as his next words. "They were all so sure of themselves. They never thought to question whether the whole RAF theory was moral or right, even when I pointed out their hubris. I told them God would not take lightly to messing with His creation like that. They gave me absolutely no credit; they treated me like a foolish child."

"You could have been one of them. You chose not to take the dendy virus pill."

Larry looked up, a flash of anger crossing his face. "Who could pervert their own brains that way? They're more machine than human. I don't trust them. I certainly wouldn't want to *be* one of them."

"Well, their lattices don't seem to have helped them out this time."

"Ha! They put such trust in their so-called super intelligence. It seems they're not all that smart in the end."

"Well, their intellectual prowess may exceed ours, but I do wonder what they've given up to achieve that." Pratt stared wistfully at the little wavelets lapping against the hulls of the boats.

"Kathy and Greg would say they've given up nothing. They're lovers now, you know."

"Oh? Does Darian know?"

"Yeah. It's just another factor to consider when he assigns work."

Pratt sensed that it was more than simple jealousy behind Larry's tone. "And how does that affect you?" he asked gently.

"They can do whatever they want," Larry replied. "It makes no difference to me. Greg changed the day he took that pill. You know, we used to be best friends, ever since the first day of grad school. We were in the same field, but we never competed with each other. We were colleagues, good colleagues. We worked together on most of our papers. In fact, our supervisor actually called us into her office one day to warn us to be careful to distinguish between each other's contributions."

Dr. Pratt worked on his burger while Larry talked. "I'm sorry you lost your friend. That must be difficult on you, to see him every day."

"If Reverend LaMontagne hadn't asked me to keep an eye on the group,

I think I would have left when Darian got back from the hospital."

"Right, the shooting. That was shocking, wasn't it? How is Darian doing? Is he recovering well?"

"He still favors his left shoulder. It seems to be healing okay but I'm sure it still hurts. It hasn't slowed him down, though. I'm not sure anything slows him down."

"What are they doing to resolve the problem?"

Larry took a few quick bites of his own sandwich, downing it with a sip of water. "All the usual. Taking everything apart: the theory, the hardware, the software. Testing everything. Checking their assumptions. Seeing if there's indication of any activity whatsoever. It's difficult because the RAF generator is binary. It either works or it doesn't. But even if the device is working, if there is no evidence of new or changed physical laws, it looks like it's not doing anything. There's no intermediate result."

"And have they found anything wrong?"

Again, Larry grinned mischievously. "Not yet."

Pratt was relieved. "Well, if the theory is wrong, and the device doesn't work, that will come as welcome news to the Reverend, won't it?"

"Oh, the theory is correct. The device works perfectly."

Pratt choked a little, as sweet, hot coffee found its way down his windpipe. "Excuse me?"

"There's nothing wrong with either the theory or the RAF generator. I've used it a number of times."

"But I thought you said the tests did *not* work."

"*Their* tests didn't work." Larry lowered his voice and leaned in closer. "I installed a slight modification to the controller BIOS. Unless I'm signed on as the operator, the RAF interrupts are routed into a side routine that adds a degree of randomness to the generated field. That randomness overwhelms the generated standing-wave resonances so they collapse without effect. None of them even thought to question the BIOS program. It's the standard externally-supplied software-on-a-chip so they just assume everything is fine with it."

"You've actually used the device?"

"Yes, I have. It doesn't do very much yet; it just alters a few physical constants."

"Like what?"

"Well, the first test altered the speed of light, exactly like Darian predicted. I've managed to alter the physical laws within a tiny microverse so light travels at about four times its regular velocity."

"That is remarkable," said an excited Dr. Pratt. "We must inform the Reverend."

"Soon. First, I have few more tests to run. Tonight, I'm going to try altering permitted electron orbitals in molecular bonds. Just to see if I can affect a bit of chemistry."

"Isn't that getting into dangerous territory?"

Larry's short, loud laugh drew attention from the other patrons. He lowered his voice to a hoarse whisper. "It's not like I'm changing the nuclear force. It won't set off an explosion or anything. I'm not insane like they are. Be grateful that God saw fit to place me where I would be first to operate this thing. In the wrong hands, say, Darian's hands, it could be extremely dangerous."

"Of that, I have no doubt."

"Anyway, I just want to see if I can change the requirement for how many electrons fulfill the outer orbitals in the atoms that form a water molecule. Make HO-water instead of H_2O. It should be interesting but, otherwise, generally inconsequential. I would not presume to tinker with things I don't understand. Unlike some people, I can make moral choices."

"I suppose I'll need to leave it to your judgment."

"I'd invite you to come have a look, but I think you'd find it boring."

"I'm sure you're right. There wouldn't really be much to see, would there?"

"Just some measurements on a computer display. A whole lot of nothing to the average layperson."

"Hmm. In that case, I'll take your word for it that the device actually works."

"Oh, it works. But only for me."

"How long before the rest of the team figures this out?"

"That's the beauty of it. They're all so smart and so noble that none of them have figured out I might be hiding something from them. I'll be able to run the RAF generator for months before anyone clues in."

"Promise me, if you get any sense they realize that they've been duped, you'll let us know?"

"Sure thing. Then you can get me out of here and move me somewhere out of their reach, somewhere inside the New Confederacy. I'll expect a very nice position. Maybe at the University of Houston."

"I'm sure that can be arranged once we have the device in our control. Until then, please be careful."

"I'm always careful, Dr. Pratt." Larry reached over and scooped up some ketchup with Pratt's last fry, and popped it into his mouth.

44

GREG WAVED HIS HANDS SLOWLY AND EVENLY, back and forth, back and forth, in rhythm with his breathing and purposeful sideway steps. This was the second last pass of *Move Hands Like Clouds*; they had about eleven minutes remaining in the routine.

He'd only begun practicing Tai Chi a month ago but already preferred the discipline over the various styles of yoga he'd studied as a child. Maybe that was because he'd never met anyone like Kathy in his yoga classes.

And now, this! This was great. Together with six other students from their school, he and Kathy were giving a public demonstration of the Yang-style 85 form in the South Corridor Courtyard of the Dr. Sun Yat-Sen Classical Chinese Garden.

They faced the corridor because, as the ancient saying went, "To face the south is to become a king." A quietly appreciative audience gathered in the open courtyard in front of them and along the other three sides of the jade green pool behind them.

Greg's lattice had enabled him to memorize the complex martial art routine almost instantly. Sadly, his muscles had yet to become accustomed to the deceptively rigorous movements, let alone the brutally slow place of this traditional Yang form. As they approached the twenty-minute mark, he could feel his heart beating rapidly and his legs shaking from fatigue. The form was surprisingly challenging, both mentally and physically. *Just a bit longer. It gets easier once we get past the last* Needle at the Bottom of the Seabed.

Over the past few months, Greg discovered he loved everything Chinese. He loved the food, the music, the architecture, the martial arts, the language and, most of all, Kathy Liang. They were happy to learn that Darian also had an appreciation of the ancient culture. When he and Kathy requested the Saturday morning off to take part in a Tai Chi demonstration at the Sun Yat-Sen gardens, Darian not only gave them permission but came along to watch.

Truth be told, Greg and Kathy welcomed a little respite from the stress of the past five weeks. They were trying their best to be a normal couple, to nurture the love that was growing between them, but it wasn't easy. They managed to steal away for a dinner date, a walk in the misty rain, or an occasional movie, but Darian granted time away from work begrudgingly, and only when exhaustion or tedium hampered productivity. By the time they got home, they barely had enough energy left to cook, eat, and crash, painfully aware that next morning's alarm would come too early for their liking.

In the meantime, the dendy lattices growing inside their heads pushed relentlessly forward, displacing and replacing biological neurons.

Ever since the shooting, which Darian now referred to as, "The Event," he had altered the lattice development program to make its host—that is, each of them—less reliant on the body's natural biology.

For now, the combination of retreating biology and aggressive semiconductor growth made all three of them more prone to total mental shutdown than they had been in prior weeks. Darian promised that would change after the system adapted. Once it did, their bodies and minds would no longer need the restorative cycles of sleep. They would be able to work as much as they wanted, provided they took care of their physical requirements.

Greg wasn't quite sure he liked the sound of that. *I guess I'm not ready to be primarily machine-driven quite yet.*

Darian's dendy program upgrade, having been implemented before the others' as a precautionary measure, was further along in its progress. He didn't need internal system checks to measure the improvements, he could tell by the dwindling hours he was able to work without rest.

The man was obsessed with solving the enigma of the RAF generator dysfunction. Like so many compulsively dedicated scientists before him, other aspects of his life were starting to suffer, notably, his hygiene, his health, and his patience. He spent his days in electronic communication with Greg in a shared virtual, computational space he had constructed on his desktop computer.

There, the two of them reworked the RAF equations from as many different starting principles as they could imagine. They compared the computed predictions with every cosmological, subatomic, and quantum experiment of the past century.

As a result of their investigations, they proposed a host of new experiments, many of which they sent out to groups around the world. At least twenty new, ground-breaking tests would be underway over the next few months at research institutes in China, Japan, Germany, Switzerland, Russia, Brazil, Pacifica, and the United States of North America.

Though politics had rearranged national alliances over the past few decades, science was as international as it had ever been. Those with the most appropriate expertise were sent proposals for new experiments regardless of their physical locations. Darian insisted that his research benefit all of humanity; borders and political alignments were irrelevant.

The team knew something was wrong, most likely with the theory. Otherwise, the RAF generator would have worked. They held to the premise expressed by one of Darian's favorite sayings, "Mother Nature is never wrong." If that were true, they must have missed some important clue in the petabytes of available experimental data. Once discovered, the overlooked data would explain why the Reality Assertion Field theory could not be correct.

But the more they probed, the better the theory stood up. Darian's frustration with his inability to spot which of his initial assumptions was faulty began to wear on all of them.

There was still a slim possibility that the theory was right, and that something had gone wrong with the implementation of the RAF generator. They'd run a cursory check early on in their testing and almost entirely ruled that out but...still. What else was left?

One day, Darian asked Kathy and Larry to log every schematic, along with videos and intermediate test results into Darian's workspace.

While the others slept, Darian reviewed all of the engineering specs and functional tests of the device. He went over everything. He checked the approach, the implementation, and the operational verifications. He proposed new tests at every step to ensure that every part was functioning to spec. He could find nothing that wasn't working exactly as designed. It was infuriating.

Everything in Darian's world moved at hyper-speed, including the questions around his competency. Within days of the publicized failure of the RAF test, the first grumblings began. "Maybe the university had been too ambitious to hire the *wunderkind*." "Maybe Leigh was more of an engineer than a *real* scientist." "Maybe the young genius had been fooled by his own brilliance or by his early successes."

Normally, fledgling tenure-track professors were granted a full two or three years to prove their academic mettle. Darian's cockiness had heightened expectations to such a degree that, in the minds of much of the Faculty, the usual honeymoon period did not apply to him.

It didn't take long for the grumblings to find the ear of the Department Chair, and Dr. Wong saw no choice but to bring the concerns forward to the Dean of Sciences. Unaccustomed to failure in any intellectual arena, Darian reacted predictably. He was defensive and arrogant.

"I would be happy for anyone to show me where I've gone wrong. However, seeing as no one outside of my team is capable of following the math in any reasonable period of time, I will likely be very old before outside help will be found to be in any way useful."

Dr. Wong was a seasoned veteran of departmental politics and knew when to withdraw quietly. He'd watched many star performers burn brightly at the beginning and flame out under the institutional pressures of constant productivity. He didn't take Darian's implied criticism personally. But while he let the comment pass, his estimation of the young man's probable long-term outlook dropped significantly.

Weeks passed without resolution of the academic or political problems picking away at the Faculty. The grumbling grew louder. Administrators from Dr. Wong to President Sakira urged patience, but the complainers enlisted the aid of those whose original protests over Darian's research were based on philosophical or religious grounds, rather than scientific or safety concerns.

Several groups organized rallies against Dr. Leigh's work. Yesterday's rally outside the President's office was sponsored by the local chapter of Yeshua's True Guard Church.

"With the birth of His Son so recently celebrated," declared the Archbishop of Vancouver, "God, Himself, has seen fit to demonstrate His dominion over the laws of nature. This experiment of Dr. Leigh's has been, is, and always will be a failure. It is an abomination to our Lord. It is the work of Satan, and it must be stopped."

When he bothered to pay them any attention at all, Darian scoffed at the ridiculousness of the protests. "They have no scientific basis whatsoever. They're just posturing for soundbites on the evening news."

He may have been right, but that did little to comfort the Board of Governors attending their first meeting of the New Year. Though academic freedom was purported to be highly valued among that eminent gathering, in the end, it came down to an uncomfortably close vote.

The decision on whether to censure Dr. Leigh's work was tabled for the following month.

* * *

THE TAI CHI DEMO moved into the final *Down Form* and *Step Forward With Seven Stars*. Greg caught his mind drifting. He brought it back to the present, finishing the form with the required mindfulness, and as smoothly as he could muster on his trembling legs. As the music came to a close, the group held the closing position, then straightened and lowered their arms in perfect synchrony. The spectators applauded as the class took three deep breaths in silent meditation and were done. Several from the audience approached the group to congratulate the instructor and students, and to inquire about lessons.

"That was great," Darian said, his broad smile echoed by others gathering nearby. "I really should think about taking it up myself."

"I'm sure you already have all the moves memorized," Greg replied. "I saw you following along with us."

"Guilty as charged. But you'll note my movements were microscopic. It's been so long since I've done anything like that, I'm afraid the body would find it hard to follow the brain's instructions on a larger scale."

"It's a really good break from working. Apart from the exercise, I find it very meditative, very calming, and deceptively challenging."

"I've always wanted to take up something like that. I like Kung Fu movies but I could never handle that level of intensity. Maybe this would be a happy medium or a good starting point. I've read that one should master Tai Chi before beginning Kung Fu."

Kathy worked her way through her classmates and joined Greg and Darian. "Well, that took care of the morning nicely. What say we avoid work a little longer and go for lunch?"

"I'm game," Greg replied. "Maybe we should change into our civilian clothes first, though."

Darian laughed. "Yeah, you go into a restaurant dressed like that," he pointed to their traditional silk martial arts uniforms with their billowing sleeves and cloth buttons, "and someone might think you're looking for a fight."

While Greg and Kathy changed, Darian finished his tour of the Garden with a brief meditation in the Main Hall. As he waited for his two assistants, he stared into the milky green water, looking for any tell-tale ripples made by the resident koi.

He pushed aside the demands of his lattice to get back to work. *The mystery will still be there this afternoon*—he thought. *Even semiconductors should take a break sometime.* He chuckled to himself over that absurd comment. He needed almost no rest these days, except from the futility of their investigations.

"Okay, where should we go?" Greg was back in his blue jeans, with his jacket draped casually over one arm; the heat generated from the thirty-minute demo was, for the time being, sufficient to dispel the winter chill.

"Why don't we go to Bojangles on False Creek," Kathy suggested, "We don't often get down this way in the middle of the day anymore and I miss it." In addition to their enjoyment of Chinese culture, she and Greg shared a love of the water. She also hoped to finagle an after-lunch walk along the seawall once they were in the area. Getting away from their problems for a few hours would do them all good.

They walked the few blocks down Carrall Street to the seawall. The first section up to the Cambie Street Bridge wasn't all that nice but, by Kathy's calculations, any sunny day by the water was a good one.

The trio walked in companionable silence, Kathy and Greg arm in arm, and Darian alongside, enjoying the sunshine and the background hum of city traffic. They arrived at the café within thirty minutes.

45

"WHAT THE HELL?" As they entered Bojangles and looked around for an empty table, Greg spotted Larry sitting with Lucius Pratt, Darian's nemesis from his first day on campus.

Larry was about to stuff a ketchup-plastered French fry in his mouth. The look of smug superiority on his face changed into a guilty frown when he spotted his three colleagues approaching. Dr. Pratt, demonstrating the value of his experience and acumen, calmly stood up, smiled, and held out his hand to greet them.

"Ah, Dr. Leigh. How wonderful to see you. Your associate, here, has been kind enough to update me on your group's progress in addressing this latest challenge. I do hope that you will find your way through to a solution soon."

"Yes. Well, my *assistant*, Dr. Rusalov, is free to spend his spare time as he wishes," Darian replied as he politely shook the philosopher's hand. "I hope he hasn't bored you with arcane details of our profession. We geeks sometimes think everyone is just like us."

"Heh, heh. No, I haven't found him boring at all. Thankfully, Dr. Rusalov has stuck to a level of generalities appropriate to my lack of training in your field. We both happened to be out on the seawall, taking in this lovely day, and quite literally bumped into each other. I trust it's alright for me to inquire how things have been going. Since I was there at the beginning, so to speak, I feel a personal interest in your research."

Darian's answering smile was reserved in its warmth. "We have no secrets, and sometimes it can be helpful to talk out one's issues with non-specialists. My father used to say, if you can't explain what you're working on to your grandfather, you don't really understand it."

"Ouch! I hope I'm not the grandfather in that story. Not yet."

"It's just a saying."

"Yes, I suppose it is. Well, as it happens, your timing is impeccable. I was just about to abandon Dr. Rusalov. There are some errands that I really must attend to. I've been enjoying our conversation so much that it seems I've lost all track of time." He turned to Larry and proffered his hand, "Dr. Rusalov, thank you so much. It's been very educational." He pulled out the chair nearest Kathy and invited her to sit down. "Please, all of you, enjoy your lunch on me. I'll instruct your waiter to leave my tab open."

"That's very generous of you," answered Darian.

"No, not at all. It's the least I can do after taking so much of your assistant's time. Have a lovely day." With that, Dr. Pratt shook hands all around and made his way to the front.

Larry couldn't mask his panic as he watched Pratt disappear out the door. He rubbed his hands too earnestly on his crumpled napkin and placed the disintegrating paper over his fries.

"I hope you weren't revealing any state secrets," Darian joked to Larry once the team was alone.

"You know I wouldn't do that," Larry asserted, his tone and demeanor more serious than Darian's teasing warranted.

Greg inspected his friend's face and body language more thoroughly, calling on the more finely-tuned observational tools of his lattice. He didn't like what he saw: nervous tics of the face and hands, flushed face, slightly dilated pupils, and an obvious attempt to control his breathing. He sent a quick private message to Darian and Kathy—*He's been talking way outside his comfort zone.*

I know—they both replied.

"Larry, relax, I'm just kidding. You can talk to Dr. Pratt all you like," Darian said aloud. "If the worst we have to endure is that our present embarrassment goes any more public than it already has, we will survive."

Larry relaxed a little, and his breathing returned to normal.

"Hey, how'd the Tai Chi demonstration go? Sorry I missed it. I forgot all about it." Larry opted for a quick change of subject to clear the slate.

"It was great," replied Darian. "Kathy and Greg's lattices give them a considerable advantage over their classmates, but everybody performed admirably."

"I think people enjoyed it. We did, too. It was fun, wasn't it?" Kathy asked.

"I'm glad we did it; I was nervous at first but it went really well," Greg replied.

The waiter arrived, took their orders, and asked permission to remove

Larry's abandoned meal. "Was everything okay?" he asked Larry, with genuine concern. "Would you like something else?"

"No, everything was fine. My eyes were bigger than my stomach, I guess," Larry answered, handing the plate to the waiter.

Their orders given, Darian shifted in his seat to better observe the boats moored in the marina, and to let himself be entertained by the rhythm of the masts bobbing gently over the sun-dappled water. *Sometimes the best approach to getting an answer is to ask no question at all*–he broadcast to the other two. Kathy and Greg followed his gaze, enduring a few minutes of uncomfortable silence.

Larry finally turned to Darian and asked, "So, do you need me to come in today, too?"

"No, we won't be doing any testing today," Darian answered. Greg couldn't tell if Larry was disappointed or relieved. He wasn't enjoying this feeling of distrust he suddenly felt toward his old friend and co-worker.

"If you'd like to go over some of the new experiments Darian and I have proposed for follow-up, I could come over tonight," Greg said.

He felt sorry for the distance that had grown between them over the past few months. *Larry must feel completely sidelined from the main action.* Still, it was his own decision to reject the dendy lattice and deprive himself of being useful. He could change that at any time.

"No, that's okay," Larry replied, "I've got stuff to do. I'll catch up with you in the lab tomorrow."

Something was definitely off, but Greg couldn't quite put his finger on it. His earlier compassion for an old friend was losing ground to unsettling suspicion. He eyed his lab mate from a new perspective. *What's going on in there, Larry?*—he wondered. The dendy lattice recognized and analyzed hundreds of micro movements in the face, but it couldn't read his old friend's mind.

Larry continued, "I'm supposed to call my folks tonight, anyway. Those video calls back to the family usually take up the whole evening, now that I work for such a famous research team."

Greg noted Larry's use of the word "for" instead of "with"; they were the team he worked *for*, not *with*. A sad but telling shift.

The food arrived, and Darian took a bite of his bacon cheeseburger. "That's right. Your mother is Svetlana Tsarkova, isn't she?" he asked between mouthfuls.

Greg was pretty sure Darian knew everything that was publicly available about Larry and a great deal that wasn't public as well. He interpreted the question as an attempt to put Larry at ease, to get him talking about something more comfortable.

Kathy saw Greg about to add his own comment and sent him a private message–*Let's leave this conversation to the boss. Larry's acting weird; let's see if Darian can pull anything out of him.*

Greg bit off whatever he was about to say, corking his open mouth with a corner of crispy panini. *Okay, let's see where this goes*–he sent.

"Yes, that's right. Have you worked with her?" Larry replied.

"No, but her work on ultrafast lasers is well known and very well-regarded. By all reports, she's an excellent scientist. Our research programs never really had much in common before, but maybe we could work her into one of the new experiments," Darian added encouragingly, and looked over to Greg for backup.

"Yeah, sure. We have a number of ideas on how the RAF could alter molecular bond formation; some of the new proposals we're working on may have some overlap with her work," Greg added. "Larry and I could meet next week to discuss which ones he thinks his mom might be interested in testing. If you'd like, that is. It wouldn't cramp your style to have your mom working with us, would it?"

"Why don't you send him the proposals now, and he can look them over later today? Then, if it's okay with you, we could talk to your mom about them Wednesday," suggested Darian.

Greg accessed his lattice, picked out a few proposals from the database server back on campus, and sent them in an email to Larry. "Done," he said a few seconds later. "They'll be in your email when you get home, Larry."

"That does come in handy sometimes," Larry had to admit.

Greg shrugged. "You can still take your pill whenever you want to, you know. No pressure at all; just keep in mind, it's never too late."

"I'm sorry you feel you can't accept installing your own lattice," Darian said aloud, making everyone squirm. *There we go; the elephant is out in the open now.*

"I do respect your decision, Larry, and I'm glad you're able to continue working with the team."

Larry looked away without saying a word.

After that, they couldn't get much more out of him on any topic, no matter how harmless. They eventually gave up, finishing their lunches in silence. Larry mumbled something about having some shopping to do and left.

Greg didn't bother inviting him to join the other three back at the lab later on. *I give up*—he sent to Kathy, a defeated look on his face.

She put a comforting hand over his. There was nothing else anyone could do.

46

It was 4:00 Sunday morning and Darian was restless.

He, Kathy, and Greg had passed an infuriatingly fruitless afternoon troubleshooting the RAF hardware, software, and theory. They pored over every detail, again and again. By the end of their day, tempers were short and nobody could focus.

It didn't make sense. The RAF should work. Every single component and idea checked out fine. Maybe they were all too close to the problem. Maybe they'd allowed themselves to be distracted by the morning off and lunch afterward. Maybe catching Larry in that clandestine meeting with Lucius Pratt had been more disturbing than any of them had thought.

Frustrated, they quit work at 6:00 p.m., or at least that was when Darian sent Greg and Kathy home. As long as he kept his lattice adequately charged, Darian was practically indefatigable.

It was his biological brain that let him down; despite its minimal role in the work, it eventually grew tired. Synaptic connections could only tolerate the enforced activity of the lattice for so long before they became recalcitrant and stopped responding.

Around midnight, he decided to give it a rest. Tomorrow would be a new start. They'd decided the best way to test the RAF generator was to build a new one from scratch, using completely different components from an alternative source. That would tell them if the defect was in their suppliers or in their design. They were getting desperate enough to start testing even relatively implausible ideas.

Darian had something even more drastic in mind for himself. A couple of weeks earlier he realized his own computational ability was at least as powerful as the laptop supercomputer they were using to control the RAF device. *Why not turn myself into an autonomous RAF generator?*–he asked himself, and went to work on the viral vectors that would construct an array of resonance-generating antennae immediately beneath the surface of his own skull. He synthesized the new DNA in-house and cultured the resulting viruses himself. If the available hardware wasn't going to work, he would try a different approach.

Eight days after taking the completed virus for the antenna, the dendies had nearly finished assembling the sub-cranial array. He waited for the ping telling him it was ready.

Darian allowed his lattice to go into a low-energy hibernate mode. His recent modifications usually took advantage of any downtime to expand the lattice domain, pushing into new areas of his natural biological neural net and learning how to assume new functionality. The process tended to produce a mild headache so Darian closed his eyes and rested while it ran its course.

You'd think that the lattice would give me better access to my own subconscious–he pondered as he drifted. *Maybe then I could figure out what's bothering me, besides the obvious.* He knew that wasn't the way the subconscious worked. He'd spent some time a few years earlier reading how consciousness was an emergent phenomenon of a highly complex web of sub-conscious processes. The "society of the mind," Minsky had called it, decades earlier.

He managed four hours of unsatisfying rest while the agitated remnants of his biological brain obsessively replayed the chance encounter with Larry in the café. Finally accepting that peaceful rest would elude him until he determined the source of his agitation, he got out of bed and went to the study.

He sat at his desk for a few minutes before giving in to the restlessness. He paced the floor, barefoot, in slow, purposeful steps. *Sometimes the body knows best what will put the mind at ease.*

The noise in his brain monetarily quieted. He reactivated his lattice, and set it consciously on the problem. *Why would Larry be meeting with Pratt, if it weren't just a random occurrence? Why had he seemed so defensive?*

A number of hypotheses came to mind, but he could think of nothing besides the welcome luncheon on his first day on campus that linked the two men. *Should I hack into their personal emails? Maybe they belong to the same church or some other organization.*

Darian didn't take such invasions of privacy lightly. Public databases, they were no problem, but areas expressly marked "Private" were different. With the professional pressure building against him, an ethical breach would give the university the justification they needed to sanction him or, worse, to fire him. Anyway, if Larry was clever enough to keep his personal communications off the net, there would be nothing to be found.

Nothing he could find on the public nets linked the two men, but his gut told him there had to be some connection he'd missed.

My gut?—he mused. *I'm thinking with my gut now? That's great. Only, I don't think my lattice has extended into that neural tissue yet.*

I could tap into NCSA surveillance records. They have no compunction about who they spy on. If he used the National Coordinated Security system to check up on Pratt and Larry, he'd have to be extra careful not to be discovered. Never mind the university's reaction, he didn't need the dark side of the feds coming down on him right now.

Am I being paranoid? Trying too hard to force a connection that isn't really there? Only one way to find out.

His lattice leaped into action. While he raked through the personal emails of both men, he simultaneously searched NCSA records, being careful not to leave any record that could be traced back to him.

Pratt and Larry had avoided direct email contact. *Or maybe Larry was telling the truth; maybe they don't know each other that well.* There were no oblique references to one another through mutual acquaintances. *If they are separated by less than the standard six degrees of separation, it's only through me.*

The NCSA telephone recordings proved more fruitful. *That's interesting*—he thought as he read a transcript of a conversation dated the day he was shot. Larry was the subject of a conversation between Dr. Pratt and Reverend Alan LaMontagne, the leader of the YTG Church.

That Pratt and LaMontagne knew each other was mildly surprising. That they would be discussing Larry, was an eye-opener.

In retrospect, it made some sense that Pratt might be a member of the Yeshua's True Guard Church, but it was odd he would be so secretive about it. His tenured status would protect him from any conceivable recrimination for belonging to a fundamentalist church.

Darian couldn't imagine any way in which being a member of a religious organization, especially one officially adopted by the government of the New Confederacy, would have hurt the philosopher's career. *Maybe he's hiding it for personal reasons, something to do with his family or friends.*

The Church of Yeshua's True Guard had too many connections to Darian's life over the past few months for him to be sanguine about this revelation. Using Larry to spy on him would be unconscionable. *I may have said some things they find objectionable but this is starting to feel entirely too personal.*

The phone transcripts indicated LaMontagne denied the church's involvement in the shooting, at least to Pratt, but Darian wasn't convinced. Even if the shooter wasn't an *official* member of the Church, it felt like something that this fundamentalist group might facilitate.

He turned his focus to the public and a few private records of Jeremiah Falton, the man who'd shot him. Collectively, the records pointed to the kind of person who would join and rapidly rise through the ranks of the YTG Church: outspoken, deeply religious, and passionately nationalistic.

He was a resident of Austin, Texas, the heart of the New Confederacy and the headquarters of Yeshua's True Guards. He had written a number of prominent public commentaries over the years that were timely and favorable to positions held by the Church. He had served in one of the most active wings of the New Confederacy Militia, where publicly professing one's faith was a requisite of acceptance into the ranks.

Darian found it more than curious that Falton had never joined the Church. Yet the name didn't appear on any of their membership rosters. Sure, it was possible, but it seemed highly improbable. *Maybe he's listed under another name, or he's a sleeper.*

Darian tried casually to penetrate the private files of the YTG Church, to see if he could find any hidden information about Falton. To his surprise, the sophisticated security around YTG's system was even tighter than NCSA's.

Their server was easy enough to locate but none of the conventional back doors would open. All of the files, including filenames and sizes, were heavily encrypted. *Even with my lattice, this could take a while to crack, especially if they've used a good algorithm.*

He moused around the system a while, hoping his activity went undetected. *With this level of paranoia, they probably keep a log of all system-level commands. They may even be trawling communications, activity looking for anything suspicious.*

He tried a different approach, injecting a monitoring virus at the router level. Routers usually had more conventional security software and could be more easily bypassed. The virus would alert him to activity over the web and, hopefully, allow him to record the required decryption key.

While he waited, he returned his attention to the NCSA recordings, expanding his search to all calls made by Reverend Alan LaMontagne. There was a lot of activity, but it was annoyingly uninformative.

An alarm chimed softly in his head, interrupting his perusal of the NCSA recordings. His internal RAF antennae were finally complete. *Excellent! I can finish the search later.* Although the machinations of church and state were intriguing, his top priority was to get the RAF generator working.

Darian sat down at one of his dining room chairs. He loaded a standard control program into his lattice and initiated the antenna array in his skull. He ran through a quick series of tests to ensure individual elements of the array were transmitting properly. Everything checked out.

He set the array to ACTIVE and fed it the settings from the first series of calculations.

A tentative bluish spherical region flickered into existence over the table a meter in front of him, sputtered for a second or two, then fizzled out and disappeared.

Darian's heart raced. *It works! It actually works! Not perfectly, but that was something! Something real. I mean, unreal. I need to send the team a message! No, they deserve to hear this in person.*

His mind raced as fast as his heart. *Focus! Focus!* He made a conscious effort to slow his breathing.

The test wasn't perfect. Given the configuration, the equations should have created a stable four-inch microverse. *They didn't. So why was the sphere so small and unstable? Think. Think! What was standing in the way? Of course! The settings weren't adapted for the presence of real matter. The air in the room would have destabilized the field. I'll need to move to the vacuum chamber in the lab to get proper results.*

He looked at the time. Somehow, 4:30 in the morning didn't seem too early to start the day, especially not when it was going to be so amazing.

The young professor threw on some clothes and headed out into the crisp pre-dawn air. The lab was only a short walk away. As he reached the edge of campus, he sent out a wake-up call through the lattice net to Greg and Kathy.

Kathy answered the call within seconds. *Darian? What is it? What time is it?*

It works—he replied, trying to keep the tone of his transmitted voice as level as possible.

It works? What works?—she transmitted. Then she realized. *It works? It works!* Several kilometers away, in the suite she shared with Greg, she squealed, "Greg, wake up! It works!" and shook her slumbering partner awake.

Kathy kept the channel open so Darian got to watch as Greg blinked sleep from his eyes and Kathy repeated the news. Greg came online instantly.

I'm sorry to wake you up—Darian said. *No, actually, I'm not sorry at all. I was going to tell you in person later this morning but I couldn't wait. We did it!* Without waiting for a response, Darian sent a synopsis of everything he'd been doing, the internal antenna array he had been growing in his cranium, the crude test that had generated a sputtering microverse in his dining room a few minutes before—everything.

I'm on my way to the lab right now. I need to use the vacuum chamber and the laser interferometer—he sent. *Can you meet me there?*

It'll take us about forty minutes but we'll get there as fast as we can—Kathy replied. *Can you wait 'til we get there before you run it again?*

Every extra minute will be torture but, for you guys, sure. Get here as fast as you can, though, okay? It was only then he remembered the fourth member of the team. *Hey, can you pick up Larry along the way? I'm sure he'll want to be there too.*

Sure—answered Greg. *I'll call him, and we'll cruise by his place. I don't think his bus will be running at this hour, and he's not going to want to miss this.* They took a collective deep breath and recorded the moment in their memories.

The lattice did a terrible job of transmitting emotions, so Darian just sent one of his favorite stock photos, a projection of the Milky Way with an arrow pointing to the tiny region just in from the outer edge labeled, "You are here." It was meant to convey how insignificant he felt before the mysteries of the universe.

Kathy laughed. *I feel like we own the entire galaxy right now.*

I know what you mean. I'll be at the lab in a few minutes—said Darian. *Get here as soon as you can.* Then he signed off.

Darian entered the nearly deserted building and practically ran down the corridor to the lab, his mind already playing out the vast number of experiments the group would perform. They'd lost some time, but they'd make up for it quickly. He realized they still didn't know why the laptop RAF generator hadn't worked. *We'll figure that out when we make the second one. If that doesn't solve it, I'll just get Greg and Kathy to grow the antennae internally like me.*

His old confidence and determination returned; it felt good to be moving forward again. He fiddled with his key in the sloppy lab-door lock—*Why do we still have this ancient technology?* He knew the answer. Everybody did. Budget cuts over the last decade had brought modernization of university infrastructure to a screaming halt. *That's going to change, too*—he promised himself.

Darian entered the darkened lab, letting the door close on its own behind him. He only caught a quick glimpse of the three small spheres floating inside the vacuum chamber, one yellow, one red, and one blue. They disappeared so fast he had to replay the last few milliseconds of visual input to be sure they had ever existed.

Then he noticed Larry sitting at the control console, his face lit by the eerie glow from the display, and everything fell into place.

47

LARRY STOOD UP AND OPENED HIS MOUTH TO EXPLAIN. "Don't bother," said Darian. "I know the RAF generator works. I know the theory is correct. And now, I know *you* know, and you've probably known for some time. What I don't know, is how you kept this from us."

Larry regained his composure. His eyes flicked over to the empty hallway and back to Darian. *He's alone.* He locked eyes with his mentor and supervisor. "You all thought you were so smart. You kept looking in all the hard places and you ignored the simple explanation—that someone was sabotaging the experiment."

Darian nodded. "So you altered the operating system?"

"The BIOS, actually. It overrode parts of the O/S in RAM after booting up. I figured you were less likely to look there than in the O/S itself. Anyway, it wasn't that hard to do. I just added a little redirection to certain interrupt handlers. You would have had to follow the machine language byte by byte to notice it."

"I was almost at that stage. I decided last night to just start over and build a second generator."

"I would have just made the same change to that one too."

"Why?"

Larry shrugged. "Lot of reasons, really. For one, I don't like the way you've all been treating me, like some half-witted lab monkey at the beck and call of geniuses." His voice shook with barely-controlled emotion.

"Larry, everything we are, everything we know, everything we can do, all of this was offered to you."

Darian's voice was little more than a whisper, so quiet that Larry had to strain to hear it. But instead of the calming effect that he was aiming for,

Darian's words only fueled the rage welling within his colleague.

Larry sat back down, putting the control console between Darian and himself. "You guys think you're some kind of young gods, altering the human brain, playing around with the laws of nature. It's just too much."

"Scientists have been doing that kind of thing for centuries."

"Well, maybe we've gone too far, too fast. Maybe there are some things we aren't meant to know."

"You don't really believe that."

"How can you claim what you're doing is for the good of humanity? None of you are even human anymore! Why should we trust *you* to do what's right for the rest of us?"

"The hardware may be different, but the program running on it is still human," replied Darian evenly.

Larry's fists clenched, and the veins in his neck and forehead bulged as he fought to control his fury.

Darian was ready to bolt. He searched his lattice for some basic self-defense moves; he hoped it wouldn't come to violence.

Larry hunched over the keyboard and tapped a few keys while Darian looked on, dumbstruck. *What's he up to?*

"I only wish the other monstrosities were here with you," Larry spat. "You are abominations before God. Someone needs to put an end to this."

"We are many things, Larry, but, come on, really? Abominations? Who are you getting this from?"

"If you'd had any shred of humility, I might not have been forced into this. But you think you know everything. I'd destroy this machine and all your notes, if I thought it'd do any good. But you'd just recreate it all, wouldn't you? How can humanity trust you to develop this for the good of all of us? You just don't know when to stop. Will you only be happy once you become immortal and all-powerful? Is it your goal to challenge God, Himself?"

Larry took a shuddering breath. His eyes, which only moments before had been projecting bitterness and raw fury, now reflected only deep sadness. The sadness worried Darian more than the anger.

"Goodbye Professor," Larry said. "Oh, and don't worry about Greg and Kathy. I have plans for them, too. And then I'll make sure the RAF generator ends up in more responsible hands than theirs. I'm sorry, but you've forced me into this. It's been nice knowing you. Or maybe not." He pressed the ENTER key.

A hazy gray field materialized around Darian, encapsulating him from the bottom of his shoes to the top of the last stray hair on his head.

Darian threw his arms out to both sides, feeling the unyielding boundary of the containment field. He tried to take a step but his foot slid down along the inside surface. He was trapped.

He instructed his lattice to connect to the laptop controller but it was already too late; the communication lines were inactive. Every system that should have been connected to the controller was offline. There was no way in.

He found a stray open line leading from some other equipment to the outside world and connected to the local power grid. Working furiously, he bypassed the university's Systems security and killed the electricity supply to the lab.

The hall light streaming in through the observation window cut out, and was replaced by the harsh glare of an emergency backup. In the lab, however, nothing changed.

He's really thought this out—Darian realized. *Well, at least the outage will trigger a maintenance alarm. They take power outages seriously in the science buildings.* Frantically, he searched for other alarms he could activate remotely—smoke, heat, water—but Larry had beat him to it. *How is that even possible?*

Larry laughed—a deranged, heartless laugh, full of hatred. "That won't do you any good. The RAF generator will work for hours on battery. In a few seconds, this microverse holding you is going to collapse. Every molecule, atom, and particle making up the great Darian Leigh will disappear from this universe forever, and there's nothing you can do to stop it."

He came around the desk, bringing his face within inches of his mentor. The transparent gray barrier was all that stood between them.

"Do you see what you've done? Do you see?" he yelled. "*You* created this...this affront to nature. You! And now, through *me*, the universe—the one true universe created by God Almighty—is going to take its vengeance and erase you from existence. Can you feel it closing in around you?"

He stepped back and pointed an accusatory finger at Darian. "I, Valeriy Illyovich Rusalov, having found Darian Leigh guilty of the greatest arrogance and hubris against God, banish you from His universe!"

For a moment, Larry's eyes softened, and Darian thought he might be feeling remorse for his actions, for his colleague's impending fate.

"Enjoy your sentence in Hell," Larry finished, his voice disturbingly devoid of emotion.

Darian struggled as the sphere began to shrink in on him. He tried unsuccessfully to control his terror. Using his lattice to clamp down on his emotions, he allowed himself to go numb. He ignored his imminent death, and filled his mind with RAF equations.

He'd learned a lot in the past few hours: the basic RAF theory was correct; fields could be formed even in the presence of matter. The fields Larry was generating permitted selective interaction between the enclosed and external universes while preventing other actions. He could hear and see through the bubble that held him captive, but he couldn't push through it.

He hoped what he'd learned could somehow save his life.

He sped through the hundreds of thousands of equations that he and Greg had devised over the past few weeks, looking for anything that might fit what he now knew to be true. There had to be a way to nullify this field before it destroyed him.

He had enough computational power to work with the equations or to operate his own internal RAF controller, not both at the same time. Whatever he came up with, there'd be no second chances.

At last, he found a set of equations that might work. A pitifully small one, but that would make it easier to generate the required field. The parameters showed enough flexibility to allow a few changes on the fly. He hoped it would be enough.

Outside, in the larger universe, Larry looked several inches taller than he'd been a couple minutes ago. This confirmed Darian's fears. *Larry isn't trying to trap me or kill me; he wants to obliterate me.*

What else have I got to work with? The laws of this microverse started out similar to our own universe, except this one is shrinking with me inside it. Oddly enough, it doesn't feel any more limiting; I must be shrinking along with the sphere. The space between electrons and the nucleus is compacting. Normal biochemistry still seems to be functioning. Electrons aren't being squeezed out like in a neutron star, not yet.

He must have set the generator to step down through a series of standing wave functions that determine the size of electron orbitals. And because atoms are mostly made up of empty space, there's potential for a lot more compression before electron shells start overlapping with protons and neutrons. At some point, though, there's not going to be enough room for everything; life-supporting chemistry is going to become impossible. Unless Larry has figured out how to convert me into a nuclear being—and I doubt that—I am going to die.

He wondered if Larry intended to keep him alive long enough to feel the electrons being crushed out of his molecules or if he'd stop before that point. His best guess was that Larry could shrink him by a factor of more than ten thousand without completely eradicating him. *Is he going to keep me alive inside this bubble or destroy me?*

Darian wasn't sure which would be worse. Either way, he would be dead pretty quickly. *I have to reverse the collapse, and now.*

He shut down the search programs and brought his RAF-generator control program to the forefront. He set his internal generator to ACTIVE, and projected fields that he hoped would return his prison to conditions more similar—according to his frenzied calculations—to the natural universe in which he belonged.

The fields he cast wove in and around the ones Larry was using to produce the collapsing bubble. Amazingly, the shrinking halted. It started to reverse. In spite of his lattice-dampened emotions, Darian was elated. His computations must be close; he'd bought himself some time. Darian felt a wisp of hope.

"What the...? Oh, no! No, you can't! No, no, no, no!" Larry babbled when he noticed the sphere growing larger. "What are you doing?" Changes were no longer being mediated through his machine alone. He ran behind the desk and sat in the operator's chair, furiously stabbing away at the laptop.

"Ahhh, very clever, Dr. Leigh! You've been busy!" He thrummed his finger on the keys. "So that's how you figured out the RAF theory was correct. You found a way to implant or grow an internal RAF generator. I'm impressed! But I imagine the amount of energy you need to power those computations must be making you very hungry by now. Isn't it?"

He strode back to the grayish bubble separating him from Darian. "You can't beat me. You know that, right? You might be smarter and faster but I have much, much more experience with this system. I know what it's capable of, and what it's not capable of. You have only theory."

He banged in some new commands and the bubble compression resumed. This time, instead of a smoothly shrinking sphere, the microverse jumped from one change to another every few seconds. It shrank several percent, and then inflated a few percent. Its net movement, though, was definitely working toward collapse.

He's attached the series to a random number generator–Darian thought. He knew the algorithms intimately. While they might appear random to the uninitiated, they were reasonably predictable as long as they were tied to the internal calculations of the microprocessor. He examined the changes to the radius of the field and tried to match the values of the pseudorandom seed number.

Darian worked out the sequence and generated opposing fields to the collapsing steps. The random oscillations of the gray sphere slowed in frequency, and the radius began to grow as Darian permitted certain favorable RAF changes to pass without interference.

Larry watched the growing sphere, momentarily confused.

Only a few more steps and the laws inside will match the natural universe again! Darian would be free in less than a minute.

Larry punched in new commands. Only seconds had passed since Darian figured out the pseudorandom field generation, and already the gray microverse had nearly regained its original size.

"Yes!" Larry cried out, and pushed a final key. The field instantly collapsed by thirty percent, and then another twenty percent.

Darian employed countermeasures, trying to follow the rapid changes Larry was generating, but he couldn't keep up. The field shrunk another ten percent, and another. He now stood under a meter tall.

The field collapsed a further fifty percent. Changes were coming too fast and the steps were too large. Darian couldn't get enough samples to counter the rapid changes.

Larry pushed another key, got up from behind the desk, strolled over to address the gray, translucent sphere containing a very small Darian.

"Nothing more to say, Professor?" Larry waited for an answer but there was none. He returned to the desk and pressed a final key. The sphere shrunk to a few centimeters.

Darian screamed in frustration, sending out wave after wave of random changes to the fields, hoping against hope that something he did would disrupt the collapse of the microverse or buy more time to work, but the collapse was inevitable.

Darian knew he was done. *I can't keep up with all of these changing configurations Larry keeps throwing at me.*

The next change shrunk the microverse to a millimeter. In a final act of desperation, Darian dumped himself—everything he knew, everything he remembered, everything he was—into one final lattice transmission to the only people he trusted.

The data that comprised the essence of Darian Leigh poured out of him on multiple channels in uncoordinated, overlapping chunks, seeking paths along any available transmission modality to its intended destination. It took up temporary residence wherever there was available memory: in bits of lab equipment, in cell phones, in smart appliances, in HVAC systems, in automobile navigation systems, in inactive computers all over the lower mainland.

Darian sent whatever he could, as fast as he could, but there was too much data and not enough time. Then an idea occurred to him, maybe a way to survive the collapse. He had one last hope to preserve the integrity of his essence—not by fighting against the fields that were destroying the very matter he was made of, but by accepting this new universe into which he was being forced. He smiled one final, peaceful, microscopic smile and sent a new configuration to his RAF generator.

In the lab, Larry watched the gray bubble shrink beyond the threshold of visibility. *Gone!* He stared at the empty spot where the microverse had been. His triumph was complete.

Now, I'd better get out of here, too. He walked back to the desk, shut everything down, and tucked the laptop inside his backpack.

Grabbing his coat off the back of the chair, he took one last look around the lab that had been his second home for the past half year and departed.

48

LARRY DIDN'T ANSWER THE DOORBELL OR HIS CELL PHONE.

"Larry! It's Greg! C'mon, dude, get up! It works! Hey, let's go! Larry, are you in there?" He pounded on the wooden door of the basement suite but only succeeded in waking up the neighbors. They were none too pleased about Larry's rowdy pre-dawn visitor.

"Hey! Do you mind? Shut up down there!" A window slammed shut immediately above their heads, making Greg and Kathy jump.

"He's either out cold or he didn't make it home last night. Let's go," Kathy suggested.

"Yeah, I guess. Hang on a sec, maybe the window's open," Greg pushed at the flimsy aluminum frame but it held tight. They cupped their hands around their eyes and tried to peer in past the cheap cotton curtains, but couldn't see or hear anything that gave them reason to stay. "C'mon, let's go."

Great. Chalk up yet another reason for Larry to be resentful. Well, he can't say we didn't try—Greg grumbled to himself. They got in the car and headed out to the expressway.

"It's weird that he's not answering his phone," Kathy said. "Do you think he's okay?"

"Yeah, he's fine. Probably just switched it off. He used to do that all the time. You'll see. He either crashed at the lab or on somebody's sofa." They rode the rest of the way in silence; it was still too early in the morning for sensible conversation.

Greg signaled, slowed down, and turned into the university parking lot.

The flood of data hit their lattices without warning.

Flashes of speculative physics, RAF electronics, and new designs for dendy lattices mixed with memories of a childhood that neither of them had lived and washed over them in an exquisitely painful, mind-wrenching torrent.

Halfway through the turn, Greg's brain became completely inundated. Without meaning to, he let go of the steering wheel and gripped his head. Darian's desperate outpouring overtook his own sensory input, and the whirlwind of images wrested away his consciousness. He heard voices crying out, and it took him a moment to recognize them as his own and Kathy's.

Unguided, the car rolled into a shallow ditch and came to rest against a spruce sapling. The two scientists were too busy fighting for their sanity and their identities to notice.

As soon as the first few gigabytes had begun pushing their way into their consciousness, Kathy had understood what was happening. *Darian is dying!*

She knew but, with all the incoming data, it was too much to process. She fought for control over a small part of her lattice and, for a split second, stemmed the incoming jumble of thoughts, images, sounds, and emotions. The narrow window was all she needed to assign her lattice the specific task of deactivating her external communications, and then she gave in to the stream.

Three more excruciating seconds passed before the isolated subroutine managed to stop the incoming rush completely.

Kathy felt her muscles relax and she slumped in her seat, letting her mind recover from the shock of trying to process all that data. She looked over at her partner, and managed a weak, "Greg? You okay?"

He was hunched over the steering wheel, unmoving. *The windshield is intact. No sign of blood*—she noted. Using what was left of her strength, she reached out to touch his arm.

As her fingers neared his sleeve, Greg let out an incoherent grunt and pitched backward, bolt upright in his seat. He grabbed both sides of his head, arched back further than she thought physically possible, and opened his mouth in a silent scream of agony. She shook him roughly and screamed, "Greg!" but couldn't break him out of it.

Desperate, she wrapped her subroutine in a viral program, opened her lattice long enough to send the package into the data torrent, and shut it down again.

Greg's body remained in catatonic rigor a moment longer and then, as suddenly as it had begun, he was free. He sagged back into the seat, exhausted and wracked by both mental and physical pain, and barely holding onto consciousness. Kathy tenderly wiped the saliva from his chin with her sleeve, and sank back into her own seat. She was conscious but still in shock.

Greg lolled his head in her direction. "What...was that?" he croaked.

49

FOUR DAYS AFTER DARIAN LEARNED THE TRUTH and paid the ultimate price, a private car delivered Larry to the Austin home of Reverend Alan LaMontagne. Larry was tired but relieved. He'd made it to safety.

The morning he'd sentenced Darian to what he considered a unique and fitting death, he'd gone straight to a payphone and called the Reverend's private number.

"I have to get out now. Right now," he'd said after identifying himself and apologizing for the early hour.

"What happened?" LaMontagne asked.

"Darian is dead. Gone forever. I did it, and I have to get out of here right away."

To his credit, LaMontagne did not panic. "Do you have the RAF device?"

"Yes, I do." Larry heard the Reverend's relieved sigh.

"Good. Do you have a car?"

"I can rent one."

"Okay. Very good. Here's what you'll do. Can you find where Interstate 40 crosses the border into the New Confederacy between Flagstaff and Albuquerque?"

"I can read a map."

"Good. It'll take you about three days to get there. Use your own passport at the crossing. Our people are in place on both sides of the border, and they'll let you through without recording the fact. Someone will meet you on the New Confederacy side and take you to a hotel in Albuquerque. You can leave your car at the border station; it will be taken care of. Do you have enough money?"

"I can stop at the ATM before I leave."

"Good. Use only cash, no credit cards, on your trip down. Travel as lightly as possible. You won't need anything else, just your basic toiletries and such. Stop as little as possible and don't use your real name anywhere; I mean it. Be careful. Don't get stopped by the police."

"How do I make that happen?"

"Drive carefully. Don't speed. Eat and rest when you need to. Relax and try not to stand out. There's a lot of traffic along that road. It's easy to cruise right through without drawing attention to yourself if you just act normally."

"They'll think I'm missing along with Darian. My picture will be all over the news."

"You'd better shave your head and buy some glasses."

"I don't need glasses."

"Neutral prescription or sunglasses, then. That should be enough. It's not a long trip."

"No, you're right, it's not. I'll be fine."

"Very well. After you've had a chance to rest up in Albuquerque, my people will put you on a flight to Austin."

"A flight? Won't they flag my passport?"

"No, it'll be a private plane, and the flight will be entirely inside the New Confederacy. Besides, the airport staff is loyal to our Church."

"Okay, thanks." Larry bit his bottom lip. "I guess that's about all. I'll see you in a few days."

"Yes. And, Larry, thank you. You've done this country and this Church a great service."

The drive was long but no one paid Larry any attention along the way. He kept checking the news on the radio, TV screens, and websites when he stopped to eat.

His and Darian's disappearances weren't reported until Monday afternoon. They were portrayed as Missing Persons, as a mystery. Foul play wasn't ruled out but no one suspected murder just yet.

Darian Leigh's face dominated the reports—way too much coverage for Larry's liking—with only minimal attention devoted to Darian's assistant researcher. Larry wasn't sure whether to feel peeved or relieved.

Reporters hounded Greg and Kathy at first, but soon tired when they found the two had little to add to the initial report. The general public's interest rapidly died down, as well. Missing scientists didn't grab headlines the way missing celebrities did.

Larry felt a twinge of nostalgia when he saw his photo alongside his three former colleagues in a front-page story about their work and the disappearances. He tapped his finger over the photo; the reporter had somehow procured their old security-identification headshots from a happier time when the team first came together.

He was sure his mom would be worried sick by his unexplained disappearance. Once he got settled in the New Confederacy, he'd call and let her know he was okay. *The Reverend will help me come up with a good story.* He was certain of it.

At dusk on the third evening, Larry reached the Arizona-New Mexico border crossing and, in keeping with the Reverend's instructions, dutifully presented his passport.

The official eyed the document, and then took a closer look at the person presenting it. "Please step inside, sir."

Larry felt his stomach crawl into his throat. All of his life, whether he'd had anything to hide or not, if someone in Customs, Security, or law enforcement asked him to "please..." well, pretty much anything, it caused him to break into a nervous sweat. This time, he had plenty to hide.

He shifted his weight back and forth from left foot to right foot, then heel to toe, and back again, while the security guard read the note attached to his file in the database and called his supervisor. The supervisor came over and the two of them eyed Larry closely. They re-checked his passport, and reviewed the computer screen. After a brief, whispered discussion, the supervisor motioned at Larry to sit down, picked up the phone, and made a call.

Larry chose the first available seat in the waiting area—a hard, orange plastic chair that was attached from below by a single metal bar to five equally uncomfortable chairs. The chairs seemed designed to throw people off balance psychologically as much as physically. He waited as calmly as he could, trying to appear casual and unconcerned. As such, he stood out as the most conspicuous person in the room.

Five minutes later, a tall, well-groomed man in a dark suit left the corresponding New Confederacy border station and walked the twenty-five meters to the Pacifica side. He conferred briefly with the supervisor, who pointed to Larry, who now sat fidgeting like a six year old in his uncomfortable orange plastic chair in the Waiting Area. The man in the dark suit came around the counter and approached Larry.

"Dr. Rusalov?"

"That's me," Larry replied, sounding more chipper than he felt.

"Leave your vehicle here and come with me, please."

"But my things are in there."

"Your instructions were to travel light."

"I don't have much, but Reverend LaMontagne will want me to bring my backpack."

The man regarded him coolly. "Please don't mention that name again," he said. "Is the backpack all you have?"

Larry considered for a moment. "I can fit everything I need in there. Give me a second."

The man followed him to the vehicle, where Larry moved his shaving kit and a change of clothes into his backpack. He slung the pack over one shoulder and closed the trunk of the car. "Where should I leave the keys?"

The man held out his hand. Larry felt the weight of the keys, more than physically, as he handed them over. His apartment keys and three for the lab shared the ring. They belonged to his old life now. He let them go.

Larry kept his head down and his eyes straight ahead as they passed through the Pacifica border. On the way by the office, the man in the dark suit dropped Larry's keys into the hands of the supervisor. The two men nodded respectfully, neither uttering a word.

The man in the dark suit escorted Larry the extra few steps into his new country, the New Confederacy, without ceremony or comment.

Almost giddy with relief, Larry risked a glance back at Pacifica in time to see the first border guard start up the abandoned rental car and drive it off the road into the desert. *Don't read too much into it*—he assured himself.

The man in the dark suit opened the passenger door of a nondescript dark sedan, made his way around to the driver's side, and got behind the wheel. Larry claimed his seat, arranged his backpack between his feet, and buckled up.

The two-hour drive into Albuquerque felt lonelier than the previous three combined. The man in the dark suit resisted all attempts at conversation, and wouldn't allow Larry to adjust the station on the radio. They were tuned in to "Rockin' Country" the entire journey. Thankfully, the radio was set to a nearly inaudible volume.

The only thing he learned from the man in the dark suit was that his name was "Jeff." Larry doubted that was his real name. What did it matter? He slumped against the door and slept most of the way into the city.

They passed a night in some nondescript motor hotel on the edge of Albuquerque. The next morning, "Jeff" took Larry to the airport where they boarded a private jet to Austin. "Jeff", Larry, and the two pilots were the only ones onboard. Hot breakfast trays waited at the separate seats to which he and "Jeff" were directed. The two men ate in silence. After breakfast, Larry stared out the window at the land unfurling far below and pondered his future.

He had considered destroying the RAF generator and Darian's server along with it until he realized that doing so would end his own scientific career as well. Instead, before leaving the city, he used the controller laptop to log into the server from home and download everything he could. As he made his own copy, he erased everything behind.

It wasn't so much that research into the physical laws of nature was inherently evil. Done with conscience and guidance, it was just another way to come to understand the mind of God.

The problem, in Larry's opinion, was that the people involved in the RAF project were reckless and drunk on their own egos. They were pushing forbidden knowledge onto a society that was not ready to receive it. Mankind would not be ready for such power until it had acknowledged the absolute supremacy of the Lord and the need for His holy guidance in all endeavors.

It might take him decades to understand the papers that Darian, Greg, and Kathy had been working on. Deciphering their work, with Yeshua's wisdom steering his heart, would make the basis for a nice career at the University of Houston. Or he could take on a post with the New Confederacy Department of Defense, if the government decided to classify the work as sensitive. That might be even better.

The loss of Darian and the RAF generator would irreversibly cripple the project at SFU and, if that didn't, the investigation into Darian's disappearance would. *Kathy and Greg are going to have a tough time, as prime suspects, getting budgets and journal papers approved. Serves them right.*

At the airport in Austin, "Jeff" escorted Larry over to another nondescript sedan, gray this time, that was parked at the end of the tarmac. They drove almost an hour out of the city and past the suburbs before arriving at the estate of Reverend Alan LaMontagne, head of the Church of Yeshua's True Guard, the official religion of the New Confederacy.

The estate was in keeping with the stature of the head of the largest church in North America. An ornate double-wide cast-iron gate complete with guard hut greeted visitors. Majestic elms sheltered the kilometer-long driveway leading to the main house. Manicured lawns butted up against carefully planted clusters of tidy shrubs. The main house was easily over a thousand square meters and featured an attached chapel.

Not as ostentatious as I expected—Larry thought, as he got out of the car and stretched his legs. *Somewhat understated and tasteful, almost traditional.*

"Ah, Dr. Rusalov, you've made it," the Reverend came down the front steps to greet Larry. "I trust you had a good journey, given the circumstances, that is. Lunch will be in a few hours. Perhaps we could enjoy a chat, first."

He invited Larry into the house. "Jeff" followed them in. They made their way through the foyer and into the study. Larry caught a glimpse of the expansive living and entertaining areas. Apart from the three of them, there was no sign of anyone else in the building.

The Reverend is more animated than the last time we met—Larry observed.

Walking more upright. Greater vitality. It must be the better climate here. It was pretty chilly in Vancouver last November. I imagine the cold, damp weather there took a toll on him.

Looking into the Reverend's eyes reminded Larry of the strong sense of purpose he used to see in Darian. He adjusted the backpack on his shoulders. *I'm sure he's excited to have a look at this.*

LaMontagne closed the door behind them, leaving "Jeff" to stand guard outside. The Reverend invited Larry to take a seat behind the desk "Perhaps you could show me the generator," he said, pointing to Larry's backpack. "I'm very eager to see it in operation."

"Of course," replied Larry, digging into his satchel to retrieve the laptop. "It doesn't look like much, just an average computer."

"But it's so much more, isn't it?"

Before he fired up the RAF generator, Larry paused. "You know, I'm curious," he said. "This thing is contrary to everything I know you believe in. Its only purpose is to subvert the Natural Laws that God gave this universe. Why are you so supportive that I should continue working with it?"

LaMontagne rubbed his chin, thoughtfully. "True. It is an abomination. But the science, as difficult as it may be to comprehend, is out in the world now. Far better that *we* should control its use than the heathens living outside of God's Grace. Don't you agree?"

Larry pursed his lips. "Well, only a few people on the planet understand the theory. Even I don't get it all, yet." He realized he wasn't helping his future position. "I mean, without a functioning field generator, it's all just speculation. And we have the only working generator in the world, right here." He patted the keyboard gently. "As far as everyone else is concerned, the failed live test proved the theory wrong."

"And now that we will have time to study it, we will know how best to use it to the glory of God."

Larry wasn't sure he liked how the Reverend used "we" in the context of studying the generator. "Yes, once I am settled into my new position, I'll have lots of time to go over the theory and to develop a deeper understanding of the device." He subtly emphasized the "I."

"Without Dr. Leigh, how will you be able to reverse engineer the theory from nothing more than a working field generator?"

"Before I left, I was able to download almost everything the entire team has produced. I have notes, papers, and design schematics all right here." He patted the keyboard again. "Greg and Kathy will have an impossible time recreating everything without their notes. Besides, they've never seen the generator work. They have no evidence the theory is even sound. I'm sure they'll be leaving in humiliation very soon."

"You erased everything? That's rather diabolical for a simple scientist, isn't it?"

Larry smiled. "I've had several weeks to think about what I'd do when the day came. I knew I'd be discovered sooner or later." The laptop beeped to indicate the system had been loaded.

Larry typed in a few commands. "You can see all the files I downloaded from the server." He indicated the directories loaded with documents, images, and simulation code.

Watching over his shoulder, the Reverend nodded his approval. "Can you show me the system in action?"

"Sure, it's actually pretty easy to use. I have to admit, Kathy designed a great user interface." A few keystrokes called up the main control program. "You have to tell it which file of basic parametric equations to use by picking from this browser." He indicated a small panel with a set of filenames.

"Ah, yes, the virtual particle resonance parameters," LaMontagne interjected.

Larry looked back at the older man, surprised. "You *have* been doing your homework. Setting up the equations is quite a lot more work than using them. I've been making copies of some basic sets and experimenting by changing just one parameter at a time. Once I've gotten deeper into the math, I'll be a bit more adventurous."

"Yes. Let's start with something simple," said LaMontagne.

"This is the most basic configuration Darian set up." Larry pointed to a small series of equations in a separate window. "The idea was to alter only the speed of light in a vacuum."

"That seems like quite a significant a goal to me."

"Yes, well, it won't give you faster-than-light travel or anything like that. The effect is confined to a small volume where the fields are properly tuned. But it's very easy to test...with the right equipment."

"Can you show me?"

Larry laughed. "Unless you have a vacuum chamber and a laser interferometer around here, it won't look like much. Wait a minute." He leaned forward and called up another set of equations, then copied a few terms from that one into the first file. "Okay, I've adjusted for the atmosphere so I can at least show you what the system looks like when it works."

"That would be very interesting," said the Reverend.

Larry adjusted the laptop so the generated fields wouldn't overlap with any of the furniture in the room. He entered a few commands and a small blue sphere popped into existence, hovering over a nearby coffee table.

The Reverend straightened and walked over to the sphere.

"Remarkable," he said. "Why is it blue?"

"That's because of the shift in wavelength of the incident light. The change in velocity causes the colors to be blue-shifted. Actually, most of the light has been shifted into the ultraviolet range so I wouldn't stand too close to it for very long. What you see here is the shifted red and infrared series."

The Reverend stepped back. "And you say this was among the simpler of the equation series?"

"Yes. I've gained a lot of experience since this level, with much more complicated sets of equations."

"Is that how you killed Dr. Leigh? Or did you use more traditional methods and hide the body?"

"No," Larry answered, a little uncomfortable talking about such things so openly. "I can show you the field I used, but I don't think you want to be anywhere near where I project it."

LaMontagne quickly took position just behind the desk where Larry sat. "I'll make it big enough so you can see it, but not as big as the one I used to hold Darian. It has very strong boundaries against the matter in this universe so once I've set it up, you'll be quite safe. You can even touch it if you like." He pushed a few buttons and the little blue bubble disappeared, but was soon replaced by a one-meter gray sphere.

LaMontagne rushed over to examine the new globe. He glanced at Larry, curiosity burning in his eyes.

"Go ahead. It's safe to touch," encouraged Larry.

The Reverend extended a finger to poke the bubble. The surface resisted depression where his finger prodded. He pushed a bit harder then tried to shove it, first with one hand, then with both. It wouldn't budge.

Larry laughed. "The field is referentially locked to the entire planet. You would have to be able to literally move the Earth to budge it. Its boundary is made up of the difference in natural laws that exists between our two universes. Except for what the equations allow to pass, it's impenetrable."

"A force field," gushed the Reverend.

"Well, I hadn't thought of that use but, yes, it could be," replied Larry. "Right now, it's set to allow light and sound to penetrate so it wouldn't be a very good force field but we could probably adjust that."

"Amazing! But how did you use this to do away with Dr. Leigh?"

"The sphere was just the trap. I set up a series of equations to slowly reduce the size of electron orbitals inside until they collapsed completely, and chemistry became impossible. The microverse that held Darian shrunk until it stopped supporting the chemistry of life and then even farther. As far as I know, it still exists; it's just smaller than a proton."

"Did he suffer? Or did he just...disappear?"

"For the way he treated me—all because I chose not to take his lattice virus and become something inhuman—and for his arrogance toward God's Creation? Yes, he suffered," Larry confirmed. His defiant chin and indignant tone challenged the Reverend to fault him.

"May his soul find peace," said the Reverend.

Larry frowned for a second but backed down, subdued by LaMontagne's humility. "Whatever is left of his soul."

LaMontagne waited for Larry to continue, expecting there to be more, but that was all Larry would say. He set the RAF generator back to INACTIVE and closed the lid.

"I hope you're satisfied; I've done what I said I'd do. I trust I will be properly compensated."

"Mmm," replied the Reverend moving toward the door, "indeed you will be, Dr. Rusalov. Although one might argue that upholding God's laws in the universe and vanquishing those foes who would seek to irresponsibly change the natural way of things might be reward enough."

Larry brows furrowed and he was about to respond when LaMontagne laughed. "Fear not, Dr. Rusalov. Larry. We deeply appreciate what you have done on behalf of our Lord and His People. You will be suitably rewarded, as we have discussed, with a tenured position." He called "Jeff" back into the room.

"Please take Dr. Rusalov to the Private Guest House so he can clean up," he instructed. "See that he is comfortable there until lunch is served."

Larry picked up the laptop back in one hand and his backpack with the other.

"Why don't you leave that here?" LaMontagne suggested. "We'll have a chance for further demonstrations after lunch."

Larry stopped mid-action, "Sure, why not?" He set the laptop back down, zipped up his backpack and slung it over his shoulders. Following "Jeff" out of the study, he turned back to LaMontagne. "See you soon."

The Reverend smiled and nodded but said nothing. He returned to his desk as "Jeff" escorted Larry to back to the car.

The gray sedan stood in the driveway where they'd left it about an hour earlier, but someone had popped the trunk. "Jeff" opened the driver's side door and started to get in. As he did, he asked Larry, "Would you mind closing that for me?" Larry walked around to the back of the vehicle.

As Larry reached up to close the trunk, "Jeff" hesitated and held up an index finger as if he'd just remembered something. He stepped out of the car. "Do you see a leather bag in there? Could you bring that up front for me, please?"

Larry could see the bag pushed to the back of the trunk. "This black one?" he asked. "Sure." He put down his backpack and reached for the other bag. He heard footsteps behind him and turned. A gloved hand held the biggest pistol Larry had ever seen, and it was pointed directly at his head. A shot rang out.

The Reverend Alan LaMontagne gazed out the window of his study in time to see Larry's lifeless body slide down the back end of the car. He watched as Jeff–that was, indeed, his real name—bent down and lifted the body into the trunk, tossed the gun in after it, and slammed the lid closed.

He continued to watch as Jeff started the car, backed up a couple of meters, turned off the main driveway, and headed toward the lush gardens at the rear of the estate.

The Reverend sat down at his desk and opened the lid of the laptop. He replayed his lattice recording of Larry's fingers as they moved over the keyboard to enter the password. The display stopped at the RAF generator control program, ready to accept his command.

The Very Reverend Alan LaMontagne smiled as he loaded a file with a simple set of equations into the generator's parameters. He pressed ACTIVE, and a small blue sphere appeared in the air a few meters in front of his desk.

Acknowledgements

Thank YOU for reading this book. If you enjoyed it, I hope you'll leave a review. For independent authors, like me, reviews are the best way of telling others the book is worth a read.
Leave a review on Amazon, click here.
Leave a review on Goodreads, click here.

Thanks to Lee for being the most patient editor imaginable, and to my great team of beta readers: Joel, Abby, Craig, Ed, Eric, Gary, Lorraine, Mike, Jeff, Kathie, Leanna, Scarlett, Barbara, Susan, and Rachel. This is a much better book for your insightful and invaluable feedback. A special thanks to the members of *Cuenca: Writing Our World* for all your support and especially to our dear friend, Scarlett Braden, for your energy, enthusiasm, and guidance along the way.

All science fiction writers owe a debt to the giants who have gone before us, many of whom still produce prolifically. I have been influenced by many of the best, though none bear the responsibility for any of my errors. Isaac Asimov, Iain M. Banks, Greg Bear, Gregory Benford, Ray Bradbury, David Brin, Arthur C. Clarke, Peter F. Hamilton, Robert A. Heinlein, Ursula K. Le Guin, Larry Niven, Jerry Pournelle, Sheri S. Tepper, and John C. Wright, you have all been great inspirations.

The scientific community crosses many borders and intellectual boundaries. My career in biology has been guided by great scientists like David Bailie, David Pilgrim, and David Wishart (I don't know why I always worked for guys named David). My love of developmental biology, molecular biology, and genetics was inspired by Bruce P. Brandhorst in my undergrad years at Simon Fraser University. I also owe a deep debt of gratitude for the exciting and inspiring researchers in synthetic biology, including: Drew Endy, George Church, Tom Knight, Pam Silver, Chris Voigt, and Jay Keasling.

I built upon a great many ideas in coming up with the speculative science, philosophies, and sociopolitical economics in the series. The following have all been sources for ideas, but none of them can be blamed for where I ran away with the inspiration: Lawrence Krauss, Richard Dawkins, Andrew Thomas, Matt Strassler, John Mauldin, John Hussman, James Rickards, and Thom Hartmann.

Further Reading

This book contains a lot of real science and speculates heavily on possible advances in several fields. If you're interested in learning more about some of the areas discussed in this book, I suggest you pick up the following:

Lawrence Krauss, A Universe From Nothing.
An excellent review of cosmology and the possible origins of the universe.

Andrew Thomas, Hidden In Plain Sight.
A great series of five books at the time of this release, covering everything from gravity, relativity, quantum mechanics, time, space, and the particles that comprise all matter.

Richard Dawkins, *The God Delusion*.
A powerful analytic indictment of religious belief that applies logic and reason to spirit and faith.

Francis Collins, *The Language of God*.
A famous scientist's perspective on reconciling belief in God with scientific studies of evolution.

Jerry Coyne, Why Evolution is True.
A fact-filled romp through the scientific evidence in support of evolution.

George M. Church and Ed Regis, *Regenesis*.
A look inside the mind of one of the world's leading synthetic biologists. Includes the origins of the field, current practices, and some stunning visions of the future.

James Rickards, *The Death of Money*.
Analysis of how modern currency wars will be fought among the major countries of the world, resulting in the collapse of the international monetary system.

Websites:

Matt Strassler (https://profmattstrassler.com/), *Of Particular Significance.*
Insightful and informative website from a theoretical physicist with essays
on a variety of topics in physics.

http://igem.org/Main_Page
iGEM is the International Genetically Engineered Machines annual
competition. This is *the* place to go to learn about the exciting research
done every year by university undergrads from around the world
.

Study Questions

The Deplosion series is not intended to be just a story. In addition to providing a thrilling read, it is meant to be a vehicle for discussing a variety of deep philosophical, religious, scientific, and social issues. Following are some questions to help stimulate further thought. Additional discussion can be found on the Paul Anlee Facebook page and science and philosophy blog (www.paulanlee.com).

1) Sharon Leigh used a genetically-engineered virus to grow a semiconductor lattice in her brain. That lattice made her smarter than any human alive but it also led to her accidental death. If such a treatment were offered to you, would you take it? What about an implanted device that gave you internet connection? What about the DirectVR briefly described in Chapter 11 that allows you to more fully experience movies, as if you were dreaming?

2) The dendy lattices were developed using synthetic biology. The "ceraffices" described in Alumston are all grown buildings, with the basic structure a genetically-engineered tree. What kinds of limitations, if any, should we place on such research and technology?

3) Two different "origin stories" are presented, one in the Prologue (natural evolution of the universe) and one at the start of Chapter 2 (Alum and Yov's Creation). Which resonated more with you? Which seemed more reasonable to you? After reading Darian's lecture at the Philosopher's Café, did you change your mind about these?

4) The idea of preserving a brain-dead mother's life so she can bring a baby to term is a controversial one, both from an ethical and legal perspective. Should the mother's wishes (say, to be removed from life support) supersede that of her unborn baby? How does this issue relate to the controversy around abortion?

5) When Darya needed to escape the Lysrandia inworld, her acolytes sacrificed three of themselves so she could get away. She left without much argument, seeing the rationality of preserving herself as leader of the rebellion. Compare and contrast human and Cybrid ethical reasoning in similar situations. For example, movies often portray a moment when a hero needs to choose between saving a loved one and a city of thousands or millions. Such choices cause

some people great anguish. How would a Cybrid evaluate such a dilemma? Is one approach "better" than the other?

6) Teenaged Darian dismisses the notion of God, the Creator, on what he sees as rational grounds, then provides an evolutionary argument for why faith is so powerful in humans. Are these two notions at odds with each other? Can a rational person dismiss God yet find reasons for faith? Is religious faith something that can even be discussed rationally and logically, or does it belong to the realm of spirit, emotion, and feelings only?

7) Darya is first introduced as if she were human, and only later revealed to be a machine. Does the notion of an electronic brain thinking of itself as a person, with feelings and self-awareness, seem conceivable? Is there an ineffable "something" about being a biological human that cannot be implemented in computational machinery? What does it mean, then, to be human? How much of our bodies or brains can we lose and maintain our humanity? How much can we enhance or replace with synthetic devices?

8) Almost everything in Darian's Philosopher's Café lecture was scientific fact. To the best of my knowledge, everything up to the first mention of "resonance" between virtual particles is factual. That's where I slip into speculation, which may or may not prove to be correct some day. How much of what came before or after that point, did you find believable?

9) Darya reveals that Alum's true intention with the Deplosion machinery is to re-create the universe according to His own version of Heaven. His Heaven would be perfect; there would be no uncertainty in it, no struggle, no pain. Why would anyone oppose such a thing?

10) One of the major differences between our universe and Alum's Heaven is that the natural universe is filled with uncertainty and risk. Do you think the universe is deterministic or probabilistic? That is, do you think it's possible (even hypothetically for an omniscient being) to know everything about the universe at any time and to predict what will happen next? Which kind of universe would you prefer to live in? If you were God, which kind of universe would you create?

11) In justifying her decision to hack her fellow Cybrids' belief systems, Darya says, "Rights are a luxury the universe can't afford right now, and free will is just an illusion based on complex decision trees with non-controlled inputs and experiences." Do you believe there is a rational basis for a "rights-based" society? Do you think "free will" is an illusion as she described?

12) Alternus is modeled on the real Earth of the near future; it faces many similar problems to those we face today. Are we smart enough to make good choices for the future of humanity and the planet? Why do you think I made "growth" such a major factor in the discussion? At one point, one of the Davos delegates—a Cybrid—decries the need for humans in the universe, and the need for Cybrids to serve and support them. Do you agree with Darya's response, and the role of "sloppy evolution" as a factor in favor of the importance of biological beings?

13) Larry states that Darian, Greg, and Kathy are arrogant and filled with hubris to think they have a right to the God-like power of changing the laws of nature. Is this adequate reason for him to kill Darian and take the RAF generator? Did the Reality Assertion Field push past the limits to places where science should not dare to go? Do you think there should be such limits to research? Why or why not? Discuss specific examples

The Reality Incursion (preview)

Deplosion: Book Two

Coming: Summer 2017

When a mysterious anomaly threatens the destruction of Earth, who will save humanity? With the help of Cybrid engineers, Greg Mahajani and Kathy Liang rush to complete the asteroid habitats before the Eater grows beyond its containment. Is Reverend LaMontagne's help genuine, or does he have other motives for cooperating?

Darya's Cybrid revolution set back Alum's Divine Plan but also caught the Living God's attention. Now she and her team have their own troubles, trying to figure out how to save Alternus, while dodging Shard Trillian who will stop at nothing until he's destroyed them. Will they be able to escape before his deadly attack traces their avatar personas back to their trueselves?

Darak and Brother Stralasi are working their way toward the Center of the Realm. Little do they know, the Angel Mika and his Wing of ten thousand lie in wait. Will they thwart Darak's journey to confront the Living God? Or will the rebels of Eso-La and the last of the alien Aelu help Darak stop Alum's plan to remake the universe in the Living God's own image of Heaven?

Chapter 1

"What was that?" Greg clutched his head with both hands.

"I think something's happened to Darian," Kathy croaked. "Something bad."

An hour earlier, before the uninvited flood of their mentor's memories overwhelmed them, before they lost control of their minds and landed their car in the shallow ditch, she and Greg had been at home, sound asleep.

Darian had called them through their private lattice network, jarring them from early-morning dreams.

It works!—was all he said at first.

It works? What works?–Kathy had replied, dragging herself toward consciousness. Her sluggish mind worked out the meaning of his simple utterance, and its significance hit like an electric shock.

"It works!" she squealed and shook Greg awake. Greg activated his lattice, joining Kathy and Darian online to share in the excitement. Darian was on his way into the lab to compile better data with the vacuum chamber and laser interferometer. *Can you meet me there?*—he'd asked after apologizing for the early hour.

Can you wait 'til we get there before you run it again?—Kathy requested. Darian promised to hold off with further testing, but she didn't believe him. Were the situation reversed, she didn't think she'd be able to hold off on playing with the most important discovery in physics this century.

After the call, Kathy sat on the edge of the bed, staring at the starry sky, remembering the image of the Milky Way Darian had shared. *You are here*—it said, an arrow pointing to Earth's solar system about half way in from the outer edge of the galaxy. It always made her feel small. But the invention of the Reality Assertion Field generator would more than compensate for that. "Wow, can you believe it? It finally worked."

"It's about time something went right," Greg replied. His voice became quiet, almost reverent. "Can you imagine what that must have been like? He produced a micro-scale universe right in the middle of his dining room. A space with its own distinct physical laws. Sure, it wasn't all that stable. But still, can you believe it? A freaking microverse!"

He threw on a t-shirt. As his face popped out the top, it wore a pensive frown, reviewing the conversation. "Hey, I didn't know Darian was growing an internal RAF antenna array in his own head. Did you?"

"No, not a clue. I'm not surprised, though. Our original RAF generator should have worked. Everything checked out: the hardware, the software, the theory. But it still didn't work. So what does a good scientist do? He starts all over, clean slate, and goes through it all again, step by step, with an independent approach." Kathy laughed. "That's so Darian, though, to grow the hardware in his brain instead of making another device."

"We better get moving," Greg said, already pulling on his jeans. "We still have to swing by and pick up Larry on the way. I'll call him right now."

Larry didn't answer their calls or his door when they banged on it some twenty minutes later. "Larry!" they'd both complained before giving up and heading to the lab without him.

Greg was easing the car into the parking lot near the Physics building when a torrent of Darian's thoughts, memories, and knowledge, everything that made him who he was, pushed past their internal neural-lattice security and gushed into the two scientists' minds unfiltered.

Unable to combat the rapid influx of data overwhelming their own perceptions, they lost consciousness. The car rolled to a stop in a shallow ditch, as they struggled against the invasion of their minds.

Just before being completely swamped by the inundation, Kathy disconnected her own communications and stemmed the inflow. Still physically incapacitated, but at least back in control of her mind, she created a cutoff routine and piggybacked it on the back of the surge of data streaming into Greg's lattice. As fast as it had hit them, they were free of the deluge and reconnecting to their own bodies.

Kathy rubbed the back of her neck. "He just blasted through our anti-virus protection like it was nothing."

Greg groaned. "I didn't know that was even possible."

"Are you okay?"

Greg stretched his neck muscles to each side. He blinked a few times, clearing his eyes. "Yeah, I think so. My head hurts, and I ache in muscles I didn't know I had."

"Me too, but I don't think there's any permanent damage." Kathy tried the car door.

"What are you doing?"

"I think Darian might be dead. I don't know why, but that's what it felt like." She stepped out of the vehicle, wincing as she stood.

Greg followed. "I feel like I ran a marathon," he moaned.

"Worse," Kathy replied. "Like I ran a marathon with a backpack full of rocks."

They left the car hanging half-in the ditch and raced to the lab, expecting to find Darian dead or in some desperate condition.

The hallway was eerily quiet this early. No lights shone through the observation window on the way by. *That's odd.* Kathy braced herself for the worst as she opened the door and turned on the lights.

They walked around the workspace and checked the shared office. Nobody there. Did Darian make it to the lab after calling? Where was he when he transmitted his message? Was he in trouble?

They tried transmitting a lattice message to him. Nothing. Greg tried calling Darian's cell phone. No answer, but Darian rarely turned on his phone. Why bother when he carried a built-in connection to the internet in his head?

Not sure how worried they should be, they took a more careful look around the room. Kathy's eyes went immediately to the project to which she'd devoted the past six months of her life. The overhead lights reflected off a dusty patch of lab bench where the Reality Assertion Field generator should have been sitting.

What the....? "Greg. It's gone!"

Darian would *not* have taken it out of the lab; he was adamant it stay in the sturdy anti-theft frame, secured to the counter. The frame was still there, unlocked and empty. The RAF generator, however, was gone.

The server!—Greg thought of the repository for the other half, the theoretical half, of their work. Without thinking, he went to log on, as normal, with his lattice but instantly hit a security wall. Kathy must have inserted a confirmation step to his comm-activation protocol when she pulled him out of Darian's thought storm. A pop-up message reminded him of the danger of opening his lattice to external communications. *Yes, definitely Kathy's work.*

He walked into the office area and tapped out his user I.D. and password using a keyboard, like any other mortal. Hundreds of folders containing all of their theories, schematics, and half-written papers awaiting data, were gone. "Uhh...Kath? Look, the directory is empty."

"This doesn't make sense," Kathy said, looking over his shoulder. "Darian called to say he was on his way to the lab. He wouldn't take all this stuff home with him. There's no reason to move it. Do you think someone broke in and stole it? Who would do that?"

Greg tried Larry's number again. *C'mon Larry! Where are you?* Still no answer. *Why aren't you picking up? Are you with Darian?* Kathy's question was a good one. Who could possibly have any motive to steal their equipment and all their data? Was Larry in trouble too, or was he involved, somehow?

Kathy's mind still reeled from the data, memories, and thoughts that had assaulted her earlier. She couldn't make sense of the flashing images, but she was sure it was an emergency broadcast from Darian's internal neural lattice to their own—a desperate effort by a dying scientist to continue his legacy the only way he could. She had no proof, only a feeling...and an empty lab.

"We have to call the police," she said.

"And tell them what?"

"Darian's missing. The RAF generator is missing. We don't know where Larry is."

Greg wasn't so sure. "Darian never sends messages over the public systems. We don't even have proof that he talked to us earlier."

"But Larry *and* the RAF device, too? That can't be a coincidence."

"How would anyone know, besides us? Maybe the two of them went out hiking for the weekend or took a trip together. Maybe they got drunk and took the RAF generator as a prank. Maybe they needed a bigger lab space or some specialized equipment in another lab. Who knows?"

Kathy stared at him. "I can't believe you're saying that. You know what hit us. Darian is dead, or at least hurt badly. That was sheer desperation, what he sent out."

Greg sighed. "Maybe. Maybe not. We can't prove anything. How do you know it wasn't just a program glitch? Think about it. There's no sign of a struggle here. Nobody but us knows Darian got the device working. Maybe he and Larry are just out for a long walk, talking about the next steps.

"I know what you *think* hit us in that transmission but, the truth is, we don't know anything yet. We're just guessing. What if they're on the way over right now with the RAF laptop and a box of doughnuts to celebrate?

"And don't forget. Our own dendy lattices are still growing and adjusting in our heads. Maybe what broadsided us was just the next level of growth, you know? Like maybe they're linking us all together or something. What if Darian received *our* brain dumps in *his* lattice at the same time, and that's why he's not answering. See? We don't really know anything. If we report it now, we'll just embarrass Darian and the lab. The university is already giving him a rough time; we don't need to add any more negative attention."

"We *can* prove the device is missing."

"We can *claim* that a non-functioning piece of lab equipment is missing. Basically, a fancy laptop, that's about all. What else do we have? An empty anti-theft frame in a lab. And we all have a key." He held up his key ring. "Darian has one, and so does Larry. Until we talk to them, we don't know whether one or both of them have the generator with them."

Kathy walked over to the lab bench where the RAF device should have been. She looked down at the empty frame. "Okay, so even with witnesses who know what was here in the lab, we have no real proof that it was stolen."

"No, and we don't have any proof that Darian and Larry are missing, hurt, or dead, either. Just a private lattice conversation that no one else can access."

"We're going to look hysterical, aren't we?"

"If we call now, hysterical is the best we could hope for. More likely, crazy. And if anyone did believe us, we'd be looking like the prime suspects."

"What do you think we should we do?"

"I'm not sure. I mean, what have we got to work with? Nothing concrete, not really. It felt like Darian blasted out all this data, the essence of his *self*, to us in a real panic. We have to report his disappearance to the police eventually; I know that. But until we have a better idea of what actually happened, until we're sure he's truly missing, I don't think there's much we can do, or should do. Let's give it a few hours. If we don't hear from him, and he doesn't show up for work—"

"You mean, *when* he doesn't show up for work. C'mon, Greg. You *know* what we experienced. That was a dying gasp."

"I know what it felt like, but I'm trying not to jump to any conclusions. Besides, the police won't do anything until he's been missing for at least twenty-four hours. So when he doesn't show up for work, we'll go talk to Dr. Wong. He can make the call."

Greg frowned and his eyes scanned the lab again. "In the meantime, let's leave a note here in case they show up, and walk the route back to his apartment. He could be somewhere between his place and the lab. Maybe he fell, or got mugged or something. If we can find some sign—his backpack, a loose shoe, or something solid—then we can go to the police."

"What about the RAF generator?"

"Until we can figure out what happened and what he'd want us to do, I think we need to keep quiet. I don't think we should tell anyone, not even the police, that Darian got the Reality Assertion Field working. It'll make no difference to their investigation, and it could make things worse. Right now, we're the only ones who know it works, besides Darian. If you're right, if somebody stole it, we don't know who's involved or what they know. If they find out that the RAF theory is right, and they know we helped design and test it, we could be next."

Kathy's eyes widened. "I wasn't even thinking about that. Do you think *we're* in danger? Darian wouldn't have told anyone else about the RAF generator working. Even Larry wouldn't have known that yet. Remember? We were supposed to tell him on the way."

"And Larry didn't answer his phone or door," Greg added. "I know I said I didn't want to jump to conclusions, but I have to admit, it's not looking good. I know, that's typical Larry, not answering. But with everything else..."

He came to a decision. "Okay, let's walk to Darian's place and see if we can come up with anything more solid to report. If we can't, we'll give it overnight. If we haven't seen them by 10 a.m. Monday—tomorrow—we'll go talk to the Department Chair. Dr. Wong will need to know what's going on, anyway, and maybe the police will take it more seriously if he reports it."

Kathy looked around the lab. Her shoulders sank. "I feel useless."

Greg pulled her into a hug. "I don't think there's anything we can do. I hate this, too, not knowing what's going on. I hate that I don't dare activate my lattice so I can think properly. I imagine all the little bits of Darian's mind out there, waiting to storm into us the second our lattices are up. Waiting to overwhelm and incapacitate us."

Kathy's face snuggled into his shoulder and she mumbled, "I don't like being just normal again. Do you?"

Chapter 2

"AND HOW LONG WILL YOU BE HERE in Casa DonTon, Mr. Trillian?" Lady Frieda, the oldest and most obviously available of five sisters, played with her dark curls.

The sumptuously appointed Family Dining Room bubbled with bravado and promise. The two-dozen guests who had bagged some game in the afternoon's hunt were the only ones invited to join the family for this intimate repast. Along with Mr. Trillian, of course. As the wealthy scion of a powerful industrialist of mysterious reputation, Mr. Trillian was an attractive catch.

The fact that he was also achingly handsome, athletic, and available, garnered him an invitation to dine with the family, despite his obvious distaste for chasing very small foxes with very large horses, slathering hounds, and ridiculously oversized guns. His intentionally dismal performance in the hunt, bordering on outright refusal to participate, did nothing to dissuade Lady Frieda and her sisters from their lavish flirting.

The object of the young ladies' attentions apologized, "Sadly, ladies, I must take my leave before the evening wears too late. I have pressing business to attend to." Five disappointed pouts appeared. "However, I do hope you will permit me the honor of visiting again soon." The bachelorettes brightened straight away.

"Well, we have you for now, and we shan't let you off without at least one dance each," chirped the youngest of the five, Lady Mirabel. Mr. Trillian bowed his head to her in polite acquiescence.

"Miry, my precious, please let Mr. Trillian finish his meal in peace," her father, Lord Chattingbaron, chastised. "He has far more important matters to attend to than some silly dancing, I'm sure."

"Nothing could be as important to me as spending the evening in the company of your lovely and charming family, my Lord." Mr. Trillian held up a hand to stem his host's mock objection. "Unfortunately, my investors insist that I elevate their mundane material priorities above my own pleasures. I must visit the office this evening." He smiled graciously at Lady Frieda, setting her heart aflutter, and sampled the roasted mutton.

"I, for one, find discussing matters of business distasteful at the evening meal," declared Lady Chattingbaron with a flick of her napkin. "Tell me, Mr. Trillian, Did you enjoy your ride today?"

"Very much so. You have the most wonderful grounds, and the forest is magnificent." Trillian flourished his fork and speared piece of meat in evidence of the family's bountiful estate. "Lady Adelle gave me quite the competition in jumping the brooks, I'm afraid."

Lady Adelle blushed to a shade befitting the dashing man's compliment. Four sets of artfully shaped brows scowled discreetly at his approval of her riding skills.

Timothy, the family's First Footman, removed the remains of the main course from in front of the young heiresses. Their figures would not tolerate the excessive ingestion of heavy meat and potatoes anyway, not if they wished to draw the attention of the likes of Mr. Trillian. Timothy nodded to Mr. Gowling, the Chief Butler. It was time to light the Peach Flambé.

As desserts were offered, some of the young men took the opportunity to engage Lady Frieda and her sisters in small talk not relating to the dashing Mr. Trillian.

Timothy started dessert service with his Lordship at the head of the table and worked his way around until he'd completed nearly a full circle. He stopped in front of Mr. Trillian and presented the polished tray holding hot brandied peaches and ice cream.

The guest didn't notice Timothy standing expectantly beside him; he was, instead, completely preoccupied with a nondescript closet door on the opposite wall.

Timothy subtly cleared his throat to draw the man's attention, but Mr. Trillian's focus remained abnormally fixated on the closet.

Timothy was about to cough quietly a second time when the room went fuzzy, and he heard a dozen bees passing within inches of his ears. Years of training and discipline helped him to hold onto the dessert tray instead of frantically batting away at the loathsome insects. He struggled to maintain his stooped position without sending the peaches flying from his outstretched hands, but it was too much.

Against his efforts, he jerked the silver platter, sending the remaining delicate cut-glass bowls to the edge of the tray, where they bumped against the rails and spilled a little juice onto the table linen. The unexpected clatter wrenched Mr. Trillian's gaze away from the closet. The buzzing in Timothy's ears stopped, as did conversation among the startled diners. All eyes turned to Timothy, who stood in uncharacteristically stunned silence.

Lady Chattingbaron jumped up from her seat. "Whatever has gotten into you, Timothy?" she demanded.

Timothy was as surprised as anyone. Well, he was as surprised as any Partial could be, which, normally, wasn't all that much. "One moment please, my Lady. I shall inquire of the DonTon Supervisor."

Initiate self-diagnostics–he sent the command to the local inworld supervisory program. The diagnostic generally reported findings within milliseconds. This time, it dragged on and on. Entire seconds passed. Most uncomfortably. People grew restless. They drummed their fingers and rolled their eyes. What was the holdup? This was most unusual.

Completely unacceptable for a game such as DonTon.

* * *

THE DONTON INWORLD SIMULATION was as stable as the classic conservative Victorian England society it portrayed. It was not a demanding inworld, being filled with activities no more strenuous than dining, dancing, visiting, playing cards, flirting, and the occasional hunt. The main features hadn't changed in millennia. The local physics were realistic, if somewhat simple. Since nobody ever examined the buildings or the wildlife too closely, they didn't need to be overly detailed.

Likewise, nobody paid much attention to the hundreds of thousands of servants, caretakers, town folk, or city folk. They were only Partials—Partial personas—a simple backdrop for the real entertainment, the endless pursuit and seduction of marriageable partners, and the creation of new family ties that carried out into the real universe.

Many hopefuls had tried to work their way into some kind of relationship with The Family; only a small percentage succeeded. The immediate Family of a few hundred Chattingbarons had dominated the DonTon inworld for ages. Their closely-guarded separation from the wider Sagittarian Cybrid inworlds lent an air of mystery to the Family and the Casa, making a visit to DonTon one of the most sought-after invitations. Though they all held perfectly normal Cybrid jobs in the outworld, here, the Family ruled as Lords.

Mr. Trillian's interest in Casa DonTon, however, had nothing to do with the Family or its eligible guests or connections.

Shard Trillian was on a mission. If he was going to successfully infiltrate the Alternus inworld, he couldn't do it by the normal, direct route. He knew that now.

This frivolous hub, Casa DonTon, would provide the ideal place, an unexpected alternative route, from which to launch the incursion.

The Living God approved his choice, and the Shard immediately instantiated inworld as Mr. Trillian, purposely setting aside his lofty title as one of Alum's most trusted agents.

Trillian's earlier attempts to enter the unsanctioned inworld of Alternus by the more direct routes hadn't worked out well. It didn't take much snooping around to discover the passcode phrase, "There's no place like home," but he'd been over-confidant and careless, and dismissed Alum's warning about the subtle thought-virus activated at Alternus' regular portal. To his surprise and chagrin, Trillian found his personal defenses nearly overwhelmed by the thing.

Outwardly, the virus appeared relatively innocuous, but it was as dangerous as it was subtle. Its touch was as delicate as Alum had intimated. It did no more than instill a willingness to consider criticisms of the Lord in minds that would have otherwise viewed such ideas as the highest blasphemy. Compounding this dangerous openness to suggestion was a tendency toward distrust of Alum's rank as the universe's Ultimate Authority.

Trillian evaded its tenacious tendrils mostly by luck. A hunch had led him to isolate his inworld interface from deeper mental structures before attempting contact with Alternus, protecting his core persona from the virus' first attack.

Even at that, the insidious virus broke through his firewall before he could program his belief matrix—his concepta—to ignore it.

The ego-checking close call and narrowly avoided catastrophe convinced him to drop any idea of a simple frontal assault in favor of a more secretive infiltration. Enter, Casa DonTon.

It made perfect sense. First, DonTon's data paths were routed close to the virus-infected hardware substrate on which the Alternus simulation ran, but were not affected by it. Second, DonTon's instantiated population was small, and its participants were shallow and silly enough that he wouldn't be overly taxed by the sim itself. He'd have ample opportunity to probe Alternus' supervisory defenses while keeping up the pretense of social niceties. Third, it seemed unlikely that whoever or whatever designed the Alternus inworld would expect an invasion from such a non-threatening neighbor as the frivolous Casa DonTon.

With his attention brought back to the room by the sound of clattering peach bowls, Trillian realized his gentle lattice probing at the edges of the Alternus sim portal—located behind the closet door on the facing wall—had been having an unexpected effect on the wait staff Partial, Timothy.

While Timothy put his concepta through diagnostic testing, Trillian reviewed what he knew about the knowledge-belief space of Partials for any clue as to how his actions might have disrupted the Footman.

* * *

TIMOTHY'S SELF-DIAGNOSTIC FINISHED, and the Supervisor program discreetly pinged the waiting Partial: *Unregistered Instantiation. Reporting anomaly now. Please wait.*

That doesn't sound very promising–thought the Footman. He straightened his posture and addressed Lady Chattingbaron. "Troubles appear to have originated in the hardware matrix as a result of anomalous solar wind activity, my Lady," he lied. "Everything is fine now." He calmly resumed serving dessert.

Unregistered Instantiation? Timothy's mind reeled though he maintained his calm external demeanor. A mind extant in the DonTon inworld without an associated physical trueself registered outworld? A full persona with no real body? Timothy knew that Partials were not supposed to become fully instantiated with independent personas unless they had been selected by the committee as candidates for embodiment outside.

How such knowledge appeared in his mind, he had no idea. It seemed as if the information spontaneously emerged in his consciousness of its own accord only seconds before. *How odd.* He looked around nervously.

His mind, his whole persona, felt richer and deeper than it had moments earlier. *As soon as the Supervisor isolates my knowledge-belief space and sees I've gone from Partial to Full, they'll scrub it. That is, once they determine how I became fully instantiated in the first place.*

What are my options? What are my options? Hang around here and wait to be erased? Try to hide? Take over one of the Family's outworld bodies? Just throw myself on the mercy of the Supervisor and hope for the best?

Timothy's hand paused mid-air, a scoop of ice cream hovering above Lady Mirabel's peaches. He was having thoughts. *I'm thinking. I'm having independent thoughts. And I lied! To Lady Chattingbaron, no less! How is that possible? I'm not sure even a Full can do that.*

For the first time in his long existence as a DonTon server Partial, he was thinking outside his simple, inworld programming. His hand remained frozen as he considered the ramifications. *Thinking for myself? Astounding!*

The ice cream, however, did not remain frozen. It dripped—once, twice—and slid perilously close to the edge of the spoon. Recovering with an elegant swoop of the wrist right before the sweet cream escaped, Timothy delivered the creamy globe neatly atop the peaches.

Thankfully, the house guests had resumed their conversations and didn't notice his hesitation. Even the eagle-eyed Mr. Gowling, busy pouring coffee, gave no indication he'd seen anything amiss.

Timothy finished serving and took his place in front of the polished oak sideboard. He kept his movements measured and his face neutral, while his mind raced. He was sure the Securitors would intervene and take him away at any moment. *I can steal an automobile and escape to London. No one would find me in those crowds.*

Then he remembered who, or rather what, he was trying to evade, the omnipotent inworld Supervisor and its ruthless contingent of Securitor agents. *It's hopeless. There's nothing I can do; I might as well face my fate with the dignity the Family deserves.*

Crestfallen but ever a professional, Timothy hid his misery. *I expect that my inexplicable, miraculous experience of consciousness outside the restrictive program of the DonTon Supervisor will be the shortest independent life the Realm has ever recorded.*

The dessert course ingested and a promising evening ahead, the Family and guests stood. "Shall we retire to the Library for a brandy?" Lord Chattingbaron asked his male guests.

The ladies shared courteous smiles, knowing that one drink would lead to a second, and the second to a third, along with a cigar or two, while the female coterie sipped sherry and played cards in the sitting room. Both groups looked forward to the dances and games to follow, once dinner had a chance to settle and the two groups were brought together again in the Grand Salon.

As the other guests filed out of the dining room, Mr. Trillian lingered behind to examine an unimportant painting displayed on the wall facing his chair. The painting just happened to be hung beside the closet door that had compelled the man's attention over dinner.

Mr. Gowling caught Timothy's attention and raised his eyebrows meaningfully toward the errant guest. Timothy walked over to see if he could be of service to Mr. Trillian, and Mr. Gowling took his leave. The maids would clear the table; he had more important things to do.

"A stirring rendition of Lord Chattingbaron's Great Grandfather at the hunt," Timothy expounded as he approached Mr. Trillian. Two steps away, the bees resumed their buzzing. This time the Footman's hand was free, and he brushed the air near his right ear.

Trillian caught the motion out of the corner of his eye and turned to face the Footman. "Are you sure the self-diagnostic was correct?"

Timothy shook his head to clear the sound, but the action served only to make the room swim unsteadily. "Quite sure," he confirmed, and rested his hand against the wall. "But perhaps I should sit a moment." He dropped into the chair beside the closet door. "I'm sure it will go away." He waved his hand, dismissing the guest's offer of assistance. "I'll be fine. Thank you for your concern."

Trillian turned back to the closet door and the buzzing noise in Timothy's head grew louder. Unseen swarms swirled around him; the room swam in and out of focus. He squeezed his eyes shut in an effort to regain his equilibrium. He heard the closet door open, and a wave of hot air washed out from the small space. He smelled the dense, complex odors of a large, industrial city.

Fighting a nauseating dizziness, Timothy pushed to his feet, steadying his balance with a hand to the wall. He opened his eyes and looked into the closet. The dark, confined space that should have been there was not. Instead of shelves of cleaning supplies, two brooms, and a dustpan, the closet opened onto a city, the likes of which Timothy could never have imagined.

Impossibly tall buildings lined a broad, busy street filled with more people than Timothy had ever seen. The people were dressed oddly. Some men wore business suits, identifiable as such despite their strange cut and the absence of proper headwear. Many individuals sported embarrassingly inappropriate casual attire. And the women! Timothy was shocked by their immodest garb. Why he could see the naked knees and thighs of those who wore dresses or short skirts.

Just then, he realized that many of the people he had thought were men were actually young women in some sort of skin-tight blue pants. They must be tradespersons. Had they not been in the middle of such a city, he would have thought them to be farmers.

While the odd vestments were surprising to the Footman, the automobiles absolutely astonished him. He had never seen such sleek machinery, not in all his days. The collective noise they emanated as their drivers impatiently roared engines and honked horns was an affront to the senses. Even worse, the language that drivers shouted at any pedestrian or vehicle that dared impede their progress was an assault on poor Timothy's sensibilities.

Mr. Trillian stood well into the other side of the closet, in the midst of that magnificent, frightful city. Timothy didn't recognize him right away; the guest's clothing had changed to match the style of the better-accoutered businessmen on the sidewalk around him. The Shard stretched out his arms and laughed as he whirled to take in the city.

Timothy stood on wobbly knees in the open doorframe watching him, too flabbergasted to move.

Trillian looked back over his shoulder and saw the stunned Footman standing at the door. He dropped his arms, amused by the anomaly. From the city side in which the Shard stood, the doorway opened into an opulently-furnished dining room from another era. Few of the frenetic passersby spared a second glance at the formally-dressed servant frozen in the open doorway. After all, this was New York.

Trillian made a sweeping motion with one hand. "Would you close that please?" he requested, pointing to the door. It was clear that he expected programmed obedience from the servant. The Shard turned without a second glance and set out down the sidewalk, disappearing into an ocean of bobbing heads. Timothy teetered indecisively at the threshold.

A gasp from the dining room pulled Timothy's attention from the spectacle of the bustling city. Lady Chattingbaron was standing at the main entrance, a hand delicately covering her gaping mouth. Over the Lady's shoulder, the Footman saw a matte black, spherical Securitor, hovering in the hallway behind her. She hadn't sensed it yet; her full attention was locked on the impossible scene behind the Footman.

"Timothy....," she began. The Securitor projected a greenish beam, encapsulating and silencing her. The menacing black sphere pushed past her frozen virtual body and floated into the room.

Timothy bolted across the closet threshold and into the strange world, slamming the closet door behind him. The city was bigger than the London he knew, in fact, bigger than any city he knew. Maybe he could hide from the Securitors here. He ran down the sidewalk in the opposite direction from Mr. Trillian, bouncing off irritated virtual New Yorkers of 2040 who did not take kindly to the Footman's flight.

Back in Casa DonTon's family dining room, the Securitor ripped the closet door from its hinges, revealing a few shelves, two brooms, a dustpan, and some polishing cloths. The city was gone.

Anomaly has escaped–the Securitor reported, its voice devoid of anger or frustration. It scanned the virtual room for any trace of Timothy. Then, without a sound, it left DonTon.

About the Author

When I was very young, a teacher asked our class to write about what we wanted to be when we grew up. My story was titled, "Me, the Everything." I've been fortunate to come close to fulfilling that dream in my life: computer programming, molecular biology, nanotechnology, systems biology, synthetic biology, business consulting, and photocopy repair, to name a few. I've spent way too much of my life in school, eventually earning degrees in computing science (BSc), and in molecular biology and genetics (PhD). I've had the opportunity to work with some of the best researchers in the world at The National Institute for Nanotechnology in Edmonton, Canada.

After decades of reading almost nothing but high-tech science fiction, I decided to take a shot at writing some. I aim for stories that are true to the best available science, while pushing my imagination beyond what we know today. I love biology, particle physics, cosmology, artificial intelligence, cognitive psychology, politics, and economics. My philosophy is empirical physicalism, and I blog regularly about the science and the ideas found in my novels. I believe fiction should educate, challenge, and stimulate as much as it entertains.

My wife and I currently live in Ecuador where, when we're not working on exciting and provocative new stories, we study Spanish and practice Chen-style Tai Chi.

Follow me on Facebook at Paul Anlee or write to me at: paul.anlee.author@gmail.com. Even better, visit me at my website, www.paulanlee.com, read the blog, and sign-up on my email list to be the first to hear about new books, posts, and special announcements. Hint: that's the best way to hear about FREE offers and exclusive deals!

Lightning Source UK Ltd.
Milton Keynes UK
UKOW04f1910221117
313147UK00001B/375/P

9 780995 844216